Ever Your Friend
E. D. E. N. Southworth

A NOBLE LORD.

THE SEQUEL TO

"THE LOST HEIR OF LINLITHGOW."

BY

MRS. EMMA D. E. N. SOUTHWORTH.

AUTHOR OF "THE MISSING BRIDE; OR, MIRIAM, THE AVENGER," "A BEAUTIFUL FIEND,"
"HOW HE WON HER," "RETRIBUTION," "CHANGED BRIDES," "TRIED FOR HER LIFE,"
"BRIDE'S FATE," "LADY OF THE ISLE," "THE BRIDAL EVE," "CRUEL AS THE GRAVE,"
"THE WIDOW'S SON," "ALLWORTH ABBEY," "LOST HEIRESS," "FAMILY DOOM,"
"THE ARTIST'S LOVE," "GIPSY'S PROPHECY," "HAUNTED HOMESTEAD,"
"FALLEN PRIDE," "VICTOR'S TRIUMPH," "THE CURSE OF CLIFTON,"
"SPECTRE LOVER," "MAIDEN WIDOW," "FORTUNE SEEKER,"
"THE TWO SISTERS," "FAIR PLAY," "FATAL MARRIAGE,"
"PRINCE OF DARKNESS," "BRIDE OF LLEWELLYN,"
"MOTHER-IN-LAW," "DESERTED WIFE," "INDIA,"
"DISCARDED DAUGHTER," "WIFE'S VICTORY,"
"LOVE'S LABOR WON," "THREE BEAUTIES,"
"THE CHRISTMAS GUEST," "VIVIA,"
"THE LOST HEIR OF LINLITHGOW."

"There are some things hard to understand;
Oh, help us, Lord! to trust in Thee!
But I'll ne'er forget her soft white hand,
Or her eyes as she looked on me."—OWEN MEREDITH.

NEW YORK:
THE F. M. LUPTON PUBLISHING COMPANY
NOS. 72–76 WALKER STREET.

Copyright, 1872,
By T. B. PETERSON & BROTHERS.

A Noble Lord.

CONTENTS.

A NOBLE LORD.

CHAPTER I.

BENNY'S HAVEN.

> It is a home to die for, as it stands
> Through its vine foliage, sending forth a sound
> Of mirthful childhood o'er the green repose
> And laughing sunshine of the pastures round.—FELICIA HEMANS.

"WHY, what a pretty boy! But surely, Charlie, dear, you never got *this* boy out of the work-house!" exclaimed Mrs. Faulkner, half in admiration, half in pity, as she gazed at Benny.

"Well, I did, then, and I have got him regularly indentured to me," answered the Captain, drawing a document from his pocket and holding it up before his wife.

"But then this fair, refined looking lad! He *never* could have belonged to the working classes! And I'm sure he'll *never* do for a servant," said Molly.

The Captain shrugged his shoulders.

"It is hard telling where such children come from. I like him all the better for his good looks. And as to his never doing for a servant, we'll see that."

"But what odd clothes he has got on!"

"It is the work-house uniform; but we'll change all that to-morrow, and put him into a page's livery—army blue, with brass buttons. Eh, my lad! wouldn't you like a dress of that sort?" inquired the Captain good-naturedly, turning to his new servant.

"Oh, yes, sir, please!" eagerly answered Benny, smiling all over his face, and gazing around upon the prettiest room he ever was in in his life, except the grand drawing-room at Brunswick Terrace, Brighton.

"You must look straight at me when I speak to you, Benjamin; do you hear?" said the Captain.

"Yes, sir," said the boy.

"Is his name Benjamin?" inquired Molly.

"Yes, Benjamin Hurst. And he is bound to me until he is eighteen years old," replied Captain Faulkner.

"He is too delicate to make a good servant. You'll repent your bargain," persisted Molly.

"We'll see! Benjamin, can you wait at table?" inquired the Captain.

"Yes, sir," answered the boy,

"Did you ever do it?" inquired Mrs. Faulkner.

"No, missus; but I know I could," said the boy, still letting his eyes wander around the charming room.

"Bravo!" exclaimed the Captain, approvingly.

"Are you an orphan, Benjamin?" kindly inquired the lady.

The boy's fair face clouded over.

"No, missus," he answered sadly.

"Well, then, where are your parents?"

The boy hesitated for a moment and then answered:

"Mother's in the 'sylum and father's runned away;" and as he spoke, the tears filled his eyes.

"Poor fellow! Well, never mind. You will be happy with us here," said Molly, pitifully.

"If you do your duty," added the Captain.

"Now come in to supper, Charley," said Molly, rising to lead the way into the neat dining-room.

"And you come too, my lad, and take your first lesson in waiting," said Captain Faulkner.

And the husband and wife went and sat down to the well-spread table, and Benny stood waiting, attentive, eager, anxious to be useful.

With his quick intelligence and ready obedience he easily learned his duties, and completely satisfied his new master and mistress.

When supper was over, Mrs. Faulkner rang for the cook, and told her to take the new boy into the kitchen and give him his supper, and then to make a bed for him in the loft over the scullery

"And mind," said the cook, as she took him away, "after this yer to clear off the table as well as wait on it."

"Yes'm," answered Benny, cheerfully.

"And you must be up early in the morning, and come down here and make the fire for me against I get up," continued the cook, who seemed to think the boy was taken into the house only for her benefit.

But Benny willingly agreed to all her requirements, for he was pleased with his new master and mistress, pleased with the cottage and the country, and pleased with his own prospects.

And when he had had a good supper and found himself in his bed, in a clean, bare, well-ventilated loft, he could not go to sleep for thinking how prosperous and happy he was.

He had always been anxious to be a "good boy." He had often run great risks to "hook" groceries, or fruit, or anything for his friends, because they would reward him by calling him a "good boy," and he would believe them. And now, lying on his bed, he aspired to deserve his prosperity and happiness by being a very good boy, yes, the very best of boys! And he resolved to rise very early in the morning to perform his duties.

Poor fellow! Proper teachers might have make a good and useful man of him, but would Captain Faulkner, the ruined gamester, be the proper teacher? We shall see.

Ah! well, there are hundreds of thousands of boys and girls as well meaning, as badly trained as Benny Hurst I take him as an example only because I knew him.

Legislators spare hundreds from the saving of the innocents, and then have to spend millions in the punishment of the criminals that neglect has left them to become! Even an old wife's proverb might teach them better economy "An ounce of prevention is better than a pound of cure."

But to return to Benny, who, in his weary pilgrimage through the desert of this world, had just now come upon an oasis.

Benny, having charged himself to do so, awoke early in the morning, and went down into the kitchen and made up the fire for the cook.

And then, as no one in the house was stirring, and as he did not know what else to do with himself, he went out into the garden.

It was midsummer. There were green trees and shrubs and grass, and ripe fruit and bright flowers, and a soft blue sky, and a pure, fresh atmosphere.

"This was Heaven! Yes, surely this was Heaven!" he mused. Benny had never in his life seen the country in the summer! No wonder he thought it was Heaven.

Presently the children, up long before their parents, ran out into the garden, and seeing the young stranger, gathered around him with child-like friendliness, and asked him what was his name, and where he was from, and whether he wouldn't like to see the bee-hive and the hen-roost.

And Benny, charmed with the beauty and brightness and kindliness of his little friends, told them that he was the new boy, and meant to do his best.

And then Charley would have taken him off to look at the duck pond, only that the shrill voice of the cook was heard, loudly calling to Benny to come into the house and learn to lay the cloth for breakfast.

And Benny, though loath to leave his little friends, ran eagerly into the house to do as he was bid.

That day Benny was put into his new page's livery—a dark blue jacket and trowsers, with three rows of buttons on the breast of the jacket. And a very pretty page he made, fit for any lady's boudoir.

And that day Captain Faulkner, Mrs. Faulkner and the cook alternately gave Benny instructions in his new duties, which, to the lad's wondering mind, seemed utterly inconsistent with and contradictory to each other.

For instance, Mrs. Faulkner said to him:

"And above all things, Benjamin, remember this: that whatever you do, you must always tell the truth."

"Yes, missus," answered the boy.

"And never, never, NEVER tell a lie."

"No, missus."

And a little later in the day Captain Faulkner said to him:

"It will be your duty, Benjamin, to attend the door bell. And when any one asks if I am at home you must say that you don't know, but that you'll go and see. Do you understand?"

"Yes, sir; but must I say it *when I know you be at home?*" inquired Benny.

"Certainly, you blockhead! You must literally obey my orders, and say that you don't know whether I'm at home or not; but you'll come and see. And then come straight to me for further orders."

"Yes, sir."

"You understand now?"

"Oh, yes, sir."

In the afternoon Mrs. Faulkner said to him:

"Benny, you must be honest, you know."

"Yes, missus."

"And never take even so much as a pin that don't belong to you."

"No, missus."

In the evening, while he sat by the kitchen window with the cook, that worthy woman said to him:

"And long as you tend on the house, boy, and see any little thing laying around loose like, such as a spool o' cotton, or a paper o' needles, or any trifle, you pick it right up, and bring it to me to put away, you know, Benny, and then I'll give you a hot cake when I bake, and you needn't say nothing about it to nobody; do you hear, boy?"

'Yes'm."

"That's a good boy."

Benny went up to his cool loft that night feeling very much confused with all these contradictory orders. But having also much pleasanter things to think of, in the children and the garden, and all the new charms of his present life, he quickly ceased to trouble himself in the vain attempt to reconcile inconsistencies.

He was very happy in his new situation; there was not a good thing in it that he did not keenly appreciate: his own clean clothes and airy lodging and good food, and the pretty cottage and fruitful garden and pleasant country, and the good-humored master and mistress and the friendly children!

And he firmly resolved to deserve his good luck by being the very best of boys.

And by way of keeping this resolution, he lied boldly whenever Captain Faulkner ordered him to do so.

Captain Faulkner had contracted some new debts in the neighborhood where he now lived, and he did not mean to pay them. The gallant Captain was in the habit of contracting debts, and *not* in the habit of paying them. And now he made Benny deny him to every man who came to the house with a bill.

"Here comes another one up the lane, boy. Go to the door, and tell him I'm not home. Tell him I'm at the seaside, and won't be home for a month," said the Captain one morning, as, looking through his bed-room window, he saw the approach of a dun.

Benny went down and opened the door to the unwelcome visitor, when the following colloquy ensued:

"I wish to see the Captain," said the visitor.

"He an't home, sir," replied Benny boldly.

"An't home! Are you sure?"

"Oh, yes, sir; certain sure. The Capting, sir, have gone down to the seaside, sir, which the doctor ordered of him there for his 'ealth, sir," answered Benny, improving upon the story that had been put in his mouth.

"At the seaside is he?" repeated the visitor incredulously.

"Oh, yes, sir; and won't be home for a month, sir, which the doctor ordered, fearing of gonstumption."

"Consumption! Yes; he looked like consumption—of beef and beer!—when I saw him at the window as I came up the lane!" said the visitor, with an incredulous laugh.

Benny was "taken aback" for a moment, but being a sharp boy, he soon recovered his self-possession and inquired:

"Did you mean the gemman as was a tying of his kervat at the windy up there, sir?"

"Of course I did. I saw him plain enough."

"Lor' bless you, sir! *that* were master's brother, sir, as is the very moral of 'im, sir; and come down from London last night, sir, to see missus and the children, sir, which he is going up to town this arternoon, sir, said Benny, telling the first plausible story that came into his head.

The dun was no match for the street boy, and whether he entirely believed the statement or not, he had to go away.

Benny went back to his master and repeated to him the whole interview.

A[illegible]! shame of manhood! the noble Captain laughed

heartily, and clapped the poor ignorant boy on the back, saying:

"Benjamin, you are the very brightest boy I ever saw in my life! that you are! You are a real treasure, Benjie! you are, indeed! I wish I had half a crown to give you!"

"Please, sir," said Benny, plucking up spirit to make his desires known, "I don't want half a crown. I'd rather have—"

"What? A whole crown, I suppose?" laughed the Captain.

"No, sir; I meant a half a holiday some o' these days, please, sir."

"What do you want with half a holiday, Benjamin?"

"Please, sir, to go and see Suzy Juniper, sir, please."

"Ha! ha! ha! ho! ho! ho! Suzy Juniper, eh? Who's Suzy Juniper? Your young woman?" laughingly inquired the Captain, who was in a very good humor with his bright page.

"She's a friend o' mine, please, sir," answered Benny simply.

"Ah! a friend of yours!" laughed the Captain.

"But a very nice girl, for all that, sir!" added Benny, who did not quite like his master's tone.

"Oh, of course! a very nice girl!"

"And a deal cleverer 'n I am, please, sir. She—" He stopped and hesitated. Ever since the double tragedy of the Flowers girls, he had associated in his own mind so much of vice and crime with the Thespian ballet, that, even little outcast as he was, he was ashamed to tell the occupation of his little friend.

"Well, what about her?" good-naturedly inquired the Captain.

"She's a carpenter's daughter, please, sir."

"Oh, a very decent origin! Well, Benjamin, when you have been with us a month, and continued to be as sharp and serviceable as you are now, you shall have your half holiday to go and see Miss Suzy. And every month, as a reward for good conduct, you shall have the same indulgence."

"Thank y', sir, please, sir," answered Benny, pulling his forelock.

And from that day, if it had been possible to have increased his zeal and diligence in the service of the Captain and his family, Benny would have done it.

The poor boy was very happy at this time. Next to his pleasure in serving his master and mistress, was his pleasure in playing with the children, with whom he mixed on almost equal terms; for children, when unperverted, are very democratic, although they *can* be trained to become the most intolerant little snobs on earth. But there was a very loose system of family government at the Faulkners', and the poor bound boy was permitted to associate freely with the children. Indeed, so much faith had his mistress in Benny, that whenever she would lose sight of her little ones for any length of time, and inquire for them and hear that they were out with Benny, she would say:

"Oh, if Benjamin is with them, it is all right; he will be sure to take care of them."

CHAPTER II.

ARIELLE.

She comes, the spirit of the dance!
Now gliding slow with dreamy grace,
  Her eyes beneath their lashes lost;
Now motionless with lifted face,
  And small hands on her bosom crossed.

And now with flashing eyes she springs—
  Her whole bright figure raised in air,
As if her soul had spread its wings
  And poised her one wild instant there!

She spoke not, but so richly fraught
  With language are her glance and smile,
That when she disappeared they thought
  She had been talking all the while.—FRANCES OSGOOD.

BUT the month drew to a close, and the day came when the boy was to have his half holiday.

But they gave it to him on Sunday afternoon, when he could best be spared, for if the family never went to church, neither did they ever work on the Sabbath day.

"I suppose you'd just as lief have your holiday now as any other day, wouldn't you, my lad?" confidentially inquired the good-natured Captain, who treated his bound boy with great familiarity.

"Oh, yes, sir, and a heap liefer! 'Cause Suzy's always off o' Sundays," smiled Benny.

"Off? what do you mean by off?" laughed his master.

Benny blushed. Not for the world would he have answered, "Off the boards," so he replied evasively:

"She an't got nothing partic'lar to do, sir."

"Oh!—well, get along with you. And be sure to be home time enough to get ready for your work to-morrow," were the last charges the Captain gave to his boy.

And at twelve, noon, Benny, in his clean linen and well-brushed page's suit, and his well-polished shoes and new cap, and feeling happy as a prince, set out to walk to London. He exulted in the consciousness of being clean, well lodged, well fed, well clothed, well *liked*, respectable and independent. Yes, even independent! for the yoke of the kindly, shiftless Faulkners was so light that he scarcely felt it, or felt it only as a protection.

He was eager to reach London and the Thespian Yard to show himself in his new clothes to Suzy Juniper.

He walked very fast, he ran, and sometimes he sprang up behind a cab and got a free ride for a mile or two before he would have to jump down again to avoid the lash of the driver.

Thus in less than an hour he found himself on Waterloo bridge, and in a few minutes more he entered the dark alley leading to the courtyard behind the Thespian theatre, at the back of which stood the old pile of buildings where the Junipers lodged.

He found the father and mother, with their large family, sitting at their early dinner.

Benny took off his smart cap, and bowed to them; but they only stopped eating and stared at him, until Suzy sprang up, overturning her chair in her haste, and ran to him, exclaiming:

"Why, it's Benny! Why, Benny, what *ever* has come to you? Where have you been? They told us you had died in the 'ospital."

"I think I must a died there, Suzy, and gone to Heaven, 'cause I'm so jolly 'appy now!" replied the boy, laughing.

But before another word could be spoken, all the other Junipers, who now recognized Benny, left their seats at the table and came around him with more exclamations than I could repeat, and more questions than he could answer.

"Let the boy sit down and have some dinner, and then he'll tell us all about it. How smart and handsome he do look, to be sure!" said Mrs. Juniper kindly, as she placed another chair at the full table, and made Benny crowd in.

"Now all on you sit down again and eat yer dinner before

it spoils. We'd only just begun, Benny, which it is a baked leg o' mutton and potatoes, and a happle tart, being Sunday," explained Mrs. Juniper.

Benny, having a fine appetite of his own, did his duty faithfully in helping to demolish the joint, and afterward the pie. But in the intervals of his exertions, he managed to satisfy the curiosity of his friends by telling them:

"As I've heerd the nusses say, Mrs. Juniper, how I were reely guv up for dead and tuk out to the dead-house, which they was just agoing to nail me down in the coffing, when all of a suddint I cum to, and opened of my eyes and sit right up in the coffing, and ast them what the blue blazes they meant by going for to bury a cove alive! I don't remember it *myself*, but that's what the nusses says I did," said Benny, giving the story with all the exaggerations that the gossips of the hospital had added to it.

"Which it's my belief as they bury many and many a poor body alive, *that* I do!" exclaimed the mother of the family.

"Lord bless my soul," groaned the father, as he left the table and lighted his pipe to smoke the subject. He could always see more clearly through the fumes of tobacco.

"And it's *my* belief," said Benny, as he cut his apple-tart—"it's *my* belief as I reely did die and go to heaven."

"How can you talk so, Benny, when you know very well as you're on earth now!" said Suzy.

"You wouldn't think so, if you knowed where I'm a living, Suzy," answered the boy.

And he told them all about his being removed from the hospital to the work-house, and his being bound to Captain Faulkner, and about his life at Woodbine Cottage.

"Well, if you an't in heaven you're in luck, that's certain, Benny," said Mrs. Juniper.

"But, Suzy, you've lost all your nice pink and white color, and you're just as pale and thin as—as—as anything!" said Benny, looking wistfully at his little friend.

"That an't polite of you, Benny," answered the girl.

"But what's the matter? Are you ailing?" he persisted.

"No," answered Mrs. Juniper, speaking for her daughter. "It's the life she leads; practising and rehearsing all the morning, and studying all the afternoon and acting all the evening. I wish the child had never seen the stage, that I do. But now I believe it would break her heart to take her off it. And besides, it do pay handsome, that's a fact, and it promises to pay handsomer still; for they do say as she'll be a star some o' these days."

"Benny, did you say as Woodbine Cottage was near the Helenic Gardens?" inquired the girl.

"Yes, Suzy; why?"

"'Cause I'm engaged to dance there to-morrow. It is only a shilling, and may be you can come."

"You going to dance at the Helenic Gardens!" exclaimed Benny, in surprise.

"Yes, Benny. Our manager have a many bids for me to dance at places. And o' Monday I'm agoing to dance at the Helenic. May be you can come and see me."

"I should like to, Suzy."

"And may be you can get your master and missus to come and bring them nice children as is so fond of you, Benny. I'm sure I'd dance my best if I thought they'd be there."

"You should always dance your best, Suzy, if you wish to rise in your profession," said Mrs. Juniper.

"I know it, mother; but sometimes I do get that tired! and then, if anything happens to put the spirits into my toes, I get over it and dance my best. I know if them children as is so fond of Benny was to be there to-morrow it would put the spirits into my toes, and I would dance like hevery thing."

"If *that*'ll do you any good, Suzy, I'll do my best to get

'em leave to go," said Benny, though his heart ached at the idea of his "respectable" master and mistress finding out that his own little friend Suzy Juniper danced on the stage.

But the very next words of Suzy relieved his mind on that subject.

"They're not agoing to put me down in the bills as 'Little Miss Juniper, the Infant Wonder,' any longer, Benny," she said.

"Ah! they an't, an't they!" exclaimed the boy.

"No; and as I am too tall to pass for an 'Infant Wonder,' and they don't care about my appearing as a half-grown girl, which is never interesting, they're going to make me out as a fairy-like young lady, and set me down in the bills as Mademoiselle Arielle. Isn't that a pretty name?"

"Beautiful name! But the people who go to the Thespian will know you are the 'Infant Wonder' all the time."

"No, the manager says not. The 'Infant Wonder' has taken leave of the Thespian forever. And now we are going on a tower through the country, where I am to appear as Mademoiselle Arielle, from the *Theatre Francais*, Paris. And I am to come back to the Thespian next winter and appear as the Signorina Zephyrina, from the Italian Opera, Florence. Don't you see? And they'll never know me again as the old 'Infant Wonder.'"

While the boy and girl were talking Mrs. Juniper was making tea.

And she soon called them to the tea-table.

After that refreshment Benny got up and took leave of the kind family, and set out to walk back to Sydenham.

He reached home in such good season as to receive the praises of his master.

The next morning, while Benny was working in the garden, surrounded by the children, who were diligently helping and hindering him, he began to tell them of the wonders of the Helenic Gardens—which, by the way, poor Benny had never seen except from the outside.

He further told them that that day was a matinee, when the price of admittance was so low that almost everybody could go, and that there would be dancing and singing and playing, and that children could go in for half price.

And he so excited the spirits of the children that they ran in with one accord to besiege their parents, and beg to be sent to the Helenic Gardens.

"There are four of you fit to go, and with Benny there will be five—five at sixpence a piece; that will be half a crown. Charley, dear, *have* you got half a crown about you to give me to send the poor children to the matinee at the Helenic? It's only a shilling, you know, and children half price. And Benny can go with them and take care of them. They will be quite safe with Benny," said Mrs. Faulkner.

And while she spoke, her "Charley dear" was feeling in all his pockets, whence he produced first a shilling, then a sixpence, then two three-penny bits, and lastly six pennies.

"There! I declare I didn't think I had so much money about me. But there you are: half a crown altogether, lacking only one penny," said the Captain, as he good-humoredly emptied his pockets for the pleasure of the children.

"Oh, I've got two pence, so we're all right! And now, children, come and let me get you ready," said Molly Faulkner, as she carried off her brood.

"Please, Charley, dear, call to Benny in the garden, and tell him to clean himself to go with the children to the matinee," she added, as she passed out of the room.

So Benny took the children to the Helenic Gardens, and arrived early enough to find them front seats, where they sat watching the curtain in eager anticipation until it arose.

There were several performers who sang and danced to the great delight of the children, as well as to that of the simple crowd that collect there at matinees.

But at length Mademoiselle Arielle flew upon the stage, alighted, and was greeted with "thunders of applause," in which Benny and his little companions heartily joined.

Suzy immediately recognized her little friend and his companions, and smiled upon them as she executed her most graceful pirouettes.

To say that the children were delighted would scarcely be doing justice to their state of ecstacy. They had never seen anything of the sort before, and the exhibition had all the charms of novelty added to its other attractions.

"But Suzy *acts* better 'n she dances though!" said Benny proudly.

"*Who* acts?" inquired little Mary.

Benny flushed.

He had forgotten, for a moment, that he wished to conceal the identity between the dancer and his little friend Suzy.

"*Who* acts?" again impatiently repeated little Mary.

"Oh! *she*—she as is now dancing. I say she *acts* better 'n she dances. I seen her act at the Thespian, you know," explained Benny.

"Oh!" exclaimed little Mary, and she looked with more interest than ever at the fairy dancer on the stage.

And Suzy, or "Mademoiselle Arielle," finished her dance with a wonderful *pas*. kissed her hand to the children and vanished.

She was applauded with enthusiasm, recalled by acclamation, and danced and kissed her hand and vanished for the last time.

The performance was over, and Benny took the children home clamorous with delight over all they had heard and seen.

"The children have been a great deal happier, and not half so much trouble, since we have had Benny, Charley, dear," said Mrs. Faulkner.

"Oh! I say! see here now, Molly, if you mean to take my page for a nursery maid, I shall take your pretty nursery maid for a page!" said the Captain.

"I dare you to do it, Charley. There are *some* things I *won't* stand, you know!"

This little skirmish took place between the married pair while Benny and the children were at work in the garden.

Benny had been very happy for the whole month that he had lived at Woodbine Cottage, and never more so than on this day; but, ah! this was destined to be the poor outcast's last happy day!

CHAPTER III.

POOR BENNY'S PURGATORY.

"One among the million, fainting on the way,
Stricken by the heat and the burden of the day;
Everywhere a struggle, and the struggle all for self,
For the wickedness of pleasure or worthlessness of pelf.
Dense are the crowds, and distracting is the strife;
Alas! for the woefulness and weariness of life!"

SOON after this last happy day, Benny fell into trouble. Partly from the goodness of his heart, and partly from the illness of his training, he committed a grave fault, by which he lost the confidence of his master and mistress, and the companionship of his little friends.

It happened in this way:

One morning Mrs. Faulkner, with the help of her cook and a famous cookery book, had make a quantity of currant jelly for winter use. After filling some dozen of common glass tumblers with this jelly, and pasting up their tops with white paper, she put them all out on a deal table in the sun to "set."

The children were all playing in the garden, where Benny was at work.

They had helped to pick the currants the day before. They had seen something of the process by which the beautiful ruby berries were turned into still more beautiful ruby jelly. They had even tasted the jelly, and found it good.

And now the sight of so many glasses glowing in the sunshine, and smelling sweeter than all the fruits and flowers together, was almost too great a temptation for the integrity of the children.

They hovered around the table, and touched and smelled, and longed to taste and eat.

Benny called them off again and again, but to little purpose, since again and again they would return to the table.

"You'll knock that there over presently, mind you, Miss Lily. That 'ere table's mighty shaky, you see," he said warningly, but fruitlessly.

"Me only want to look," persisted the little willful one.

"Miss Ada, 'deed you mustn't lift up that big tumbler; you'll let it fall presently."

"No, I won't, Benny. I only want to smell."

"Master Charley, sir, if you keep putting your tongue to the edge of the tumbler, you'll wet the paper and make it come off."

"You shut up! I only want to taste the jelly, where it is leaking here."

"'Deed, Miss Lily, dear, if you try to climb up on the end of the table—"

CRASH!

Down came the table, glasses, jelly and all, cutting short the expostulations of poor Benny!

The slight table had tilted under the weight of the willful children, who had persisted in climbing or leaning upon it, and a heap of spilled jelly, mingled with broken glass, lay upon the ground.

The crash was followed by a dead silence, as the panic-stricken children stood gazing on the wreck.

"We've done it now!" said little Mary, gravely.

"And won't we catch it now, neither? Oh, my eye!" exclaimed Master Charley.

Ada and Lily began to cry.

"There, now, don't tune up your little pipes for nothink! *Crying* never does no good. So what's the use o' crying? Besides, what could you expect of *tumblers* but to tumble down? Didn't the tumblers at the Helenic Gardens tumble? And they was people. And if them flesh and blood tumblers tumbled, and got praised and paid for it too, what can you expect of these poor insensible glass tumblers?" said Benny, by way of cheering up the fallen spirits of the children.

"O Benny! don't tell on us, please!" pleaded Ada. And Lily and Charley chimed in and added their petitions to hers.

Mary said nothing, but looked gravely on.

"Don't tell on us, Benny! Don't tell on us!" pleaded the other three children.

"*Who* tell? ME? Why, I never split on a pal in my life! I'd die first. And I've had *rich* chances! Why, lawk! there were Sneaking Sam, and a 'ward o' fifty pound offered for him. And *I* knowed where he were all the time. And me and Rosy and granny all but starved to death that time. And I never spilt on him. 'Cause why? It would a been *mean*. And besides, if he'd been lagged, they'd a made him a lifer," said Benny heroically.

The children stared at him in utter astonishment. They comprehended not one word of what he said. At length Charley spoke:

"I don't know what you're talking about, Benny. But I want to know one thing—you won't tell on us?"

"*No!*" said Benny, "I won't! And now all on you cut and run, and leave me to face this here music!"

"The children all gladly ran away from the scene of the disaster, and left Benny on the spot.

He stood for a moment reflecting how he could best cover the children's fault. He had some little instinctive misgivings as to the right of deceiving his kind mistress, but then he would deceive her only to protect her own children from punishment, and so he dismissed these misgivings as so many weaknesses.

"I'm sorry for missus a losing of all her jelly, arter taking sich a deal o' pains to make it! But splitting on the kids won't do *her* no good, and punishing o' *them* won't fetch back the jelly! So, blowed if *I* split!"

With this resolution Benny wandered away from the spot, and resumed his work of weeding out the flower-beds.

It was not until sunset that the misfortune was discovered. Then the cook went out to bring the glasses in, and seeing the catastrophe, ran back into the house, calling to her mistress.

"O ma'am! ma'am! what a dreadful thing has happened!"

"Heaven have mercy upon us! Which of the children is it?" exclaimed the terrified mother, naturally supposing that one of her little ones had been tossed by a bull or bitten by a dog.

"I don't know which on 'em it were, ma'am; but every bit o' the jelly is ruined!" answered the cook, speaking at cross purposes.

"The jelly!" exclaimed Mrs. Faulkner, puzzled.

"Yes, ma'am; the jelly! which them little plagues of my life have knocked over the table, and broke every one of the glasses. I say it, and I stand to it, ma'am, begging your pardon, as children *is* the devil!" exclaimed the cook.

"For goodness' sake, let me come and see what's the matter!" said Molly.

"Come then, ma'am, and see for yourself! And then, if you don't think as them ere little ones deserves a good switching, *I'll* give up," said the cook, leading the way to the scene of the catastrophe.

Molly gazed on her lost treasures, and could have cried.

"Where are the children?" she inquired.

"Oh, away down in the bottom of the garden, ma'am, like little thieves as have set fire to a barn and run away by the light of it!"

"Where is Benny?"

"There he is, ma'am, a weeding out the flower beds But lor' ma'am, *he* never did the likes o' that! A more steadier or a more carefuller lad don't live, ma'am."

"Oh, I know it wasn't Benny! But he may know something about it. Call him here, cook. And call the children."

"What's the row?" inquired Captain Faulkner, walking up as the cook walked off.

"Oh, Charley, dear, look there! About three pounds' worth of red currant jelly utterly destroyed! And we haven't any more currants on the bushes, and no more sugar until the children's fairy grandmother sends the next month's supply! And, oh, Charley, dear, it was for *your* sake I made it! I know you are *so* fond of game, and game is nothing without currant jelly!"

"And who the devil did this mischief, then?" inquired the Captain, waking up to a realization of the misfortune.

"Of course, the children. There was no one else in the garden, except Benny, and he would never have done it."

"Molly, these children want to be taken in hand. Upon my word and honor, they are growing up as wild as unbroken colts. Where are they?"

"They are coming now. And here is Benny," said Mrs. Faulkner, as the boy advanced, followed by the four terrified children.

It was ridiculous and it was pitiable, the contrast between the abject terror of the children and its cause—the destruc tion of a few dozen glasses of jelly. But then the poor children possessed a papa who doted on his stomach and a mamma who doted on him.

"Benjamin, come here! Do you know anything about this?" inquired Molly.

"Yes, missus," answered Benny promptly.

"Who did it?"

"Please, missus, Farmer Greenfield's black bull."

"What?" exclaimed Mrs. Faulkner.

"How is that?" inquired Captain Faulkner.

"Tell me all about it, Benjamin," said Mrs. Faulkner.

"Please, missus, Farmer Greenfield's black bull do be in Farmer Greenfield's meadow, behint the garding. And the bull, he lep over the hedge and came a rampaging through the garding, and he run over the table, so he did, and upsot all the jelly afore I could stop him."

"Good gracious! Why didn't you come to the house and tell me at once?" inquired Molly.

"Please, missus, I druv him out fust, and then I did just turn 'round to come and tell you when cook called me, so she did."

"Charley, you must really complain of that bull. I can't have him jumping over the hedge and destroying everything in our garden. And, good gracious! he might toss or gore one of the children some of these days, and then there! I always was afraid of him ever since he was put in that paddock, and often and often have I warned Benny against him," said Mrs. Faulkner earnestly.

Captain Faulkner laughed a heartless, sardonic, wicked laugh. And then his face grew still and stern, and he said:

"Molly, don't you see that that infernal little rascal is lying as fast as a horse can trot? The idea of Farmer Greenfield's black bull jumping over a hedge of six feet high to get into our garden! Preposterous! Look here, you lying little villain! The next time you undertake to lie, just be sure that you know what you are talking about. A bull *couldn't* leap over a six-foot hedge! It would be impossible. And now, do you see, your extravagant invention has betrayed you! It was you yourself who knocked over the table, and destroyed all this valuable jelly. Confess at once, sir, if you would escape a worse punishment than that I mean to give you!"

"I didn't never turn no table over, master; nor no more did I break the tumblers, nor spill the jelly," said Benny firmly.

"How dare you to tell me such a lie as that? Don't you know that it is mean, wicked, abominable to lie?" demanded the Captain, totally oblivious of the fact that he himself had taught the boy to do so.

"I'm telling on you no lie, sir, this time; for I didn't never knock over the table and spoil the jelly," persisted the boy.

At this moment the conscious faces of the children caught the eyes of the Captain.

"*You* were with him in the garden most of the time. You may know all about this thing. Say, Charley, do you know who knocked over that table?"

"The black bull did it!" answered Master Charley boldly endorsing the statement of Benny.

"How dare you utter such a falsehood, sir? You! the son of a gentleman, to tell a lie! Shame on you, sir!"

"Oh, Charley! Charley! how *could* you tell a story?" added his mother.

"Go to the house, sir, and stay there till I come. I'll cane you well for this," said the Captain.

And the boy, crestfallen, crept away.

"Now, then, you little ones; you will tell the truth WHO DID IT?" demanded the Captain.

"The blat bull did it," answered Ada.

"De bat bud did it," added Lily.

"There now, you see, Charley, dear, you have been un just. The black bull *must* have done it!" exclaimed Mrs Faulkner.

"My dear Molly, how absurd! It is just simply impossible! No black bull, or any other sort of bull, could possibly have leaped over a six-foot hedge to have done this damage. This boy here did it. There is no doubt whatever about that. And he has so corrupted our children that he has induced them to join him in telling this lie. Look at Mary, there. She has said nothing as yet. Now I will question her, and I will guarantee that we hear the truth. Mary, who knocked over the table and destroyed the jelly?"

"We did, papa," answered Mary, hanging her head.

"Who? You?" inquired the Captain, puzzled by her answer.

"Yes, papa, we did: I and Charley and Ada and Lily We got upon the edge of the table to lick the jelly where it leaked. And we were all at one end, and so we pulled it over, papa," answered Mary, weeping.

"That is right, my little daughter; always tell the truth. There, don't cry any more. You sha'n't be punished," said the father, patting her head.

Then turning to Benny, he sternly demanded:

"And now, sir, what about the black bull?"

The boy turned his eyes on little Mary, and kept silence. By the rules of his thieves' code of honor, the only one he had ever learned, he was condemning little Mary for "splitting" on a faithful "pal," and he felt himself betrayed and deserted.

"How about that black bull of Farmer Greenfield's, sir?" fiercely repeated the Captain.

"It were a Irish bull o' my own, sir, I'm thinking," answered the boy, with a faint smile.

"None o' your insolence, sir. How dare you! Sir, you have lied to me! And by your example, sir, you have taught my children to lie. Charley, Ada and little Lily have all repeated the falsehood you put in their mouths—"

"I told the story to keep 'em from being punished, please, sir; I didn't know as there was any harm in it, please, sir. And I didn't tell 'em to jine me in it, please, sir," said poor Benny, standing alone, pleading his cause as well as he could.

But he left out the best argument he could have used in his defence. If he had only thought to say to his virtuous and indignant master:

"You also taught me to lie, sir, and rewarded me when I did it well."

But Benny did not once think of calling his master's consistency in question. He had made the best defence that he could, and now he stood patiently waiting his doom.

"You thought there was no harm in it!" exclaimed the Captain, taking up the line of prosecution again. "You thought there was no harm in lying, and in teaching my innocent children to lie! for, by your example, which they imitated, you did teach them. Sir, I do not know anything so base, so cowardly, so infamous as falsehood, except perhaps theft, which is as bad, but no worse. And those who lie will certainly steal—"

"Please, sir—"

"Be silent, sir! I know of no punishment that I could inflict upon you too severe for your fault—" continued the Captain.

But just at this point little Ada and Lily began to cry.

"Please, sir—" again began Benny.

"Hold your tongue!" thundered the Captain. "And go instantly to the house, and up into the loft where you sleep, and wait there till I come. Then I'll decide what to do with you."

"Please, sir, let me speak just one word. Please, sir, take it out on me like blazes; but please, sir, don't take it out on poor little Miss Ada and Miss Lily! Please, master, they's such little things, they don't know nothink!" pleaded Benny for the weeping children.

"How dare you dictate to me about my children, you wretched young work-house vagrant! Be off with yourself. And see here; this association between you and these children must be stopped, sir! And now listen! if ever I catch you speaking so much as one word to one of these children again, I will take you and cane you within one inch of your life. I'll break every bone in your body. I will, by ——! Begone!"

As soon as the poor bound boy had left the spot, the noble Captain turned to his progeny.

"You see, my dears," he began, "the disgrace that follows falsehood. And falsehood, let me tell you, is much more reprehensible in little ladies and gentlemen than in persons of that boy's order. Well, what the blazes do *you* want?" He broke off to speak to the cook, who came down the garden walk.

"Only this, sir," said the latter, "there's that man with the livery stable bill again wants to see you."

"Tell him I'm not at home. Tell him I've gor e to town," said the Captain impatiently.

"The woman might have had the sense to have said that without coming to bother me. Benny would have had! But then he is in disgrace now, so it's no use talking of him," growled the Captain.

"And now, my children," he continued, taking up his lecture, "bear this in mind; always, in future, to shun falsehood and speak the truth. You have all offended in that respect except Mary. Mary, my dear, I commend you for your courage and truthfulness. Charley, Ada and Lily, I am sorry I cannot commend you for the same qualities.

Ada and Lily are but babies, and could not be supposed to know better than to do as they did—though they must never do it again. But *you*, Charley, my son, I am deeply pained by your conduct. However, I see that you yourself are thoroughly ashamed of it, so I will trust you will never repeat it. And I will say no more than this: you must bear in mind that you are a gentleman, and a gentleman never lies! And now let us go in to tea."

CHAPTER IV.

BENNY'S BURDEN TOO HEAVY TO BE BORNE.

And he was bound a helpless slave,
With no one near to love, to save,
In all the world of men.
A friendless, famished, work-house child,
Morn, noon and night he toiled and toiled,
Yet he was happy then.

But weeks and months had passed away,
And all too soon the bitter day
Of wrath and ruin burst.
The children feared him for his fate,
And mistress' scorn and master's hate
Him, their poor servant, curst.—TUPPER.

BENNY went away to his loft and sat there alone. He was quite unconscious of having done any wrong, but bitterly conscious of having suffered injustice; for now he remembered what he had before forgotten—namely, that his master himself had often ordered him to tell a falsehood at the street door to any unwelcome visitor, and had praised him when he had told it well.

"To think as he'd order me to tell bouncing whoppers over and over ag'in, to keep a great big man like he from being ill-conwenienced with bills, and then come down on me only just for telling a little story to keep the little bits of children from being punished! I say it's blamed hard, I do! And a cove don't know what to make of it," said

Benny to himself, as he brushed the indignant tears from his eyes, and waited for the coming of his master.

It was not the threatened punishment he dreaded. He was no coward, and besides, he was inured to pain; but to be banned from the society of the children he had loved and lied for and suffered for, seemed very bitter to the lonely boy.

He did not dread any other punishment, and indeed he had no occasion to do so.

The anger of his master was very short-lived. And the good-humored, unprincipled Captain had no more intention of keeping his word and beating his boy, than he had of performing his promises and paying his debts.

After a while Benny was called down stairs to wait on the supper table.

His master and mistress were at the table, but the children had gone to bed. He waited on them in silence, for they never spoke to him. He was glad, poor boy, when his duties were done, and he was at liberty to return to his lonely loft.

He got up early the next morning, to try to recover, by zeal and diligence in his work, the lost favor of the family; for his young heart was aching in solitude, and longing for sympathy.

He waited on the table at breakfast. The children, as usual, ate this meal with their father and mother. But again the bound boy had to serve in silence. Neither master nor mistress spoke to him, except to give a brief order. And the children seemed afraid to look at him. Benny's heart was so oppressed by this silence and coldness that he felt as if he should suffocate, or as if he must speak and be spoken to, or die.

Remember that he was the son of Willie Douglas and Eglantine Seton, and derived a delicate and sensitive organization from both parents.

He could bear very much; he could bear and had borne hunger, cold and pain; but he could not bear to be shut out from sympathy with his kind.

Benny took up a plate of muffins for an excuse to speak, and he offered them to one of the children, saying:

"Won't you have a muffin, Miss Ada?"

He had better kept silence. Even kind-hearted Molly looked up, and said coldly:

"I don't want you to speak to the children, Benjamin. I am very angry with you for teaching them to tell stories. And they have our commands not to have anything to say to you."

"Yes, sir," added the Captain sternly, "and you have had orders not to address one of them again. How dare you do it, sir? Leave the room this moment, sir!"

Benny went out, his heart almost bursting with grief and indignation.

The cook in silence gave him his breakfast, but the food seemed to choke him.

To wash the dishes and rub the knives formed part of his daily duties. He accomplished this task, and then went out to weed the garden.

The children were there as usual, and his own boyish heart yearned toward them; but they walked apart, and he did not dare to approach them.

Like Cain, he was banished, and like Cain, he felt his burden too great to be borne.

This exclusion continued for days and weeks. And every day he felt his isolation more and more oppressive.

The autumn came, and Captain Faulkner had a visitor staying with him at Woodbine Cottage. This was a visitor whom Molly did not like at all, but whom she tolerated for "dear Charley's sake." This was a certain Colonel Brierly, late of her Majesty's service, now retired upon half pay. This Colonel was a childless widower, who lived in London lodgings whenever he did not get an invitation to some good country house. He was a great epicurean, an amateur cook with specialties in salads, soups, and punches and "cups." It was not easy to keep him out of the kitchen; and more than one cook, in houses where he visited, had given warning on his account; more than one kitchen maid had slyly pinned a dish towel to his coat tails.

But nothing could break the Colonel of putting his finger in the family pie, or helping to improve "the broth;" for, to do him justice, he never spoiled it.

He was addicted to telling the most marvellous stories of his campaigns and adventures in India. By his own account, no living man had ever fought so many duels, hunted so many tigers, or broken so many ladies' hearts, as the invincible Colonel. In person, however, he was certainly no Apollo, but a tall, thin, hard-featured, red-faced, grey-headed old gentleman, with a rough voice, which he was much given to exercise in very objectionable language, especially while emphasizing some of his incredible stories.

This last-mentioned habit Molly Faulkner could not tolerate in their visitor, and so she often arose and withdrew from the dinner table where they would be sitting, long before it was time for her to leave the gentlemen to their wine. On such occasions even Charley Faulkner would be half inclined to call his guest out.

But if the brave and gallant Colonel was somewhat objectionable in the dining-room, he was ten times more so in the kitchen—to every one except Captain Faulkner, who liked the guest all the better for his cooking proclivities.

The cook not only gave warning, but actually left the house, declaring that she would not stay in any place where the gentlemen demeaned themselves down to the level of sauce-pans and gridirons, and gave her so much extra work, cleaning up after them in the morning.

And then they had to get a char-woman to come in every

day, to fill her place until they could provide themselves with another cook. But the char-woman went away every day directly after dinner.

It therefore fell to Benny's lot to help to get the next meal.

Colonel Brierly and Captain Faulkner seemed to like this arrangement very much. They now had the kitchen all to themselves, with Benny to do their will.

Every afternoon, after their early tea, Molly Faulkner would take her children and go up stairs in disgust.

The Colonel and the Captain would smoke in the garden until it was time for them to think about supper.

Then they would call Benny and betake themselves to the kitchen, where the Colonel would throw off his coat, turn up his wristbands, and go in to the compounding of some rare salad, soup, or something of the sort.

Benny was their most obedient slave, and did their wil. submissively until one fatal evening.

On that evening the Colonel had procured a terrapin, which he was going to cook after a famous receipt.

The fire was made in the kitchen range, and a pot of water was boiling.

"Take the terrapin out of the tub and bring him here, boy," said the Colonel.

Benny was half afraid to touch the ugly beast, whose long, snake-like head and neck were protruded from his shell, and reaching around as if in search of something to snap up; but nevertheless the boy conquered his fear, and took the creature up in his hands and carried him to the Colonel.

"Please, sir, here he is," said Benny.

"All right; now drop him into that pot of boiling water," said the Colonel.

Benny stood still and stared.

"Well, why the deuce don't you do it?" demanded the Colonel.

"Please, sir, he's alive!" said Benny.

"Of course he's alive, you idiot! He wouldn't be fit to cook if he wasn't alive. Drop him in the boiling water at once!"

Obediently Benny approached the boiling water, and held the struggling creature over its hot steam for an instant, and then, shuddering, drew back.

"Why the blazes don't you drop him in? Are you quite a fool?" demanded the Colonel.

"O sir! please, sir, don't make me do it! It is boiling so hard! It will scald him to death! Oh, please, sir, kill him easy before you drop him in!" pleaded the boy.

"You infernal little son of a gutter, if you don't do what I order you in one second, I'm blasted if I don't take and chuck the terrapin into the pot and you after it!" exclaimed the Colonel in a voice of thunder, as he sprang toward the boy.

With a start of terror, Benny inadvertently let the terrapin fall into the boiling water so suddenly, that the water splashed up into his own face and scalded him.

And then he burst into tears, not from the pain of his burns, but from pity and horror.

That mode of putting a living creature to death may be necessary and proper, for aught I know, but little Benny, outcast as he might be, was no more fit for the cruel work than was either of his dainty little sisters and brothers at Cheviot House.

"I say Faulkner," began the Colonel, with half a dozen abominable expletives, "this fellow of yours wants the discipline of your horsewhip. Why don't you give it to him?"

"I know he wants thrashing, Brierly; and I don't know why I don't thrash him. And, indeed, I don't know why I don't send him about his business. He's an awful little liar, for one thing," answered the Captain.

"He is, is he? I'd like to have the training of him for a little while. S'pose you let me have him up to London?"

"Perhaps I will. I'll see," answered Captain Faulkner. And then, as the dressing of the terrapin demanded all their attention, they left the subject of Benny and devoted their minds to cookery.

That night Benny, lying alone in his loft, thought over all the loneliness and misery of his position, and felt a longing to return to his old companions in Junk Lane. Beggars and thieves and worse they were, but they had never been cruel or unkind to him.

He could bear anything better than this loneliness. His heart felt breaking in his solitude.

He took a sudden resolution. He would run away and go to London, to his old friends the beggars and thieves, who would hide him away from cruel Captain Faulkner and horrible Colonel Brierly.

He would never see the pretty, friendly children again, and the thought gave him pain, until he said to himself that that would not be worse than to see them every day and not to be allowed to speak to them.

So Benny got up and dressed himself very quietly, and went down stairs from his loft to the scullery below it. There was no one to hinder him. He unbolted and unbarred the door, and opened it and went out.

It was a dark and drizzling night in November; but he did not mind the weather; it rather favored his flight.

He passed around to the front of the house, and down the front garden walk, and through the gate, and out into the lane.

The lane was very dark, but it was narrow and straight, so that he could not miss his way.

The lane led to the high road, where there were gas lamps and sidewalks.

Benny hurried along as fast as he could walk, until he suddenly stopped short in great surprise and delight.

A man was leaning against a lamp-post.

The man turned around, and Benny recognized his step father, Tony Brice.

CHAPTER V.

THE BURGLARY.

Shadows there are, who dwell
  Among us, yet apart,
Deaf to the claim of God,
  Or any kindly heart.
Voices of earth and heaven
  Call, but they turn away;
And Love, through such black night,
  Can see no hope of day.—A. A. PROCTOR.

YES, it was Tony Brice! big, bull-necked, bullet-headed, red-haired Tony Brice; but oh, so altered—so aged, haggard, ragged and wretched!

Benny could scarcely recognize him.

They stared at each other for a moment in doubt and then both at once spoke:

"Why, daddy!" cried Benny.

"Why, Benny, my man!" cried Tony.

"Oh, daddy, I'm so glad to see you!" said the lonely lad, bursting into tears.

"So am I you, Benny, my brave boy!" said the wretched man.

"They told me as how you had runned away to forring parts, never to come back no more!" wept Benny.

"They told you a lot o' lies, then, 'cause you see I have come back. And what's more, they told me a lot o' lies also. They told me as you'd died in the 'ospital. And here you are!" growled Tony.

"Well, they thought I died. I 'most did die. And the

undertakers was going to nail me down in the coffing; but I was too game to stand *that*, daddy!" exclaimed Benny, suddenly drying his tears and laughing.

"Eh? too game for what?" inquired Tony.

"Too game to let them nail me down in the coffing, when they thought I was dead. Oh, you don't know how game I was, daddy! Just as they was going to hammer away, I come to, and lept up, and guv 'em a black eye apiece, I did!" said Benny, repeating another version of the exaggerated stories that, half in jest and half in earnest, had been circulated about his sudden resuscitation in the dead-house.

"Well, I swow! Benny, that's a bouncer!" said Tony.

"No 't an't. You go ask the nusses in the 'ospital," replied the boy, who fully believed the stories that had been told him.

His faith convinced Tony, who exclaimed:

"Well, dash *me*, but that's the queerest go as ever I hear in all my days! And they told me in Junk Lane as you'd died in the 'ospital. You didn't go back to Junk Lane, Benny?"

"No, daddy. 'Cause why? They sent me from the 'ospital to the work'us. And from the work'us they binded of me out for a gentleman's servant."

"Blow their imperance! To bind a man's only son out, without his knowledge and consent! So you're bound out, are you? Who's your master?"

"A Capting Faulkner. But I've run away. I run away this wery night, and were on my road to London when I met you," explained Benny.

Tony gave a long, low whistle, and then he said:

"Come along wi' me, my boy. We mustn't stand here. The bobbies will be a spotting on us. Let's walk a spell."

They sauntered on together, and Tony said:

"So you ran away? Quite right, my bully boy. But

what did you run away for, aside o' the nateral love o' liberty?"

"I couldn't stand it no longer, daddy. I couldn't indeed. I tried hard, for love o' the children, but I couldn't!"

"They mistreated you, did they? Like 'em! Tell me all about it, my man!"

Benny told him.

"And so you slipped out after they were all asleep?"

"Yes, daddy."

"*Who fastened the door after you, Benny?*"

"Nobody didn't, in course. There wa'n't nobody to do it. The cook went away all along o' Colonel Brierly's goings on. And the nuss-maid sleeps long o' the child'en in the front part o' the house up stairs. And lor, daddy, how queer you do talk! In course I wasn't a going to call anybody to shet the door after me when I was up to cutting away!" said Benny, in surprise at his daddy's unusual stupidity.

Tony Brice chuckled.

"And so, Benny, you left the door open?"

"Why, in course, daddy!"

"And they was all fast asleep in the house?"

"In course, daddy!"

"Do them two gemmen, that Capting and his wisitor, sleep sound?"

"Well, I just think as they do, daddy. They set up drinking punch till they can hardly stand on their feet, and then they help each other up stairs and off to bed. And they sleep that sound a cannon wouldn't wake 'em."

"Any man-servant about the house, Benny?"

"No, daddy, nor servant whatsomedever, 'cept 'tis the nuss-maid."

"Any dog?"

"No, daddy."

"And the house is at the end of a lonesome lane?"

"Yes, daddy."

"Benny, I think as you was werry wrong to leave that door open. Some murderer might get in and kill them child'en as you're so fond of," said Tony, shaking his head.

"Oh, so there might!" said Benny, starting, and changing color. "I never thought of that before. I might have locked it on the outside too, mightn't I, daddy?"

"Yes, you might. Benny, I think I must go back and lock that door to purtect the innocent child'en, you know," said Tony, with a cunning leer, whose wicked meaning escaped poor Benny's observation.

"I think I must go back and lock that door to purtect the child'en, Benny."

"Yes, daddy, so do," eagerly exclaimed the boy.

"Is the house far off, Benny?"

"No, indeed, daddy."

"I wonder what o'clock it is?"

"I heerd the clock o' St. Mark's strike one, just afore I met you, daddy."

"Then I've got time enough. Come along, bully boy, and show me the way," said Tony, turning back.

They went on together until they reached the entrance of the lonely lane leading to Woodbine Cottage.

"Is that the house down there, where you can see nothing but chimneys through the trees?" inquired the man.

"Yes, daddy, that's the house. And you go through the garden gate, which, in course, I had to leave that open too. And you go round on your left hand to the back o' the house, and there you'll see the kitchen door open. There's a vine growin' over the top of it, and a bee-hive close by. So you'll know it."

"Oh, I'll find it fast enough. You stay here, Benny, till I come back," said Brice, as he walked on down the lane.

Benny sat down on a stone under the hedge and waited. He was very tired and very willing to rest for a while. But as soon as he sat down he began to grow sleepy.

He watched and listened until Brice's burly form disappeared in the darkness and the echoes of his footsteps died away, and nothing was tc be seen but the lonely lane, and nothing was to be heard but the drizzling rain.

Benny nodded, recovered himself; nodded again. And he repeated this process some half a dozen times before he finally fell fast asleep.

He had slept some time, when he was suddenly aroused by a quick succession of violent noises. There was the report of several shots fired fast, one after the other, and there was the swift rushing of feet.

Benny started up in a panic and rubbed his eyes. He saw lights glancing from windows in the cottage at the end of the lane, and he knew at once that the whole household had been aroused. Two men were running up the lane—the pursued and the pursuer. The foremost one had a large pack upon his back, which retarded his progress. The hindmost one was disembarrassed and was gaining rapidly on the foremost, who suddenly wheeled around and fired a pistol. The hindmost man dropped, and laid perfectly still.

And the next moment Benny recognized Tony Brice in the man who carried the pack and fired the pistol.

"Up, bully boy. Cut and run for your life. London, you know. Cracksman Jack's," exclaimed Brice, as he flew past the boy.

Benny, suddenly startled from his deep sleep, perplexed, bewildered, terrified, scarcely realizing what had happened, yet feeling that his only safety consisted in instant flight, staggered to his feet and ran off as fast as his legs could carry him.

Outside, on the high-road, everything was as quiet as if nothing terrible had occurred in the lane. It was very dark, and Benny slackened his pace and peered about to see if he could catch a glimpse of Tony anywhere. Brice was nowhere to be seen. Then Benny heard some one coming from the direction of the lane. The boy shrank into still deeper shadows, and watched for the passing of the new-comer.

The figure that walked rapidly by seemed only a denser shadow than that which enveloped and obscured all other objects. Yet Benny thought it was Captain Faulkner, and he now knew also that the man who had been shot by Brice must have been Colonel Brierly, and that the Captain was now hurrying to give the alarm to the police.

Captain Faulkner walked rapidly a few yards ahead of the spot where Benny crouched, and then turned sharply off, and went on in a direction at right angles to that which the boy meant to take.

Benny watched him out of sight and hearing, and then arose to resume his flight.

But at that moment a hand was laid on his shoulder, and a voice whispered into his ear:

"Hold on. Yer mustn't go this road, yer'd be nabbed in half an hour. He's gone for the bobbies. Cut across this common and on to the Westminster Road, and so to London. I must take another track. But you make for London and Cracksman Jack's. Do you mind now?"

"Yes, daddy, I mind. Was you here all the time?"

"Sartain. And so close a hint you, as you might a felt my panting at the back o' your head. There, cut away, now! There ben't a minute to lose."

With these words the robber and possible murderer was off.

Benny clambered over a hedge and ran across a field, and then clambered over a second hedge and got out upon a common, ran across the common and came out upon the high-road.

The darkness of the night and the drizzling rain favored his escape. And the dawn of day found him in London, and in the neighborhood of the Seven Dials.

He knew the den of thieves indicated to him by Tony Brice, and known to the craft as Cracksman Jack's. It was a tumble-down old house, in a court, in the darkest, dirtiest and densest part of the neighborhood.

Benny passed in and found himself in the midst of its wretched denizens—beggars, tramps, thieves and worse, of men, women and children. He was a stranger to most of them, and they were jealous of the entrance of strangers. They looked at him suspiciously, and then recognized him as the little tramp that he was, and therefore one of themselves.

"What d'yer want here, boy?" inquired a good-natured looking, poor wreck of a girl, who was loitering on a miserable door-step.

"Why, please, Miss Mary Hann, I wants the cracksman," answered the lad.

"Why, it's Benny!" exclaimed the girl, recognizing an acquaintance. "I declare, child, I didn't know yer. But then I ha'n't seen yer for more than a year. Yer want the cracksman?"

"Yes, Miss Mary Hann."

"Jack!" called the girl, turning her head toward the door.

A low-built, thick-set, bettle-browed, black-headed and altogether very ill-favored fellow made his appearance from the inside of the house, growling:

"Wull, wot d'you want now?"

"Here's some 'un wants to see yer," said the girl, pointing to Benny.

"Wot do *you* want, kid?"

"Please, Mr. Jack, daddy, he—"

"Hello!" exclaimed the cracksman, interrupting the boy. "Why, it's Tony Brice's lad! Where did *you* come from? He thought as how you was gone up the spout!"

Before Benny could explain where he did come from, and

why he had not "gone up the spout," the cracksman hurried other questions upon him.

"Hello! I say; where's your daddy? Did he send you to me? But in course he did. Why didn't he keep faith with an old pal? There I kept watch by the blasted elm more'n three hours, waiting for him. Did he give you a message for me? But in course he did. So out with it! Wot's up with him? Was he copped?"

"No, Mr. Jack, but he told me to come 'ere to you, and he'd be along by and by," said Benny.

"Why, wot's he been up to now? Have he cracked a case?"

"No, Mr. Jack, not cracked, sneaked."

"Any swag?"

"Lots! He's coming on with it too."

"That's bully!"

"But oh, I say, Mr. Jack," said Benny, turning suddenly very pale.

"W'y, wot's the matter, bully boy?" demanded the cracksman.

"Daddy'll have to go in lavender." *

"Eh! wot! wot's he been up to now, besides sneaking?"

"Oh, Mr. Jack, he have shot a man down dead as run after him in the lane," replied Benny, in a low, faint voice, as he reeled and leaned up against the door-post.

"Whee-ee-ew!" commented the cracksman, with a long whistle.

Benny burst out crying, and sobbed hard.

"Come, come, my bully man! Brace up! Daddy'l. be all right soon as he gets here, you know. And as for you, you're safe enough anywhere," said the cracksman cheerfully.

"I don't know that. But I wasn't a thinking on myself

* In hiding from the police.

I was a thinking on poor daddy, and how I saw him shoot the man down dead, and if so be the bobbies cop him and me, they'd make me swear his life away," sobbed Benny.

"Bosh! they couldn't make you do it! You'd never go for to swear away your own daddy's life, you know."

"But I saw him shoot the man down dead!" sobbed Benny, whose instinct was to tell the truth—on all occasions upon which he had not previously been instructed to lie.

"S'pose you did? That's nothink. Swear you didn't. Swear you saw another man do it. And let's see—your daddy's red-headed and freckle-faced. Swear now to a man as different from him as possible. Swear it was a tall, black-headed man, with a long face and a hook nose, you know! That'll get your daddy clean off from being scragged—though I doubt as they'll give him fourteen years for the robbery—that is, if so be they'll catch him, which they won't—not if we know it, eh, bully boy?"

"No," said Benny, as his face brightened, for although he had been terribly shocked by the sight of the murder, and was deeply depressed by the memory of it, yet now that he was told that it was his duty to swear his father clear of the crime, he felt his spirits rise.

"And here he comes now," added the cracksman, as a ragged man with a pack on his back, entered the court, singing:

"Old clo'! Any old clo?"

"Hello, old chap! What have you got there? Old clo' sure enough?" inquired the cracksman.

"Not much!" said Tony, as he took the pack from his shoulders and set it down with a rattle on the ground.

"Whee-ee-ew! Silverplate!" commented the cracksman.

"And watches and sich. But it was by the old clo' dodge that I got 'em safe through the streets under the merry eyes o' the bobbies," said Tony, with a boastful and defiant air that ill concealed the trouble of his guilty breast.

"Bring 'em in!" said the cracksman hurriedly, leading the way into the house.

And there we must leave them engaged in devising some way by which they could conceal their plunder and protect Tony.

CHAPTER VI.

THE NIGHT ALARM AT WOODBINE COTTAGE.

What's the business,
That such a hideous uproar calls to parley
The sleepers in the house?—SHAKESPEARE.

FOR an hour after Benny had left the house, the sleepers therein remained undisturbed.

The extreme quiet of the situation favored deep repose, but at the same time made the senses of the sleepers more susceptible to any unusual sound about the premises.

That night Mrs. Faulkner had retired early, with her children and nurse, and they were all very fast asleep in their apartments in the second floor front.

Captain Faulkner, somewhat overcome by punch, had been helped up to his wife's room by Colonel Brierly, and had dropped down in his clothes on the sofa to sleep himself sober.

Colonel Brierly, seasoned old toper that he was, had drank about twice as much as his younger companion, but yet retired to his bachelor bedroom on the first floor back as sober as a saint. Having a good digestion also, he slept lightly, and dreamed pleasantly, eating all his best dishes over again in his visions, until a very slight noise in his room quietly awakened him.

It was so dark that he could see nothing; but he lay and listened, not without some disturbance of his nervous system; for it is rather trying to the firmest heart, to wake in the night and hear some unknown person prowling about in the darkness around your bed.

Colonel Brierly at length slipped silently off his mattress, and felt his way cautiously to the gas-burner and the match safe that hung beneath it, and drew a match.

By its sudden flash he saw a man with a full sack on his back, and a pair of pantaloons in his hands.

The man dropped the pantaloons and ran off with the sack.

Colonel Brierly lighted the gas and then gave chase to the man, halloing out as he went:

"Ho! Faulkner! Faulkner! Thieves! thieves!"

The thief ran down stairs, through the back-passage and out at the kitchen door, the Colonel pursuing him and shouting at the top of his voice:

"Stop thief! stop thief!"

But the burglar darted through the garden, out at the gate, and up the lane as fast as his legs could carry him.

The Colonel, who had caught up his revolver when leaving his room, now fired three or four shots, in quick succession, after the flying thief, who, notwithstanding, continued his flight.

Meanwhile the family at the cottage had been roused by the uproar.

Molly was the first to wake, and on hearing the cries of:

"Ho, Faulkner! Faulkner! Thieves! thieves!" she sprang up, and ran over to the sofa on which her husband was sleeping off the fumes of his punch, and she laid hold of him and shook him vigorously, while she shouted in his ears:

"Charley! Charley! There's some robber broke into the house, and Colonel Brierly is calling you to help to catch him!"

Over and over again, and with many hard shakes, she had to cry these words into the ears of the intoxicated man, before she could arouse him to a comprehension of the case.

Even then he only stared stupidly at his wife, and asked which of the children was in fits.

"Go wet your head, Charley, and come to your senses! *There are thieves in the house!*" she shouted in his ears.

Then indeed he sprang up, dipped his head in a basin of cold water, wiped it hastily, and seized his revolvers, sobered and ready for action.

"Where?" he inquired.

"There!" answered Molly, pointing through the front window, which she had opened. "There! You can't see anything, but I heard them run out of the gate, and Colonel Brierly after them. Listen! There! some one is shooting!" she exclaimed, as the sound of several pistol shots reached her ears.

Captain Faulkner darted out of the room, ran down stairs and out of the house, hurrying as fast as he could to the assistance of his guest.

But the lane was now dark and silent; nothing but the dim outlines of the hedges could be seen, nothing but the drizzling of the rain could be heard.

Still he went on, calling:

"Brierly! Brierly! Where the deuce are you?"

But there was no answer.

Near the outlet of the lane he stumbled over a prostrate form and fell to the ground.

At the same moment a faint voice spoke and said:

"For Heaven's sake, help me! I am bleeding to death!"

"Brierly! Good Heaven! Where are you hurt?" exclaimed Captain Faulkner, recognizing the voice of his guest, and struggling to his feet in the darkness.

"In the leg; but I'm faint from loss of blood. I believe

an artery is severed. That scoundrel of a burglar turned on me, and fired just as I was about to seize him."

"Well, I wouldn't talk if I were you. You'll waste your strength. Now what the deuce am I to do? If I had a light here, I might stanch the blood at once; but I haven't. And how the deuce am I to get you to the house? Do you think, if I were to help you up, that you could manage to walk by leaning on me?" inquired the Captain, in great perplexity.

"No, no, no—couldn't think of it! If I were to stand up I should bleed to death in a very few minutes," answered the Colonel, in a fainting voice.

"I could run back to the house and fetch the two women to help to carry you; but I am afraid to leave you here. You might faint. What the deuce had I best do? What would you rather I should do, old fellow?"

"I don't know, I'm sure," groaned the wounded man, growing fainter every minute.

"Wot's the row, masters?" inquired a countryman who had quietly come up.

"A gentleman has been shot by a burglar while pursuing the miscreant. And I want help to take him to the house at the other end of the lane," explained the Captain.

"Here I am at your service, master. And glad I am to be on hand. I was going home, after sitting up with a sick neighbor all night, when just as I was passing the high-road near the opening of the lane I heard your voices in distress, and I thought I would just come and see what was amiss. No offence, I hope?"

"Of course not. Only lend us a hand here."

"Certain. Master, if you'll support the gentleman's head and shoulders, I'll support his legs."

"Yes, that will do," said Captain Faulkner.

And between them they raised the wounded and groaning man, and bore him gently on toward the cottage.

The whole house was lighted up now, as if light was the very best protection against hidden dangers.

And all the members of the little family, mother, nurse, and little children, half dressed and half frightened, were assembled in the front hall.

Seeing them standing in the blaze of the gaslight, as he drew near with his burden, Captain Faulkner called out:

"Now, Molly, don't be frightened; for we're bringing home a wounded man."

"Is it the robber?" inquired Mrs. Faulkner, hastening out to the gate to meet them, and fully believing that Captain Faulkner and Colonel Brierly had wounded and captured the burglar, and were bearing him home in triumph.

"But, good Heaven! It is the Colonel himself!" exclaimed Molly, as she recognized the wounded man.

"Yes, my dear lady, it is I. And the scoundrel has done for me, I do believe," groaned the Colonel, as they bore him into the house.

"Oh, come now, master! Not so bad as that, neither," said the countryman cheerfully.

They carried him to his own chamber and laid him on his bed, and then began carefully to undress him. They found the wound in his leg already almost stanched by the clotting of the blood. They bound it up as it was, until they could procure the services of a surgeon.

"Now where is Benny? I must send that boy for Dr. Herby at once," said the Captain.

"Oh, Charley, dear, I'm sure I forgot to tell you! I was so shocked at seeing the Colonel wounded that I forgot all about that boy," said Mrs. Faulkner, who was standing by the Colonel's bed.

"What about him, Molly?" inquired the Captain.

"Oh, Charley, he's gone!"

"Gone!"

"Yes; run away!"

"Are you sure?"

"Oh, Charley, dear, yes. As soon as you ran out in the lane we were all frightened at not having a man in the house at such a dreadful time, and we all went together to Benny's room to call him, and we found that he was not there. And we called him, and searched for him all over the house, but he was certainly gone."

"Well, I swear! That diabolical little miscreant—I see it all now—has opened the door to the burglars, and let them in!" exclaimed the Captain.

"I always thought the little sneak looked like a snakesman," murmured the Colonel.

"A snakesman!" echoed Molly, in perplexity.

"Yes, dear lady; but you don't know what that means. In thieves' Latin, a snakesman is a thin, lithe boy, trained to wriggle himself, like a little serpent, through a small window, side light, or panel, into a house, and open a door to bigger burglars."

"Oh, Benny was thin enough, goodness knows; but he didn't look wicked."

"Ah! his innocent looks made him all the fitter instrument of evil. But what the deuce, Faulkner! are you going to leave me without surgical help until my wound inflames?" groaned the Colonel, trying to draw up his suffering limb and failing to do so, and then groaning worse than ever.

"I beg your pardon, Brierly! This new discovery has quite upset me. I'll go for a surgeon at once, and to the police quarters too, while I'm about it," said the Captain, preparing to be off.

"Oh—oh—oh! The rascals have got both my watches, with their chains and diamond seals. One is a chronometer—a heavy gold chronometer; and the other—oh, oh, oh! blast the fellow! how my wound smarts!—the other is a small gold, enamelled watch, studded with diamonds. But you would know them, should the scoundrel be taken with the property on him."

"Oh, yes, of course! Don't disturb yourself," said the Captain, drawing on his gloves.

"And I suppose you have suffered equally, Faulkner, my poor fellow?" said Brierly.

The Captain burst out laughing.

"I should like to know what they could find worth carrying off in our house. Molly and I have no money, nor do we own a watch or an article of jewelry between us, nor a single piece of plate, unless Britannia ware will pass for such," he said.

"And they've taken all that, and our spoons and forks to boot!" said Mrs. Faulkner ruefully.

"Electro-plate! Oh, how the rascals are sold! They took this for silver, in the dark, you see!" said the Captain, roaring with laughter.

"Faulkner, *will* you go for a surgeon?" impatiently demanded the Colonel.

"My dear fellow, I am off now! Friend, will you oblige me by remaining here with these frightened women until I return," inquired the Captain.

"With all my heart, sir," answered the countryman.

But Captain Faulkner scarcely waited to hear the reply, before he bounded down the stairs and out of the house on his errand.

On the high-road, as we know, he passed close by the burglar and the boy, without suspecting the proximity of either.

He hastened first to the residence of the nearest surgeon, knocked him up, informed him of the outrage, and gave him directions how to find the cottage in the lane.

The doctor promised to hasten immediately to the assist ance of the wounded man.

And Captain Faulkner left him and hurried away to the police quarters.

He found the night-watch at the station house, just about to be relieved. He inquired for the principal officer who might then be on duty, and he was at once shown into a stuffy, musty, close little office, where the gas was still burning and the weary official at the desk still watching.

He went up to this person and gave his name and stated his case, all of which was taken down in writing by a clerk seated at the end of the same desk.

He charged his bound boy, Benjamin Hurst, *alias* Benjamin Brice, with being associated with a burglar or burglars, and with having, on the just preceding night, opened the doors to one or more thieves, who robbed the house of money, gold watches and other articles, and seriously wounded a gentleman visitor of the family, while he was in pursuit of them, and then made off with their booty.

"Have you any suspicion as to who were the parties that robbed your house, Captain Faulkner?" inquired the Inspector.

"Not the slightest suspicion as to the identity of any one among them except the boy. It is certain that he opened the door to the burglars," answered the Captain.

"Where is that boy?"

"He ran away with the thieves after the robbery. I thought I had mentioned that."

"No, you had not. And it is important. You know the boy, and you do not know the others?"

"Exactly."

"Do you happen to know any of the boy's friends, associates, or haunts?"

"No; he is an orphan, and I got him from the workhouse last spring. Yet, stay! Yes, I do know some of his friends and places of resort, or rather I know one of each."

"Let us hear what you know, if you please, Captain."

"He has some friends that he visits in London, called—let me see — a curious name — Beech? — Hazel? Pine?

No—Juniper? That's it—Juniper! There is a carpenter and his family of the name of Juniper. They live in the yard behind the—the—the 'Victoria?'—no—the Thespian Temple theatre."

"Oh, yes; I know. And they have a girl named Suzy—a pretty little dancing girl?"

"That's it! 'Suzy'—a friend of Benny's; though I didn't know she was a dancing girl. Benny spent his half-holidays with her. She is the only friend he has in the world, as far as I know."

"We must watch the stage carpenter's family. We shall probably thereby light upon Master Benny, and through him discover the perpetrators of this daring robbery. In the meantime also, we shall set our most experienced detectives on other tracks," said the Inspector.

And then he asked Captain Faulkner a number of other questions, to which he received some satisfactory and some unsatisfactory answers.

And then he gave his client a number of valuable hints, all tending toward the discovery of the robbers.

And finally, as it was now broad daylight, the Captain arose and took his leave.

When he returned to Woodbine Cottage, he found the Colonel in a deep, wholesome sleep.

"The doctor says he will be all right in a week or ten days, if he will keep quiet and abstain from stimulants," said Molly, as she met her "dear Charley" in the hall.

"The devil himself can't make the Colonel do that," replied the Captain.

Then they went in to breakfast.

"And only think, Charley, dear," said Molly, as they sat down to the table, "the horrid burglars have taken away all our electro-plate service, and we have got to use the tin coffee pot from the kitchen."

"Never mind, Molly! Revenge is sweet! This happen

ed all through the treachery of that little serpent, Benny! But we will have *him* in limbo before a week is over our heads. You'll see," said the Captain with assurance.

CHAPTER VII.

THE DETECTIVE.

A most seemly fair and reverend gentleman!
We'll trust him.—MESSENGERS.

BENNY could not be found, although he was diligently sought for by the most experienced detectives—not that they cared so much to capture the boy, except as a means of capturing the man, and perhaps the gang of men, engaged in the burglary.

A skillful detective, in the disguise of a home missionary clergyman, visited the Junipers, and under the pretence of seeking the boy for the purpose of entering him as a resident pupil in one of the public charity boarding-schools for boys, made many inquiries concerning Benny.

Good, motherly Mrs. Juniper was at once interested.

"And a good job, sir, it will be, to take the poor, misfortunate orphing and put him to school, to have him reared up in the way he should go according to the Scripter," she said, suiting the style of her conversation to the cloth of the supposed clergyman.

"But I do not know where to find the lad unless you tell me," answered Spry, the disguised detective.

"Lor, sir, I can tell you that easy enough. He be a page living along of one Captain Forkiner, at Woodbine Cottage, Hawthing Lane, Sydingham."

"He *was* living there, but he is not now. He was enticed away some ten days ago."

"Lor! see at that now! Who could a done it? Old

Kutt Drug she's dead, and a good job too! Madge she's in the mad-house, which is another good job! And that raskilly ruffing—begging your parding, sir, it's that bad Tony Brice, his pappy-in-law, as I mean—he's been run away this ever so long, and a good riddance of bad rubbish, sir! Any way, they're all gone, them male and female reporates as were leading of the boy to his everlasting ruing. And so I can't think who have enticed him away."

"No more can I," said Mr. Juniper, who happened to be present.

"I had hoped that you would be able to assist me in rescuing this interesting lad from his evil associates," said the pretended clergyman.

"So we can, sir. Indeed we can!" put in eager, affectionate, confiding little Suzy. "No matter where Benny is, he will be sure to come to see us soon. Benny is good, sir. Oh, indeed, indeed Benny *is* good, sir. Ever since I knew Benny, he was always doing the very best he could to please everybody—old folks and children, and the poor dumb creatures too! for Benny felt for them all, sir, he did! Oh, you don't know what a heart poor Benny has! Oh, if he was only a great rich gentleman, he would do so much for the poor, sir. Oh, I hope you'll find him soon, and put him to school, and give him a good education, and then, may be, he'll make the riches for himself."

"You are quite enthusiastic and eloquent in praise of your young friend, my little maid, and no doubt he deserves all your encomiums," replied the pretended minister, who saw in this innocent and confiding little girl his most effectual aid in the capture of the boy.

"Oh, sir, he does deserve all the good one can say of him; he does indeed, sir. Poor Benny! he never thinks of himself; he always thinks of others! Nothing is too mean for Benny's pity, sir. I've seen him give his own crust to a poor famished dog, and go hungry himself. Oh, I'm so glad he is to go to school!"

"And you, my little maid, you seem to go to school to some purpose. You speak well," said the disguised detective, wishing to draw the child out.

"No, sir, I don't go to school. But I learn how to speak properly through studying my parts."

"Your 'parts!'" echoed the cunning detective.

"My parts in the play, sir. I am an actress, sir. I hope you don't think it very wicked of me to be an actress?" inquired Suzy, glancing timidly at the professional black coat of the pretended minister.

"Oh, not at all, my child! It is the person, not the profession, that is concerned in Christianity. The illustrious Sarah Siddons was at the same time a good Christian and a great actress," replied the pretended minister.

"Oh, I'm so glad to hear that!" exclaimed Suzy, with sudden animation; "that's what I want to be—just! I want to be a good Christian and a great actress! For oh! I do love the church service. I never miss it on Sundays. It warms my heart, and sets my whole soul in a glow. And oh! I love and honor more than tongue can tell, Him whose very name I reverence too much to speak except in prayer or praise," murmured Suzy reverently.

"How the child talks! But then she is a little actress—the 'Infant Wonder' of the Thespian—and that makes all the difference between her and other children," thought the disguised detective, as he gazed at the eloquent face of the little *artiste*. Then speaking kindly to her he said:

"And you also love your art?"

"Oh, yes, yes; I do indeed! It makes my heart burn."

"And you wish to be at once a good Christian and a great actress? Well, you can be both."

"And I'm so glad to hear that. For Mary Kempton, you must know, told me that I could not be both; that I couldn't be any sort of an actress and any sort of a Christian at the same time; and that I must either give up my art or give up my Christianity. She almost broke my heart. What is to become of my family," said the little bread-winner, looking protectingly around upon her father and mother, and her elder brothers and sisters. "What is to become of my family if I give up my art?"

"Certainly, what indeed! It would be very unchristian in you not to provide for them."

"Oh, sir, I'm so glad to hear you say so. And you a clergyman too. For oh, sir, it is not only my family that I have been thinking of, but Benny, sir. Poor Benny! I see 'no light in Heaven or earth' for poor Benny, unless I succeed in making a fortune on the stage."

"And when you have made a fortune on the stage, what then?" inquired the detective, with a smile.

"Oh, then, sir, I mean to provide for my father and mother, and set my brothers up in business, and give marriage portions to my sisters—and—"

The little girl stopped suddenly, but the pretended clergyman continued for her:

"Then you will marry Benny and so make his fortune?"

"Yes, sir; and we'll live in a pretty place in the country, with trees and lambs and things that Benny likes. And we'll give away a great deal.

'We will feed the hungry and clothe the poor,
And all shall bless us who leave our door,'

said the child, quoting a poem* that she had often recited with great effect, and which, no doubt, had had its influence in forming the best parts of her character.

"A very pretty little programme for the future," said the detective, rising, as if about to take leave.

Mr. and Mrs. Juniper, out of respect to the supposed minister, whom they believed to be professionally catechising and "improving" their daughter, had kept silence during the interview between the detective and the child.

* Whittier's Maud Müller.

Now the interview seemed over, Mrs. Juniper could hold her tongue no longer. Her maternal pride broke forth in these words:

"Which them as is good judges do say, sir, as my gal has great talents for the stage, and is bound to make her fortune when she grows to be a woman."

"There is no doubt of it," said the obliging detective; "and let me tell you, my good woman, that all the greatest actresses and singers in the world have sprung from the same rank of life with your little girl here."

"Indeed, sir! Well, it do seem as if the poor and humble ought to have something sometimes to encourage them."

"Certainly they ought."

"Yes, sir, she's right there where she says she will make a fortune for herself and all her family; but as to her talk about ever marrying of Benny, that's all nothing but childish nonsense, you know, sir."

"Of course; of course. It is not likely that the future queen of the stage will so lower herself," agreed the compliant detective.

"As if I hadn't said, over and over again, that success itself would not be sweet unless shared with Benny," said Suzy.

"Well, well, we will see," said the detective.

"Yes, yes, we will see," agreed Mrs. Juniper.

"And I'll tell you all what—it's all childish talk, and it's no use to mind it. But let our gal get to years of discretion, and then, fortin or no fortin, fame or no fame, if she's then a mind to marry Benny, blowed if she shan'n't marry him! If she makes our fortin, must we pay her by breaking of her heart? And who's got a better right, I'd like to know, to have her own way, than her as wins all our bread? When she's twenty years old, if she wants to marry Benny, she *shall* marry Benny! Blowed if she sha'n't! Do you hear that, girl? If you want Benny when you get to be a woman, you shall have Benny!"

"Yes, papa, dear!" answered Suzy.

"Well, now, my friends," said the disguised detective, "I feel so interested in the future well-being of this lad, that I shall call again to-morrow."

"Do, sir, in welcome," replied Mrs. Juniper.

"*I* shall not be here, sir. I am going down to-morrow to commence a week's engagement at the Brighton Theatre with Madame Vesta's troupe. But oh! I hope you will find Benny! And I shall feel so anxious until I hear. Wouldn't you please condescend to write to me, sir, just one little line, to let me know when you find him?"

"Certainly, my dear. Where shall I direct my letter?"

"Oh! to Mademoiselle Zephyrine, care of Madame Vesta, Brighton Theatre, Brighton."

"Mademoiselle Zephyrine?" echoed the detective.

"Yes; that is my stage name. I hope you don't think it is wicked for me to call myself by another name?"

"Nonsense, nonsense, my child. Even ministers of the gospel sometimes preach under their own name and write under another name, that they call their *nomme du plume*, Mademoiselle Zephyrine is your *nomme du theatre*," said the pretended minister encouragingly.

"And indeed I'm so much obliged to you, sir, for setting of her mind at ease on that and her profession too. It was very ill convenient to have Mary Kempton a coming here with the best of intentions, and upsetting of her mind so about its being sinful to act on the stage and that, as the child couldn't reely half do her duty," said Mrs. Juniper.

"And who is this Mary Kempton, whom I hear you quote so often?"

"A very good girl, sir, barring her being a bit of a fanatic all along of attending the Reverend Mr. Sturgeon's preaching," answered Mrs. Juniper.

"Oh! a dissenter. That accounts for it all. But set your mind at ease, my good woman. Your daughter is fulfilling her duty in that state of life to which she is called."

"Oh, sir, you make us so happy when you say that! And coming from a reverend gentleman like you, of course it sets our minds completely at rest. Suzy, you hear what the reverend gentleman says? And now you won't worry any more, will you?"

"No, mamma, no more," answered the little girl.

The pretended clergyman then took leave, with a promise to come again the next day.

And the next morning Suzy joined Madame Vesta's opera troupe at the London Bridge Railway station, and started with them to commence that engagement at Brighton which was to have such a great influence on all her future life.

The Junipers left at home watched for Benny, but the boy did not come.

The detective, in the disguise of a benevolent clergyman, came every day, only to be disappointed.

At length the detective went and reported his ill-luck to the party supposed to be most interested—to Captain Faulkner of Woodbine Cottage.

"Oh, leave the lad alone!" said that good-natured good-for-nothing, who had got over his short-lived anger against Benny, and only remembered the affectionate boy's winning ways. "Leave the lad alone. There's been no murder done. Brierly is on his legs again, all right. He never was half so badly hurt as he was scared. And he was scared, badly scared, in spite of his boasted feats of valor in the Indian warfare," added the Captain, with a jolly laugh. "So leave the lad alone; I don't wish to have him punished, for—blame you!—your punishments are ten times worse than the sins punished."

"We do not care to get the boy for the boy's sake, sir. But we believe him to be connected, as snakesman, with a band of burglars to whom we attribute the many daring robberies of the past month. And we wish to get him in our hands as a means for the discovery of the band. Young lads are timid, and can usually be terrified into giving up their older accomplices."

"I somehow think that Benny cannot be. There is a sort of crude, untrained heroism about the child, that would lead him to sacrifice himself on a false sense of honor to his accomplices," said the Captain.

"No. Benny 'll never peach on a pal," added Maste. Charley.

"There!" exclaimed the Captain, beginning to lose a little of his good humor. "You see what it is to have a boy of that class in one's house! Already he has taught my son his thieves' honor in good set thieves' Latin. Pray what is the meaning of "peaching on a pal?"

"Betraying an accomplice," answered the detective.

"Telling on a playmate," at the same instant answered Master Charley.

"With your leave, Captain, I must still prosecute my search for the boy," said the detective, who thereupon took leave and went away.

But days passed and still Benny was not found.

Meanwhile Captain Faulkner, through his most unfortunate intimacy with Colonel Brierly, was fast relapsing into his former bad habits.

He staid out every night to a very late hour. He spent about three evenings in the week at the lodgings of Colonel Brierly.

Their friendship, if it could be called such, was of the most uncertain quality.

Both were hard drinkers. Captain Faulkner, though good-humored, was very reckless in conversation; while Colonel Brierly was decidedly quarrelsome and insulting, in his cups.

A careless jest from the Captain, an insulting repartee

from the Colonel, might at any moment break the bond that bound these *bons vivants* together.

The "impending crisis" came at last.

It happened that, one evening, Captain Faulkner was invited to meet a few gentlemen at supper, at the lodging of his friend Colonel Brierly.

The company met in due time, and supped sumptuously, the dishes having been prepared after the Colonel's own receipts. Choice wines "graced" the board, and were freely imbibed by the guests.

At the end of the supper, when every guest had already drank a great deal too much, Colonel Brierly rang the bell, and ordered a punch-bowl, a kettle of boiling water, half a dozen different sorts of liquors, half a dozen different sorts of fruits and spices; and having obtained all that was necessary to this hell-broth, proceeded to brew his own celebrated Punjaub punch, which he afterward served out with his own hand to his guests.

It was while they were sipping this punch, and agreeing that if the Olympian gods had ever been so lucky as to have tasted this exquisite beverage, they would never have condescended to nectar more, and while they were uttering other nonsense of the same sort, that their host, *tête-monté* with his punch, suddenly mounted his hobby of marvellous story-telling.

On this occasion the scene was changed. It was no longer tiger hunting in India, but deer-stalking in the western wilderness of North America.

"Where, sir," he said, addressing more particularly his nearest neighbor at the table, "I was once on leave, and on a visit to a friend stationed at one of the frontier forts—commanding the fort, in fact," he added, correcting himself

"A fine country that, by all accounts," said his neighbor.

"Fine country, sir!" exclaimed the Colonel, turning off a bumper of punch. "Fine country, sir! You never saw, heard of, or read of so fine a country in your life, sir! Stupendous forests! Magnificent game! I tell you, sir, I have seen forests of titanic oaks, whose boles were yards in circumference, standing scarcely three feet apart, and with their limbs and twigs so interlocked and interwoven as to form an impenetrable green thicket! Yes, sir! And I have seen bounding through these forests magnificent deer, sir! —majestic creatures six feet high, whose splendid antlers branched *ten feet* apart! Yes, sir!" exclaimed the Colonel, glancing around the table.

"Wonderful!"

"Amazing!"

"Stupendous!"

So exclaimed all the gentlemen at the table, with the exception of Captain Faulkner, who was in one of his most reckless, jolly and chaffing moods, and who now pursed up his lips and gave vent to a long, low, offensive—

"Whee-ew!"

Colonel Brierly, quarrelsome as usual when in his cups, turned fiercely upon him and demanded:

"What do you mean by that, sir?"

"Oh, nothing particular," answered the Captain, laughing.

"Death, sir! Do you mean to doubt my word?" demanded the Colonel in a loud voice, and with a heightened color.

"Oh, no, certainly not. I never doubt a gentleman's word," replied the Captain, with a very questionable laugh, that infuriated the Colonel.

"Then, if you do not mean to impugn my veracity, sir, what the devil do you mean? I insist upon knowing!" exclaimed the Colonel.

"Oh, well, if you must know," coolly returned the Captain, "I was but wondering how the deuce those majestic deer, with antlers branching *ten feet wide*, managed to *bound through* those magnificent forests where the titanic oak-trees stand but *three feet apart.*"

For a moment the Colonel was dumbfounded, and then he exclaimed :

"By Jupiter, sir, that was *their* business—not mine, or yours!"

A laugh at this retort went round the table.

"You have him there, Brierly," said one.

"Ah, yes, he has you there, Faulkner," said another.

"So much for asking inconvenient questions, old fellow," added a third.

The good-natured good-for-nothing laughed with the rest, and soon forgot the little contest.

Not so Colonel Brierly; he never either forgot or forgave it; though, at the separation of the supper party and the departure of his guests, he received the adieus of Captain Faulkner as politely as he received those of the other gentlemen.

And the two boon companions met as usual, three or four evenings out of every week.

CHAPTER VIII.

THE DUEL.

Indeed, at last, close scrutiny must show
A duel cowardly, and mean and low;
And men engaged in it compelled by force,
And fear, not courage as its proper source:
The fear of tyrant custom, and the fear
Lest knaves should censure and lest fools should sneer.
It is to trample on our Maker's laws,
To hazard life for any such ill cause.—COWPER.

At length the opportunity offered itself to Colonel Brierly to take his revenge, and he took it.

The occasion was another little supper, given by a literary Bohemian at the Red Lion Inn, Strand

There were about half a dozen gentlemen present, among whom was Colonel Brierly. The supper was over, and the wine was circulating very freely, when Brierly proposed a game of loo.

The table was immediately cleared, and the cards were brought.

About three rounds had been played, with more or less luck to each player, and the cards were dealt for the fourth round, and the usual question:

"What do you do?" was asked of each player in succession.

"I take 'miss,'" answered Colonel Brierly when the question came to him.

"I beg your pardon, but *I* have taken 'miss,'" said Captain Faulkner, whose turn was before that of Colonel Brierly.

"Why didn't you say that before, then? It is too late now," said the Colonel, taking up the "miss" cards, and putting down his own.

"Colonel Brierly," said the astonished Captain, "I *did* say that I would take it."

The Colonel contemptuously shrugged his shoulders.

"I tell you, sir, that I *did* say I would take it," repeated the Captain, flushing to his temples.

"Did any gentleman hear Captain Faulkner say that he would take 'miss?'" inquired the Colonel, with a tone and manner intensely insulting to the Captain.

"I did not."

"Nor I," answered several.

"Did *any* one?" persisted the Colonel.

It appeared that no one had heard the Captain declare for "miss," though several suggested that the Captain might have spoken, though they had not heard him.

"There, you see, sir, your assertion is unsupported. None of these gentlemen heard you say that you would take miss,'" sneered the Colonel.

"Colonel Brierly," said Captain Faulkner, his face deeply flushing, "do you venture to express a doubt of my veracity?"

"I do."

"SIR!" exclaimed the Captain, changing color.

"I do most distinctly assert that I doubt your veracity, Captain Faulkner," scornfully repeated the Colonel.

A murmur of disapprobation passed around the table.

"Colonel Brierly, there is but one answer a gentleman can make you," said Captain Faulkner, turning deadly pale, as he threw down his cards, arose and left the table.

"Let him go," said the Colonel defiantly. "And now, gentlemen, to our game. *I take 'miss.'* Fitz-John, it is your lead."

"Thanks. I shall not play," said Fitz-John, an innocent young Bohemian enough, but with a lion's heart to back a friend, and he laid down his cards, left the table and followed Faulkner, whom he considered to have been insulted without just cause.

He overtook the Captain in the hall outside.

"Faulkner, you have been grossly and unwarrantably insulted. Brierly is a bully and a coward. And whatever you mean to do, I am with you," he said, drawing the Captain's arm within his own.

"Thanks, my dear Fritz. I knew you would be with me, and I meant to have sent for you. Thanks, dear old fellow, for your prompt anticipation of my wishes," said the Captain with emotion.

"What do you intend to do?" inquired the young man.

"My dear Fitz, what but one thing can a gentleman do under such circumstances? Come with me into the coffee-room. We can find a private corner somewhere there at this hour," replied the Captain.

They went together to the coffee-room and found a table in a box, at which they sat down.

Captain Faulkner called for writing materials, which were supplied to him.

"You will go to the scoundrel on my part, my dear Fitz-John, and demand from him a retraction of his words, and a public apology for the public insult he has offered me. Should he refuse, then demand from him the last and only satisfaction he can give me. *That* he dare not refuse."

"No, the miscreant! because he knows he is a dead shot," thought the young man, as he went away upon his errand.

Captain Faulkner called for cigars, and sat smoking and waiting for the return of his messenger.

Half an hour passed, and then Fitz-John returned, and reseated himself at the table looking very grave.

"Well," inquired the Captain.

"The scoundrel is stupid and stubborn. He absolutely refused to retract his words, although every man at the table, with one exception, entreated him to do so," replied Fitz-John.

"The villain! I expected this. Of course you told him of the only other alternative?"

"No, I did not. I am with you, as I said, Faulkner, and whatever you do I will see you through it. But I thought, before giving your challenge, I would come back to you once more. You have a wife and children, Faulkner, and—that infernal rascal is a dead shot," said young Fitz-John very gravely.

"I know, I know. Poor Molly! poor babes. But a man's honor should be dearer to him than wife or children, Fitz-John. You will therefore take my challenge to that fellow, and ask him to name some gentleman on his own part to act with you in arranging the details of the meeting."

Young Fitz-John once more entreated the Captain to consider well before going further in an affair of so grave a character.

But Faulkner was firm of purpose.

"You know," he said, "that I am no professed duellist so far from being one, I have never in my life been engaged, either as principal or second, in any hostile meeting. Besides, I love my wife and children—" Here the Captain's voice broke down, and his face turned pale. "But a man cannot pass over an insult such as I have received. You know it, Fitz-John. Now go, good fellow, and deliver my challenge."

"To the worst man and the best shot in England!" sighed the young man, as he went upon his fatal errand.

Captain Faulkner lighted another cigar, and smoked and waited. He waited a full hour, at the end of which Fitz-John once more entered the box, and eated himself at the table, looking even graver than before.

"Is it arranged?" inquired Faulkner, in a low voice.

"Yes," replied Fitz-John. "Do you know a place called the Devil's Dyke, down on the south coast, near Brighton?"

The Captain burst into a loud, harsh laugh.

Fitz-John looked shocked and inquisitive.

"I was only thinking what a deuced appropriate name that is for the ground upon which a duel is to be fought, if it *is* the ground. Is it?"

"It is the ground. It is a solitary place, well suited to the work."

"'Excellently well.'"

"The weapons to be used are pistols. We are to leave town quietly, by the midnight express, for Brighton; on our arrival, to take rooms at the 'Ship' hotel; and at five o'clock to-morrow morning—an hour when the spot is sure to be deserted, and the tide low—we are to meet on the sands below the Dyke."

"And should there be a fatal termination to the duel, the survivors can easily reach New Haven in time to take the early boat for Dieppe, and thus escape," added the Captain.

"Yes; that has been thought of in the selection of the spot," said Fitz-John.

"What is the hour, old fellow?" inquired the Captain

"A quarter to eleven."

"We have just an hour and a quarter left before we must catch the train. That leaves me about three quarters of an hour in which to settle up all my worldly affairs, supposing I had any affairs to settle, which I haven't. I have only to write to Molly—poor Molly! and poor babies! But old Melliss, when I am gone, will take much better care of them than ever I could have done; for he only hated me," said the Captain, with a deep sigh, as he drew writing materials before him.

He wrote but a short letter to his wife, but it took him a long time to finish it; for he frequently paused and sighed, as he told her of the insult he had received from Colonel Brierly, and the obligation that rested on him, as a man of honor, to demand satisfaction. He begged her forgiveness for all he had caused her to suffer, and recommended her, in case of his death, to seek the protection of her father for herself and her young family. He concluded with sending tender messages to his children, and he signed himself her "Poor Charley."

In a postscript he begged her, if she could possibly avoid it, not to prosecute Benny.

He folded, sealed and directed this letter, and gave it in charge of Fitz-John, saying:

"If I should fall, Fitz, you will take this to my poor wife at Sydenham, and deliver it yourself."

"Yes, certainly. But let us look forward to a more righteous end."

"After giving that letter to my wife, you will call on Mr. Melliss, the great banker, who lives in Charles street. Tell him that his good-for-nothing son-in-law is killed off out of his way, and ask him, in Christian charity, to look after his widowed daughter and orphaned grandchildren. Will you promise me that, Fitz-John ?"

"Yes, certainly; I promise to do that, if it should be necessary: but it will not be necessary. We do not mean to have any widows or orphans in the case, or anybody killed out of anybody's way. We intend only to wing our scoundrelly antagonist, to teach him to keep a civil tongue in his head, that's all," said the young man, speaking more cheerfully than he felt.

"I believe that is all I have to say now, Fitz. And it must be nearly time for us to be off."

"Very nearly. The carriage was ordered at half past eleven to take us to the station, and it wants but five minutes to that time," said Fitz-John.

And even as he spoke, a servant came in and announced the carriage.

Both gentlemen arose, took their hats and went out as upon an ordinary journey.

They reached the London Bridge station in time to catch the train for Brighton. This train was the last for the night, and it stopped at Sydenham. It was the train by which Captain Faulkner usually returned home, after spending the evening out. He thought of that now, as he went up to the ticket office and took tickets for himself and his friend. He thought of it as he passed Colonel Brierly and his second, who were standing on the platform, waiting for a guard to give them a first-class carriage.

By the judicious administration of half a crown to the guard, Captain Faulkner secured a coupé for himself and friend.

They had scarcely got seated when the train started.

Captain Faulkner felt as if he were going home as usual, to his wife and children. He could scarcely realize that he was going to fight a duel.

Very soon the train ran down to Sydenham, which was the first station, blew the signal, and stopped

Captain Faulkner arose, as if to get out as usual; then recollecting himself, he sank back in his seat with a groan. Then a sudden impulse seized him to jump from the coupé to the platform, and hurry home through fields and lanes now rich in Autumn's beauty, home to his cozy cottage and lovely wife and little children, and to leave Colonel Brierly to go to the Devil's Dyke, or the Devil himself, alone.

But the train started, and his fate was sealed.

In due time it ran in to the Brighton station, where a few cabs were still waiting to take late travellers to their destinations.

Captain Faulkner and Mr. Fitz-John took a cab between them to the "Ship" hotel, where they were followed by Colonel Brierly, his second and the surgeon, in another cab.

The whole party ordered rooms, and soon retired.

Captain Faulkner and Fitz-John took a double-bedded room between them, and then feed a waiter to bring them coffee at five in the morning, and also to order a cab for that hour.

These arrangements having been made, Mr. Fitz-John would have persuaded his principal to lie down; but the Captain said that he wished to write another letter, and begged that his second would lie down and leave him to himself.

Fitz-John then threw off his coat and laid down on the outside of his bed, meaning to watch with his principal. But fatigue soon overcame him, and he slept soundly.

Captain Faulkner sat down to write his second letter This was to Mr. Melliss. Now that he was so near an event that might terminate his earthly existence, "poor Charley" was forced into a stricter self-examination than he had ever instituted before. For the first time he felt remorse for having first "stolen the old man's daughter," and then brought her and her children to such misery.

He wrote to Mr. Melliss as he felt, as a dying man; tell

ing him that in his present crisis, when all the seriousness of life and death weighed upon his spirit, he felt, for the first time, the enormity of his sin, and would, if possible, atone for it. He begged the bereaved and outraged father to forgive him, and to forgive his wife, the erring daughter. He said he did not ask that father to protect his widowed daughter and her orphan children, because he knew that father would do so. And he ended, as he had begun, by entreating forgiveness.

He folded, sealed and directed this letter, and laid it aside to give to Fitz-John in the morning.

Then he threw himself on his bed, not expecting to sleep. Yet sleep soon overtook him, and he slept until he was aroused by the knocking at his door.

He and his friend sprang up at the same moment.

Fitz-John opened the door, and found the waiter.

"If you please, sir, it is five o'clock. Here is the coffee, and the cab is waiting," said the waiter.

"All right. Bring the tray in and put it on the table, and let the cab wait," said Fitz-John.

"Yes, sir. Any further orders?"

"No. I'll ring if I want anything."

The waiter touched his forehead and went out.

"Come, Faulkner. Douse your head into a basin of cold water, dry it with a coarse towel, brush your hair and come to coffee. We can breakfast when we return," said Fitz-John, as he cheerfully set the example of making a hasty toilet.

"Yes, when we return!" sighed Captain Faulkner.

Then he took the second letter from the table and gave it to Fitz-John, saying:

"Fitz, I feel now as if I would like to be at peace with all the world, even with my unrelenting old father-in-law. Yes, even with that wretched man who is thirsting for my blood this morning, and only because I happened to turn one of his boasting stories into ridicule; for *that* is the real origin of this duel, Fitz! Well, wishing to be in charity with all mankind, I have written to my father-in-law. This is the letter. In case I should fall, will you take it to him?"

"I will. But come now, none of that! Take your coffee and brace up!" said Fitz-John encouragingly.

They sat down to the little table and drank two or three cups of coffee each.

Then they took their hats and went down and got into their cab, and directed the cabman to drive to the "Devil's Dyke."

"And not over the downs, but by the beach," said Fitz-John.

"But the tide, sir," suggested the cabman.

"Oh, it is ebbtide now. It will be low tide by the time we get there. And we shall return before the tide turns. Go on."

The cabman touched his hat and went on.

A strange weird drive of death was that through the gray of the autumn morning, along the sands of the seashore; on one side the beetling rocks, on the other the rolling sea. And a long ride it seemed, considering the distance; but at length they neared the spot.

Fitz-John ordered the cabman to stop. And he and Faulkner alighted, taking their pistol-case with them.

Fitz-John directed the cabman to wait there. And then he drew the arm of his principal within his own, and they both walked on toward the duelling ground.

They reached the foot of that yawning chasm known as the Devil's Dyke, and found themselves alone there.

"The other party has not come up," said Faulkner.

"No. I am glad of it. I am glad that we are the first upon the ground," said Fitz-John.

But even as he spoke, they discovered three persons

approaching from an opposite direction, and whom they soon recognized as Col. Brierly, his second Mr. Aiken, and the surgeon.

They lifted their hats as they approached, and our friends courteously acknowledged the greeting.

The seconds — Mr. Fitz-John on the part of Captain Faulkner, and Mr. Aiken on that of Colonel Brierly—proceeded to step cff the ground and place their principals.

They planted their men ten feet apart, standing sideways toward each other, with their backs to the downs, their faces towards the sea.

The seconds then retired.

An instant afterward Aiken gave the signal.

"One, two, three. *Fire!*"

At the fatal word both antagonists wheeled around and fired.

Captain Faulkner sprang into the air, fell forward upon his face, and lay motionless.

Colonel Brierly, who was unhurt, forgetting all the "points of honor," threw away his pistol and ran towards his fallen foe.

But Fitz-John and Aiken had reached the fatal spot before him.

Fitz-John had raised the head of the fallen man upon his knee.

"My friend is dead!" he groaned. "Fly, and save yourself, Colonel Brierly.

CHAPTER IX.

AFTER THE FATAL DUEL.

Since ill-respected honor bade me on,
I held as little counsel with weak fear
As you. What I did, I did in honor,
Led by the impartial conduct of my soul;
And never shall you see that I will beg
A ragged and forestalled remission.—SHAKESPEARE.

"BRIERLY, we must fly! There is not a single instant to lose! The cab still waits. We must take it and drive like the very demon, if we wish to get to New Haven in time to take the boat to Dieppe!" exclaimed Mr. Aiken, Colonel Brierly's second, speaking in great excitement.

"By my soul, I'm very sorry for this! Is he dead? Are you quite sure?" anxiously inquired the Colonel, of the surgeon, who was kneeling down beside the body of poor Faulkner.

"He is quite dead," answered the surgeon.

"Brierly, we can do no good here. We shall all be in a devil of a mess, if we don't clear out!" urged Aiken.

"I know it! By——, I never was so sorry for anything in my life!"

"Sorrow 'll do no good now. Save yourself!" said Aiken, taking the Colonel's arm and hurrying him off the ground.

Then seeing that young Fitz-John still lingered, looking upon his fallen friend, he called to him:

"Come, Fitz! Heaven and earth! Come! We can wait no longer for you."

"Go, then. I have a duty to do here!" said Fitz-John.

"Man! you'll have duties to do in the Pentonville Penitentiary. Do you know what we have been doing will be construed felony by the law, and that it is punishable by imprisonment and penal servitude?"

The young man started! "Imprisonment!" "Pena servitude!" Horrible fate! More horrible than death And had he really made himself liable to such degradation?

He could have braved pain or death for the sake of remaining by the body of his fallen friend; but not imprisonment! not penal servitude!

He cast a look of sorrow and remorse upon the face of the dead man, and then hastily followed the others.

They found the cabs waiting where they had left them.

He thought of the letters in his pocket, and of the solemn promise he had made his friend, to deliver them to their destination in the event of his death; but—imprisonment! penal servitude! disgrace! He could not meet that.

"I will send the letters by mail. That will do quite as well," he said to himself.

And he entered the cab, ordered the cabman to drive to New Haven, and promised him a guinea over and above his fare if he would get him there in time to take the boat for Dieppe.

The other cab was already far ahead.

His cab bowled along as if life depended on its speed.

In a word, both cabs reached New Haven in good time, and the survivors of the fatal duel embarked upon the early boat for Dieppe, and made good their escape to France.

Meanwhile poor Molly Faulkner had passed a restless and anxious night at her home in Woodbine Cottage. She had sat up to a very late hour waiting for her "poor Charley."

She had heard train after train blow the signal whistle, as it slowed and stopped at the Sydenham station. And as each in turn came on and stopped, she had said to herself:

"There he is now!" And she had waited ten or fifteen minutes, and then sighed and said to herself:

"He didn't come by *that* train; but he will come by the next."

At length, however, the twelve midnight train from London came shrieking. She thought he was on *that* train certainly, for, after all, that was the train he usually came down on.

And he *was* on that train, as we know, but he was also on his way down to Brighton to fight that duel.

When the train started again, shrieking out of the station on its way, poor Molly sat and watched and listened, expecting every moment to hear the familiar, welcome sound of her Charley's footsteps coming down the lane, and the pleasant click of the gate latch that always announced his arrival at home.

She watched ten, fifteen, twenty minutes, and did not even then give him up.

"He may have met some friend at the station, and, late as it is, stopped to talk to him. Poor Charley is the very mischief for talking, both *in* season and out of season," she said to herself, and she waited five, ten, fifteen minutes more. And then her courage broke down.

Charley had not come home by that train, and now it was certain that he would not come home that night, for there would be no other train until morning.

Watching, suspense, anxiety, and finally disappointment, completely overwhelmed her spirits. She also felt horribly lonesome and sorrowful. She felt that she must see some one, speak to some one, or die.

The clock struck one, with a preternaturally loud detonation.

She jumped up from her seat by the front window, and walked rapidly into the nursery, where her sleeping children lay. She looked at them in their little beds, and then went on to the cot occupied by her young nurse, Bessy Morriss.

"Bessy! Bessy!" she said, gently shaking her.

"Yes, ma'am! Please, the baby's all right," answered the girl, half asleep.

"Bessy! Bessy! I'm sick to death. I'm so nervous I could scream. Wake up!"

"Law, ma'am! Whatever have happened?" cried the girl, now thoroughly aroused.

"Nothing has happened that I know of, except that the last train from London has gone by an hour ago, and Captain Faulkner has not come in."

"Law, ma'am! he have missed the train, that's all," said the girl consolingly.

"Yes, I suppose that *is* all. But, oh, I'm *so* nervous!"

"That's along of sitting up so late, ma'am. Please, I think you'd better go to bed, ma'am, and sleep it off. The time passes quick in sleep, so it do, ma'am, and before you'll know it, the morning will be here, and the Captain too."

"Yes; probably. At least, I think your advice very good, and I will follow it," said Mrs. Faulkner.

And good little Bessy, though it was no part of her duty to do so, slipped out of bed and helped her mistress to undress, and waited affectionately on her until she retired to rest.

And poor Mollie Faulkner, ignorant of the trouble in store for her, fell asleep, and for the remainder of the night slept well.

She slept until very late in the morning.

The young nurse arose at the usual hour, and dressed the children as quietly as she could, that they might not disturb their weary mother.

Mrs. Faulkner continued to sleep until near noon. Then she woke up, and finding how late it was, immediately rang her bell, which was answered by the little nurse.

"What did you let me sleep so long for, Bessy? Why didn't you wake me up as soon as the Captain came home?" she inquired.

"Please, ma'am, the Capting haven't come home yet; and I let you sleep 'cause I thought you wanted of it," said the little nurse.

"The Captain not come home yet!" echoed Molly turning pale. "Why, do you see what o'clock it is? It is nearly twelve, noon!"

"I know it be, ma'am; but the Capting haven't come."

"Oh, my Heaven! my Heaven! what keeps him? What can have happened?" exclaimed Molly, wringing her hands.

"May be, ma'am, he were at one of the Colonel's suppers last night, and is enjoying of one of his bad 'eadaches to day," suggested the little girl.

"That is very, very likely," admitted Molly.

"In course it is, ma'am. You know, if he had a catched the train and got home, he would 'ave 'ad 'is 'eadache here all right. But as he missed of the train and 'ad to stop in London all night, he got caught with his 'eadache in town, and can't come home till he gets better."

"I see! Yes, that must be the reason of his absence. But oh! these irregularities do cost me so much anxiety! Oh, Charley, dear, if you knew how much trouble you give me, you wouldn't do it, love! I'm sure you wouldn't," sighed poor Molly, apostrophizing her absent husband.

"I told cook to make some fresh tea and cream toast for you, ma'am. Will I bring it up?"

"Yes; no, I don't care! Oh, if I only knew where in all London my poor Charley is stopping, I would go to him; but—in all London!" sighed Molly hopelessly.

"You may depend, ma'am, if so be he were sick enough to need you, he would find somebody to send for you," said the little nurse consolingly.

"Yes, I think he would," agreed Molly.

She saw no reason for any extraordinary anxiety now. She reflected how often her erratic Charley had caused her the deepest anxiety for nothing. She was refreshed by her sleep besides, and so she was the more fitted to be patient.

She dressed herself as usual and went down stairs, ate

her breakfast, nursed her baby, walked in the garden, played with her children a little, and then came back into the house and sat down to her needle-work, to wait for the hours to pass that would bring the evening, when "Charley," recovered from his penal "headache," should return.

Still, though she waited calmly, she could not dismiss all anxiety from her mind. Vague fears tormented her at intervals.

"What could have happened to him?" she asked herself.

"Probably a headache, after a revel! But possibly another arrest for debt!" she answered to herself.

"Another arrest for debt!" This was the very worst she feared for him. The idea of such a calamity as death in a duel never once entered her mind.

"And if he were arrested for debt, he would send me word. Oh! it is only his usual wine headache that has overtaken him in London, because he couldn't catch the last train last night and get home in time to have it here. But oh! I wish he would come! I wish I knew exactly where he was, or even where that horrid Colonel Brierly could be found! But I don't know anything about their haunts. Oh, my poor Charley, how much trouble you *do* give me, my dear!"

So, waiting, sighing and gently complaining, Molly passed the day.

Evening came, and the children were called in from their play in the garden, to get their supper of milk and bread, and to be put to bed.

But their mother interposed on this occasion.

"I don't want them to go to bed until their father comes in. Remember that they haven't seen him since yesterday morning. Give them their supper, and then wash and dress them nicely, and bring them in here to wait till their papa comes," she said to the young nurse, as she took her place at the front parlor window to wait for the early evening trains, as on the preceding evening she had watched from her bedroom window for the late night trains.

After a while the children, nicely dressed, and delighted with the privilege of sitting up for papa, joined her there, and half distracted her mind from her anxiety with their innocent prattle.

The gas was lighted in the parlor, hour after hour passed, train after train came shrieking and thundering into the station, and went shrieking and thundering out again, and still he came not.

Anxiety was just beginning to be insupportable again, when the sound of carriage wheels was heard in the lane, approaching the house.

"That's Charley, at last! Poor fellow! he must have been quite ill, to have to get a cab to come from the station in! Children, papa has come!" said Molly, jumping up as the carriage stopped at the gate.

But at that moment little Lily pulled a flower-stand over on herself, and her mother stopped to pick both up, which occasioned a few moments' delay, at the end of which the young nurse, Bessie Morriss, opened the door and naïvely announced:

"A lady as come in a carriage to see Mrs. Faulkner."

Molly started with surprise. A lady to see her! Such a very unusual circumstance! What could the lady want? And at such an hour too? Oh! she must be some one come to her from dear Charley! Dear Charley was too ill to come home, so he had sent for her! Or else he was arrested for debt, and had sent for her all the same! concluded poor Molly, as a spasm of terror for Charley's safety seized her heart, and in some degree prepared her for what she had to hear.

All this occupied but an instant of time.

"Did the lady give her name, Bessie?" inquired Mrs. Faulkner.

"No, ma'am. When I asked her for it, she said I need only say that a lady wished to see you."

"Where have you shown her?"

"Please, ma'am, I haven't shown her anywheres. She's standing at the hall door yet."

"O Bessie! how stupid of you to leave any lady standing at the hall door! Never do such a thing again! Show her in at once!" said Mrs. Faulkner impatiently, and trembling, but more with alarm than from any other cause.

The little nurse retired for a moment, and then ushered in the visitor.

Mrs. Faulkner turned, and saw standing before her a graceful young woman, elegantly dressed in black.

The lady threw aside her vail, revealing a lovely young face, lighted by large tender hazel eyes, and shaded by golden-brown curling hair.

"It is Fay Dammer!" cried little Lily.

"Fay-ee Dammer!" exclaimed Ada.

"Fairy Grandma!" said Charley.

And the three children ran to her and seized her skirts.

"This lady is our Fairy Grandmother, mamma," explained little Mary, as she went up to the visitor and demurely offered her hand.

Yes, it was Angela Melliss, the banker's young wife, Molly's hated step-mother, the children's "Fairy Grandmother."

What had brought her here?

We must go back and see.

CHAPTER X.

BAD NEWS AT CHARLES STREET.

Can honor set a leg? No. Or an arm? No.
Or take away the grief of a wound? No. * * *
Who hath it? He who died o' Wednesday.
Doth he feel it? No. Doth he hear it? No.—SHAKESPEARE.

ABOUT three hours before her visit to Mrs. Faulkner, Angela Melliss had come in from her afternoon drive, and had gone to her room to dress for dinner.

As was her frequent custom, she sat down before her dressing-glass, with the evening paper in her hand, that she might look over it while her maid was combing her hair.

On this occasion, while glancing down the columns of the paper, she suddenly started, and hurriedly exclaimed:

"Put up my hair in any sort of way, Mary, as quickly as you can, and hand me my dressing-gown. This is most horrible!"

"What has happened, dear Madam? I hope nothing dreadful has happened," said the maid impulsively, as she hastily gathered up her lady's golden-brown ringlets, and put them into a net.

Mrs. Melliss was trembling too much to answer.

She drew on the dressing-gown handed her by Mary, and taking the paper from the floor where it had dropped, she hurried with it to her husband's room.

The banker was under his valet's hands.

"Send your man away, Walter, dear; I must speak to you," said Angela, dropping into a chair.

"Leave the room, John," said the banker, taking the hair-brush from the servant's hand.

"Now then, what is it, my love?" he inquired, as soon as the man had gone. Then seeing how pale she was, he exclaimed: "Good Heaven, Angela! what has happened?"

"Read!" she faltered, laying the paper before him on the dressing-table, and pointing to a certain paragraph.

The banker took it up and read:

A SHOCKING EVENT NEAR BRIGHTON.—Devil's Dyke was, early this morning, the scene of a tragedy. A duel was fought on the spot between Colonel Barrett Brierly, late of the Honorable East India Company's service, and Captain Charles Faulkner, late of the Royal Guards, which terminated fatally in the case of Captain Faulkner, who, at the first fire, fell, shot through the heart, and died instantly. The surviving principal of the duel and the two seconds succeeded in making their escape to France. The body of the unfortunate Captain Faulkner is lying at the 'Ship,' where an inquest was held, and a verdict of manslaughter returned against Barrett Brierly as principal, and John Fitz-John and James Aiken as accessories. The cause of this hostile and fatal meeting has not yet transpired."

The banker finished reading the paragraph, laid down the paper and looked into the pale face of his young wife.

"Where is his widow? You know, I am sure, Angela," said Mr. Melliss, speaking with forced calmness.

"Yes, I know where she is. She is living at Sydenham," replied Mrs. Melliss, in a low, sorrowful tone.

"Go, then, at once, my love, and bring her and her children home. Tell her I forgive—" His voice broke down, and his frame shook as with an ague fit. "Tell her anything you will, my love; but if she has not heard of her husband's dreadful fate, do not tell her that. But tell her that she will find him here. I should rather she should be here, in the bosom of her family, when she meets the shock the news of his sudden death will bring. Go to her, Angela. It will be a sorrowful errand, my child, but you will perform it well. I will go down to Brighton by the next train, and see to the removal of the body. The funeral must take place from this house," concluded the banker as he rang the bell.

His valet answered the summons.

"Order Mrs. Melliss' brougham to be brought around immediately, and send one of the grooms to fetch a fly for me," said Mr. Melliss.

And the man, wondering what on earth was the matter, went out to obey his master's directions.

"I will go and get ready at once," said Mrs. Melliss, and she arose and returned to her own room.

She quickly dressed herself in a black driving dress, and was in the act of drawing on her gloves when a parlor maid rapped softly at the door, and being told to come in, entered and said:

"If you please, ma'am, cook says as you are going out just as dinner is ready to be dished, she begs to know your wishes about it."

"Oh! Never mind about dinner, Jane! I cannot think about that now! Mary Kempton, go and use your judgment in the matter," said the lady.

The next servant who came to the door announced Mrs. Melliss' brougham. And the lady being quite ready for her drive, went down stairs.

She found her husband in the hall, waiting to hand her into the carriage.

"Be very, very prudent in your mission, my dear Angela! If it be possible, do not even permit her to suspect the calamity that has befallen her until she is safely housed here," said the banker, as he led her out.

"I will do my very best," replied his wife, as he placed her in her carriage.

His own ordered fly was waiting. And his servant was standing by with his hat, gloves and shawl.

So he took leave of his wife, closed the carriage door, and told her coachman to drive to Sydenham.

Then he sprang into his own ordered fly, and directed the driver to go at his utmost speed to the London Bridge Railway station, promising him an additional fee if he should catch the Brighton express train.

The fly whirled away first.

Mrs. Melliss' brougham left the door.

As it passed out of Charles street, Mrs. Melliss, looking from the window, saw Rachel Wood turning the corner, with a parcel of work in her hands, which she was bringing home.

The banker's wife immediately pulled the check-string and stopped the carriage, and beckoned the seamstress to approach.

Rachel came up to the door, which the footman had already opened for her.

"Oh, Rachel, my good girl, I am so fortunate to meet you! Come right in here and sit by me, and I will explain as we drive along," said the lady.

The seamstress, much wondering, got into the carriage, and took her seat as requested.

"Tell the coachman to drive on," said the lady.

And the footman closed the door, gave the order, and resumed his place.

"I hope you have the evening at your disposal, Rachel, for I need you very much just now," said Mrs. Melliss.

"Yes, madam. I have completed the work you gave me to do, and I was bringing it home when you called me, that is all," said Rachel.

"Never mind the work, Rachel. I have a terrible thing to tell you. Captain Faulkner was killed in a duel this morning, and I am on my way to Sydenham, to bring his poor widow home to her father's house, before breaking the news to her," said the lady.

The seamstress gazed upon the speaker in silent horror and amazement.

"Heaven and earth! what an awful calamity! Oh, how will you ever tell her?" at length exclaimed Rachel.

"How, indeed?" shuddered Mrs. Melliss.

"When did you hear this? How did you hear it?" inquired Rachel.

Mrs. Melliss told Rachel all that she had learned from the newspaper paragraph.

"Oh, Heaven have mercy on the poor widowed wife and orphaned children!" fervently breathed Rachel Wood.

"Heaven has mercy on them, for the heart of the grandfather is moved to send for them and bring them home," said Mrs. Melliss.

And then she told Rachel all that had passed on the subject between herself and Mr. Melliss.

And the lady and the seamstress talked of nothing but the fatal duel, the dead man and the poor unconscious widow and orphans until they reached Sydenham, and turned into Hawthorne lane.

The lights in the front windows of the Cottage drawing-room, placed there for "poor Charley," quite illuminated the house and the upper end of the lane.

The scene looked cheerful. But its very cheerfulness depressed the spirits of the tender-hearted women, who knew what sorrow was presently to change all that light to darkness.

They had, however, scarcely time to think about it before the carriage drew up at the garden gate before the cottage.

The footman jumped down and rang the bell.

And Molly's poor little simple maid answered it, as has been said.

She could not tell whether her mistress was at home or not; but she would take the visitor's name in and see, she said.

But Mrs. Melliss directed her to say only that "a lady" had called to see her mistress.

And the little maid took in the message, and soon returned with a request that the lady would walk in.

"Come, Rachel," said the banker's wife, as she entered the house.

"Dear Mrs. Melliss," said the seamstress, trembling, "give me a few minutes to recover myself. Go on before. I will follow in a moment."

The lady then entered the house, and was shown into the drawing-room.

She was instantly recognized by the children, who crowded around her with exclamations of:

"Fay Dammer!"

"Fay-ee Dranma!"

"Fairy Grandmother!"

"You will kindly pardon my little ones, madam. They know no better than to be so rude in their welcome. And you will please to let me know who it is that honors us with this visit," said Mrs. Faulkner, as she rather formally greeted her visitor.

"I come from your father," murmured the banker's young wife, in some embarrassment.

"I am aware of that, dear madam. I am also aware that you have often come from my dear father, and that you have been the trusted medium of countless benefits from him to me and my children, though I have never had the pleasure of seeing you before, or even of hearing your name. But sit down, dear madam; please sit down," said Molly, drawing forward the best resting chair.

Mrs. Melliss accepted the offered seat just as Rachel Wood, recovering from her agitation, entered the room.

"Ah, Rachel, you here! I am very glad to see you. You have just come in good time. I am sure you know this lady. I wish you to introduce her to me, since she does not introduce herself. She comes from my father *again*, dear Rachel," said Mrs. Faulkner eagerly.

"Madam, have I your permission to tell, *at last?*" inquired Rachel.

Mrs. Melliss nodded assent. She was too much disturbed to speak.

Rachel turned to Mrs. Faulkner, who was waiting impatiently.

"Madam," she said, "this lady visitor of yours, who calls herself your children's Fairy Grandmother, and who has been your benefactress from the beginning, and who is now the best friend you have in the world — this lady, madam, is Mrs. Melliss, the wife of your father!"

Molly gazed from the seamstress to the lady, in stupid amazement.

"You—my—father's—wife?" at length she slowly inquired.

"Yes, dear Mrs. Faulkner, I am your father's wife, and his daughter's friend," gently answered Angela.

Again Molly stared from the lady to the seamstress, and then she slowly inquired:

"You—my—friend? What then turned you from being my bitterest enemy into being my friend?"

"Dear child, I never was your enemy! I have always been your friend," answered Angela.

Molly stared at her in silent wonder.

"I always warned you that you did your young step-mother cruel injustice, Mrs. Faulkner; but you would not believe me without proof, and I was not at liberty to tell you before, what I am happy to tell you now—that it was and it always was your step-mother, and no one else, who has helped you in your trouble, and who has heaped upon you the blessings that you are now enjoying, and who has been striving for years to bring about a reconciliation between your father and yourself, but has never succeeded in doing so until to-night."

"Dear Rachel," interrupted the banker's young wife

"you must do my husband justice. He this evening, unsolicited, quite voluntarily, sent me here to ask his daughter to come home with me, bringing all her children."

"Oh, Rachel!" said Molly, piteously clasping her hands—"Oh, my dear Rachel, is this really true, that you tell me about my step-mother?"

"True as truth, Mrs. Faulkner."

"Oh, then, how bitterly cruel and unjust I have been in my harsh judgments, and in my deep hatred! Oh! how can you ever forgive me, Mrs. Melliss?" inquired poor Molly.

"My child, you have never offended against me; so I have nothing whatever to forgive. The bugbear of a step-mother that you feared and hated so much was never I, but it was only a grim chimera of your own imagination!" said Angela pleasantly.

"That's so!" eagerly exclaimed Molly, delighted to see such a clear way out of her dilemma; "that's so, indeed! Of course it was never you, it *could* never have been *you*, that I hated; for who could hate such an angel as you? No one could—not even such a little devil as I! No, indeed, my dear lady! It was not you I hated! It was a chimera of my own imagination. You never said a truer thing than that. I had made unto myself an image of a step-mother who had been an old maid, tall, raw-boned, skinny, with a sharp nose and thin lips, and with false hair and false teeth and enamelled complexion, as to her person; and with a false heart and artful mind and vindictive temper, as to her soul! And I hated her with all my might. But *I* never hated you."

"No, you never hated me! So, therefore, let us say no more about that. But your father has sent for you to come home to him, with all your children, to-night, my dear. Can you do so?"

"I am delighted at the thought of going—but it is very sudden."

"Yes; but it's best to 'strike while the iron's hot,' as the old proverb advises. I should go at once, if I were you, Mrs. Faulkner," said Rachel.

"I should be only too glad to do so, but you see I am waiting here for my poor Charley, whom I expect from London by every train," said Molly.

The mention of the dead man's name by his unconscious widow produced a sudden silence, that lasted until Molly herself again broke it, by saying:

"You see, Charley hasn't been home since yesterday morning. I *did* expect him last night, but he did not come. He either missed the train last night, or else he has run down to Brighton or to Worthing, or some other place, as he sometimes impulsively does, for a day's airing. Ah, you don't know how much anxiety my poor Charley causes me by his thoughtlessness!" said Molly, shaking her black curls.

"To be sure," said Mrs. Melliss, who now saw her way clear to draw her poor step-daughter home before revealing her heavy bereavement. "And you are right in your conjecture, my dear. We happen to know that Captain Faulkner *did* go down to Brighton last night with a party of gentlemen."

"There! I said so!" exclaimed Molly.

"Your father, who has his own reasons for desiring an immediate and complete reconciliation, has gone down to Brighton to bring him up this very night. Your father desires that the family meeting shall be at his house. So now you have no objection to go, have you?"

"Oh, none at all. Not the least."

"Then get ready, dear," said Mrs. Melliss.

Molly called the nurse to bring the children after her, and then ran up stairs.

"Oh, how fortunate you have been, Mrs. Melliss, to gain her consent to go to London without exciting her suspicions that anything was wrong, and without tampering with truth either!" said Rachel, as soon as they were left alone.

"Ah, yes, Rachel!" But what am I about to do? To 'keep the word of promise to her ear, and break it to her hope.'"

"It seems cruel, but unavoidable. She *must* be at home before she is told," said Rachel.

"Yes, she must. She must be under her father's protection, and in reach of medical assistance; for I warn you, Rachel, that this great sorrow will go very hard with both her mind and body," sighed Mrs. Melliss.

She had no time to add more, for just at that moment Molly entered, followed by all her children, the nurse carrying the youngest baby.

"I was not long, was I? Fortunately, you see, the children were all dressed to receive their father. And I had only to put on their wraps," said Molly pleasantly, as she entered.

The children crowded around their Fairy Grandmother, and seized her hands and skirts, and wanted to know if she were now going to take them to Cinderella's Palace.

Rachel Wood called them off, and took them to the brougham, where they were all, with some difficulty, crowded in. Mrs. Melliss and Molly followed the children into the carriage.

Rachel Wood and the nurse were left to shut up the house and to follow in a hired fly that was to be sent from the Family Hotel.

The drive back to town was, to the children and their mother, a journey full of glee. The children romped and laughed and babbled, and jumped and tumbled about over each other and over their Fairy Grandmother to their heart's content.

And their mother laughed to see them.

In due time they reached London, the West End, and

finally Charles street, and drew up before the banker's residence.

The fly, with Rachel and the nurse, came up almost at the same moment.

Mrs. Melliss led her step-daughter into the house, and installed her into a handsomely furnished suite of spare rooms.

And there Molly took off her own and her children's wraps. And then the children were allowed to run through the house for a little while, and then they were given some light and wholesome refreshment and put to bed

Rachel Wood went home in the hired fly.

Mrs. Melliss ordered supper to be served for herself and her visitor.

"Will you not wait, dear, for papa and Charley?" inquired Molly, with a look of anxiety.

"I think not. Your papa will scarcely return before the last train; that will make it much too late for our supper," said Mrs. Melliss, who thought it much the best that Molly should be fortified by a good meal for the shock she must shortly sustain.

So the two ladies supped alone together.

And then Angela would have persuaded Molly to go to bed, in the faint hope that she might also go to sleep, and thus escape hearing the bad news until morning.

But Molly very naturally insisted upon sitting up until the return of her papa and Charley.

They sat together until one o'clock, and then began to listen for the door bell to ring. At length, near two o'clock after midnight, the door bell did ring.

And as all the servants had been sent to bed, Mrs. Melliss herself went out to answer it.

"Stay here, my dear, until I return," she said to Molly.

She ran and opened the door to her husband.

"Well, dearest, have you brought my daughter home?" whispered the banker.

"Yes, and her children," answered Angela.

"Does she know anything?"

"Nothing. She thinks she comes here to meet her husband and to assist at a family reconciliation."

"Poor child! poor child!"

"Dear, you look so weary. Will you not take something before you see her?"

"No, no; I require nothing," said Mr. Melliss, as he mechanically hung up his shawl and hat.

Angela had been trembling to ask another question. She asked it now, in two whispered words:

"*The body!*"

"It will reach town to-morrow, in charge of the undertaker. The funeral will be held at this house. Now let us go to my daughter."

Angela opened the back drawing-room door, and went before her husband to the sofa where her step-daughter sat eagerly expectant.

"Your father, my dear," she said.

Molly sprang up and ran, and then stopped, trembling.

Her father came to her, put his arms around her, and silently folded her to his breast.

"Papa!" she murmured, kissing him — "dear papa, though I cannot say I am sorry for having married my poor Charley, yet I can say, with earnest truth, that I am very, very sorry my marriage should have so displeased you. You forgive me, dear papa?"

"I forgive you from the bottom of my heart, my own dear daughter!"

"And my poor Charley! You forgive him too?"

"I forgive him with all my soul."

"Then where is my Charley? Lurking behind, I suppose, so as not to interrupt our first meeting! Poor Charley is always so considera e in these little matters. But you will let him come in n w?"

The hour had come in which she must be told of her horrible bereavement. Yet neither the banker nor his young wife could summon courage to tell her.

She looked from one to the other, and saw that there was something withheld from her knowledge.

"Where is Charley? Why does he not come in?" she inquired, in a slightly tremulous tone.

"My dear child, your husband did not return with me," said the banker gravely.

"Not return with you! Oh, why? Is anything wrong with my dear Charley?"

"Come and sit down, my darling," said the banker, leading her to a sofa, and placing her between himself and his young wife.

"Oh! why don't you answer my question? Oh, papa! what is it that you are keeping from me?" she cried, in a piteous voice.

The banker covered his face with his hands, and his young wife wept.

"Heaven of Heavens! What do you both mean? What has happened? Is Charley ill? Is Charley—Oh, my heart!—Is Charley—*dead?*"

Her father took her in his arms, and tried to soothe her.

Her step-mother kneeled down beside her, and begged her to try to be calm.

But she declared that she knew some terrible calamity had befallen her, and she insisted upon knowing what it was.

Then they gently, tenderly told her the terrible truth.

And here I would willingly draw a vail over the scene that followed.

Poor Molly had never in her life possessed the least self-control. And now she abandoned herself to the wildest anguish and despair, ending in strong convulsions.

Her father laid her on the sofa, and her step-mother loosened all her clothes.

The household was aroused, and a physician was summoned.

And she was conveyed to bed, and by medical advice she was put under the influence of a strong narcotic, that finally gave her agonized spirit rest.

The next morning, while the young widow was still sleeping under the influence of morphia, the body of her husband was brought to the house and laid out in the front drawing-room.

That forenoon the letters from poor Faulkner, mailed from Paris by Fitz-John, his absconding second, arrived.

Mr. Melliss laid carefully aside the letter addressed to his daughter. Then he opened and read the one written to himself. And if he had never forgiven poor Charley before he must have done so now.

On the fourth day, while Molly was still very ill in bed, the funeral took place. Before the coffin was finally closed, the young widow, at her own earnest prayer, was lifted out of bed and carried to the room where the dead lay, that she might take a last look at all that remained of her gay and handsome Charley.

But the ordeal was too severe for her. Again she gave way to the wildest agony of grief, and again fell into spasms, and so was carried off to bed and quieted only by powerful narcotics.

Not the least trying scene in this tragedy was the grief of the poor children beside the open coffin of their dead father, where they too had been taken, that they might kiss the cold face before it was forever hidden from their view.

But Angela Melliss took them to herself and soon consoled them, for the grief of innocent children is happily very short-lived.

The remains of Captain Faulkner were finally laid in the

family vault of Walter Melliss, in the Kensal Green Cemetery.

Days passed before the young widow could sleep without opium, or take any food except in a liquid form, or even bear the sight of her own children.

Weeks passed before she could be persuaded to leave her own room, or take an airing with Mrs. Melliss in a carriage.

But at length youth and nature conquered sorrow and despair, and the active duties of life drew her from her seclusion.

It was on the third day that she had made her appearance in the drawing-room, when she was told that a person at the door wished particularly to see her.

She directed the servant to admit the "person," who entered the drawing-room, and proved to be Adams, the detective employed by the late Captain Faulkner to look up Benny.

He greeted the mourning widow with deep respect, and apologized for intruding on her privacy in these early days of her widowhood, but pleaded the compelling force of the law.

"The fact is, Madam," he said, "that desperate young snakesman, Ben. Hurst, who let in the burglars on the night of the robbery at your house, is taken at last, and is now in the hands of the police. And you are wanted, Madam, to give evidence against him."

CHAPTER XI.

HOW BENNY WAS BETRAYED.

Then earth arose, and in her might,
To vindicate her injured right,
Thrust him in deeper dens of night.—A. A. Ipocrea.

This was the manner in which Benny came to be arrested.

For weeks he had hidden himself away in that miserable den in that wretched court with Tony Brice, the Nut Cracker and other pickpockets, snakesmen and burglars—not that he for an instant suspected that he himself was in any degree implicated in the robbery at Woodbine Cottage, and the assault with intent to kill in Hawthorne Lane; but that he feared to be taken as a witness against his father.

When some weeks had passed, however, without any apparent cause for alarm, Benny became more confident of safety, and he also grew sick to see his playmate, Suzy Juniper.

So one Monday morning he stole out of his den in the court, and glided through lanes, alleys and back streets, until he reached the court-yard behind the Thespian Temple and the back buildings where the stage carpenter and his family lodged.

He opened the door and went in to the large family room, where, as usual, he found the father, mother, and all the girls and boys gathered for their midday meal, which was not yet quite ready to go on the table.

Suzy was the first to recognize Benny, and she ran eagerly to meet him. She looked worn and weary, but flushed with excitement as she accosted him with:

"Oh, Benny! I am so glad to see you! Wherever have you been this long, long, long time?"

"I've—I've been away," said Benny, still careful not to betray his father by any chance. "But I'm so glad to find you home, Suzy! I tried to time my visit so as to catch you just after you came home from rehearsal."

"I don't go to rehearsal no more, Benny. Oh, such news! I have left the London stage for good, Benny! Oh, I have got such lots to tell you! But come in and speak to mother and father and the children first; they're a looking at you, ever so!"

Benny went further into the room and shook hands with Mr. and Mrs. Juniper, who greeted him with cheerful kindness, and said that he must stay to dinner, "which it was their favorite dish of tripe and inyons, with a pot of beer round." And then he shook hands with all the little Junipers, and they greeted him noisily, and informed him that "Suzy was a going to France along of the great Madame Vesta, and was a going to make all their fortunes right off!"

"Yes," said Suzy, "that's so, Benny! Come and sit right down here by me on this little bench, like we used to do, and let me tell you all how and about it, Benny."

Benny, much pleased, and also a little bewildered by all that he saw and heard, took the seat beside his little playmate, who immediately put her left arm around his waist, and drew his right arm around hers, "like we used to do in Junk Lane, Benny," she said, and then prepared to tell him all her news.

"You know the last time you was here, Benny, when I told you so many offers was made for me to sing and dance and act at other theatres?"

"Yes."

"Well, one come to our manager, from the agent of the great Madame Vesta, who was forming a troupe to go to Brighton for a short season. Well, you see, our manager was trying it on with Shakespeare again, which he can't come it, you know, Benny, and never could. Howsever it was to be a Shakespeare go for two weeks, and so I wasn't wanted here, and was let of to go to Brighton along of Madame Vesta's troupe. So I went. Oh! it's a heavenly place compared to London, Benny—is Brighton."

"I know. I've been there," said Benny.

"Yes, you told me all about that, you know, and how the beautiful children on Brunswick Terrace took you in and gave you a slice of the Twelfth-day cake, and all that!"

"And how I got the ring, and was made king!"

"Yes. Well, Benny, I had good times at Brighton, too. I played every night in such beautiful and splendid dresses as a'most dazzled my own eyes, and mostly with wings too! I was one time a Flower Fairy, a Diamond Queen, an Air Spirit, a Fountain Fay, a Spring Sprite, and, oh! once I was the Angel of the sun, in a glorious dress of golden gauze spangled with diamonds, and wings of the same, to represent the sun's rays, you know!"

"That must a been splendid!"

"It just was! Well, you see, Madame Vesta took notice of me and picked me out from all the rest, and so—and so —and so—"

"And so the long and short of it is," interrupted Mrs. Juniper, "the great Madame Vesta wants to take my gal to France with her, to be under her own pertection, which she offers her sich good wages—"

"Salary, mamma," amended Miss Suzy.

"Sich good salaries then, an' me and her father don't feel justified in refusing of her."

"Specially as the great Madame do promise and vow that our gal shall have private chutors and time to get her schoolin'," added the stage carpenter.

"Which Madame says I must have some education to make the most of my gifts," put in Suzy.

Benny looked from one speaker to another in sympathetic pleasure, though upon the whole he seemed rather bewildered by all this.

"And so, in fine, she is to go to Paris with Madame when Madame returns from her engagement in Vienna," said Mrs. Juniper.

"When will that be, Suzy?" inquired Benny.

"About the first of January, when Madame will open her new theatre. An't you glad, Benny?"

"I'm glad o' your good luck, Suzy; but I'm sorry you're going away."

"Oh, but, Benny, I'm going to begin to make a fortune. And that'll be for your good as well as mine, dear. And, oh! Benny, I forgot to tell you!—oh, how selfish it was of me to be a thinking only of myself! Benny, there's a stroke of good luck for you too!"

"For me!" exclaimed the little outcast in astonishment.

"Oh, yes, indeed! You know these missionary gents as go about looking up poor boys and girls to put them to school?"

"No, I don't. I never see none on 'em. I don't know what you mean."

"O yes, you do, Benny! Good gents in black coats as—"

"Oh! you mean Gospel Grinders, as puts a printed pamphlet in your hand when you're starving for a piece of bread! And tells you to be good and read it when you don't know one letter from t'other!"

"Oh, Benny, Benny, that's not the way to talk of the pious clergy!"

"That's the way Tony and the Nut Cracker talks on 'em, and *they* knows."

"No, they *don't* know, Benny. And you mustn't mind 'em. They try to make you a bad boy, Benny. And they've been trying to do it all their lives. But they can't make a very bad boy of you, Benny, that's certain, because you've got such a good heart! But you mustn't speak ill of dignities, Benny."

"Well, then, I won't, Suzy, if you don't like it. I won't do nothink to tease you."

"That's you, Benny. I knew you wouldn't."

"And now what about the parson, Suzy?"

"Oh, Benny, yes! The parson is a real sweet-spoken gentleman, as does a great deal of good, which he is connected with a public school which he wants to put you to, Benny."

"Put me to school? What does he know about me?" inquired Benny, distrustful and alarmed.

"Oh, I'm sure I don't know as he knows anything more'n we've told him! And we've told him nothink but what's good of you, Benny. And he comes two or three times a week to inquire after you, Benny."

"I don't like him. I'm going home, Suzy," said the wretched boy, whose life, passed among thieves and beggars, had sharpened his wits to detect a detective.

"What are you afraid of, Benny? Don't go till after dinner. See! I'm dishing of it up now. And only smell how good it is! Tripe and inyons! We don't have that every day, I can tell you," said Mrs. Juniper, as she sat a large bowl filled with the savory mess steaming hot upon the table.

"But I want to go home. I don't want to see that man as is looking after me," persisted the boy, notwithstanding the tripe and onions.

"Well, you shall go home the minute you've had your dinner," said the good mother of the family.

"And a pot of beer," added the kind-hearted father.

"And you sha'n't go home a minute before that," said Suzy positively.

And Benny yielded to the will of this innocent little Delilah.

They gathered around the table and made very merry over it.

But ah! the meal was scarcely concluded, and the little pots of beer were not half empty, when the door opened and the disguised detective walked in.

The stage carpenter and his wife and his daughter at once arose from the table and most respectfully greeted the visitor.

"Oh, keep your seats, keep your seats, my friends, and go on with your dinner. There is no pleasanter sight in this sinful world, than a father and mother with their young brood gathered around the family board," said the pretended parson.

"Would your reverence do us so much honor as to join us?" inquired Jerry, who honestly believe tripe and onions to be an irresistible temptation to all classes of society.

"No, thank you. Have you heard anything yet of our interesting young friend, Benjamin Hurst?" inquired the disguised detective.

"Why, Lor' bless your reverence! there he is now!" said Jerry, pointing with his fork to Benny, who, poor boy! had already recognized in the pretended parson the disguised detective—not that he had ever seen the individual before, but that he had a thorough acquaintance with the species.

"Oh! Ah! So that is our interesting little friend, is it? That is Benjamin Hurst, is it?"

"Yes, sir, that's the boy; and a better boy, barring the bad example of his companions you won't find nowhere, sir," said honest Jerry Juniper.

"No, that you won't, sir," added Jenny Juniper.

As for Suzy, she looked wistfully into the supposed minister's face, to see if he really were so well disposed to Benny as he professed and she believed him to be; but she could make nothing that she had not already made out of that smiling countenance.

"So this is our young friend, is it?" said the pretended parson, going around the table and standing beside Benny

"How do you do, sir? And where have you been this long while, away from your anxious friends?" he inquired.

"Please, sir, I an't been up to nothink to be tuk for, sir!—please, sir, indeed I an't!" pleaded Benny.

"Why, of course you haven't. Who said you had?" jocosely inquired the visitor.

"Please, sir, nobody didn't! But, please, sir, I knows you, sir! Please, sir, I know as you an't no parson, sir. Please, sir, I know as you're a detective. But, please, sir, I an't been up to nothink to be tuk for, sir!" pleaded Benny.

It was wonderful, but from the moment that Benny had instinctively detected the detective, every one in the room believed him, and followed suit.

"I wouldn't 'ave 'ad this 'appened in my 'ouse for a ten pound note down!" said the stage carpenter indignantly.

"What ever has the boy been up to, sir?" demanded Mrs. Juniper.

"Benny hasn't been up to anything bad. I know he hasn't," added Suzy positively.

"I am sorry to undeceive you, my good friends, but this young rascal is about *the* greatest young rascal now in London!"

"He's not! Benny's not! You great, big, ugly, hairy, clawry, old story-telling fie-for-shame, you! Pretending to be a good parson, coming to put Benny to school, and all the time being of a deceiving old detective, coming to take him to prison—like the wickedest old willian in all the plays I play in—so you are!" burst forth Suzy, in a torrent of childish indignation.

"Whe-ew, my dear! It's clear to me that the great Madame will need to have you educated, before she can make a great actress of you," said the detective, with a laugh.

Suzy turned away from him in childish scorn, and addressed herself to Benny.

"Oh, Benny, Benny, I'm so sorry! I didn't know he was a detective. None of us didn't, or we would never a let him darken our doors, so we wouldn't."

"Don't cry, Suzy. You couldn't help of it. Them sort's a deal too sharp for the likes o' you. Lord bless you, Suzy! they'd deceive—yes—they'd deceive each other. And I couldn't say more'n that," said Benny.

"And you an't mad long o' me, Benny?" pleaded the little girl.

"Mad long o' you, Suzy? I never was mad long o' you in my life. And no more I couldn't be."

"And you an't been up to nothink they can hurt you for. I know you an't, Benny."

"Lor' bless you! no; not a thing. I know what they want: they want to make me 'peach; but they'll have a healthy time doing that, you mind!" said the boy, overcoming his own fright and plucking up a spirit to reassure his little friend.

"But what have he been a doing of?" inquired Mrs Juniper.

"Yes; what *ever* is he took for? You haven't told us that yet," added Mr. Juniper.

"He's took for being implicated in a burglary where there was a very considerable amount of property stolen, and an assault with intent to kill made, and all but a murder committed. That's what he's took for," said the detective, who had now laid his hands on the accused.

"What! *that* child!" exclaimed the stage carpenter, staring.

"Yes, sir, that boy. And it was his master's house that he helped to rob."

"What! the place where he was living page, and run away from?" inquired Mrs. Juniper.

"The same, ma'am. He admitted a set of burglars to his own master's house to rob and murder."

"I didn't, Suzy. I didn't do no such a thing," exclaimed Benny, bursting into indignant tears.

"I know you didn't, Benny," said his little friend, in perfect trust.

"And I wouldn't never a helped to rob no house as Lily and Charley and Mary and Ada lived in, so I wouldn't!" wept the boy.

"I know you wouldn't, Benny. You needn't tell me," said Suzy.

"Then, pray, how came you by this, sir?" inquired the detective, who had been quietly searching the person of the boy, and now produced from his pocket a small gold thimble, marked with the name of M. M. FAULKNER.

"That was give to me in London here, sir; indeed, indeed it was, sir; and I was a bringing of it for a gift to Suzy."

"Oh, it was given to you. Of course it was! And by whom?"

Benny did not understand, or would not.

"Who gave you this gold thimble?" inquired the detective, varying the form of his question.

Benny could not or would not tell.

"Come, then, my fine fellow. We'll see what the magistrate will say to you!" said the detective, taking the boy by the shoulder, to march him off.

"Oh, sir," said Suzy, smothering her resentment, that she might plead the cause of her friend—"Oh, sir, please, you won't hurt Benny, sir! Please, he's a good boy, sir! Indeed he is! He didn't do it, sir; indeed he didn't! You may take my word for that!"

"Oh, yes! we'll take your word for that! Of course we will! Come along, you young rascal!" said the detective, first answering the little girl, and then giving the boy a jerk.

"Oh, sir! please don't hurt Benny! I'm sorry I sauced

at you just now! But I won't do it never no more, if you will please not to hurt Benny," she pleaded.

"Suzy, don't you cry! *I'm* all right! I an't been up to nothink. And if I an't been up to nothink, they can't do nothink with me. They want me to peach; that's what they want. And they'll have a healthy time a getting of me to do it!" said the boy, defiantly.

"Come along, sir!" said the detective, dragging him.

"Well, I'm a coming along, an't I? But you'll let a cove take leave of his friends first, won't you?" cried Benny, breaking suddenly away from his captor, and giving his hand to Mrs. Juniper and then to Suzy to say "good-bye." But when he offered his hand to Mr. Juniper for the same purpose, the honest stage carpenter took up his old hat and said:

"I'll go along and see you through this, my boy.

"Thank y', sir," said Benny.

"Oh, papa, thank y' too from me!" added Suzy.

And then the detective walked off with Benny, followed by Mr. Juniper.

CHAPTER XII.

HOW BENNY WAS COMMITTED FOR TRIAL.

"True to the only faith he knew."—DEEMS.

WHEN they reached the magistrate's office, which was but a short distance off, they found the place still full of the usual morning crowd of petty delinquents who had been arrested on the previous evening for such minor offences as drunkenness, disorderly conduct, and so forth.

Many of these had to be examined and disposed of before Benny's turn came.

When at length it did, the detective led the boy up before the magistrate and said:

"Please your worship, this is the young snakesman the police have been in search of so long, and I arrested him this morning."

"Ah! What is the charge against him?"

"Please your worship, he was concerned in the robbery at the late Captain Faulkner's place, Woodbine Cottage, Hawthorne Lane, Sydenham, where there was a quantity of property stolen, and an assault with intent to kill, that almost ended in a murder."

"Ah! ah!" said the magistrate, putting on his spectacles and leaning over his table to take a nearer look at such a precocious young criminal.

"Please your worship, this is one of the worst young villains in all London, and connected with the most desperate set of thieves and burglars to be found anywhere. With the Nut Cracker and his gang!" continued the detective, with much unction.

"Ah! ah! Now what have you got to say to all this, boy?" inquired the magistrate, still staring through his spectacles at the little prisoner.

"Please your vorship, I an't been up to nothink at all!" answered Benny, raising his blue eyes frankly to the face of the magistrate.

"Ah! you haven't! Where are your witnesses, officer?"

"The witnesses are Mrs. Faulkner, widow of the late Captain Faulkner—she is now with her father, Mr. Melliss of Charles Street—and a Mr. Riley of Sydenham, and a Mr. Briggs of Lower Norwood."

"When can you produce them?"

"To-morrow morning, your worship."

"Then the prisoner must be detained in custody until to-morrow morning—half-past eleven, officer. That will give us time to clear off all smaller cases before this comes up. Take him away."

And Benny was taken to the station-house and locked up.

The stage carpenter went with him to his temporary lodging, and took leave of him at the door, advising him to keep a stiff upper lip.

"Never you mind," said Benny; "I'm not scared. Give my love to Suzy, and tell her as I'm all right."

And the stage-carpenter went home and reported, and tried to console his weeping little daughter, by telling her that he felt quite sure the boy would come out all right in the end.

The next morning, at half past eleven o'clock, the little prisoner was again brought before the magistrate, where he found assembled his late mistress, in her deep mourning, and with her two men whom he had never seen before.

As soon as the prisoner was brought up, the clerk dipped his pen in ink and prepared to take down the charge which Mrs. Faulkner, being duly sworn, was requested to make.

Poor innocent Molly began by saying:

"Mr. Magistrate, I want you to understand that I don't wish to have this poor boy punished at all. All I want you to do is to frighten him a bit, so as to make him tell where the stolen goods are and give them up; for you see, sir, they are many of them relics and memorials of my poor, dear, dead Charley."

The magistrate looked puzzled for a moment, and then asked:

"What is it that you want, madam?"

"I *don't* want to have the poor boy sent to prison. I only want you to frighten him a bit, to make him give up the stolen goods, and then let him off."

"O! Then, if I *do* understand you, madam, you wish to—COMPOUND A FELONY?"

"Yes " said Molly eagerly, as if glad to have her kind intentions so briefly expressed; "*that's* what I want to do —to 'compound a felony.'"

But, mind you, poor Molly had no more idea of what compounding a felony meant than—than you or I have.

The magistrate smiled in a sour sweet sort of way, and without taking any further notice of her innocent intention to "compound a felony," he requested her to make her statement.

"And mind you, missus, you needn't to go for to confound no felonies, not on my account, 'cause I hadn't nothink to do with it. They want me to peach! that's what they want me to do! which I hope they'll get it," said Benny.

"Hold your tongue, sir!" commanded the magistrate.

And then Mrs. Faulkner made her statement. She told all she knew of the boy, from the time he entered her late husband's service, to the time he was supposed to have assisted in the robbery of their house.

And the clerk took her words down in writing.

Then a Mr. Riley, from Sydenham, testified that he had been walking in the neighborhood of Hawthorne Lane about one hour after midnight, on the night of the robbery and attempted murder, when he was startled by a cry for help, and had gone to the lane, where he found a man lying on the ground, bleeding from a wound in the leg, and another man, Captain Faulkner, endeavoring to raise him; that he had helped to carry the wounded man, who was called Colonel Brierly, down the lane to Woodbine Cottage, the residence of Captain Faulkner, where they found drawers broken open and rifled, and other signs of the recent robbery; that he had remained with the wounded man and the terrified family while Captain Faulkner went to call a surgeon, and to give information of the robbery to the police.

The third witness, John Briggs, stationer at Lower Norwood, testified that he had been to a convivial party at Sydenham, and was standing under the shelter of a tree just at the point where the lane went in from the high-road, waiting for an omnibus to take him home, when he saw the prisoner approach, followed by a tall, stout man. He saw them both pause at the entrance of the lane, and saw the prisoner point up the lane, and heard him whisper to his companion that that was the house, and that it was the kitchen door which was open. And then both disappeared in the shadows of the lane. And the witness saw no more of them, for the omnibus he was waiting for came by, and he immediately got into it and rode home.

And that was all he knew of the robbery at Woodbine Cottage.

Although this testimony bore very heavily upon the young prisoner, he seemed really to brighten under it.

And why?

Because he learned from it that Colonel Brierly, whom his "father" had shot, had not been killed, as he had supposed, but had been only slightly wounded—that therefore his "father" was no murderer, and in no danger of the gallows.

Nevertheless Benny resolved to be true to the only faith he had ever been taught, and not upon any account to betray his father to imprisonment or transportation.

"What have you got to say to this charge?" sternly demanded the magistrate.

Now Benny might have fully and entirely exculpated himself from all suspicion of complicity in the robbery, by only revealing the truth, telling how he had run away and left the door open behind him, and had accidentally met his "father" and told him all about it, and how his "father" had offered to go back and shut the door, and made that errand the pretence, unsuspected by Benny, to commit the robbery.

But to vindicate himself in this manner would have been to betray his supposed father. And Benny would have died before he would have done such a thing.

So he hung down his head and kept silent.

"What have you got to say to all this, I ask you, sir?" again demanded the magistrate.

Still Benny kept silence. And there was a strange blending of native gentleness with acquired defiance in the look and manner of the boy, utterly incomprehensible and perplexing to those who knew nothing of the dreadful fatality that had given him gentle birth and ruffianly training.

"Answer, sir! What have you to say to this charge?" a third time was demanded of the boy.

And now he lifted his fair, refined face and fixed his mild blue eyes upon the questioner, and answered calmly:

"Nothink, sir."

The magistrate, meeting those innocent eyes, pitied the poor boy, and said:

"Now attend to me, you sir. You are very young—quite a child; and on account of your tender years, you may be let off, if you will do what you ought to do."

At the unexpected kindness expressed in this address, tears filled the eyes of the boy. And the magistrate, encouraged by these signs of sensibility, went on to say:

"If you will give such information as shall lead to the arrest of the miscreants concerned in this robbery, you will only be retained for a short time as Queen's evidence against them, and will afterwards be discharged free of any penalty."

The magistrate ceased to speak, and waited for the prisoner's answer.

But Benny fell into silence.

"Will you do this?" he inquired.

Benny did not answer.

"Will you give up your companions?"

"Benny! answer, child! If you will tell who robbed the house, you will go free, you know," whispered Mrs. Faulkner, approaching him.

But Benny shook his head.

"My lad, you'd better tell his worship all you know, if you want to get out of this clear," whispered Jerry Juniper.

But Benny shook his head.

"Are you going to give information, sir, or not?" inquired the magistrate.

"No, I an't!" said Benny, taking up his mood of defiance. "I won't peach on my pals—no, not for nothink as you could do to me. *I* an't afeard!"

"You see before you a very hardened young offender, your worship; tender in years, but hardened in crime," said the officer who had the boy in charge.

"Hold your tongue, Adams!" said his worship.

Then turning to the little prisoner again, he said:

"Do you know that by your obstinacy you incur a very great penalty? and that unless you will give the required information, I shall have to commit you to Newgate, to answer to the charge of burglary at the Old Bailey?"

At the sound of those terror-striking words, "Newgate," "Old Bailey," Benny turned sick and pale, and leaned against the railings in front of the justice's table.

The magistrate noted these symptoms of yielding, and tried his subject again.

"You have only to give us the names of the men who have drawn you into this trouble and tell where to look for them, and you need have no fear for yourself. Will you do so?"

Benny was silent.

"Will you do so? Answer boy!"

"No, your worship; I won't peach, not for nothink as you could do to me."

"He is incorrigible," sighed the justice.

"Oh, Benny, just think! They'll put you in jail, and try you in court, and may be send you off to Bottomy Bay, where you'll never see Suzy no more!" said Jerry Juniper ready to cry.

"I wouldn't mind it if it wasn't for Suzy," sobbed the boy, as his chest heaved with a great swell, and the tears rained down his face.

"Suzy's heart would break, Benny. Tell his worship what he wants to know, for Suzy's sake!" pleaded Jerry.

"Do, Benny," added Mrs. Faulkner.

"I'd do most anythink in the world for Suzy 'cept peach, but I can't peach on my pals; no, not even for Suzy," wept the boy.

"Your worship," said Jerry, coming up before the bench and tugging at his forelock, "might I be so bold, as for to speak?"

"Yes, man, if you can speak to the purpose."

"I think I can, your worship. Which I meant to say, if as how it be more of a hobject to catch them burglarious willains as misled this boy into this here trouble, than it be to punish this here boy hisself, I think as I have a little gal at home as can coax him to tell where them reprobates is to be found—which they was play-fellows ever since they was babies, sir, and are mightily wrapped up in each other."

"Very well. I am exceedingly unwilling to commit a child like this upon so heavy a charge. I will give him another chance. I will remand him until this hour to-morrow. And, in the mean time, if you or your girl can persuade him to give up the villains who really committed the robbery, and to turn Queen's evidence against them, you or she will be the means, at the same time, of saving the boy and serving the community," said the justice.

"Thank your worship. We'll try," said Jerry, touching his forelock, and retiring.

"Officer, remove the prisoner," was the next order.

And the magistrate arose from his seat, and the policeman cleared the room.

"Give my love to Suzy. Tell her never to fear. I am all right," said Benny, as, in the custody of the officer, he passed Jerry Juniper.

"Suzy and I'll come to see you to-morrow," answered the stage carpenter, turning to shake hands with the boy.

"And please, Mrs. Faulkner, give my duty to Master Charley and the little young ladies, and tell 'em as how I never done it, and I would a died sooner'n cracked a case where they lived."

"I'll tell them, Benny," said the lady through her tears.

"And Mr. Juniper!" said the boy, calling after the retreating stage carpenter.

"What is it, Benny?"

"Don't let poor Suzy cry about me. Tell her as how I'm all right!"

CHAPTER XIII.

THE LITTLE PRISONER.

Branding him with a deeper brand,
A shame he could not understand.—A. A. Proctor.

"Oh, father! how about Benny?" breathlessly inquired Suzy Juniper, who had been for hours on the watch for her father's return, and now ran out to meet him.

"I can't tell you quite just now, my little maid. 'Tan't decided yet," answered Mr. Juniper, as he entered his own home.

"How about the boy?" inquired Mrs. Juniper, placing

a chair for her husband, while all the young Junipers gathered around him with eager, questioning faces.

"I've just told Suzy as nothing is decided yet. But this I know, he's got a chance to get clear off, if he *will*," said the stage carpenter, nodding his head as he took his seat.

"Oh, father, I'm so glad! For of course he *will*," exclaimed Suzy, while her mother joined her in expressions of delight.

"Well now, you see, I don't know so much about that," said Jerry dubiously, shaking his head. "This here is what it is—whether he be guilty, or whether he be innercint—"

"—Oh, innocent, father!" This from Suzy.

"Well, innercint be it then. Which, innercint as he may be, he's unfortinitly known to be cornected with a gallus bad lot of cads. Which, on account of his tender age, and on conditions he will give such infermations to the perlice as shall lead to them being took up and brought to justice, he will be received as Queen's evidence on the trial, and so get clean off hisself."

"Of course the boy'll do that," said Mrs. Juniper.

"I'm not so sure, do you see! But if he *do* do it, he'll get off hisself scot free."

"And if he don't do it?"

"It'll go gallus hard with him. He'll be lagged for seven or ten or may be fourteen year. Not only house-breaking, you see, but 'sault with intent to kill mixed up along of it," said Jerry sorrowfully, shaking his head.

"Oh, father!" breathed Suzy, clasping her hands. "Can nobody persuade him to give up the wicked men?"

"I don't know, dear. *I* couldn't, and his Worship couldn't, and the lady, his former missus, couldn't. But the magestrit wouldn't commit him yet a while, but just remanded of him until to-morrer, to give him another chance. And I'm thinking, my little maid, that if I take you to him in prison to-morrer, you can persuade him to blow on them fellers and save hisself."

"Oh, yes, yes, yes, father! I know I can. Benny'll do anything in the world for me. I'm so glad that you thought of it, you good pappy!" said Suzy eagerly.

And so delighted was she at the prospect of being the means of saving her young friend, that she forgot all about her own fine fortune as the protégée of the great Madame Vesta, and she talked of nothing but poor Benny.

And very early the next morning, Jerry Juniper and his little daughter presented themselves at the police station-house, and requested admittance to see Benny Hurst.

Being recognized by the policeman who had Benny in charge, they were at once admitted.

Benny was not in the large common room, where all the crowd of transient prisoners were detained. By order of the magistrate, he had been placed in a cell to himself, lest "evil communications" with older and more hardened offenders should confirm him in his resolution to shield his supposed confederates in crime.

As soon as the cell door was opened, Suzy ran in, and found him sitting alone on the side of a narrow little bench that had served him as a bed, and that was the only piece of furniture in the bare den. He was playing idly with his finger, and his sad blue eyes were fixed on vacancy.

As soon as she saw him, so lonely and forlorn, she threw her arms around his neck and burst into tears, crying:

"Oh, Benny! Benny! Benny! Benny! to think of your being here in such trouble! And it all *our* fault too! for it was just the same as if we had betrayed you into the hands of that detective. Oh, Benny, I don't know how you can ever forgive us, or be friends with us, or even so much as bear the sight of us, any more! But we didn't mean to do you any harm. Indeed we didn't, Benny, dear! We never thought that man was a detective, looking after you! We truly thought he was the city missionary, as he pretended to be."

"I know it, Suzy. Don't cry, please. I an't mad long o' you. How could I be? You couldn't help it, Suzy, dear. There, don't cry! please don't!" pleaded Benny, beginning himself to shed tears, of which he felt ashamed.

"You are so good, Benny, so good! and to think we have brought you to this! But we didn't mean it," repeated the girl.

"*You* never brought me to this, Suzy. Neither you nor yourn didn't. You was always the best friends as ever I had, you and yourn. So 'twa'n't you, you see. It was them detectives—bust 'em!" said the boy.

"There, my lass," now began Jerry Juniper, coming forward; "that'll do! Don't take on no more. You see you break the lad right down! Just take a consideration on to it, that you couldn't help his being brought here, but you *can* help to get him out of here."

"And simmerlerly just think, Suzy, as how even if I *be* here, and even if I *should be* lagged, I'll never do nothink dishonoble. They may put me in prisin, or they may send me to Bottomy, or they may scrag me, but they'll never make me blow on anybody!" said the boy triumphantly.

"Oh, Benny! Benny! don't say that! I come here a purpose to beg you give up the wicked men that did the robbery as you are took for. You know who did it, Benny. And you know where they are!"

"If I do—and mind, I don't go to say as I do—but if so *be* I do, I'd die afore I'd tell!" said the boy stubbornly.

"Oh, Benny! not even for my sake?"

"No, not for yourn!" shaking his fair head.

"Oh, Benny! do you love them bad—bad—men better'n you love me?" wept his little friend.

"No, I don't love 'em one bit—even supposing I knows 'em, which I don't own I do—and I love you a great deal, Suzy!"

"Well, then, why won't you tell on them for my sake, if you love me more than you love them?" urged the girl.

"I say as I don't love them a *bit*—s'posing as I know 'em, as I don't say I do—and I love you *heaps*. But I never *did* peach, and I never *will!*" said the boy, still very stubbornly.

Suzy burst into fresh tears, and wept as only a distressed child can.

"Oh, please don't cry any more! It *cuts*, Suzy! It do, indeed. Don't, Suzy! I would do a most anythink in the world to please you, Suzy; but I *can't* peach, you know, dearie; I *can't* no how."

Poor Suzy was not at this time gifted with much power of logic or eloquence. She could only cling to her little friend, and weep and plead, but all in vain; for though Benny was moved by her tears to weep with her, he still shook his head and repeated that he "couldn't peach no how, not even for her sake, not even if they killed him."

Jerry Juniper looked on and listened, half in anger, half in sorrow. At length he broke forth with:

"I'll tell you what, my lad, if you don't peach, you'll be lagged may be for fourteen year."

The boy raised his sad blue eyes to the face of the man, and said:

"I'm sorry, Jerry, but I *can't* peach! don't you *see* as how I can't? And don't you know as if so be I *could*, I'd do it for Suzy in a minute?" And here he burst into tears and clung to Suzy, sobbing hard.

But he was true to the only point of honor he had ever been taught. Poor little outcast that he was, he could no more have betrayed his companions to save himself than his father the Duke of Cheviot, or any grand old Douglas of his line, could have committed any act that they deemed dishonorable.

But still Suzy wept and pleaded, and Jerry argued and scolded, and Benny resisted, sobbing the while as if his heart would break, until at length the policeman came to take the boy before the magis

Even then Jerry and Suzy did not desert him, but followed on to the magistrate's office.

The office was crowded with spectators of the very lowest class, for somehow or other the report had got around that the police had arrested the little snakesman of the Nut Cracker gang, and that they were trying to get him to "peach."

Benny was led through this crowd, and placed once more before the justice's bench.

The witnesses against him having all given their evidence on the day before, there was nothing new to be heard, and nothing more to be done than to commit him to prison, either as a culprit to await his trial at the Old Bailey, or as a witness to appear as Queen's evidence against the older and harder criminals.

"Well, my boy, I hope you have made up your mind to do your duty," said the magistrate.

Benny lifted his head with a strange pleading look in his clear eyes.

"Will you give up the names of your confederates in this robbery?" continued his worship.

"Please, sir, I can't peach," answered the boy.

"'Can't!' you mean you *won't*, don't you?"

Benny looked directly, though very meekly, in the magistrate's face, and answered nothing.

"Do you mean to say that you *won't* give up your confederates?"

"Please, sir, I said I couldn't peach, and I can't."

"Does that mean you *won't*, I ask you?"

"Yes, sir, it do," answered Benny, without withdrawing his gentle eyes from the face of the justice.

"Well, of all the incorrigible little cases! Officer, what does this mean?" inquired the magistrate, turning toward a policeman.

"Why, your worship, he won't give information," answered the latter.

"My good man," said the magistrate, turning now to Jerry Juniper, "did you not tell me that you thought you could induce this wretched boy to save himself by giving up his confederates?"

"I told you as I had a little gal at home as might, your Worship, which here she is; but werry sorry I am to tell you as we've both on us failed so to do," answered Jerry Juniper, coming forward hat in hand, and pulling his red forelock.

Here Suzy began to weep again, and to plead with the little prisoner, saying:

"Oh, Benny, it isn't too late yet! Tell his Worship, Benny; do, dearie! Save yourself, for my sake."

"I'd do anythink in the world as I *could* do, for your sake, Suzy; but I *can't* peach," replied the boy, bursting into tears.

"Make out the warrant for the committal of Benjamin Hurst to the prison of Newgate, upon the charge of burglary and assault with intent to kill," said the magistrate, addressing his clerk.

Suzy threw her arms around the boy's neck, and in an agony of sorrow and terror implored him to yield before it should be too late.

But Benny, weeping bitterly, persisted in his purpose "never to peach on his pals."

"Take him away," said the magistrate, as soon as he had signed the warrant.

And the policeman took Benny by the arm to lead him off.

"Good-bye, Suzy! *Don't* cry, Suzy! I'm so sorry I hurt you, Suzy; but I couldn't peach, you know," said the boy, holding back to shake hands with his friends.

Desperation gave the pretty little maiden courage.

"Oh, Mr. Policeman, don't take him off just yet! not *just* yet! Let me speak to the magistrate *one* minute"

Oh, sir! Mr. Magistrate, please don't send Benny off to prison yet? not *just* yet? Oh, please give him *one* more day to consider, and give me *one* more chance to try and coax him to tell you what you want him to tell? Benny's a *good* boy, sir; indeed he is! He never had nothing to do with robbing his master's house; indeed he hadn't! And if he knows who *did* rob it, or who shot the gentleman he'l' tell *me*, sir; indeed he will! Only give him *one* more day to think about it, and me *one* more chance to coax him?"

"You are very good at coaxing, as I perceive, my poor little girl. But I'm afraid your efforts would be lost upon the prisoner. I know the sort of boy that he is. My good man, you had better take your little daughter home. Officer, remove the prisoner," said the magistrate, rising.

And Benny was immediately carried off by the policeman.

And Jerry Juniper led his weeping little daughter away

"Hush crying, Suzy! Crying don't do no good. Let us be thinking of something as *may* do good. Who was that lawyer as defended of Benny's mother when she was tried for the murder of the ballet girl, and who saved her life, you know?" inquired Jerry Juniper of his daughter, as they passed down the street, after having left the magistrate's office.

"I don't know, father; I was so little then. But oh! I tell you who does know," said Suzy, between her sobs.

"Who then?"

"Rachel Wood; she knows!"

"I wonder if she lives in Junk Lane yet."

"I don't know. We could go and see, father."

"So we could; turn about now, and let's go there without loss of time. For if we can only get hold of that young lawyer, as has a heart in his buzzum, we may get him to defend Benny! And then he may get the boy clean off, or else with a very light penalty," said Jerry, as they turned into the Strand and bent their steps toward Low street.

They turned down Low street and down Ship Alley and into Junk Lane, and soon reached the old tenement house.

They climbed to the fourth story and rapped at the left-hand front room.

The pleasant voice of the seamstress bade them enter.

They did so, and found Rachel Wood sitting in her low sewing-chair, with her hands busy with her needle-work and her foot on the rocker of her adopted baby's cradle.

"Why, Suzy, dear, is this you? And how do *you* do, Mr. Juniper? And who would ever have thought to have seen you here?" she inquired, rising and giving them her hands.

"And what wind blowed us here? ye would like to ask, if it weren't impolite, Miss Rachel. Ah! but it was a werry ill wind, Miss Rachel," said the stage carpenter, shaking his head.

Suzy said nothing, but put up her hands and wept behind them.

"Sit down. And then tell me what is the matter," said Rachel quietly, as she placed two chairs for them and re-seated herself in her own.

Then, while Suzy wept in silence, Jerry Juniper told Rachel Wood of Benny's arrest and imprisonment on the charge of having been concerned in the robbery of his late master's, Captain Faulkner's, house.

Rachel Wood was dreadfully shocked.

She had not been near Mrs. Melliss or Mrs. Faulkner since the funeral of Captain Faulkner, and she had not heard of the arrest.

And to go further back than that, as she had not been at Woodbine Cottage from the time she helped to install the family there, until she went with Mrs. Melliss to bring them away again, she had never even known that Benny Hurst was alive, and had been in their service, much less that he had been charged with admitting burglars to rob their house.

All this was new, startling and dreadful intelligence to Rachel Wood. She wept over the fate of the poor, friendless boy, whom she firmly believed to be innocent of the robbery

"I know," she wept, "that he was taught to pilfer, as a duty he owed to his grandmother; but there was a rough honor about the poor mistaught boy, that would for ever have prevented him from robbing those whose bread he ate."

"There an't a doubt as he knows who *did* rob the house, but he won't tell, even though he was offered to be let go free if he did," said Jerry Juniper.

"The same rough honor prevents his 'peaching' as he would call it, poor boy!" sighed Rachel.

"But what we want for to do, Miss Wood, is for to get hold on that young lawyer as defended of his mother, Madge Brice, and saved *her* neck, you know! If we could get him to defend poor Benny, he might get clean off, or only with a little punishment."

"You mean Mr. Percy Melliss?"

"Aye, aye, *that's* the gentleman! I couldn't think of his name before."

"Oh! I'm so sorry!" said Rachel, with a grieved look. "I am so very sorry! If he were on the spot, I do believe he would take up the case at once with zeal. But he is not in town—not even in England. You see, he broke himself down with his labors at the bar, and he has been ordered by his physicians on a sea voyage for his health."

"And he's gone?" groaned Jerry, with a look of despair.

"Gone! I told you so. He sailed for New York last Saturday."

"And he was my last hope! Now, what's to be done? sighed the stage carpenter.

"Nothing that I know of can be done but endeavor to persuade that poor mistrained boy that it is his duty to turn Queen's evidence in this case," said Rachel.

"But an't it too late?" inquired Jerry, while Suzy suddenly stopped crying, and looked up with new hope in her eyes.

"No, indeed. Of course it is too late now to prevent his having been committed to answer the charge of burglary. But it isn't too late even now for him to give up the robbers, and turn Queen's evidence against them, and so appear at the Old Bailey in the witness box, instead of in the felon's dock. It an't too late for that. And I have no doubt in the world but that the prison chaplain will bring all good influences to bear upon the boy, to make him give up the wretches who have brought him to this pass," said Rachel Wood.

"Lord grant it!" sighed Jerry Juniper.

"Oh, Miss Rachel, and won't you please to go to see poor orphan Benny? And won't you please try to coax him to do what's right, to save himself?" pleaded Suzy.

"Indeed I will, dear. I will go to-morrow."

"And oh! will you please to call for me and take me with you, so as to add my coaxing to yours?"

"Yes, Suzy, I will."

"And now, my lass," suggested Jerry Juniper, "it is time for us to be going. Mother will be wondering whatever have become of us."

"Good-bye, Miss Rachel! Mind you be sure to call by for me," said Suzy, as she kissed and took leave of the seamstress.

"Good-afternoon, Miss Wood," said the stage carpenter, picking up his old hat to take his daughter home.

There was lamentation in the stage carpenter's house that night, when the mother and the children learned from the father that their favorite, Benny Hurst, was a prisoner in Newgate.

There was pity and sorrow in the banker's house in Charles street, when the ladies there heard from Rachel Wood of the condition of the poor, friendless boy who had been the faithful little slave of one lady, and the grateful little beneficiary of the other.

"Poor Benny! And he was so fond of my children! Oh, never let them know about this! They would cry their eyes out!" said Mrs. Faulkner.

"He is the same lad, you say, Rachel, whom I once remarked in the hall outside your room door, and who attracted my notice at once by the singular fairness and delicacy of his features and complexion, and his most extraordinary likeness to the little Earl of Wellrose?" inquired Mrs. Melliss.

"The very same, madam."

"How did the unfortunate child fall into such misery?"

"His wretched old grandmother took him from our house on a begging tramp, and I lost sight of him for a long time. And indeed I had the strongest reasons for believing him to be dead until this very day, when I heard all at once from his friends that he was alive, that he had been living as page at Woodbine Cottage, and that he was in prison under the charge of being concerned in the robbery of the house. But, before Heaven, I do not believe the poor boy to be guilty."

"Neither do I," said Mrs. Faulkner. "He didn't look like that sort of boy."

"At any rate, his extreme youth pleads for him. You say that there is a chance for him to clear himself, by giving up the names and abodes of the real robbers?" inquired Mrs. Melliss.

"Yes, madam; for the authorities are very anxious to get hold of the band," answered Rachel.

"Then I shall try very hard to induce the boy to give them up, when I go to see him in prison; for I shall certainly go to see him, Rachel."

"Heaven bless you, Mrs. Melliss!"

"And although my dear Percy is on mid-ocean now, and not available for this service, yet some other able advocate may be found, and the funds shall not be wanting to retain him. All this I will see about to-morrow."

"Heaven bless you, Mrs. Melliss," repeated Rachel, as she arose to take leave.

CHAPTER XIV.

THE LITTLE OUTCAST IN PRISON.

> Defiled
> By the air he breathed in a world of sin;
> But the truest, tenderest, gentlest child
> Man ever trusted in.—MEREDITH.

POOR Benny, inured to misery from his very birth, bore his fate with a patient fortitude that casual observers might have taken for sullen defiance.

He even slept through the first night in his cell at Newgate. And with a courtesy that was as much a part of his inherited nature as was the clear hue of his complexion, he thanked the turnkey who brought him a mug of coffee and a hunk of bread for his breakfast, and who took him to the rude wash-room allotted to the prisoners of his ward, and afterward gave him leave to walk in the closed and grated court-yard.

As soon as the hour for the admission of visitors arrived, Rachel Wood and little Suzy Juniper presented themselves at the gate and begged leave to see Benny Hurst.

They were taken to a central yard closed in with stone-walls and iron gratings, where they found Benny, sitting by himself on a wooden bench, and looking very lonely and forlorn.

There were several other prisoners sauntering about in

the yard, but they neither spoke to nor glanced at the solitary boy.

Rachel and Suzy hastened toward him, and spoke to him before he perceived their presence.

"Benny, dear, good-morning," said the seamstress very gently. And,

"Good-morning, Benny," at the same instant said Suzy.

The boy jumped up, his face radiant with surprise and pleasure.

"Oh, Miss Rachel, is it you? I'm so jolly glad to see you! It's wery good in you to come and see a poor cove as is in quod for nothink, and to bring Suzy too; which, to be sure, she never could a come 'less you had brought her, 'cause her father can't leave his work every day along o' me," he said.

"I'm very sorry to see you here, my poor boy," said the gentle seamstress, weeping.

"And I didn't do it, Miss Rachel! I didn't indeed!" said the poor child a little obscurely, as he lifted his blue eyes frankly to her face; "indeed, indeed I didn't do it. Suzy knows I didn't!"

"No, *that* you didn't, Benny. I told Miss Rachel so," added the girl.

"I know you didn't, Benny," calmly answered the seamstress.

"Oh, *do* you know it? I'm so jolly glad you know 'cause—"

"'Cause what, Benny?"

"'Cause, if you didn't know it all out of your own head as Suzy knows it, you mightn't believe *me*, when I tell you I didn't. The magistrate he didn't believe me, bust him!"

"He didn't know you as well as I do, Benny."

"No, and so he sent me here. And I'm to be tried for burgl'y in the first degree; for they do say as it's burgl'y in first degree when there's housebreaking with 'sault with to kill. And I didn't it, Miss Rachel."

"I know you didn't, my poor boy; so you need not trouble yourself to say so again."

"But for all that, here I am to be tried for burgl'y in the first degree, and lagged for ten year, or for fourteen, or may be for twenty year, or may be for life; for they do say as they can make me a lifer for burgl'y in the first degree."

"No, Benny, my dear, not so bad as that! And there is a way of escape for you, Benny, by which you can not only clear yourself, but confer a great benefit upon the whole community."

"I know what you mean, Miss Rachel. You mean as I can peach! But I can't, Miss Rachel; I can't, indeed!" said the boy, shaking his head.

"My poor child, it is your bounden duty to give up the men who committed this robbery."

"No, it an't, Miss Rachel. Beg your parding, but it an't no cove's duty to peach on his pals," persisted Benny.

"My poor, poor boy! will you sacrifice yourself for those bad men?"

"They wouldn't peach on me—not one on 'em wouldn't, and I won't on them!" persisted the lad.

And though all the old arguments and entreaties were used with him, neither the reasoning of Rachel Wood nor the weeping of little Suzy could move him from his purpose.

While they were still pleading and expostulating with the boy, Mrs. Melliss, attended by the prison chaplain, came into the yard.

It would appear that, on first coming to the prison that morning, she had asked for the chaplain, had been shown into his room, and in half an hour's interview had succeeded in interesting his reverence in the little prisoner, Benny Hurst.

And now they had come together to see him.

Rachel Wood, after respectfully returning the kind greeting of Mrs. Melliss, took leave of Benny and led little Suzy away, to leave the field free to Mrs. Melliss and the chaplain.

"Do you remember me, my boy?" inquired Mrs. Melliss kindly.

"Yes, ma'am. You are the lady who gave me a suit o' clothes once, the werry best suit as ever I had in my life. I thank you kindly, ma'am," said Benny, smiling, and pulling his fair front locks, by way of a respectful salute.

"And do you know this gentleman?" she inquired, indicating the chaplain.

"Oh, yes! I know *him* fast enough!" replied Benny, laughing. "He's Lady Green!"

"Lady—*who?*" inquired Mrs. Melliss, much perplexed.

"Lady Green. Lor', don't you know?—Lady Green," said the boy, laughing.

"Child, are you out of your senses? This is a gentleman—a reverend gentleman, the chaplain of the prison," replied Mrs. Melliss, in a sort of consternation.

"*I* know who he is! And I know his little game too. But he can't come it! not on *this* child!" said Benny, shaking his fair-haired head in good-humored defiance.

"My poor boy, you must not speak so of this good gentleman. It is very disrespectful to him, and unbecoming in you," said Mrs. Melliss seriously, laying her hand on the head of the lad. "And what in the world, sir," she inquired, turning to the chaplain, "does he mean by 'Lady Green?'"

The reverend gentleman smiled good-naturedly as he explained:

"It is a name that a class of prisoners bestow upon their prison chaplain, for what reason I cannot possibly imagine, unless it be because they think him very 'green,' to be so often imposed upon by their professions of penitence.

"Oh, I see," said Mrs. Melliss.

"You say you know me, my boy, and know my little game. Now, what do you suppose my little game to be?" inquired the chaplain, with an indulgent smile.

"Why, to get me to peach on my pals. Which, begging of your parding, sir, I can't do it," said Benny.

His words were the signals for Mrs. Melliss to commence her attack upon his fatal resolution.

She went over the same ground taken by all who had preceded her in trying to persuade the guiltless boy to give up the guilty parties, and with no better success.

"I must leave this poor little fellow to you, reverend sir. You have more experience than I have, and will be better able to cope with his perverted ideas of honor than I am," said Mrs. Melliss, rising to take her leave.

The chaplain courteously attended her out to her carriage.

Before entering, she said:

"I hope that unfortunate child may be induced to save himself by giving up his guilty companions. But, in any case, I shall lose no time in seeking out able counsel to defend him."

"I thank you in the name of all humanity, dear madam," said the chaplain, as he put her into the carriage.

The next day Mrs. Melliss succeeded in engaging the services of a learned and eloquent young barrister, a Mr. Frederick Freefield, for the defence of the forlorn little prisoner in Newgate.

She took Mr. Freefield to Benny's cell, and she implored the child to confide in him as his counsel.

But Benny, turning his tearful eyes from the lady to the gentleman, answered:

"Missus, and your honor, I'd do anythink in the world to please you but peach. Please don't ask me to do that, 'cause I can't. If I couldn't do it for Suzy Juniper, couldn't do it for nothink nor nobody."

It was utterly useless to assure the boy that to enable his counsel to defend him successfully, he must confide in him entirely; and that his confidence would be held sacred.

Benny could not be moved from his point "not to peach." He held his secret with the tenacity of death. So his counsel could get no help from him for the defence.

Nevertheless Mr. Freefield felt all the more deeply interested in the fate of the poor, mistaught, but loyal-hearted boy.

In attending Mrs. Melliss back to her carriage, he said:

"We will not be discouraged, madam. It will be some weeks yet before the opening of the Sessions at the Old Bailey. In the mean time continued imprisonment may so break the boy's spirit as to bring him to listen willingly to our advice to save himself by becoming Queen's evidence against the miscreants who have brought him to this pass."

"Oh, try your very best to persuade him so to save himself, sir," pleaded the lady.

"I certainly shall. No doubt also the chaplain of the prison will use all his influence," replied the gentleman.

And they took leave of each other.

Benny felt all the weary irksomeness of "continued imprisonment." Each day it grew heavier and still heavier.

Neither his foster-father, Tony Brice, nor his friend, the Nut Cracker ever came near him, though they must have known his condition. And their neglect hurt Benny more tnan all the rest.

Yet for all that he would not "peach" on them—no, though the chaplain and the lawyer and the lady argued with him, and though Rachel Wood and Mary Kemptcn and little Suzy Juniper wept over him, he stood steadfast upon the false principle of honor he had been taught.

The chaplain of the prison became deeply interested in the poor, mistrained, but true-souled child, and began at once to improve the time and beguile the tedium of his long imprisonment by teaching him to read, write and ciphes.

This was the very first opportunity the boy had ever had of learning anything of the sort.

With gratitude and eagerness he gave himself up to his lessons. Never had teacher a more willing, attentive and intelligent pupil. To use the words of Mr. Jerry Juniper, "Benny devoured his books."

The chaplain set him lessons every day; and whenever any of his friends, either Mrs. Melliss, Rachel Wood or Mary Kempton would come to visit him, and to renew the subject of his turning Queen's evidence, Benny would decline that discussion, and say:

"But if you would only please to hear me my lesson."

And of course they always complied with his request.

And thus, by his bright intelligence and zealous attention, and with the help of several teachers, Benny rapidly advanced in this rudimentary knowledge.

He also received moral and spiritual light from the religious instructions of the good chaplain.

He was grateful and docile, and he was also quite obedient, except upon the one point of refusing to give up the burglars. There was no moving him from that.

By the time the Sessions opened, Benny had learned to read the New Testament, to write his own name, and to work sums in the first four rules of arithmetic. Besides this he had committed to memory the Ten Commandments, the Sermon on the Mount, and several of Dr. Watts' hymns. But he never learned to inform against his confederates.

When he was engaged in his simple studies he seemed almost happy. And at all times he was very patient—he never complained. Only once in a while, with a sigh that seemed to come from the bottom of his heart, he would breathe forth his deepest want.

"Oh, I wish I could get out!"

And then he would go patiently back to his lessons.

At length the day came, and the Sessions opened.

CHAPTER XV.

BENNY'S FATE.

The felon outcast of the land.—A. A. P.

THE sessions of the Central Criminal Court opened.

It was a wintry morning when Benny was taken from Newgate jail to the Old Bailey Court.

And London saw the strange spectacle of a fair child in the felon's dock! a gentle child, who should rather have been in some humane reformatory school.

Overawed by the bench of wigged and robed and ermined judges, and the bar of wigged and gowned lawyers, and the crowd of spectators that filled the hall, the poor boy stood panic-stricken for a moment.

Then his eye wandered timidly over the assembly, in search of some friend who might be in it. But he saw not one kind or familiar face. If his friends were there, they were hidden in the crowd.

He raised his blue eyes deprecatingly to the bench of judges, and then turned them timidly toward the bar of lawyers and pleadingly to the box of jurors.

They all seemed to him to be very busy about something that he could not understand. Again his weary eyes turned from them and wandered anxiously over the sea of heads, searching for some kind face to comfort him, and finding not one.

If only he could have seen his foster-father Tony Brice, or the Nut Cracker, or any of the villains for whom he was innocently suffering, he might have found strength to bear his troubles.

But to be deserted by them all in this hour of his utmost need! To stand alone in the dock with a multitude of enemies around him! His burden was too hard to bear. His childish heart sunk in his bosom, and he burst into tears.

"Come, come, bully boy," whispered the rough turnkey who had him in charge, "brace up! They can't *hang* you, you know! It's only transportation at worst!"

"Oh, sir," said Benny, nervously catching hold of the turnkey's trowsers, "don't leave me! Stay by me, please! stay by me, please!"

"I'm going to. It's my duty, you know. Here now, take my pocket handkercher and wipe your eyes. *I* wouldn't let 'em see me cry, if I was you."

"No more I won't," said Benny, industriously drying his eyes. "'Cause I an't been up to nothink whatsomedever."

"All right, then; if you can prove that, you're cleared."

"But I can't prove nothink. *They* proves whatsomedever they pleases!" said the boy.

At this moment an awful personage in a long black gown and a full-bottomed white wig came to the side of the dock, and said:

"Well, my boy!"

Benny, appalled by the gown and wig, lost all his new-found fortitude and trembled from head to foot, as if he thought his last hour had come.

"You don't seem to know me, my boy! Your advocate, Mr. Freefield," smiled the apparition.

"Oh, is it you, sir? Beg pardon, sir—I didn't know you, indeed," replied Benny, gazing in ever increasing awe upon the black gown and white wig.

"I came to tell you not to be so cast down. Be of good courage. We hope that all will go well. When you are arraigned—that is to say, when the clerk asks you if you are guilty or not guilty—you must stand up, bow to the presiding judge—the stout old gentleman in the red gown, ermine cape and curled wig, sitting in the middle of the others on the bench—look honestly in his face and say, 'Not guilty, my lord.' Can you do this, my boy?"

"Yes, sir; 'cause I an't been up to nothink," answered Benny.

"I believe you, my poor child. Be of good courage. Now!" said Mr. Freefield, as he moved from the side of the dock.

At that moment the Clerk of Arraigns arose, with a formidable document in his hand, and proceeded to read the indictment, which, divested of its unintelligible jargon, seemed to charge the prisoner, Benjamin Hurst, with feloniously breaking into the house of one Charles Faulkner, gentleman, then living at Sydenham; with purloining thence a large quantity of valuable property belonging to said Charles Faulkner; and with making an assault with intent to kill, by shooting a loaded pistol and wounding seriously the person of one Barnabas Brierly; and so forth, and so forth, and so forth.

Benny scarcely understood a word of this rhodomontade; but when asked whether he were "guilty, or not guilty," he bowed to the judge, lifted his head, and answered clearly:

"Not guilty, my lord."

The counsel for the Crown took the indictment from the Clerk of Arraigns, and proceeded to open the case by telling the gentlemen of the jury that they had now before them one of the most abandoned and dangerous young criminals in England, if not in the world—a monster of juvenile depravity — one in whom crime seemed to be hereditary and inexterminable—the son of a man who was a confirmed pickpocket and burglar, who was much more frequently in jail than out of it, and of a woman who was a murderess, and had been tried for her life at that very court, and had only escaped the extreme penalty of the law upon the doubtful plea of insanity, and who was now expiating her crimes by life-long imprisonment in the Criminal Lunatic Asylum; that this wretched boy had been a thief from his infancy up to his present age; that imprudently received into a respectable and benevolent family, where he was treated as a child of the house, he had thanklessly and basely repaid their protection and fostering care by bringing into the house the band of burglars with whom he was known to be connected, and by robbing them of a large quantity of plate, jewels, money and other valuable property, and by murderous assault upon a friend and guest of the house. And though the learned counsel for the defence might pretend to say that *his*, the prisoner's hand never fired the pistol that wounded Col. Brierly, yet did the law hold him guilty of that deadly assault, inasmuch as he was confederated with the wretches who made it. And he hoped that both judge and jury would do their duty by punishing with the utmost rigor of the law a crime that was known to be fearfully on the increase—and so forth, and so forth, and so forth.

At the end of his opening speech, the counsel for the Crown called his witnesses.

The first who took the stand was the widowed Mrs. Faulkner, who, weeping bitterly, gave her evidence regarding the robbery, which bore very heavily upon the little prisoner.

The next witness was John Briggs, the man who had seen Benny in company with a suspicious looking individual at midnight, on the night of the robbery, and who had heard the prisoner give his companion particular directions how to find and enter the house, by a door that he, the prisoner, had left open.

This evidence was still harder on the little accused. And the severest cross-examination of the witness by the counsel for the defence did not tend to weaken it in the least degree.

The third witness was Mr. Riley, the man who had come to Captain Faulkner's assistance, and had helped to carry the wounded Colonel Brierly to the house.

He testified to these facts, and also to the confused condition of the house, several of the rooms of which bore signs of forcible entry, and also the absence of Benny from the bed where he usually slept.

This witness was also cross-examined without effect.

The last witness was the detective who had arrested the prisoner, and had found upon his person the little gold thimble, which was here produced and identified as the property of Mrs. Faulkner.

When these witnesses had all been examined and cross-examined, the counsel for the Crown summed up the evidence for the prosecution, and called upon the jury to convict the prisoner.

But then Mr. Freefield, the counsel for the accused, arose for the defence.

Of course he went over and politely contradicted all that the counsel for the Crown had stated concerning his client.

He begged the gentlemen of the jury to look upon that poor child in the dock, and see if they could find in his fair face and open brow any signs of that hereditary depravity and personal guilt ascribed to him by the learned counsel for the Crown.

This boy had been a most unfortunate and pitiable child from his very birth—a worse than orphan, cast upon the tender mercies of the thief and murderess who had brought him up, and yet who, thief and murderess as they were, were much less culpable than the unnatural parents who had given this fair child life, and then abandoned him to his fate.

He would prove that this boy, so far from being the "monster of juvenile depravity" he had been called by the counsel for the Crown, had been, from his infancy up, gentle, obedient, kind-hearted and generous. Even in still tenderer years he had worked, and begged when he could not work, to support an aged woman and a sick girl.

He would prove that, while the boy had been in the service of Captain Faulkner, he had been the affectionate com panion and protector of children but little younger than himself; and that when he left their service, he did so in fear and horror of their guest, who had terrified him with threats; that he could have had no share in the robbery with which he stood charged.

He would prove further, that while the boy was in prison he had been perfectly gentle, docile, obedient and anxious to please. And finally the advocate said he should confidently expect, from the gentlemen of the jury, the acquittal of his young client.

Then the counsel for the prisoner called the witnesses for the defence. These were Jeremiah Juniper, and his wife Jane Juniper, Rachel Wood and Mary Kempton. Each, sworn and examined in turn, testified to their intimate knowledge of the little prisoner from his infancy to the present time; they each bore witness to his gentleness of manner, kindness of heart, obedience, docility and generosity; but, Oh sorrow! when cross-examined by the counsel for the prosecution, they could not bear witness to the honesty or truthfulness of the poor child, who had been taught theft and falsehood as sacred duties from his infancy up! So their testimony in favor of the poor boy broke down.

Mrs. Melliss and the jail chaplain were called, and in turn testified to the perfectly blameless conduct of the gentle boy while suffering imprisonment.

But being cross-examined, they were in turn forced to admit that the little prisoner was obstinate in his determination never to give up the names of the burglars who had robbed his master's house.

So their testimony in favor of the little prisoner was also much weakened.

The defence rested.

The Judge arose and summed up the evidence on both sides, bearing very heavily on the young prisoner.

In conclusion, he said that the accused, being confederated

with the criminals who had perpetrated the burglary and made the assault with intent to kill, and shielding them now by his silence, was in law held equally guilty with them of the burglary and the attempt to kill, and that the jury would find a verdict in accordance with the facts.

And so he left the case in their hands.

The jury asked and obtained leave to retire to consider their verdict.

And they left the court room in charge of a bailiff.

Then, there being nothing else to do, the judge fell to reading his *Times*, and the lawyers lounged about, or went out to get a glass of—*pure water*, of course.

Benny's friends took the opportunity of coming up to speak to him.

The chaplain and Mrs. Melliss came first.

"Oh, missus," said the child, "I *do* thank you for speaking a good word for me. And do you think they will let me off?" he asked pathetically.

"I don't know, my poor boy. But even if you should be convicted, there may be still hope; for you may receive a full pardon on condition of giving up that band of burglars," said the lady.

"I never will get off on them terms, missus," sadly replied the boy.

Then he turned to the chaplain, and said:

"Your reverence don't think, *do* your reverence, as I'm as wicked as that first gentleman made me out to be."

"No, my poor boy, I certainly do not," answered the chaplain.

Rachel Wood and Mary Kempton and the Junipers were waiting modestly for their turn to come up and speak to Benny; but before the opportunity came there was a stir at the upper end of the hall, caused by the entrance of the jury.

The friends around the prisoner dispersed to their seats

The crier called order. The judges settled their wigs. The lawyers resumed their seats. The spectators became attentive. And the Clerk of Arraigns inquired:

"Gentlemen of the jury, have you agreed upon your verdict?"

"We have."

"Do you find Benjamin Hurst, the prisoner at the bar, guilty, or not guilty of the felony wherewith he stands indicted?"

"Guilty."

There was a pause of a few minutes. Then a few formula were gone through with; and then the little prisoner was told to stand up.

Benny arose and once more bowed to the bench, thinking, perhaps, poor child! that a little politeness here might help his sad case.

The judge, in pronouncing sentence, told the little prisoner that he had had a fair and impartial trial; that he had been convicted of burglary in the first degree, by an intelligent and conscientious jury; that the crime of burglary, as the learned counsel for the crown had stated, was fearfully on the increase; that there seemed really no security for life or property in the metropolis; that the most skillful and effective aids of the burglars were the boys, called among themselves "snakesmen," and employed to enter houses through such apertures as small panels, windows, or side lights, as would be inaccessible to the passage of men; that but for these 'snakesmen" many successful burglaries could not be accomplished; that he, the prisoner at the bar, had proved himself a most daring, expert and unscrupulous abettor of the burglars whom he had admitted to rob his master's house, and all but murder his master's guest; that his crime was all the more heinous and detestable, because that master had been his kind protector and confiding friend; that it behooved judges, in the face of all these facts, to punish such crimes with the utmost rigor of the law; that the extreme penalty of the law for burglary in the first degree, where there had been assault with intent to kill, was transportation for life; but that, in consideration of his, the little prisoner's youth, he—the judge—should sentence him to transportation to the penal colonies for the term of fourteen years only; that, in conclusion, he would remark, if he, the young prisoner, could be brought into such a frame of mind as to understand his duty to his sovereign and his country, and could be induced to give such information to the proper authorities as should lead to the apprehension and conviction of the dangerous band of burglars with whom he was connected, then he might be considered a proper subject for the mercy of the crown, and find it in the commutation of his sentence, if not in a full pardon.

Having concluded, the judge ordered the prisoner to be removed.

And the crier of the court called the next case.

The turnkey and another officer led Benny from the dock. The boy was too bewildered by the address of the judge to have any very clear conception of his own condition. Many who watched him thought him stupid and insensible; but he was not either.

As they led him away, Rachel Wood and Mary Kempton met him.

"Don't be discouraged, Benny. You may yet be saved," said Rachel.

"For you heard what the judge said about the pardon," added Mary.

"I know; but I can't be pardoned 'less I peach, and I'll never do that. No, I'll be lagged for fourteen year! Think of it! Might just as well be for life, you know. And—and—I wouldn't mind so much if it wa'n't—wa'n't for leaving Suzy!" added the boy, bursting into tears and sobbing as if his heart would break."

Mary and Rachel would have tried to comfort him, but the turnkeys were obliged to hurry him out of the way.

As the little prisoner passed out of the hall he noticed in the crowd of miserable wretches around the building, two men more miserable looking than any of their companions.

They were Tony Brice and the Nut Cracker!

"Daddy!" cried the boy gladly, eagerly stretching out his hand toward his foster-father.

Tony heard him, but immediately slunk away and hid himself in the crowd.

"And I only wanted to whisper to him that I would never peach," said the child to himself, weeping from his wounded heart, as they led him away to his cell in New gate.

Meanwhile Tony Brice and the Nut Cracker slunk away to the den of guilt they called their home.

Even Tony Brice, low as he had fallen, bad as he was, felt ashamed of himself for having deserted the boy and left him to suffer for *his* crimes.

"It's *hard* on the kid! It's *deuced* hard on the kid!" he said, blowing his nose.

"Oh, bosh! none of that, you know. Hard on the kid! *What's* hard on the kid? To go a sea v'yge? Why, lots of b'ys run away and go to sea for the fun o' the thing," answered the Nut Cracker.

"It *is* hard to be lagged for fourteen year, for a thing he never done—*that* it is," said Tony.

"Oh, the devil! What's fourteen year in a forring country at his age, and come back a young man in his prime, with plenty of experience? Nothing! If it had a been *you*, now, 'stead o' he, *you* wouldn't a got off with no fourteen year! *You'd* a been a lifer, *you* would!"

"That's so," agreed Tony, with a sigh.

"And besides, he an't gone yet. You heard what the judges said about a parding?"

"Yes, on conditions he'd peach."

"Well, he *may* peach yet."

"Who? Benny? Benny peach? I wish I was as sure of a ten pound note to-day as I am that Benny'll never peach. Benny'd *die* before he'd peach!"

"Well, may be so! And now let's talk of something else.—*There's a plant!*" added the man in a whisper, as they both entered the dilapidated house in which they lived.

CHAPTER XVI.

BENNY'S STRUGGLE.

God will judge thee and them aright.—A. A. P.

There was a convict transport ship to sail in a few days, and Benny was doomed to be sent out in her.

It was ascertained, however, from the highest authority, that a full pardon would be given him on condition that he would give such information as should lead to the apprehension and conviction of the burglars whose "snakesman" he was supposed to have been.

But the poor boy had still his mistaken spirit of honor within him, and would suffer anything rather than betray his foster-father and false friends.

A day or two before the transport was to sail, and while yet there was a last chance left for the little prisoner, his true friends resolved to make one final appeal to him.

Mrs. Melliss, Rachel Wood and little Suzy Juniper went to him in company.

They found him in his cell, at his lessons, pale and patient, as usual.

"What are you studying this morning, my poor boy?" inquired Mrs. Melliss, after the first greetings were over.

"Only my reading lesson in my 'Second School Reader,' missus," answered Benny, lifting his sad, blue eyes to the lady's face.

"Does the Chaplain still hear your lessons?"

"Oh yes, missus, every day."

"And you like his instructions?"

"Better'n anything in the world, missus."

"And you wouldn't like to lose them forever?"

"No indeed, missus."

"But, my poor child, unless you follow our counsel and do as we wish you to do, you will have to give them up in two days, and give them up forever. You will find no instructors in Van Dieman's Land, my boy," said the lady, with her eyes full of tears.

Benny turned a shade paler and looked down at the open book on his knees.

"But, my child, if you *will* do as we wish you—if you *will* win your full pardon by giving information against the evil men who have brought you to this pass—if you *will* do this, *then* you shall have even better instruction, under better circumstances than you can possible get here. You shall learn not only what you are learning here, but every thing else that you have the inclination and capacity to learn."

The boy raised his head, his whole face beaming with a look of eager longing and delightful anticipation; but the next instant its expression changed to one of sadness and despair, and he dropped his eyes once more upon his book.

"There is to be—" began the lady; but watching the boy with his sensitive and changing face, her voice broke down, and she faltered, "Tell him the rest, Rachel. The child distresses me so, I cannot continue."

"Listen, Benny," said Rachel, sitting down by him and taking his hand.

"You have heard—for even *you*, poor little fellow as you

are, *must* have heard of the beautiful Duchess of Cheviot, who is so distinguished for her benevolence?"

"Oh, yes, indeed," said Benny, his whole face brightening at the recollection; "I *seen* her once too. At Briting, you know. I told you all about it."

"Yes, I remember; it was at the Duke's marine residence on Brunswick Terrace, Brighton, where the little Ladies Douglas had you called in, and gave you a piece of their Twelfth-day cake."

"Oh, yes; I seen her then. She was lovely."

"Have you ever seen the Duchess since?"

"No; but I've dreamed of her—oh, so many times. I never told nobody; but I have."

"I don't wonder."

"And at the 'Ospital, you know; when I was ill, you know. I used to dream as she'd come and look over me, and lay her hand on my head. And once I dreamed as her tears fell warm on my face. And then, bless you! I dreamed as it wasn't no dream, and I tried to wake up. Wasn't that funny?"

"My poor child! That was no dream at all. The beautiful Duchess went to see the sick children in the Hospital very frequently. And she used to linger by your bed, and bend over you and sometimes weep for pity. And in your semi-delirium you must have been half conscious of her presence, though we never suspected it."

"You—don't—say—so!" said Benny, pondering. "And that lovely lady came to see me when I was ill, and I didn't know it! I thought as it was nothing but a dream. Oh, I wish I had knowed for true! I think then, if I had knowed it for true, I could a waked up to see her, I would a tried so hard. Oh, I *wish* I could get out and go to the Park once more. And then I would watch till I would see her carriage go by. And the little Earl—oh, an't *he* a swell, neither? He gave me a pair of shoes once, he did Oh, I *wish* I could get out!"

"My poor boy, even if you could get out, you could not see the Duchess, nor any of her children. They are all spending the winter in Florence, on account of the little Lady Hester's health, which is delicate."

"*I* know her. She was the littlest lady of all. But wasn't you agoing to tell me something about something?"

"Yes, my boy. I was going to tell you that the good and beautiful Duchess, whose wealth is almost equal to her benevolence, feeling a deep compassion for poor neglected children like you, is about to establish a poor boys' boarding school, where boys are to be lodged and boarded, clothed and taught."

Benny listened with his whole face intent with interest.

"And where boys of superior talents—like you, Benny—are to be instructed in the higher branches of science and literature, and even prepared to enter a college or to study a profession.

Benny's face ever increased in interest.

"And, child, a highly educated young curate is to be the Head Master of the school. And I, your old friend, am to be the matron, and to look after the boys' clothes and meals."

"Oh!—My!—Won't that be BULLY!" exclaimed the boy, with a short gasp of surprise and delight. "And Billy and Tommy and Johnny Juniper can go, can't they?" he added, in his sweet unselfishness.

"Yes, Benny, perhaps; though the school is to be founded for a much poorer and more needy class of boys than the stage carpenter's. But *you* can certainly go, Benny."

"Oh, I *wish* I could! Oh, I *wish* I could!" said the boy, clasping and unclasping his hands nervously.

"And so you can, Benny. It lies with yourself. Does it not, Mrs. Melliss?" said Rachel, appealing to the lady.

"It does indeed, my boy. You have only to give the in

formation that is required of you, to win a full pardon Then you will be set free from this prison. Then you wil be entered into the Duchess' school, where you will be cleanly and comfortably lodged and boarded, clothed and instructed; where you will be under the constant care of your old friend, Miss Wood here, who will always be like a mother to you; and where you will frequently see the beautiful Duchess who was so kind to you, and who will of course, be a frequent visitor at her own school; and finally, where you may not only learn the common and indispensable branches of knowledge, but where you may be instructed in the higher branches of literature and science, and be prepared to enter college, or to study the profession of your choice, as Rachel has already told you."

"Oh! I *wish* I could! Oh! I *wish* I could!" pathetically repeated the boy, still nervously clasping and unclasping his hands.

"And so you can, my child, if you please."

"Oh, no, no, no, I can't, missus! I can't, unless I inform against—never mind who. And I can't turn informer against them."

"What lamentable folly to think that you cannot! My child, it is your sacred duty to inform against those lawbreakers," said Mrs. Melliss.

But Benny only shook his head, resolving to remain silent as death upon that subject, no matter what might become of him.

"Please, ma'am, let *me* try now," whispered Suzy to Mrs. Melliss.

The lady nodded assent, and Suzy went and sat down on the bench beside Benny, and said:

"Listen to *me*, Benny."

"Don't Suzy! don't say nothing to tempt me to peach. It's no use, and it hurts so to refuse you," pleaded the boy.

"But I *must*, Benny. There's only two more days to try

and save you! Oh, Benny, dear, just listen to me! I'm going to talk about myself now."

"Well, I'll hear you talk about yourself, willing."

"Well, then, Benny, next week I am to go to Paris with Madame Vesta, to enter on the course of study and practice that is to make me, *she* says, a celebrated prima donna. Think of that, Benny."

"Oh! that *is* bully! I'm so glad, Suzy! How happy you will be!" exclaimed the boy, smiling brightly, in sympathy with her good fortune.

"Yes, but *I'm* not glad; and I shall not be happy. No matter how fortunate I may be, how could I be glad or happy, knowing that *you* were away out there among strangers and taskmasters in the convict colonies for fourteen long years? I should be so miserable, Benny, that I don't believe I ever *could* become a great prima donna," said Suzy, weeping.

Benny burst into tears, and sobbed until his whole small frame shook with emotion.

"Oh, don't cry so hard, Benny! Please don't," said the little girl, embracing him. "You know you can change it all, and make us quite happy."

Benny shook his head sadly.

"But now look on the bright side just one minute Benny. Supposing you should give the information that is wanted, and win your full pardon and get out of this, then you'd be put into the Duchess' school, and be *so* clean and comfortable and happy. And *you* would be training for a profession there, while I should be training for the opera in Paris. And in the holiday times you could even come over to Paris to see me; and whenever I should come to London to see my mother, I would go to your school to see you. And so we could visit each other and compare notes about how we got on in our education, and be a pleasure to each other and to our friends. But you would be the best of all pleasures to me, Benny," said the little girl, her face beaming with bright anticipation.

"Oh, I *wish* I could! I *wish* I could!" sighed the boy from the depths of his troubled heart.

"And then," continued Suzy, who saw she was moving him, "then, Benny, in a few years we should both of us grow up. And I should be a prima donna at the grand opera, and you—they say you've got *such* talents, Benny—you would be a great lawyer, and may be a member of parliament. And we, who lived together when we were babies in Junk Lane, would live together in a palace in May Fair! And we two would clothe the ragged and feed the hungry, and build schools for the poor children."

"Oh! I *wish* I could! I *wish* I could!" sobbed Benny.

"Oh, you can, child! You can, if you will only think so!" said Mrs. Melliss, Rachel Wood and Suzy Juniper, all speaking at once.

"Oh, no, no, no, I can't! I can't! It an't for me! It an't for me!" sobbed the boy, falling and rolling on the stone floor of the cell, utterly overcome by the agony of renunciation.

"You might tear that boy limb from limb with wild horses, but you'd never move him from that point, mum," said a turnkey, who now made his appearance to tell the visitors that "time was up," which meant that they were to take leave and go.

"Good-bye, Benny! Oh! you poor child, good-bye!" said Mrs. Melliss, holding out her hand to the boy.

He raised himself from his fallen position and gave his hand to the lady, sobbing.

"You're not mad long o' me, because I can't peach, missus, be you?"

"Mad! no, my poor child, only deeply grieved; for certainly your inability to do so, wherever it comes from, harder on you than on any one else."

"And you'll come and see me once more, missus, before they take me away?"

"Yes, my boy; I will come again to-morrow."

"And bring Suzy?"

"And bring Suzy."

"And you, Miss Rachel—will you come? And tell Mr. Juniper and Mary Kempton. I want to bid 'em all good bye, before they take me away."

"Yes, my poor child. All shall come to take leave of you," answered Rachel.

"Oh! I *wish* I could see the little Faulkner children once more before I go. But that's impossible. But, oh! please Mrs. Melliss, ma'am, please tell 'em as I never helped to rob the master's house."

"I will tell them, Benny, and they shall believe it," answered the lady.

And then they all took leave of the boy, and followed the turnkey out of the cell.

In the hall outside they met the chaplain, on his way to visit the little prisoner.

The reverend gentleman warmly greeted Mrs. Melliss and her companions, and then eagerly inquired:

"Have you succeeded in persuading him to give information against those burglars?"

"Ah, no! he is immovable on that point although the prospects we held out to him were so bright and alluring. Oh! sir, if you had seen that poor child's agony, in renouncing all that we offered him—liberty, home, education, friends, prosperity—all upon a false idea of honor!"

"Ah! what strength to do and bear and suffer is in that young heart! Oh! if it had but been trained aright!" sighed the chaplain.

"And I am so pained to think that now he must go out in that transport ship, among the most hardened criminals and with no good influences around him!"

"But be comforted a little, madame. He will have good influence. A Christian missionary is going out in the same ship. I have recommended this boy to his especial attention."

"Oh, I am so pleased to hear you say that!" said the lady.

But the turnkey who was to see the visitors out, seemed so very impatient, that the lady and her companions immediately took leave of the chaplain and left the prison.

Faithful to their promise, they went the next day to Newgate, to make still another appeal to the young prisoner, and if it should not prove successful, to take a final leave of him.

On applying at the gate for admission, they were told—HE WAS GONE.

"'GONE!'" they echoed simultaneously.

"Yes, gone," answered the turnkey; "took off by Black Maria* at seven o'clock this morning."

"But was not that a day sooner than was expected?" inquired Mrs. Melliss.

"It were, ma'am, certainly; but it's none o' my business."

"Where is the transport ship?"

"At Gravesend, ma'am if so be she have not sailed; which they were to sail as soon as the tide served, after getting the convicts aboard."

"Rachel, Mary, Suzy, we will speed down to Gravesend We *may* be in time to take leave of him on the ship," said Mrs. Melliss.

And they hurried out of the prison and into their cab. And they feed the cabman heavily to make double time And they sped to Gravesend and down to the water-side.

They inquired for the convict transport ship.

They were told that she had sailed, but that they might yet catch a glimpse of her canvas as she stood out to sea.

* The prison van.

CHAPTER XVII.

TRIUMPHS OF TIME.—THE YOUNG PRIMA DONNA.

Hers was the spell o'er hearts
  Which only Acting lends,
The youngest of the Sister Arts,
  Where all their beauty blends;
For, by the gifted Actress brought,
  Illusion's perfect triumphs come;
Verse ceases to be airy thought,
  And Sculpture to be dumb.—CAMPBELL.

FOURTEEN years have passed since our poor little outcast, Benny Hurst, was transported to the penal colony of Van Dieman's Land, to expiate a crime he never committed, and since our pretty little "prodigy," Suzy Juniper, was taken to Paris to be trained in her beautiful art.

These years have brought their trials and triumphs, and wrought their changes for good or for evil, upon all the persons concerned in our true story.

The Duke and Duchess of Cheviot, first in honor as in place, are now a stately couple in early middle age.

They have a grown-up family around them: one handsome and talented son, and six beautiful and amiable daughters.

Their son, the Earl of Wellrose, has faithfully kept the promise of his boyhood as to the good he should do when he should "grow to be a man." He now represents his native borough of Cheviot, in the House of Commons, and devotes all the powers of his fine mind to originating, supporting and forwarding all wise, good and great measures for the prevention of crime, the relief of suffering, the elevation of the working classes, and for the general improvement of the human race.

Their eldest daughter, the Lady Jessie Douglas, after having been presented at Court, and having been crowned the reigning belle of the season, gave her hand in marriage to the Viscount Moray, eldest son and heir of the Earl of Ornoch.

Their second daughter, Lady Clemence Douglas, in her turn presented, admired and flattered, ended her first season by marrying young Elphinstone of Elphinstone. This was not so brilliant a marriage as that of her elder sister, but it was, nevertheless, a very happy one, and, as such, quite satisfactory to her parents.

Their next two daughters, Ladies Hester and Eva, had been but very recently presented. They were as beautiful and as much sought in marriage as their lovely elder sisters had been, but they were still unwedded.

Their two youngest daughters, the Ladies Maud and Mary, were still in the school-room.

So much for the Duke and Duchess of Cheviot and their family.

Of the Earl of Ornoch and of his Countess, whom we first knew as the beautiful Anglo-Indian, Hinda Chimboza, it is only necessary to say that, having married their only son the Viscount Moray, to the lovely Lady Jessie Douglas they had but one remaining wish—to give their one sweet daughter, Lady Hinda Moray, in marriage to the handsome and distinguished young Earl of Wellrose.

And Rumor says that the Earl is "nothing loath" to accept the priceless gift.

The Elphinstones of Elphinstone, whom we knew in their youth as Captain Frank Harry and Lady Margaret Douglas, are blessed with a numerous family, the eldest of which, a son, married, as we know, the second daughter of the Duke of Cheviot.

And the wealthy banker, Walter Melliss, and his lovely young wife Angela? What of them?

In years the banker has grown old, but he is still enjoying a vigorous and "green old-age."

His lovely wife is no longer young, but is if possible more

beautiful in her ripe maturity than she had ever been even in her youth.

Poor Molly Faulkner never married again; but devoted and still devotes herself to the care of her children now grown, or fast growing up. They live in a pretty villa at Brompton.

The Duchess' School for Indigent Boys still flourishes under the care of the Reverend Mr. Miles as Head Master and Miss Rachel Wood as Matron. Rachel has kept her word never to marry. Her whole affections are fixed upon her adopted boy. He is a pupil in the school, and promises soon to take its very highest honors.

Mary Kempton is well married to a dissenting minister, and having no children of their own, they work diligently among the neglected children of the ignorant and the poor.

The Juniper family have long since emigrated to Australia, where they are prosperous sheep farmers.

I have had to record many changes in these few pages; but then—fourteen years had fled.

It is now the middle of April and the height of the London season. Parliament is in session; the Queen has held her first drawing-room; and the Italian Opera has opened at Covent Garden.

Three sensations in chief occupy the fashionable mind and employ the fashionable tongue.

First the rising young statesman, Lord Wellrose, who now represented the borough of Cheviot in the house of Commons, and had first taken his seat at the meeting of Parliament in the preceding February, had just made his "maiden speech," which had waked up the dozing old Conservatives to the knowledge that they had now for an opponent a very strong young giant-killer indeed, and that his war upon the worn-out policy of the past would be to the death.

Secondly, the new beauty, the Lady Hinda Moray, the daughter of the Earl and Countess of Ornoch, had been presented at the Queen's first drawing-room, and was voted by all the clubs in London to be the most brilliantly beautiful girl in England—save one.

And that brings us to the cause of the third sensation—the lovely young prima donna of the Italian Opera—the fairy-like, wondrous "Arielle," of whom men said that she was more a "spirit" than a woman, and whose beauty, grace, genius and goodness were the themes of every tongue.

She made the greatest sensation of all. Her worshippers were unnumbered. And among them were to be found the most noble, princely and imperial dignitaries in Europe.

But her only favored lover, Rumor said, was the new lion of the liberal party, the rising young statesman, the handsome and talented Earl of Wellrose.

It had been thought natural, proper and probable that the Earl should marry his distant young relative, Lady Hinda Moray, the reigning beauty of Belgravia. It was certain that such a marriage would be highly gratifying to the respective families of the youthful pair; certain also that the attentions of the young Earl to the young beauty and her evident pleasure in receiving them, had given strong color to the rumor of their intended marriage; finally it was equally certain that the Duke and Duchess of Cheviot and the Earl and Countess of Ornoch looked forward with confidence to this desired union, which they considered merely a question of some little time.

But this was before the Italian Opera came, and before the fair young prima donna electrified London with her marvellous beauty and genius.

The Earl of Wellrose, in his character of constant attendant, went with Lady Hinda and her mother to hear the celebrated singer on the night of her first appearance in London. Arielle that night carried the hearts of her audience by storm It would be scarcely too much to say that every man present, young or old, gentle or simple, fell more or less in love with the most lovely songstress.

Among them, the Earl of Wellrose.

The next night he avoided the private boxes occupied by his mother and her friends. And he took a stall in the orchestra where, undisturbed, he could feast his eyes and ears on the beautiful vision before him.

That next night also, after the performance was over, he went behind the scenes and effected an introduction to Arielle.

The fair singer looked at him with so much surprise and interest as to excite the wonder of those present, and to draw from herself an apology and explanation :

"Forgive me, my lord. I was startled a little. But what shall I say? Your lordship's face and voice seemed to me so familiar, so intimate—like those of one that I had always been used to see and hear. Ah! pray forgive me, for after all I find it quite impossible to explain, or even to understand myself," she said, with a very sweet, naïve smile.

The Earl bowed.

"If face, or voice," he said, "recall to you any pleasant association of the past, I shall begin to set a value upon both, that neither ever had before."

She looked up at him again, and caught the warmth of his smile and the light of his eyes, and—she forthwith invited him to supper; a very imprudent thing to do on such a short acquaintance; but then Suzy—for of course you know this *was* Suzy—did many an imprudent thing, though she never did a wicked one; and then, to be sure, the Earl of Wellrose was not like other young men: *he* was a young man of perfectly unimpeachable conduct and character; and then, again, he was so like Benny! He was the very image of Benny, grown up and well dressed—of poor lost Benny, fourteen years gone, never heard of, but never forgotten, and never unloved.

Through all the successes of her brilliant youth she had remembered and mourned the companion of her childhood —mourned him all the more for the deep sadness of the contrast between his fate and hers.

With the world at her feet, she sighed for the poor boy who had played with her in her infancy.

Crowned with fame and wealth and surrounded with luxury and adulation as she was, she often sighed for the poor old days in the tenement house in Junk Lane, where they were often cold and always hungry, and where they had nothing in the world to comfort them but only love.

Ah, but how much love she had had then!—father's and mother's love, sister's and brother's love, and her dear playmate, Benny's love!—nay, his whole, *whole heart!*—for Benny knew neither father nor mother, sister nor brother, to divide his affections with Suzy.

Ah, even in the midst of her brilliant fortunes, how she longed sometimes to go back, if only for a few days, to the poor old times and poor old places, dearer to her memory, dearer to her faithful heart, even for their poverty, and to live over again the poor old life, sweetened by the presence of all she had loved and lost!

Then and there they were all together, and though often half-famished or half-frozen, yet they were all fond of each other; and then, when food or fire were attainable, how passing sweet they were, enjoyed by all together!

Now they were scattered far and wide—father, mother, sisters and brothers, except one—were all at the antipodes, and though she was glad to know that they were all prospering in their distant homes, still there were times when she longed, with an unutterable and insupportable longing, to hear some dear home voice, to see some familiar old face.

And Benny?—where was he? A guiltless convict in a distant penal colony beyond the seas. Lost, gone and unheard of for fourteen long years.

Fourteen years that had developed herself, the poor little prodigy" of the Thespian, into the most celebrated prima donna of her time.

Fourteen years that had done—what, for Benny?

Thus, looking back upon the past, thinking of the number of years that had gone by, she recollected that they formed the exact term for which Benny had been transported to Van Dieman's Land; and that should he now be living, he might now return again to his native land.

If he should now be living? But who could tell whether indeed he were? Was it likely he could have survived the long years of exile, sorrow and shame that he must have suffered? Who can tell?

It was while these thoughts were passing through her mind, and the memory of old times was revived all the more vividly by the presence of old places and old associations, on her return to England, that Suzy, as we shall call her when off the stage, first met the young Earl of Wellrose, to be startled and overcome by his wonderful, his perfect likeness to her dear, lost old playmate, Benny.

Do you wonder now that she was startled into suddenly inviting him to supper?

Somewhat surprised and amused, but also quite pleased with this unexpected mark of confidence, the young Earl accepted the invitation as frankly as it was given.

That evening he forgot or disregarded all other claims upon his time and attention, and went to sup with Suzy at her elegant little palace in Park Lane, that had been engaged, furnished, for her use before she left Paris for London.

There she now lived, guarded by her elder brother William, whom we used to know in Junk Lane as Billy Juniper, chiefly remarkable for his love of "horse cake," but now grown up to be a very fine looking young man indeed, with a full tawny beard, and, alas! also a very fast young man with a taste for cigars, wine and dice.

He had emigrated to Australia with the rest of his family, but not liking colonial life and agricultural labor, light as it was with him, and hearing that his sister had made a most brilliant *debut* in Paris, and thinking that she was going to have a very good time, and loving pleasure himself better than anything else in the world, he had made up his mind to come back to England and live with Suzy—to take care of her, as he said. He had joined her in Paris, and accompanied her to London, and was now living with her in her miniature palace in Park Lane.

And there is no doubt that in one sense he did take care of her.

Besides her brother there was also a grave matron, the childless widow of a poor curate, who lived with Suzy as housekeeper and companion.

These were the people that the young Earl met, the first evening he supped with Suzy. And certainly he was somewhat surprised at the very quiet domestic life of the celebrated prima donna, and somewhat disappointed also, that there was not the slightest chance of a tête-á-tête with his charming hostess.

As for Suzy, she was deeply delighted with her guest. It seemed to her that her old playmate, poor Benny, sat opposite to her, as she had always dreamed and hoped that he would—grown up, well educated, well dressed, good and happy!

The Earl was such a perfect counterpart of the outcast, that, as she looked at him, she almost deluded herself into the belief that he was really Benny redeemed and transfigured before her.

This imbued her looks and tones, when addressing her guest, with an involuntary friendliness and tenderness that was as free from the least shade of immodesty or coquetry as from any other sort of guile. And the young Earl did not misjudge the purity of her heart, though he could not quite understand her manners.

But every moment he found her more lovely, and every moment it seemed more difficult to leave her.

He did not overstay his time, however; but when it came, he arose and took leave—feeling that he had spent one of the happiest evenings he had ever seen in his life.

As soon as their guest had gone, Mr. William Juniper turned upon his beautiful sister, and said:

"I say, Suzy, this won't do, you know!"

"What won't do, Willy?" she inquired, raising her brows.

"How long have you known this swell?" he demanded without answering her question.

"The Earl? Only since this evening."

"Whee-ew!" exclaimed Master Willy, with a long whistle—"this *is* getting on! But I say, you know, Suzy, this really *won't* do!"

"*What* won't do, Willy, I ask you again?"

"*This* won't. This *swell* won't. He's a flight above *your* reach, I can tell you, Suzy, if you *are* a prima donna! He's the Earl of Wellrose, the Duke of Cheviot's son, and heir. That's what *he* is."

"I know what he is. And I do not care for that. I liked him at first sight, because he didn't seem like a stranger at all, but like an old, *old*, dear, *dear* friend. He felt *near* to me, Willy."

"Well, I swear! If that isn't the softest rubbish I ever heard in all the days of my life! It's well I sacrificed all my prospects in Australia and came over here to look after you, blest if it isn't! See here, Suzy! That swell's over head and ears in love with you, and don't take no trouble to conceal it. And similarly you act as if you were over head and ears in love with him and didn't care about hiding it

Blest if it isn't a good thing I *did* come to take care of you!"

"Willy, I can take care of myself. I am of age. And you *may* go a trifle too far. I will not have my guests affronted. You know nothing of the exigencies of my life. I must live here as I lived at Paris, Berlin, St. Petersburg and other continental cities. I must give elegant little suppers here as I did there. And you are not, because you are kind enough to 'take care of me'—you are not to fancy every gentleman an ogre, and affront my visitors. I shall receive the Earl, as I receive others. Good-night," said Suzy.

And she retired, and left her rough but well-meaning brother to his own reflections.

Did Suzy receive the Earl as she received her other guests? No doubt she intended to do as she said, for she was the very soul of truth and honor.

However that might be, it is certain that from that evening forth, the brilliant young patrician, Lady Hinda Moray, missed from her circle the most favored of her admirers, while the lovely prima donna numbered among her worshippers the handsome and talented Earl of Wellrose.

Rumor soon connected the name of the rising statesman with that of the renowned songstress, and whispered that Arielle would add one more to an illustrious list of artistes raised by marriage to the peerage.

Of course this rumor never, by any chance, reached the ears of the Duke or Duchess of Cheviot. They believed their son was pleased with the Lady Hinda, and that in due season he would propose and be accepted by her.

The Duke, however, though a handsome, healthy man in the prime of life, was growing rather impatient to see the perpetuation of his race insured.

So one day he took his son to task.

"As my heir and only son, Wellrose, I confess that I feel anxious to see you married. You admire Hinda Moray, and she likes you. What should delay your early marriage?" he inquired.

"I'm sure I don't know," answered Lord Wellrose, "unless it is that I feel there is still a plenty of time to spare."

"Ah, yes! 'plenty of time,' if all my daughters were sons, Wellrose, or if a few of them were. But as I have but one son, I confess that I should like to see half a dozen grandsons or so. Now I do not know what should hinder your marriage."

"*Hinda* might hinder it," laughed the young Earl.

"Find that out immediately for yourself, my son. Ask her, ask her. The sooner the better," said the Duke.

Lord Wellrose laughed, but gave no pledge.

He had really not made up his mind on the subject.

He was very fond of his distant cousin, the beautiful Lady Hinda; he was also very much charmed by the lovely young singer. He said of them that they were beyond all question the two most perfect beauties in Europe—Hinda being the most beautiful brunette, and Arielle the most beautiful blonde.

But at this period he was not really very deeply in love with either of them, or with any one else. His mind was more occupied with a great and comprehensive bill that he was about to bring before the House for the reclamation of juvenile offenders and the amelioration of the condition of the destitute classes, than with any question of love or marriage.

And yet every evening when he was not in his seat at the House of Commons, he might be seen in an orchestra stall at the Italian Opera, and afterwards in the elegant drawing-room of the young prima donna, at Park Lane.

Ah, if he had only known that then his sole attraction for Suzy was not his manly beauty, his brilliant talents, his rank or wealth, but—his perfect likeness to her early friend Benny!

CHAPTER XVIII.

THE PRIMA DONNA AND THE RETURNED CONVICT.

Yet scorn not thou, for this, the true
And steadfast love of years,
The kindness that from childhood grew,
The faithful to thy tears.—FELICIA HEMANS.

It happened one evening after the opera was over, that Lord Wellrose was conducting the beautiful prima donna to her brougham, that was waiting at the stage door.

As usual a great crowd was around the door waiting to get a glimpse of Arielle as she passed.

One young man in particular, pale, emaciated and poorly dressed, was pressed so near the carriage as to be seriously in the way of the Earl, as he handed the actress to her seat.

"Stand aside, my good fellow; you impede us," said his lordship.

But at the same instant a slight scream from Arielle startled him.

"Stand aside, sir!" he repeated sternly. "Do you not see that you are really frightening the lady?"

"Oh, no, no; he doesn't!—he doesn't frighten me, my lord! He is Benny—my dear old playmate Benny, whom I have not seen nor heard of for fourteen long years! Move a little, my lord, if you please. And oh, Benny, come here to me, my dear!" said Suzy, leaning from the carriage, unceremoniously pushing the Earl out of the way, and beckoning the pale spectre to approach.

He came at once, the crowd still pressing closer behind him to get a sight of the beautiful singer, whose unvailed face was now leaning from the carriage door in full view of all.

Suzy neither cared for them, nor even saw them. She only saw the friend of her childhood.

"Oh, Benny! I am so glad to see you, and so—so grieved to see you this way!" she added, bursting into tears of mingled joy and sorrow.

"And to think you should know me, after all that is come and gone! And to think you should speak to me, now you are so famous and so wealthy!" murmured the poor young man, in a voice choked with emotion.

"Oh, Benny, did you think *that* could make any difference with me? Oh, get in here and come home with me, and tell me all that has happened to you since we saw you!" she said, clasping both his hands and drawing him toward herself.

Almost involuntarily he yielded to the impulse. And before he realized what he was doing, he found himself seated opposite to her in the pretty little brougham.

Once more she leaned from the carriage window, and said to the astonished Earl, who was standing near:

"Lord Wellrose, will you kindly beckon a policeman to clear the way? These people are so rude! And please also tell the coachman, "Home!" she added.

"I wonder if I am awake," muttered the Earl to himself, as he obeyed all the orders so cavalierly given him.

The police cleared the way. The coachman started his horses, and in due time the little brougham drew up to the miniature palace in Park Lane.

"Open the Rose parlor, Smith; and mind, I'm not at home to any one at all this evening!" she said to the servant who attended the door.

"If Lord Wellrose should call as usual, Miss?" inquired the man, hesitating.

"Not at home to *him* either. Not at home to *any* one, I tell you! Now open the Rose parlor!"

The man, after a furtive glance toward his mistress strange companion, led the way to the back of the house, and opened a door leading into a lovely bower, fitted up and decorated with rose-colored furniture and hangings, and opening upon a conservatory of the rarest and riches roses.

"Serve supper here as soon as possible. Tell Mrs. Brown she need not join me this evening," said Suzy to the bewildered servant, who went out, muttering to himself:

"Vell, if this 'ere an't the rummest go as hever I see! That young cove be some poor, misrepertable relation or other of hern, as is a blackmailing on her, or something!"

Meanwhile Suzy turned toward her poor guest, and noticed again how very thin and pale he looked, and yet how perfect, notwithstanding, was the likeness between him and the Earl of Wellrose!

The outcast seemed but the faded and defaced counterpart of the Earl.

"Oh, Benny, dear, sit down! Oh, Benny, I am so glad —and so grieved to see you! Sit down, Benny!" she said, as she threw off her own light opera hood and cloak, and dropped into one of the luxurious little chairs.

The poor outcast turned his eyes around the room with a dazed and bewildered look, and then fixing them on her compassionate face, answered:

"I am not fit to sit down here."

"Oh, don't say that, Benny! Don't say that, brother, or you'll make me wish, for all that has come and gone, that we were both children, back in Junk Lane again. *Please* sit down, Benny," she pleaded, beginning to weep.

He looked around again upon the rich and delicate chair coverings—white satin, embroidered with roses—and he sighed as he sank into the nearest seat.

"Dear Benny," she said, drawing her chair toward him, "when did you get back? Have you been in London long? And why didn't you find me out, and come to see me?" she continued, hurrying question upon question with breathless eagerness.

"My time was out last Michaelmas, you know," said Benny, answering a little aside from her questions. "And I longed to get home. Oh, Suzy, you don't know how one *longs* to get home when they're in a foreign land and not allowed to come. I used to dream of home."

"Home! Ah! poor boy, what sort of a home has England been to you? What sort of a home has the world been to you, poor Benny!" she said, and her eyes filled with tears.

"But it was *home*. And all I loved in the world was here. And all these long years of exile I did so long and weary to get home. At length I think Heaven took pity on me, and sent me home every night."

"Sent you home every night, Benny?"

"*In dreams*, I mean. Yes, every night as soon as my eyes would close in sleep, I would be at home. I used to long for night to come, so I could go to sleep and go home. And every day I used to tire myself out with more work than I need to have done, so I might be sure to go to sleep at night and go home in my dreams. At last, when the long, long years all rolled by, and my time was out, I took passage in the very first ship that was homeward bound. And, Suzy, I never was so happy in all my life, as I was when I stood on the deck of that ship, and she stood out to sea with her head toward home!" said the poor outcast, his pale face lighting up again with pleasure at the recollection.

"Home! Oh, poor boy! home!" repeated Suzy, with sorrowful sarcasm.

"Yes, *home!* Ah! you've never been outcast from your native land, or you'd know the feeling on getting back again. It was a long voyage though. And we only reached London three days ago. It was night when we dropped our anchor, Suzy; but I was one of the first to come ashore

I bent down and kissed the ground, Suzy! *I did!* I cried too. I could not help it. That same night I went to the house in Junk Lane. But all the people that I used to know there are gone, not only from the house, but from the neighborhood. And the house is turned into a ragged school by day and a lodging for the homeless by night."

"Yes, Benny, that is Mrs. Melliss' charity."

"Is it? How good she is! I remember her so well! Suzy, I lodged in that house that night. I slept in your mother's old room, where you and I used to play together and have grand parties out of ha'pennies' worths of gingerbread or taffy," said the poor outcast, with the old tenderness melting his blue eyes, and the old sad smile wrinkling his pale cheeks.

"Oh! did you, Benny? Did you, really? Oh! I should so love to see the poor, dear old place again! Some day you and I will go there and see it together, Benny, for the sake of old times," she answered, with a sympathetic smile.

But the outcast sadly shook his head.

"That will never do, Suzy," he said. "For the sake of 'old times,' you may let me sit and talk to you here in your own house. But you must never be seen in public with such as I."

"Oh, Benny, Benny! You hurt my very heart when you talk that way! Don't I tell you *all* that has come and gone can make *no* difference between you and me? You are Benny and I am Suzy!" She wept.

"You are a renowned prima donna and I am a returned convict," he answered.

"Benny! Benny! you will break my heart. You never deserved to be cast down so low; I never deserved to be lifted up so high. And it makes me wish I could roll back all these years and find ourselves children again, in the poor, dear old tenement house, with all our dear friends around us!" she said, weeping abundantly.

"Don't cry, Suzy! Indeed I didn't mean to hurt you. But you must look facts in the face, dear. It is not *fit* that *I* should be seen with *you*."

"And *why* is it not? You *look* like a gentleman, Benny; you *speak* like a gentleman; you *are* a gentleman, Benny, notwithstanding *all* that has come and gone; and in heart and soul you always *were* a gentleman, Benny. And you need only to be well dressed to be seen anywhere with anybody. Well, there! you are the living image of Lord Wellrose—that is, Lord Wellrose in poor health. If you could get your health and a fashionable suit of clothes, I do not believe any one could tell either of you apart. Yes, you are a natural gentleman, Benny; while I— Nothing on earth can ever make a lady of me; and I have sense enough to know it."

"I am no fit judge of a lady or a gentleman, Suzy; but I know one thing; that your good, true heart is worth a kingdom, if a man had it to give you."

"I wish all that was so, for your sake, Benny. But now tell me what you have been doing since you got back to England, and why you did not seek me out and come to see me. You say you lodged in the poor, dear old room we used to play in. Now what did you do the next day?"

"The next day I walked to the Strand. And the first thing I noticed there was the great bills posted everywhere, with 'ARIELLE!' I knew the name, Suzy. I knew it must be yours. I remembered that day, at the Helenic Gardens, when you danced under the name of Arielle. So I went to Covent Garden, and hung about the Theatre all day, in the hope of seeing you go in or come out from rehearsal. But I did not see you."

"I was not at rehearsal that day. But why, Benny, didn't you go to the box-office, and find out my address and come to see me?"

"Look at me, Suzy. Was it likely that I would *wrong*

you so much as to go inquiring after you, as if I were an acquaintance? No, Suzy. But I watched again at night. And I saw a very elegant little brougham drive up to the stage door. And I heard the loungers on the corner say 'That is she!' And I saw you come out of the carriage closely vailed, and go in at the stage door."

"Oh, Benny! *Why* did you not make yourself known to me, then and there?"

"Why? Ah, Suzy! *I*, a poor, returned convict! *You*, a celebrated prima donna. Would it have been likely that I should affront you so grossly as to claim acquaintance with you there? No, dear, no! But from that hour I watched morning and evening, and I saw you every time you came and went."

"You did! And you never made yourself known to me! And I never saw you! And I suppose, if I had not chanced to see you to-night and speak to you, you never *would* have come to me."

"Never, Suzy—never, for your sake! But I should have watched you from a distance, and I should have delighted in your triumphs, all the same. It was the pressure of the crowd that forced me up against your carriage and precipitated this *denouement.*"

"Yes. I bless the crowd, though I blamed it, only this evening. But—*denouement*, Benny? I have been noticing all this evening that you no longer speak as you used to speak when a boy. You have improved yourself, Benny?" she said, looking in his face.

"Yes, perhaps, a little. You know I learned to read and write while I was in prison here. Well, when a boy knows how to read and write and wishes to gain knowledge, he can learn almost anything else. I have taken every opportunity to learn as much as I could."

"I am so glad to hear you say that, dear Benny! But I think, Benny, that when you showed such a good disposition to improve yourself, they might have pardoned you and sent you home! *I do.*"

"Why, Suzy, did they acquit me because I was innocent? No! They convicted me because I would not betray my supposed accomplices. And do you think that they would pardon me because I had been unjustly convicted, or because I behaved well under that ordeal? No! because still I would not betray my supposed accomplices, whom the authorities were so very anxious to arrest. No, Suzy! I had to 'dree my weird,' as the Scotch say. In other words, I had to bear my doom. And now, Suzy, since you are so kind and good to me, tell me what has become of all our old friends; for I have not been able to find any of them, or to hear news of any of them. And first of all, your own family, Suzy."

"They are all in Australia. You see, my father and my brothers were unwilling to be always dependent upon me, though I could have kept them all in comfort all their days, and would have been willing to work for them all my life, if I could only have kept them with me. But they took the Australian fever, and must needs go out there and try their fortunes at sheep farming. So the first thousand pounds I made, clear of expenses, I gave to my father and sent them all out."

"And they all left you?"

"Every one! And I thought my heart must have broken, for I had not a soul near me who loved me, or whom I loved. And, Benny, the very night that I achieved my first and greatest triumph, when I knew that all the city was ringing with my name, I sat down and wept in solitude and homesickness, and longed for the poor old times in the poor old house in Junk Lane, with my father and mother and *you* to love me!"

"Ah, Suzy! Suzy! I wish you could accept your brilliant destiny with gratitude and joy."

"But I cannot. Never mind that. Whom else do you wish to hear of, Benny?"

"My poor mother."

"Still hopelessly insane, Benny! I visit her, for your sake, on every visiting day."

"The Kemptons?"

"Mary is married to a Baptist preacher at Corydon, and is doing well. The rest of her family went out to Australia with mine. Mrs. Melliss paid their way."

"Rachel Wood?"

"Is matron of the Duchess' School for Destitute Boys. But you knew she was going to be, before you left."

"Yes. Captain Faulkner's widow and children?"

"They live at Brompton, supported by Mrs. Faulkner's father. The children are grown up, as you and I, Benny. Is there any one else you would like to hear of?"

"No, no one else."

"And here comes the footman, to announce supper," said Suzy, as a man-servant drew aside a sliding door that divided the little apartment, and displayed an elegant little supper-table set for two.

Suzy took the arm of her poor friend and went to the table.

Her glance compelled the waiting footman to show as much respect to her poorly clad guest as if he, that guest, had been the Earl instead of the Outcast.

A few minutes after supper was over, Benny arose to take his leave.

"Come to me at two to-morrow afternoon, Benny. I have something particular to say to you," said Suzy, as he bad her good-night.

The poor outcast bowed, and promised.

CHAPTER XIX.

TWO FATES.

Why, let the stricken deer go weep,
The hart, ungalled, play;
For some must watch, while some may sleep,
Thus runs the world away.—HAMLET.

SUZY slept little and wept much that night. And it took a great deal of rose-water to cool her eyes the next morning, before she went to rehearsal.

In the green-room she found Lord Wellrose, apparently waiting for her—evidently curious to hear some explanation of her strange conduct, and some account of her stranger acquaintance of the night before.

Though courtesy obliged him to be quite silent upon the subject until she should speak, yet she quickly perceived his uneasiness, and in the intervals between her business in the rehearsals, she talked to him of her early life and humble friends.

"You know, my lord," she said, "that I am a child of the people—"

"Like Rachel, Ristori, Jenny Lind—"

"And all the rest," she added. "But, my lord, I was much humbler born than any of those. I could scarcely have been poorer, lower, than I was in my childhood. If Madame Vesta had not seen me and pitied me, I should never have been richer or higher, I think."

"You 'think.' Well, let that go, for the present."

"In my childhood I had a friend, dearer to me than any one else in the world. We were of the same age. My mother used to tell me that we were fond of each other in our cradles, and that strangers always took us for twins. When we were but a few months old, Benny's mother used to leave him with my mother when she went out to work. In the same way on Sundays, my mother used to leave me with Benny's mother while she went to work. That was the way in which the baby love began. I do not remember that; but so far back as I do remember, we two were inseparable companions. There's the prompter's call " she exclaimed, breaking off from her narrative to run upon the stage and sing her part.

Lord Wellrose walked up and down the green-room, his soul flooded with the tide of harmony that swelled from the stage and filled the building.

After a while she came back to him, and took up her subject just where she had left off.

"We were very, very poor! As I told you, we could scarcely have been poorer. We were very often half famished and half frozen. But we shared everything with each other. When Benny had no fire, I brought him in to ours. When we had no fire, Benny took me in to his. If Benny had a ha'penny roll, he always divided it with me. If I had one, I shared it with him. We two poor little heathen were like the primitive Christians in one respect—we 'had all things in common.' The call-boy again!" she exclaimed, breaking off and running away.

There was another rapture of divine harmony, that filled the place and transfigured the world for a time, and then again she came back and resumed her reminiscences.

"You may judge, Lord Wellrose, how dear to my soul was this friend of my childhood."

"I can judge."

"But I could never make you realize how gentle, affectionate, compassionate he was; how true and faithful he was; how utterly unselfish, how devoted to his friends. And yet, Lord Wellrose, there were those about him, those he loved and trusted, who taught him always evil for good; who led him into sin by his own purest affections; who taught him, for love of them, to break the laws of God and man, and to believe that he was doing a brave and good deed. My lord, you, in speaking of your own pure childhood, have told me how you used to boast of the great things you would do for humanity, when you 'should grow to be a man.' Benny would caress his starving companions and beg them not to mind, for that he would 'crack a case' and get them plenty of 'prod' when he should 'grow a big man.' All this, you see, out of the misled goodness of his heart."

"It is very deplorable."

"Yes; but I loved Benny dearly, notwithstanding all. You may judge, therefore, Lord Wellrose, what a deep, lasting, incurable sorrow it was to me, when I was entrapped by an artful detective into betraying my dear playmate to the hands of the police, to trial, to conviction, to transportation for fourteen years! And all for a crime that he never committed!"

Here Suzy dropped her face upon her hands and wept.

Lord Wellrose was deeply touched. He laid his hand upon her bowed head, and in earnest, tender tones, inquired:

"Can I do anything for him, for you?"

Suzy sadly shook her head.

"No; thanks, but no, you can do nothing. He had to 'dree his weird!' It is over now. He is back here again. It was he whom I met last night. You do not wonder now at anything I did, do you?"

"Indeed, no. And I should like to do something for the young man."

"If there should be anything that you—There! I must go again," she said, hastily drying her eyes, and hurrying off to take her part in the last and longest scene of the rehearsal.

When it was over, she once more rejoined Lord Wellrose in the green-room.

He asked permission to attend her to her home.

"Thanks, no; not this morning, if you please, my lord.

Come this evening, after the opera, if you have no other engagement, and I shall be very glad to receive you," she said, with a smile.

Lord Wellrose handed her to her carriage, bowed, and went away very thoughtful.

And Suzy drove home to her pretty house in Park Lane, to keep her appointment with Benny.

As soon as she entered the hall, the footman in attendance touched his forehead and said:

"If you please, Miss, the person that was here last night have come again, and is waiting to see you."

"Where is he?"

"In the servants' hall, Miss."

"In the servants' hall!" echoed Suzy angrily.

"If you please, Miss, he rang the servants' bell at the servants' door, and said he would wait in the servants' hall, himself," said the footman, who strongly suspected that the strange visitor was some poor, shabby, disreputable relation of his young mistress.

"Then show him into my sitting-room. And never keep him waiting in the servants' hall again. He is a very old friend of mine. Do you hear?"

"Yes, Miss," said the man, touching his forehead as he turned to go upon his errand.

Suzy went into her bright little sitting-room, fragrant and blooming with the bouquets that had been showered upon her the evening before; and she threw off her bonnet and vail, and her rich India shawl, and sat down to wait for Benny.

He came at last, ushered in by the same doubting foot man, who immediately shut the door and withdrew.

He was still very pale and thin—still like the faded out fac-simile of Lord Wellrose; and his clothes were very, very shabby, but his face and hands were as clean as those of any gentleman and his fair hair, combed back from his broad, pale forehead, turned into the soft curls so familiar to Suzy's memory of his childhood.

"Good-morning, Benny. I am very glad to see you. Oh, dear! I didn't mean that. I should have said that to the Earl or anybody. Benny, dear, I am gladder, much gladder to have you back in England, than I have been of anything else that has happened to me since you were forced away," she said, giving him both her hands, as her eyes filled with tears.

"You are!—oh, you are wonderfully good to me, Suzy!" he faltered, with much emotion.

"No, I'm not. I'm a heathen, I think, to have let you go away, Heaven knows where, last night, when I had four or five empty rooms in the house. A very heathen, Benny!"

"Suzy, you are a saint, more like. And you were right to let me go. Besides, my dear, I would not have staid for a thousand guineas," he answered gravely.

"But why? But sit down first, Benny. Sit down, and then tell me what you mean—why you would not have staid in my house; and, moreover, why you went to the servants' door this morning, and waited in the servants' hall?"

"Because, dear Suzy, dear, fortunate sister, I could not do otherwise without injuring you. It is not fit or right that I should visit you at all. Much as I longed to see you, I should not have come here at all, if I had not so faithfully promised to do so. When I did come, I purposely rang at the servants' door and waited in the servants' hall, as became the poor fellow that I am. For, Suzy, what am I? Not even a ticket-of-leave man! Worse even than that! I am a returned convict, who had to serve out his full term of punishment."

Suzy burst into tears and wept vehemently, saying, between her sobs:

"Oh, Benny, Benny, never, never say anything like that to me again. It cuts through and through my heart like a knife! You were sent out there for the sins of others, not for your own. You ought at least soon to have had a ticket-of-leave, and chance and help to recover and improve! But no, you had neither. Oh, Benny, why was it that you had neither? I know you deserved both."

"Ah, no, Suzy; in the law I deserved no indulgence. My fate followed me even out there. Listen, dear Suzy."

"Yes, Benny."

"You knew Tony, my step-father?"

"Of course, Benny."

"And you knew the Nut Cracker?"

"Nut Cracker? No, Benny."

"No, of course you didn't. Well, he was a pal of my step-father's, after my step-father went entirely to the bad. It was my step-father who committed that burglary for which I was lagged. I beg your pardon, Suzy; I should have said transported. I am trying to forget the thieves' Latin as fast as I can, but the force of habit is very strong. Well, it was Tony, my step-father, who committed the crime for which I was transported. And it was the Nut Cracker who received the stolen goods and disposed of them, and who harbored father and me. I had nothing to do with the burglary, and knew nothing about it until it was done and over."

"Of course I always knew that you had nothing to do with it, Benny."

"But, you see, I knew who did it, and where the thieves and the goods were both to be found. And then the evidence was very strong against me also. And I tell you Suzy, it was a great stretch of clemency, or of policy, to give me the chance, as the Court did, to clear myself by turning Queen's evidence and giving up the burglars!"

"Oh, if you had only, only done it and saved yourself!

You might now be a graduate of the Duchess' school, with a presentation to Oxford," wept Suzy.

"Well, well, it was my fate to be compelled to do as I did. I could not tell on them then, Suzy. I only tell you now, because my doing so can now in no way hurt them while it will explain much in my after misfortunes."

"Yes, Benny. Go on."

CHAPTER XX.

BENJAMIN'S STORY.

> "She bowed her head on her breast in ruth,
> With the rose-buds loose in her languid hands,
> While he told her tales of his outcast youth
> In the far-off convict lands."

I MUST explain that, on the voyage out to Van Dieman's Land, the chaplain on the ship was very kind to me and gave me instructions. When we reached the convict colony, I was still kindly treated and put to light labor. I tried to do right, and to please all in authority over me, and I succeeded in doing so."

"You were always sure to please, dear Benny; you always did."

"Ah! but my fate! After some months I was placed out, as a gardener's boy, in the house of a wealthy colonist. There also I tried to do right, and to please my master and mistress, and still I succeeded."

"Of course, Benny."

"But, ah! my fate!—I had been in that service about fifteen months, and was liked and trusted. One night, during the temporary absence of my master, I was ordered to sleep in the front hall of the house, for the better protection of the mistress and children. I slept in the hall four nights, and nothing happened. On the fifth night I was waked up by screams. I started to my feet. It was pitch dark in the house, and through the darkness there was the sound of rushing feet and muttered oaths, and above all, continued screams. I was groping toward the room from which the screams came, and which was my mistress' room, when there was a sudden rush of some one past me, and a sudden flash of light and crash of sound, that was so close it nearly blinded and deafened me. But in the instantaneous flash I saw the face of my step-father, with a pistol in his hand, and I saw the fall of the woman he had shot, and whose screams he had silenced forever."

"Oh, Heaven of Heavens! how horrible!" cried Suzy, covering her face with her hands.

"Then there was the silence of death in the darkness. And then a gathered group and a muttered conversation, and then the flash of a match and a lighted candle, which showed me my step-father Tony, the Nut Cracker, the Drum Breaker, Cracksman Jack and two ill-looking men who were strangers; and the murdered woman in a pool of blood, on the floor at their feet.

"'All quieted,' said one of the strangers, as the light flashed.

"'Hello! that's not so. Here's a kid must be silenced!' swore the other stranger, drawing a knife.

"'Let the kid alone! He belongs to me!' swore my step-father, snatching the knife from the hand of his comrade. 'That's my son, that is, and I'm proud of him! As skillful a snakesman and as faithful a pal as you'd find in the world. Why, bless you, he was lagged for us, when he might a been let off if he'd listened to the gospel-grinders and peached on us! An't that so, Cracksman?'

"'That's so,' said Cracksman Jack.

"'Well, then, he must go along with us any ways,' said the stranger.

"In horror of them, Suzy, I refused to go. They laughed

in my face, and the Nut Cracker took hold of me, while the others packed silver plate, jewelry, money, clothing and even food into sacks brought by them for that purpose. I implored my step-father by all I had suffered for him to leave me alone.

"'Would you stay here to be found and to be forced to put the bobbies on our track, you little sarpint?" inquired Tony.

"I reminded him that I had never yet betrayed him.

"'Well, then, you know if we was to leave you here, and you the only one left alive, you'd be forced to give a full and partic'lar account of this here ewent, or else to be scragged as an accomplish. And you might be scragged whether or no. And so the long and short of it is this, that we must do one thing or the tother with you—we must either take you with us, or kill you where you stand.'

"'Kill me where I stand,' said I.

"'Now, it's all for your own sake, you know, so I think we'll take you with us. What do *you* say, pals?' he inquired of his companions.

"'Brain him, and be done with it!' said one.

"'Yes, quiet him that way!' said another.

"'Fetch him along with us,' said the Nut Cracker. 'He stood by us in our trouble, and was game through the whole on't.'

"So, Suzy, they decided to take me with them. I resisted to the last. I had rather died then and there, than have gone with them, I had such a horror of them. I had been used—too used to thieves, but not to murderers! And oh! I had by this time found out, that in order to escape with all their booty, they had murdered all in the house—mother, babes, female servants — all but myself, who implored them to finish their bloody work and kill me."

With a slight cry, Suzy hid her face.

"Forgive me, dear, for telling you these horrible things," said Benny.

"Go on. If you could live through them, I can surely listen to them. Go on."

"I resisted to the last: but what could a slight boy do against six determined men? I hoped that they would kill me when one of them raised his pistol; but instead of firing it, he struck me a stunning blow on the head. That was the last I knew, until I opened my eyes and found myself in the bush."

"Your captors were the terrible Bushmen of the Colonies, then?"

"They were. I learned afterward that my step-father, Tony, and the Nut Cracker and Cracksman Jack and the Drum Breaker had all been arrested and tried at the Old Bailey, for the robbery of a bank and the wounding of a watchman; and that they had been convicted, and sentenced to transportation for life. As very desperate characters, they had been sent to Tasman's Peninsula, and set to the hardest labor, under the severest restrictions. By a deep concerted plot, they murdered their guard and made their escape. Subsequently they joined the most formidable gang of bush rangers in the colony, and they lived by murder, robbery and rapine."

Suzy shuddered.

"But their end was drawing near, dear Suzy! I wandered with them in the bush, their most unwilling captive, until at length a strong body of soldiers, in conjunction with armed police, was sent in pursuit of them, traced them to one of their rendezvous, laid in ambush there, and surprised and surrounded them. There was a desperate fight, for they were desperate men. But every one of the gang was killed or taken. My wretched step-father was mortally wounded, and he died in jail before his trial came on. Cracksman Jack was killed outright in the fight. The Nut Cracker and the Drum Breaker were afterward executed."

"Oh! horrible! most horrible! But you, Benny? you?"

"I, Suzy, told my story—told how I had been violently carried off by the Bushmen. There was really not evidence enough to convict me of any complicity with them, but the circumstances of my near relationship to the most notorious of the Bushmen were so suspicions, and also the record of my trial and conviction at the Old Bailey was so much against me, that all late good conduct was forgotten, and I was sent to Tasman's Peninsula, to join a gang of the very worst convicts."

"Oh, Benny! Benny!" moaned Suzy.

"Don't weep, dear. I carried with me the memory of all the good instruction I had received from the chaplain at Newgate, and from the missionary on board the convict transport ship. This saved me, Suzy, even in that hell, with devils for my companions. It saved me. There were very few chances of improvement there, but I made the most of all. After five years of bitter slavery there, I was given a little liberty to work for myself, under certain restrictions, and to receive a part of my wages. I then tried my best to do right, and to please those in authority over me, and again I succeeded; but, Suzy, the old black cloud hung too heavily over me. And I never got a ticket-of-leave. I had galling restrictions upon my liberty. The weary years rolled on, and I grew more and more home-sick and heart-sick, as the time of my exile approached its end. But every night, just so soon as my head would be upon the pillow, I would fall asleep and dream of home. In effect every night, in my dreams, I came home. But I have told you all this before, dear."

"Yes," said Suzy, weeping still, "yes. Oh, how I wish you had found my dear father and mother out there! They are wealthy sheep farmers now, Benny, and *they* would have employed you, and took you right into the bosom of their family and loved you like a son. I know they would. How strange and unfortunate you did not meet them!"

"More unfortunate than strange, dear Suzy. Australasia is a large place—Australia alone nearly as large as Europe To what part of the island did they emigrate, dear?"

"To Carpentaria, in North Australia."

"And I, you see, was on Tasman's Peninsula, a thousand miles or so south of them, with no knowledge of their being out there, and with no liberty to seek them, if I had known where they lived."

"Benny, dear, what do you intend to do, now that you have come here?"

"I have not thought yet. You know it will be difficult, if not impossible for me, a returned convict, to get employment from any one, for no one will employ a stranger without a recommendation. And who could give me a recommendation?"

"*I* could, Benny. And I would, heartily."

"But you should not, Suzy. I would never consent to that."

"But why?"

"Because it would bring reproach and trouble on you."

"I do not care if it should. But how could it do so?"

"In this way. You would give me a recommendation and a reference to yourself. Upon the strength of that, some one would employ me. Then some one else would be sure to find out that I was a returned convict, and would expose me. Why, Suzy, you would even be liable to criminal prosecution, for giving a false character, my dear."

"But it *wouldn't* be a false character. If I were to say all that is good of you now, Benny, it would be true."

"Ah, but, dear, opposed to all your faith in me would be the hard fact of my being a returned convict."

"Oh, Benny, my poor brother, what can I do for you?"

"Nothing, Suzy. I am fit for nothing but service, and no one would employ me."

"Benny I am your sister—your heart's dear sister! Let

me do a sister's good part toward you, as I do for Bill. Let me advance the funds to set you up in some business that would be to your taste, Benny."

"I thank you deeply, dear, happy little sister; but I cannot accept your generous offer. I cannot and will not sponge upon your resources, little sister."

"Oh, Benny, to let me advance the funds to set you up in some business would not be sponging on me. I only want to loan you the money, Benny. You would pay it back to me again."

"No, Suzy, I should lose it and never be able to repay it. No, Suzy, I know nothing of business, and I should be sure to fail."

"Benny, you will break my heart if you don't let me do something for you! Benny, I have no agent but my brother, and my business bores him. Couldn't you be my agent, Benny?"

"And supplant your brother? No, Suzy!"

"You need not supplant him, but only supplement him. I have business enough to employ two such agents as Bill makes. Be one of them, Benny."

"No, dear Suzy, I am not fit to be your agent or your brother's co-laborer. I should bring discredit on you both; and that I never will do."

Suzy burst into tears and wept passionately, sobbing and gasping forth her lamentations.

"I am wretched! I am miserable! And people think me so fortunate and happy! Oh! if they only knew how I suffer, they would pity instead of envying me, who cannot even save or help my own old playmate in his bitter need! What is fame or fortune to me, when my heart is bleeding and aching all the time? My dear father and mother are far from me! I shall scarcely ever see them any more! My sisters and brothers, all except one, are gone! And a stranger fills my mother's place in my home! And I am lonely, lonely, lonely! And now when my fortune *could* at least bring me some happiness by enabling me to help my old playmate, he is too proud to let me help him!"

"Suzy! 'proud?' I, proud? Of what, oh! Heavens! have I to be proud? I, who have been ground down to the dust! No, dear sister, I am not proud, but I hope that I am too just and generous to take the least advantage of your magnanimity," said the poor young man earnestly.

"But you will not let me help you! You will not let me do a single thing for you! And I wish, I do! that you and I were back again in the poor, old house, in the poor, old times when we used to hunger and shiver and play together; for we loved one another like true brother and sister then, and we were happy in our poverty! Oh yes! I wish that you and I could go back to the poor, old times, in the poor, old tenement house again; or else that we were both in our quiet graves," she said, with a fresh burst of grief.

The poor outcast bowed his head, but whether in assent to her words, in amen to her prayer, or in submission to her will, she could not know until he spoke.

"Suzy, little faithful sister, weep no more. You shall help me, if you will, in the only way in which you can do so without compromising yourself—in the only way in which you can make me happy.

"Tell me! Tell me! Tell me quickly!" she exclaimed vehemently.

"'Make me as one of thy hired servants,'" he said very gravely.

"Benny! Benny! What do you mean?"

"I told you, dear, that I was fit for nothing but service. Take me into your service, Suzy. Give me a footman's place in your household."

"A footman's place in my household!"

"I will never, never, *never* degrade you so, my brother!" she indignantly exclaimed.

"It will be no degradation, little sister. It will be a service of affection and devotion that I shall render you. Besides, I shall have the comfort of honestly earning my own bread; and above all, the happiness of living in the same house with my happy little sister, and of seeing her every day. Take this into serious consideration, Suzy."

"I will not take it into consideration for a single moment. I will never, never do such a thing as that, Benny."

"I think you will, dear Suzy; because you will come to know that it will be the only thing you can possibly do for me. Good-morning, Suzy."

"You are not going?" she said, drying her eyes.

"Yes, dear, I must not stay long, and set your household wondering what business such a poor fellow as I am can have with their mistress."

"What do I care, and why should you care, how much they wonder at us, so that we do right? You will come again at this hour to-morrow, Benny?"

"No, Suzy. I must not come again to see you. It is not fit that I should do so."

"Not fit! Oh, Benny! when so many not half so good as you are come to see me, and whom custom obliges me to receive! Oh, Benny, come again to-morrow."

"No; I cannot come here again as a *visitor.* I cannot come here again until you take me into your service—which you will sooner or later do, Suzy; and when I can see you every day, and watch over you faithfully. And then it must be no longer Suzy and Benny between us, since we will be no longer little children on terms of equality; it must be— How do people address you, Suzy? On the bills you are 'Arielle'—nothing else. But surely your visitors and servants do not call you 'Arielle.'"

"No, Benny, they do not. It is so extremely ridiculous They call me 'Mademoiselle Arielle,' as though I were a French woman—because I was educated in France, and because I sing in the opera, I suppose. Lord knows why they do it, *I* don't. My English servants call me simply 'Miss.'"

"Either will do. Good morning 'Mademoiselle.' When you require a footman, and are willing to take one without a character, I shall be at your orders," said the poor young man jestingly, so as to raise her spirits, as he turned to leave the room.

"Benny, come back to me! Where are you stopping?" she anxiously inquired.

"In the old house at Junk Lane by night. Nowhere in particular by day."

"And you *will* not come to see me to-morrow?" she pleaded.

"No, dear Suzy; for your own sake I must not."

"But if I consent to take that proposition of yours into consideration, will you not come to-morrow to talk it over with me?"

"No, Suzy; for it would be quite useless, and I must not visit you here unless in a case of the greatest necessity, if such should arise. No; I have said all that can be said in favor of my plan. You will think of it, and if you think favorably of it, as I trust you will, you can send to let me know that you have decided to engage me. Then I will come to you as your faithful servitor, and upon no other terms. I would die before I would do anything to compromise you, Suzy. Good morning, little sister."

She held her hand out to him. He raised it to his lips, bowed and withdrew.

And Suzy, left alone, fell to weeping again.

"The only one who has come back to me out of my lost childhood, and the dearest one of all, and he will not let me lift him up!" she complained

Her lamentations were interrupted by a knock at the door

"Come in," she said crossly

It was her costumer.

"This new dress for Mary Stuart, Mademoiselle, will you have it trimmed with gold or silver lace, or seed pearls?" inquired the costumer.

"Trim it with black crape, if you like, I don't care, what you trim it with," snapped "Mademoiselle." Then blaming herself, she said, "I beg your pardon, Madame. I did not mean to speak so uncivilly; but indeed I am vexed. Pray use your own perfect taste in the decoration of the robe, and I shall be quite satisfied with it."

The costumer smiled, nodded and withdrew.

At the same hour Benny went back to his poor lodgings in the house at Junk Lane, where he had been permitted to leave his box of clothes with the old woman who had charge of the place.

As the ragged school was dismissed for the day, Benny got leave to go up to the room where he slept at night, and where he had left his trunk.

The room had six small single beds in it, but nothing more.

At this hour there was no living creature in it except himself.

He drew his box out from under his bed, unlocked it and took from it a little parcel.

He sat upon the side of the bed and unrolled and looked at it.

It consisted of a baby's fine white merino sack embroidered with white silk, and a baby's little fine white knitted woollen sock, with white silk cord and tassels.

He took the sack in his hands and narrowly examined the embroidery, thinking:

"That poor, wretched Tony Brice gave me this on his death-bed. He had managed to keep it through all the vicissitudes of his miserable life He had hoped, he said, that some day it might make my fortune and his own. And he went on to tell me that I was not the son of Madge Hurst whom he married, and consequently that I was not his step-son. He told me that I was the son of a lady; that I was palmed off upon Madge Hurst in place of her own child, which died soon after birth; that this was confessed to Madge by the midwife who attended her, and who, in conjunction with the doctor, had practised the fraud upon her; but that was all, even the midwife could tell, for she died before she could utter the doctor's name. And a parcel containing this little sack and this little sock, supposed to be a part of my infant outfit, and the work of my mother's hands, and which was found by Madge among the effects of the midwife, is all that they could find to afford a clue to my birth. Madge kept it carefully as long as she retained her senses or her liberty. Then Tony took charge of it and contrived to keep it safe through all the troubles and changes of his life, hoping some time to profit by it. Ah! if they had only possessed the wit and knowledge to discover what I now see, they might have been more successful in their search for my parents. For here is the sure clue. On the top of the little slipper, and around the border of the sack, *among the embroidered wreaths of eglantines, is wrought the crest of the Barons of Linlithgow.*"

CHAPTER XXI.

THE TWO.

> She with jewels on head and hands,
> And I in the garb of a servant poor,
> While between us both there stands
> A thousand years or more!
>
> There are some things hard to understand;
> Oh, help us, Lord! to trust in Thee!
> But I'll ne'er forget her soft white hand,
> Or her eyes as she looked on me.—OWEN MEREDITH.

THREE days passed, during which Benny haunted the neighborhood of Covent Garden Theatre, morning and evening, for the pleasure of catching a glimpse of Suzy, as she went back and forth to the rehearsal or to the opera.

But while thus watching for her, he tried to avoid attracting her attention, or that of any one else.

On the evening of the third day, after he had seen her go in at the stage door for the opera, and while he was waiting weary hours to see her come out at the end of the performance, a man from the theatre came up and addressed him.

"Be your name Benjamin Hurst?"

"Yes," said Benny, wondering.

"Then I were to give you this. It's a bank note, I shouldn't wonder. Marmselle is werry charitable, and flings money about like dried leaves in Nowember. And you look as if you might be a hobject," said the man, as he handed Benny a sealed envelope and hurried away.

Benny was not acquainted with Suzy's handwriting, but he suspected this note to be from her.

He took it to the nearest gas-light, opened it and read as follows:

"DEAR BENNY—Come to my house early to-morrow morning. Come on your own terms.—SUZY."

He pressed the little note to his lips and put it in his bosom.

He waited until she came out, wrapped in her soft white-hooded opera cloak, and escorted by Lord Wellrose, who carefully handed her to her carriage.

He saw the door close, and then he turned away to his humble lodgings in Junk Lane.

Very early in the morning he arose and carefully brushed his poor clothes, and washed his face and combed his hair; and thus having made himself as clean and neat as his circumstances would permit, he set out to walk to Park Lane to keep his appointment with Suzy.

The distance was long, but he had no money to pay his omnibus fare. Therefore he had started early to walk all the way.

It was ten o'clock when he reached the little palace

In opposition to Suzy's repeatedly expressed wishes, he rang again at the bell of the servants' door.

On being admitted, he inquired for Mademoiselle Arielle, saying also, that he had been ordered to wait on her at this hour.

He was told in reply that Mademoiselle was at home, and had given orders that he should be shown to her presence immediately upon his arrival.

Benny took off his poor hat and followed the footman, who conducted him up stairs to the Rose Parlor, where he had last seen Suzy.

"The young man Hurst, if you please, Miss," said the footman, throwing open the door for Benny to enter, and then closing it and retreating.

Suzy was dressed in a plain white muslin robe, and seated at a little table, upon which lay some sheets of music.

She immediately arose and held out her hand, saying earnestly:

"I am very glad to see you, Benny, though you do come only on your own hard terms. And I only agree to these terms because you will not permit me to help you on any others, and because also, having you near me, I hope to induce you to let me serve you, my brother, in some better way. Pray sit down."

"I thank you, Suzy," said the young man, seating himself, for in truth he was very tired with his long walk.

"Now, brother, dear, we can talk plainly with each other, can we not?"

"Yes, little sister, but it must be for the last time. After I become your servant there can be no more such talk between us."

"Oh, dear me! dear me!" mourned the poor child, wringing her hands.

It seemed very hard to her to speak of wages to her old playmate. In fact, after several efforts, she gave it up, and said:

"Benny, I would rather write what I have to say to you in regard to one particular of your engagement, if you don't object."

"Anything you please, Suzy."

"Everything else but that, I can talk about. I hope you will feel no scruple in accepting this small advance on account, Benny?" she said, slipping a sealed envelope into his hand.

"No, Suzy, especially as it is really necessary to procure my livery before entering your service. Your livery is blue, white and silver, I think. I wonder who makes it up."

"You are not to go into livery! I won't have that!" exclaimed Suzy, bursting into angry tears. "You wish quite to break my heart, Benny, I believe! But I can be obstinate as well as you! And I say I will not have you degraded by any badge of servitude! Livery, indeed You in livery! I should as soon expect to see the Earl of

Wellrose in livery! the Earl of Wellrose, who is so much like you that you and he might be taken for own brothers!"

Benny started and changed color.

Suzy, too much absorbed in her own passionate denunciations, did not perceive his emotion, but continued vehemently:

"Yes, *that* he is! enough like you to be your own brother! And he *may* be your own brother, for aught I know!" she added maliciously.

"Suzy," said the young man, speaking with forced calmness, "as you are so well acquainted with the Earl of Wellrose, do you happen to know whether he is in any way related to the Scottish house of Seton-Linlithgow?"

Suzy looked up at him from the corners of her tearful eyes and answered saucily:

"Is the Earl of Wellrose related to the Scottish house of Seton-Linlithgow? Well, I should really think he was On the surest side of the house, too: on his mother's side Why, I thought every one knew that his father, the Duke of Cheviot, married Eglantine Seton, Baroness Linlithgow in her own right. What's the matter, Benny?" she suddenly inquired, seeing the young man grow very pale, and throw his hands to his head.

"A sudden turn. Never heed me, Suzy. What were you saying, dear, about the livery?"

"I was saying that you should never, *never*, NEVER be degraded by such a badge of servitude," began the young girl, flushing up again with indignation at the ideas recalled. "I say that I should just as soon expect to see the Earl of Wellrose in livery! there!"

"You are right, Suzy; I will not wear the livery."

"Thank you for conceding so much, Benny. I was afraid that you would hold out for the livery. Now listen to me further. Since you *will* serve, at least you shall serve no one but me. You shall stand near my chair at meal times, and never leave it. You shall not so much as hand a chair, or a plate, or a glass, or anything whatever to any person present except to me. The footman in livery shall wait upon every one else. You shall wait on no one else but me. And no one shall wait on me but you. That will be a bond between us. And oh, Benny, I have just thought of something, and I wonder I did not think of it before!"

"Yes, Suzy."

"This is what it is: You shall be my butler and house steward. Since you insist upon taking nothing better than a service with me, you shall take the best service in my gift. You shall be both butler and house steward."

"But, little sister, shall I not be displacing some one else?"

"No; for I have neither butler nor steward, nor ever have had."

"Nor ever would have, but for your goodness in trying to make a better position for me," said the young man with emotion.

"I am not so sure of that. I certainly need both butler and house steward; and you shall be both, Benny, and be at the head of my household, and keep the keys of the wine cellar, and pay the wages of the servants. And when we go back to Paris, you shall go with us there, Benny, if you will. And we shall never be parted in this world again, Benny, unless you wish it," said Suzy, in a tremulous but happy tone.

"Heaven knows I never wish to leave you," answered the young man, in an agitated voice.

"Then that is settled, my good brother. You will come to-morrow, to enter upon your—office?" inquired Suzy, after hesitating for a word.

"Yes, little sister, I will come to-morrow."

"For, after all," said the young girl cheerfully, "it will be an office, rather than a service, that you will have with me. Why, dear me! a Queen has always a domestic officer called the 'Master of the Household.' And they call me the 'Queen of Song.' So why may not I set up a 'Master of the Household?'" she added, laughing.

So delighted she was to think that she had found a place in her establishment that Benny would take, and that was not quite menial.

"Little sister," said the young man, "I cannot now say much—my heart is too full. But I am deeply grateful—"

She put her hand upon his lips.

"Hush, Benny, hush! That word has no business between you and me. We have been brother and sister in our infancy and childhood, with but one interest between us. If I had had my will, we would have been brother and sister up to this day. But fate was against us both. But as far as you will let it be done, we will be brother and sister again, and to the end of our lives. And now, good old brother, it is time for me to go rehearsal."

While she spoke there came a rap at the door.

"Come in," she said.

A footman entered.

"If you please, Miss, the brougham is at the door."

"Very well, Smith," she carelessly answered the footman. Then turning to Benny, she said very formally:

"Mr. Hurst, I shall expect you to enter upon your duties to-morrow morning."

Benny bowed low in reply, and then left the room.

"The house steward, Smith. You will in future take all your orders from him," she said in careless explanation, as she put on her hat and mantle, that were lying on the sofa beside her.

"Yes, Miss," answered the footman.

And when he had attended his mistress to her carriage, and returned to the servants' hall, he informed his fellow-domestics that their young mistress was about to provide for one of her poor relations, by making him her house steward.

"One of the Yerl of Wellrose's poor relations, you better say, for there never was two peas so much alike as them two," said Miss Jenny Smith, the footman's sister and Suzy's dressing maid.

And so it was quite settled, in the servant's hall, that the new house steward was some poor, unacknowledged kinsman of the noble Earl of Wellrose, whom his lordship had recommended to their mistress.

Meanwhile Suzy went to her rehearsal at Covent Garden Theatre, where she sang with even more animation than usual.

And Benny walked very thoughtfully away from the house. He had much to occupy his mind.

A week before this he had arrived in England, after his fourteen years' absence, and had been filled with the deep delight that only a returning exile knows, once more to touch his native soil, to view his native sky, to breathe his native air.

But then had followed the feeling of deep desolation, the sense of his own solitude in the crowded city.

But now all that was changed!

Suzy, once his dear little child friend, but whom he had not ventured to seek, not knowing how prosperity, wealth and fame might have affected her, Suzy — the celebrated singer whom he worshipped only at a distance—Suzy had found him out, had sought him and drawn him to her home and had shown herself the very same dear, loving, trusting little sister that she had been to him in their poverty-stricken infancy and childhood.

And now she had made an office for him in her house, in which he could really be of use to her, and which would also make him independent.

She had done all that he would permit her to do for him,

and he knew that she would do much more, if he would only let her—that she would do quite as much for him as for one of her own numerous brothers.

While thinking of all these things, he came upon a large old church, standing back from the street in its shaded church-yard. He saw that the door was ajar. He opened the iron gate and walked in from the roar of the street to the quietness of the church-yard.

He entered the old church. It was at this time quite empty. And the subdued light shining through its stained glass windows filled it with a rich, solemn, pleasing gloom. Benny sat down in one of the lower pews, bowed his head upon its front, and earnestly thanked the Lord for the peaceful life that was opening before him, and earnestly prayed that he might be able to serve and benefit his little adopted sister, and that she might be forever saved from the great temptations and perils that surrounded and pervaded her art-life.

Then he arose comforted and strengthened, and went forth out of the church.

And not only on his constant friend Suzy did his thoughts run, but on that mystery of his unknown birth that was beginning to possess a morbid and absorbing interest for him.

As he walked down Oxford street, he mentally summed up his case, so far as it was known to him.

He knew, for Tony Brice on his death-bed had told him, that he, called Benny Hurst, was not the son of Madge Hurst, but that he was the offspring of unknown parents, who had found it necessary to conceal his birth, and who had effectually done so, by the agency of a midwife and a confidential medical attendant, who had palmed him off on his delirious foster-mother, in place of her own dead child which was taken away and buried; that this much had been confessed by the midwife, who had died before she could divulge the name of the confidential medical attendant; that the name of the latter had never been ascertained; that the only mementos of his abandoned infancy were the little sack and the little sock, both embroidered with a wreath of eglantines, and with a family crest.

He knew, for he had looked into a book of heraldry on the table of a street vender of old books—he knew that that crest was the crest of the ancient and noble Scottish house of Seton Linlithgow.

He knew, for Suzy had told him, that the Duke of Cheviot had married the sole heiress and last representative of that house — Eglantine Seton, Baroness Linlithgow in her own right.

He knew, for his own eyes assured him, that there was the strongest possible resemblance between himself, poor Benjamin Hurst, the abandoned son of somebody, and the noble young Earl of Wellrose, son of Eglantine, Duchess of Cheviot and Baroness of Linlithgow.

He knew, from his own personal experience, that the beautiful Duchess had more than once encountered him in his wretched childhood, and had shown strange emotion at the sight of him.

He remembered that wintry evening at Brighton, when he had stood on the sidewalk in front of her house on Brunswick Terrace, and by the whim of the little Lady Jessie, he had been brought in by a footman, and after having been washed and brushed and polished up a little, and made decent, had been taken to a parlor where the children were holding a Twelfth-night festival; how the children had made much of him, and little Lady Jessie had given him a slice of the Twelfth-day cake; and the ring having been found in that slice, he was jestingly made the King of the festival, and told to crown his Queen; how he had gone trembling up to the beautiful Duchess, and laid the crown at her feet, and tried to speak the words set down for him, but she had looked on him with such compassionate t[illegible] tender eyes, that he had lost all his self-control, and burst into a storm of passionate tears and sobs, for which he could not account; and how the Duke had ordered him to be kindly sent away.

He remembered, later on, lying ill of a fever in the hospital, and in a dreamy, half-conscious state, seeing the lovely face of the Duchess bending over him, hearing the tender tones of her voice murmuring words of love and pity, feel-the light, warm rain of tears upon his face, and trying to wake up and speak his thanks, and failing to do so.

He had thought this all a dream until he had been assured by Rachel Wood that it was a reality.

He had not seen the beautiful Duchess since that time, now fifteen years past.

Why was there such a perfect likeness between his poor self and her noble son?

Why had the crest of Seton-Linlithgow been embroidered on his own infant sack and sock, and the eglantines also?

Why did the beautiful Duchess weep over him, as he lay in the hospital bed?

Was he perhaps her poor little disowned brother? or rather *half*-brother, he meant. And did she know it, or suspect it?

If so, why should she have left him in the hospital then, and never inquired for him again?

Ah! he remembered the reason now.

Of course he was too ill to be removed at that time. And the very next day he had been taken to the dead-house for dead, and his death had been reported to the Duchess, as well as to others.

And how should she know, more than others, that he had recovered from the deathly trance that had been taken for death?

And besides, as Rachel Wood had told him, she had gone abroad almost immediately after his reported death.

And he himself had been transported within a year afterward.

And fifteen years had passed, and no doubt she had quite given him up for dead, and utterly forgotten him.

But the whole subject so troubled his soul that he resolved to go into a bookstore and examine the Peerage, to find out all he could about the ancient and noble Scottish House of Seton-Linlithgow.

Then he looked down upon his shabby clothes, and doubted whether any bookseller would let him examine his books.

So he decided to go to an outfitter's first.

He kept on his way until he reached the Strand and found a shop that suited his purposes. He went in and selected the articles he wanted, and took out the sealed envelope that had been placed in his hand by Suzy. He opened it, and found that it contained four five pound notes. He took one to pay for the complete suit that he purchased, and then taking his large parcel under his arm, he went with it to an humble tavern on one of the side streets, and asked for a bed-room, where he proceeded to change his dress.

His next visit was to a barber's shop, where he got his hair and whiskers trimmed and dressed.

CHAPTER XXII.

THE OUTCAST IN SEARCH OF HIS PEDIGREE.

> Howe'er it be, it seems to me,
> 'Tis only noble to be good.
> Kind hearts are more than coronets,
> And simple faith than Norman blood.—TENNYSON.

AND now, being neatly clothed in a suit of clerical black, with spotless linen and fresh gloves, he looked more than ever like a gentleman, more than ever like his unknown brother.

He walked on until he reached a bookstore.

He went in and requested a young shopman to allow him to look at "Burke's Peerage" for the year.

"Certainly, my lord," answered the young man very deferentially, handing down the great red volume in question. "Will your lordship please to take a seat?"

"You mistake," said Benny very quietly.

"I beg your lordship's pardon. I'm sure I understood your lordship to ask for 'Burke's Peerage,'" the shopman apologized.

"So I did. You have not mistaken the book; but you have mistaken *me* for some one else," said Benny, with a smile.

"Oh! I'm sure I hope you'll excuse me. I *did* take you for Lord Wellrose, who comes in here quite often," the young man explained, losing much of his deferential deportment.

"Oh, there is no offence at all," Benny answered, with a little laugh, as he sat down, laid the great book on his knees, and began to turn over the leaves in search of the Barony of Linlithgow. He found it.

LINLITHGOW.

LINLITHGOW, BARONESS (Eglantine Douglas) of Seton-Linlithgow, Co. Inverness, North Britain, born June 15th, 18—; succeeded her father December 20th, 18—; married, July 25th, 18—, to William Douglas, tenth and present Duke of Cheviot, (see *ante* CHEVIOT, DUKE.) By this union her grace has issue—.

Here followed a list of the children of that distinguished marriage, commencing with the eldest and only son and heir.

"William-Alexander-Cromartie-Seton Douglas, Earl of Wellrose, born October 30th, 18—," and going on with the names of the daughters in due order.

Then followed the history of the long lineage, beginning nine hundred years back, when the founder of the family, one Madoch Seton, for some important service rendered to majesty, was rewarded with the Lordship of Linlithgow by Malcolm First, King of Scotland.

Benny ran his eye down the lines, where the family history of nine centuries was compressed into two double-columned octavo pages, until he came to—

John-Alexander-Madock Seton, eighteenth Baron, who was born March 7th, 17—; succeeded his father May 14th, 18—; married, August 25th, 18—, the Lady Anne Moray, daughter of the Earl of Ornoch, and had issue—

Eglantine, present Baroness.

Benny closed the book, and holding it upon his knees, fell into deep thought.

"There were no other children of the late Baron, so I cannot be her unowned nephew. The late Baron died December 20th, 18—. That must have been more than five years before I was born, so I cannot be her unowned younger brother. Yet I must be *something* to the beautiful Duchess; all circumstances go to prove that. I was born in her own native neighborhood, in Scotland; I was an unowned child, outcast from my birth; I bear a perfect likeness to the Earl, her son; she once or twice manifested the deepest and tenderest interest in me; and the only mementos I have of my infancy are the little garments marked with her family crest. Let me be sure of that," he said to himself, as he once more opened the big red book, and turned to the article LINLITHGOW, and examined the arms and crest of the family.

Yes, the crest engraved and described there was the same that was embroidered upon the little sack and sock—a lark with expanded wings, rising from a baron's coronet, and holding in its beak a spray of ripe eglantine rose berries.

He closed the book with a sigh, and fell into still deeper thought.

But the article "LINLITHGOW" had referred the reader for further information to the article, "CHEVIOT, DUKE OF," *ante*.

So again he opened the book and turned back the leaves until he found

CHEVIOT.

CHEVIOT, DUKE OF, William-Angus Douglas, Earl of Wellrose, Viscount Angus, Baron Douglas of Douglas, and a baronet, County of Inverness in North Britain, born April 3d, 18—; succeeded his uncle as tenth duke August 7th, 18—; married, July 25th, 18– Eglantine Seton, Baroness Linlithgow, and has—

Here followed a list of the children similar to that given under the head of Linlithgow; and a pedigree even more ancient, noble and renowned than that of Seton-Linlithgow; and the arms and quarterings of the family; and last of all a list of the numerous seats. Among them the inquirer particularly noticed Seton Castle, Seton, County of Argyle.

He closed the book and took it to the counter, saying:

"I will buy this book, if you will put it up for me."

"Certainly, sir," said the shopman, still a little sulkily, in remembrance of having mistaken "this plain gentleman" for the noble Earl of Wellrose.

"In the meantime, will you let me look at a map of Scotland?" inquired Benny.

The shopman handed down the required article, and laid it before the inquirer.

Benny opened it on the counter and began to examine it closely.

On the west coast of Argyleshire he found the little port of Kilford, and a few miles inland the village of Seton, above which Seton Castle was known to stand.

So close together stood the little fishing hamlet to which he had been taken to be concealed, and the ancient feudal hold of the renowned house whose crest was wrought upon his infant garments!

"I will take this map also, if you please," said Benny, handing it back to the salesman, who put it into the parcel with the other large volume, and inquired:

"Where will you have these sent, sir?"

Benny gave the address of the little hotel where he had engaged a room.

"What name, sir?"

"Never mind the name; the number of the room will do —No. 7."

"Very well, sir; the books shall be sent immediately."

Benny took his hat to leave the shop, but recoiled toward the back of it, where he leaned on the counter pale and faint, for there, before the door, stood the equipage of the Duchess of Cheviot!

A footman in livery of purple and gold was in the act of letting down the steps.

At the same time the beautiful Duchess quietly, but richly dressed, descended from the carriage and entered the shop.

"Why, Wellrose, my son, you here?" she exclaimed, in a low, quick voice. Then, as something in the pale face of the young man seemed to correct her mistake, she dropped her tender eyes, and said very gently, "I beg your pardon, sir; I took you for—some one else," and passed on to the counter.

He caught his breath and stood for a moment, feeling deadly cold, with his heart beating like a hammer, and then, as a man walking in darkness, he put out his arm and groped his way from the shop.

The Duchess looked wistfully after him for a moment, as some strange emotion, half of pity, half of pain, disturbed her bosom. Then turning to the shopman, she inquired:

"Who is that young gentleman?"

"Beg pardon, your Grace, but I really do not know. I never saw him before," answered the shopman, with a low bow.

"He looks ill," said the Duchess in a compassionate tone, gazing after him as he passed out of sight.

'There *is* something odd about him, your Grace. He has been for two hours poring over the 'Peerage,' and over the map of Scotland, and ended in buying both and ordering them to be sent to—"

"Thanks. That will do," said the Duchess gently, arresting the garrulity of the shopman.

She made her purchases, children's books, each of which she carefully examined before selecting.

She directed them to be sent to her school, and then she re-entered her carriage and gave the order:

"Home."

Meanwhile Benny returned to his room at the Black Lion, where he sat down and took himself to task for the most unreasonable emotion he had betrayed at the sight of the beautiful Duchess.

After some slight refreshment, he went out again.

He spent the afternoon in collecting his scanty effects, which had been left in the care of the old porteress of the lodging-house in Junk Lane, and in purchasing the articles necessary for a respectable outfit.

All these things were directed to be sent to his room in the Black Lion, where, later in the afternoon, he returned to pack them into the large new trunk he had purchased.

In the evening he went to Covent Garden Theatre, to hear "Mademoiselle Arielle" sing.

He had not had the opportunity of doing so before, for he had had neither proper clothing to wear, nor money to buy his ticket.

He might now have gone into the boxes; but in the very shyness and sensitiveness of his nature, he preferred to lose himself in the dense crowd of the parquette.

He found a seat there and waited impatiently for the rise of the curtain.

And when at length it did rise, he was indeed disappointed.

Mademoiselle Arielle was not on the stage, and though the chorus had been a choir of angels, he could take no pleasure in their singing.

The scene changed, and a solo and a duet, and then another chorus, were sung.

And then the drop-scene fell upon a grand tableau, but Arielle had not appeared.

The young man was so surprised, disappointed and anxious, that he could not resist the desire to question his next neighbor.

"What has happened? Will Mademoiselle Arielle disappoint the audience to-night?"

"Oh, no; but she does not come on until the second act."

"Oh!"

"Hush! The Royal party are coming in," whispered his neighbor.

At the same moment there was a half-suppressed excitement sweeping through the crowded audience, like a breeze through the leaves of a forest.

The band struck up—

"God save the Queen!"

The audience arose *en masse.*

Benjamin Hurst stood up, and looking toward the Royal box, saw the Royal family taking their seats.

And in close attendance upon her Majesty stood the beautiful Duchess.

Benjamin looked at neither queen nor princesses after that. He looked at only *her*. And he asked himself:

"Why is it that my heart is so troubled at the sight of that lovely lady? That I am something to her I know. But what of that? I am not worthy so much as to 'touch the hem of her garment!' I, whose infancy and childhood were passed in sin and shame; I, whose youth was spent in the penal colonies; I, who hold myself unworthy even to enter my old playmate's house, except as her hired servant. I will never trouble the beautiful Duchess—no, even though I should discover myself to be—but that's impossible—her own lawful son."

While these sad thoughts were passing through the mind of Benjamin Hurst, the band finished playing the National Anthem; the audience sat down; the prompter's bell rang, and the curtain rose, revealing the fair Arielle alone on the stage.

Her appearance was hailed by the most enthusiastic applause. And Benjamin, forgetting the trouble of his soul, so rejoiced in her triumphs that his blue eyes fairly danced with delight.

She sang a solo, that so enraptured her audience that it was encored and encored.

As she was retiring the third time amid a storm of applause, a gentleman, sitting in the front row of the orchestra seats, arose and threw a bouquet of the richest and rarest roses, in the midst of which was a diamond, that, in dropping, blazed like a falling star.

As this gentleman stood up, Benny recognized him.

He was the Earl of Wellrose.

Arielle picked up the bouquet, and smiled and courtesied to the giver, and then raised her eyes and encountered, afar off, the intense blue orbs of Benjamin Hurst fixed earnestly upon her. She smiled on him also, and with a courtesy for the whole audience, glided off the stage.

She came on again in a duet, and then with the chorus.

And whether she sang alone, or with one or two or many, or whether she came on or went off, she was greeted or followed with "thunders" of applause and showers of bouquets But no other bouquet was so choice as that one with the blazing star, thrown by the Earl of Wellrose

When the curtain fell upon the last magnificent tableau, the evening of triumphs ended in one grand ovation to the fair prima donna.

And the crowded audience slowly worked itself out of the theatre.

In a strange delirium, half of delight, half of despair, Benjamin Hurst pushed out into the street, and posted himself where, unseen, he could see Suzy when she came forth.

She came at length, wrapped in her soft white opera cloak and hood, carrying in her hand the rich bouquet with the blazing star in the midst, and leaning on the arm of the Earl of Wellrose, and smiling sweetly to herself.

The Earl put her in her carriage, lingered to speak a few words in a low tone, then bowed and withdrew.

The footman put up the steps, shut the door, gave the order to the coachman, and leaped up to his place behind just as the coach started.

Like a sleep-walker, Benjamin Hurst sauntered along in the direction of his lodgings at the Black Lion.

All that had passed that evening seemed to him like the phantasmagoria of a midnight dream. The magnificent scene, the splendid audience, the beautiful Duchess in the Royal box, the divine songstress on the stage, the dazzling lights, the glowing colors, the entrancing music, the transcendent procession of scenery and incident in the opera, the supernal tableau and the final grand ovation, seemed rather to belong to the visionary than the real world.

He reached his lodgings and went to bed, and passed from the waking dream to the sleeping one. And in the last, as in the first, the forms of the beautiful Duchess and the fair prima donna passed before him.

He awoke early, and recollected, in his first conscious moment, that that morning he was to enter the service of the young prima donna.

He arose and made his simple toilet, and ordered his frugal breakfast.

And when he had eaten it, and had called for his bill and paid it, he sent for a cab and had his large trunk strapped on behind, and his small effects packed inside, and then he got into it himself and directed the driver to take him to number —, Park Lane, and to stop at the servants' door.

In good time he reached the miniature palace, drew up at the servants' entrance and alighted.

He directed the driver to bring in his effects, and then paid and dismissed him.

He went into the servants' hall, where, before he had time to announce himself, the footman, Smith, accosted him with:

"If you be the new house steward and butler, sir, my mistress left word as you was to come up to her immediate."

"Very well. I am quite ready to go," replied Benjamin.

"Then come with me, if you please," said the footman, leading the way.

The man took Benjamin up stairs, and to the door of the Rose Parlor. He opened the door, announced:

"The new house steward and butler, if you please, Miss," and immediately retired.

Benjamin found himself alone with Suzy.

CHAPTER XXIII.

MISTRESS AND MAN.

"GOOD-MORNING, Benjamin. I am glad to see you here to-day. I saw you at the Opera last night, and I was glad to see you there too," said Suzy, holding out her hand.

Benny took it and bowed over it, but did not speak. Emotion that he could neither understand nor conquer, kept him silent.

"Please sit down, Benjamin," she said, pointing to a chair beside her.

He shook his head slightly, bowed and remained standing.

"Oh, well, if you will not sit, you must stand, I do suppose. 'A willfu' mon maun ha'e his way,' as the Scotch say. Benjamin, you enter upon your duties to-day. And I need scarcely tell you that I will make them as light and as pleasant as possible. The housekeeper, Mrs. Brown, has prepared a room for you—a very pleasant room on the third floor back, looking upon the little inclosed shrubbery. It has been fitted up for you very nicely. I have seen it myself, and I like it. That will be your own private apartment, Benjamin, where you can retire when you wish to get away from everybody."

She paused and looked at him. But again he only bowed in silence. And so she continued:

"Besides that, Benjamin, there is a little office in the front basement where you can sit to transact the business of the house. It is fitted up with book-shelves and cupboards, and a writing-desk and table and comfortable chairs. I think you will like it, Benjamin, I did, I'm sure," she added.

And then again she paused. But again he only bowed and remained silent.

"You do not speak to me, Benjamin. You have not spoken to me since you came into the room. Why is it?"

"Oh Susan, Susan," he said, in a choking voice, "it is, perhaps, that my consciousness is so darkened and burdened with the memory of my past life. When I remember what my life has been—when I recall my stained and defiled infancy and childhood, my disgraced and dishonored youth, my cursed and ruined manhood—I feel that I ought not to be here."

Susan covered her face with her hands and wept. He continued:

"I feel that I am unworthy to be here. I feel, Suzy

that your very meanest lackey, if he knew my past, would not obey my orders, nay, that he would not even tolerate my presence in the house, but would give you warning."

Susan wept bitterly. He went on:

"That, perhaps, was the reason, Susan, why at first I felt unable to reply to you," he concluded, and then he stood meekly before her.

Susan lifted up her head and dashed the tears from her eyes, as she answered:

"No one shall ever know your unfortunate past life, Benny. It is not given to the ignorant and narrow-minded to know some things of which they are incapable of forming just judgments. You are not responsible for your past, Benjamin. You were and are naturally honest, true, just and generous, affectionate, self-devoted, magnanimous. I who have known you as long as I have known myself, am sure of this. The sins of your childhood, Benjamin, were habits taught you as duties. They were no more a part of yourself than were the little ragged jacket and trousers that I remember so well. In the greater misfortunes of your youth, you were without a shadow of blame; you were then, indeed, a blameless victim who suffered a criminal's punishment. But your manhood, Benny, if you will only think so, need not be blighted by these antecedents. They were misfortunes that still darken your inner life because you are so sensitive; but they should not be permitted to affect your outer life at all. Oh, dear boy, accept what good I can do you, and spend your leisure time in self-improvement, that you may be prepared for something better," she added, as she held out her hand to him.

And never knight touched the hand of a queen with more reverence than Benjamin Hurst showed, when he bowed over the hand of Susan and pressed it to his lips.

Then she rang the bell. And to the page who answered it, she gave a direction to send her companion and housekeeper to the room.

The latter soon made her appearance.

"Mrs. Brown," she said, "this is the new house steward and butler I told you about. You will please show him his office, and take the keys of the wine cellar and the household account-books to him there. You will also send all the tradespeople's bills to him for settlement. He will pay the servants their wages, and be in authority over them. You will have his meals served to him in his office."

"Very well, miss," answered the housekeeper.

"And now, Mr. Hurst, here are certain instructions for your own guidance," said Susan, turning to the young man and placing in his hand a letter.

Benjamin took it and bowed, and left the room with the housekeeper.

"I will take you up stairs first and show you your bedroom," said Mrs. Brown, leading the way.

She took him to the third floor back, and opened the door of a spacious chamber, neatly but plainly furnished with every possible comfort, and having two lofty windows that looked down upon a back yard, where green trees, sweet shrubs and climbing vines were very pleasant and refreshing to the sight.

Benjamin looked around it with evident satisfaction.

"You will know where to find this again. And now I will show you the house steward's office," said the matron.

And she led the way down four flights of stairs to the basement story, where she showed him a front room of good size furnished as Susan had described.

"And now, if there's anything else you need, I have orders to supply it," she said.

"Thanks. Nothing more whatever at present," said the young man.

And the housekeeper left him, to return in a few moments, bringing with her the household account-books.

"Up to this time they have been under my charge. And I think you will find them correct," said Mrs. Brown.

"I have no doubt of it," answered the young man, with a smile, as he received them from her.

And when the matron had left the room he proceeded to open the books, to make himself familiar with their contents.

His front window commanded the sidewalk before the house, and his desk was immediately below the window. He sat poring over the account-books until he heard the sound of carriage wheels, and looking up, saw Susan's brougham draw up before the door.

He watched until he saw her come down and enter the carriage and drive off.

He knew that she had gone to rehearsal. And then he applied himself again to the revision of his account-books.

It was only to become familiar with an unfamiliar subject that he now studied.

He saw no more of Suzy that day.

He had chosen his own lot, chosen it in his self-humiliation, at the memory of his poor, degraded childhood and youth. And of course he must abide by it.

He might have been her agent, in place of her very inefficient brother Bill.

And brother Bill would no doubt have been well pleased to be relieved from the duties of his office, while still enjoying its privileges, which consisted mainly in the freedom of his sister's house and table and pocket and fame.

But he, Benjamin, was, as we have said before, overshadowed and overwhelmed by the memory of his sinful and shameful, though irresponsible childhood. How little he was blameworthy, all our readers know. But in his morbid remorse and humiliation, he felt that he would be less unhappy in an humble position than in any other.

Did he love Suzy then?

As a sister, *yes;* he loved her as never brother loved sister before. But as a lover who longed to become a husband? No, *not yet.* His love was disinterested.

Did Suzy love him? As a brother, yes; she loved him as sister had never loved brother before. But as a lover, and a possible husband? No, indeed!

She was beginning to love the Earl of Wellrose in that light.

Drawn to Earl Wellrose, first of all, by something in his face that at first sight had reminded her of her best beloved early friend and playmate, she had received him with pleasure.

Later on, charmed by the fascination of his manner and the profundity and brilliancy of his mind, she had learned first to wonder at him, then to admire him, and now—*to* love him.

Benjamin Hurst knew nothing of all this, as he sat patiently poring over his account-books. He knew that his beloved foster-sister was the worshipped of all London; but he suspected not that she favored one more than another of her worshippers.

The moment of his illumination was, however, at hand.

That very evening, after the opera, "Mademoiselle Arielle" was to give a "little supper."

Arielle's little suppers were very elegant, *recherché* and refined affairs. Usually there were but four present, seldom more than six, never more than eight.

On this occasion, there were to be but six: the Earl of Wellrose; Mademoiselle Zephyrine, the secunda donna of the opera; the Honorable Stuart Fitzroy, the younger son of the Viscount St. Paul; Arielle, the hostess; and Mr. William Juniper, her brother, and La Pettite Fée.

The supper was to be served at half-past eleven P. M. I might have been a breakfast if it had been ordered to be served half an hour later.

And Benjamin Hurst, in his capacity of butler, was to

stand behind the hostess' chair, and according to particular arrangement, to wait only on her.

The matron who stood in the double character of companion and housekeeper to Mademoiselle Arielle — our Susan Juniper—informed Benjamin Hurst of what was afoot, and gave him a hint of what would be expected of himself.

Therefore, as the hour for the supper approached, Benjamin went into the elegant little supper room, opening from the drawing room, to see that all things were in order. Not that he was any sort of a judge of supper tables, poor boy! but his hard life had made him an excellent judge of men, and he was sure he should know, by the very looks of the footmen under him, whether they had faithfully performed their duty and all was right.

When he saw the supper table, he had no complaint to make.

It seemed to him, with its rich decorations of the most fragrant hot-house flowers, its splendid service of gold, silver, porcelain and glass, and its rainbow lights from stained gaseliers, to be just perfect. He did not need to look at the confident faces of his underlings to see this.

"You have done very well indeed, Smith and Jones. Nothing could be more elegant," he said, happy to be able to approve so heartily.

"Thank you, sir; glad you like it, sir," said Smith and Jones, who had come to the wise conclusion that it might be prudent for them to stand well with the new house steward and butler, whether he were simply an ordinary person, or an unacknowledged poor kinsman of the Earl of Wellrose, whom their mistress certainly distinguished above all her other adorers.

Benjamin Hurst then went to his room to make a toilet proper to the occasion—a fine black cloth dress suit with white vest, white cravat, white gloves and white handkerchief—very like a gentleman's

At eleven o'olock, "Mademoiselle Arielle" came home bom the opera.

She hastily changed her carriage suit for an evening dress, ind then sent for Benjamin Hurst to attend her, in the Rose Parlor.

He went in and found her seated on the sofa. She was 'ery richly dressed, in a light blue satin, with a point lace verskirt, and jewelry to match, of fine pearls and turquoise, nd a bouquet of blue and white violets on her bosom. Her ight golden hair, parted on the top of her small head, and arried back from her temples and caught up behind with a omb of silver filigree set with pearls and turquoise, fell in a hining shower of curls upon her neck. She held in her and a fan of blue satin spangled with silver, and a larger ouquet of blue and white violets.

"I have asked you to come up here, Benjamin," she said that I might say to you this. You need not attend at the upper table to-night unless you really wish to do so. There no necessity, you know."

"But I wish to do so," said Benjamin.

"Then it shall be as you please; but you will wait on no ne but me, remember. And a service of affection it will e," she said.

And Benjamin, understanding that the little interview as over, bowed and withdrew.

Half an hour later, Arielle and her guests were assembled the elegant little drawing-room, when the doors of the ining-room were drawn back, as by invisible hands, and the oung butler appeared and said:

"Mademoiselle, supper is served."

CHAPTER XXIV.

THE LITTLE SUPPER.

Then all was jollity,
Feasting and mirth, light heartedness and laughter.—Rowe.

Arielle arose and took the offered arm of the Earl of Wellrose, and led the way to the supper table, followed by the Honorable Stuart Fitzroy with Mademoiselle Zephyrine, and Mr. William Juniper with La Petitie Fée.

It was a round table, and as each gentleman handed his companion to her seat and sat down beside her, it happened that a lady and gentleman were placed alternately around the board.

The supper was composed of the most choice dainties of the season, in meats, fruits, pastry and confections, with the rarest wines and cordials.

Benjamin Hurst waited behind the hostess' chair, and changed her plates or filled her glass; and waited on no one else, but kept his eye on the two footmen who were in attendance under him, to see that they did their duty. And Smith and Jones, who thought that they were now overlooked by a man who, in spite of his youth, understood the duties of his office, exerted themselves to win his approbation.

Jest and laughter, raillery and repartee ran around the table, and "all went merry as a marriage bell."

But very early in the feast the tastefully dressed young butler, standing behind Arielle's chair and waiting exclusively upon her, attracted general though covert attention. His rare personal beauty and delicacy, and his perfect resemblance to the Earl of Wellrose, excited much admiration and astonishment.

"Who the deuce is that languid swell of a new butler of yours, Suzy?" inquired Mr. William Juniper, who sat on the left hand of his sister, while the Earl of Wellrose sat upon her right.

"Hush! I will tell you after supper," replied Arielle, in a very low tone.

And the wine circulated and the feast went on amid much merriment.

Benjamin, watching from his post behind the hostess' chair, observed much: first, that Suzy took no wine, only lifting her glass to her lips when invited to do so by a guest; secondly, that the Earl of Wellrose took very little; and thirdly, that the Honorable Stuart Fitzroy and Mr. William Juniper drank a great deal too much.

He also noticed that the attentions of the Earl of Wellrose to Arielle were at once tender, delicate and respectful, and she took a shy delight in his society. But that the admiration of Mr. Stuart Fitzroy for her was freely and somewhat coarsely displayed, and that she shrunk from it in ill-concealed disgust. Furthermore, he noticed with astonishment that her brother clearly favored the vulgar advances of Mr. Fitzroy, while he discouraged the delicate attentions of Lord Wellrose.

Not having the key to Mr. William's strange conduct, he could not understand it at all.

The little supper came to an end at length.

The party adjourned to the drawing-room for a few moments to exchange a little more raillery and repartee, jest and laughter, and then to prepare to separate for the night.

Tho two young ladies from the opera went away in their brougham. Then the Earl of Wellrose made his bow and departed.

When all the other guests had gone, Mr. Stuart Fitzroy lingered.

Suzy stood up where she had received the conges of her friends, and, though she was very tired, she forbore to sit down, lest the Honorable Stuart should take her act as a tacit invitation and follow her example, and then prolong his stay.

So she remained standing, as if waiting for him to bow and go, until her wise brother, Mr. William, said:

"Sit down, sit down, Mr. Fitzroy; it's early yet—quite early."

Yes; indeed it was "quite early"—only two o'clock in the morning. So, to Arielle's extreme annoyance, Mr Stuart Fitzroy sat down and made himself at home.

Arielle dropped heavily into her seat, without making the least effort to disguise her weariness and dissatisfaction.

That was not the worst of it; for, after a very few minutes of light conversation with Mr. Fitzroy, Mr. William, who had been standing with his back to the fireplace, now deliberately sauntered out of the room, leaving the obnoxious suitor alone with his sister. Arielle darted a glance of indignation after the deserter, who should have been her protector, but who had become in a manner her entrapper.

But she had little time to think. Mr. Stuart Fitzroy, somewhat inflamed by the wine that he had drank, approached her, took her hand, and said:

"Mademoiselle, this is an hour that I have long looked for, hoped for, sighed for, in vain!"

She withdrew her hand and rang the bell.

A footman answered it.

"Smith," she said, "ask Mr. Hurst to be so good as to come here."

The footman disappeared.

"Mademoiselle, for heavens! before we are interrupted, hear me! I—my intentions are honorable. I—I—explained them to your brother. In fact, I—I wish to lay my heart and hand and fortune at your feet—*hand*, observe, Mademoiselle! I am aware that many hearts and many fortunes are ready to to be laid at your feet, but I lay also my hand and name! I—"

Here the door opened, and the young house steward entered the room.

"Mr. Hurst, attend this gentleman to the door; put his hat on his head; give him his cane, umbrella or gloves, or whatever else he may have left about; see him safely to his carriage, and tell his coachman to take him home, and to look well after him when he gets him there."

And so saying, she swept out of the room.

Benny immediately approached the Honorable Stuart Fitzroy, and saying very politely:

"Will you take my arm, sir?" drew that gentleman's arm within his own.

But the Honorable Stuart was not so far gone as not to know that he was contemned and despised and dismissed."

He jerked his arm away from Benjamin's, and exclaiming elegantly:

"Well, I'm dashed," pushed out of the room, seized his hat, and decamped.

Benjamin ordered the footman to turn off the gas, and then he retired to his own room in the third floor back.

Late as was the hour, Suzy — as we shall always call Mademoiselle Arielle in the privacy of domestic life—was too indignant to go immediately to her much-needed rest, but went impetuously to a little smoking room off from the conservatory, where she knew she should find her hopeful brother.

"Well, sir!" she exclaimed, as she threw open the door and found him enjoying his *otium cum dignitate*, leaning back in a resting chair, with a pipe in his mouth and his heels on the mantel shelf—"Well, sir: a very honorable young man, and a very good brother, and a very safe protector I have found in you! I think you had better convey your invaluable qualities back to Australia. I shall write to our father and tell him so."

"Hallo! I say now, Suzy, hold on, you know. You're

coming it a little strong, an't you? What do you mean? what's the row?" he inquired defiantly, taking the pipe from his mouth.

"I mean, you cowardly— Oh, I will not speak to my mother's son as he deserves! I mean, William, that you entrapped me into an interview with that man Fitzroy, whose every word was an insult."

"Hallo, I say! Is that so? Because, if it is, he's got to account to me for it, if he is twenty times my Lord Viscount's son. But he told me he meant to offer you marriage."

"*His* offer of marriage, couched in the terms that it was, was an affront."

"Oh! he *did* keep his word to you, then, and offer you marriage. Well, now, let me tell you, Suzy, that that's a deal more than that magnificent swell the Earl of Wellrose ever did, or ever will do," said Mr. William, coolly resuming his pipe.

"SILENCE, SIR!" she indignantly exclaimed, her blue eyes blazing on him. "Never let me hear you speak one word against the noble Earl of Wellrose again, lest I break with you in good earnest."

"Now, Suzy, don't be stagey, whatever you do. Leave heroics in Covent Garden, and let us have common-sense in Park Lane. I'm not saying anything against the Earl. But I warn you not to set your heart on him. Because such a magnificent swell as he is will never go to propose marriage to you. Besides, he's engaged, as all the world knows, to the great beauty, Lady Hinda Moray, the Earl of Ornoch's daughter. So what hope can you have?"

Suzy wheeled her chair around, turning her back full upon him, for an answer.

"Yes, you may treat me with contempt, Susan, but what I tell you is the truth. And I tell it to you for your good. I warn you to expect nothing from Lord Wellrose; and at the same time I advise you to accept the honorable proposals of my friend Mr. Fitzroy."

"A spendthrift, wine-bibber, and gambler! How dare you advise your sister to take such a man for her husband?" demanded Suzy, without turning around.

"Come now, Suzy, you would not let me speak one word against *your* friend the Earl, and here you are abusing *my* friend Fitzroy the worst way! I don't say that he has not his little faults; all men have; but—"

"His little faults!" echoed Suzy scornfully.

"Yes, his little faults, for that is all *I* consider them; but with all his little faults he is a gentleman. And even you can't deny that he has made you honorable proposals. He has laid heart, hand and fortune at your feet."

"His fortune!" echoed Suzy contemptuously. "And what *is* his fortune? A load of debts that he cannot pay."

"Well, he offers you the best he has to give.

"'He gives you all, he can no more,
Though poor the offering be;
His heart and lute are all the store
That he can offer thee,'"

sung Mr. William, in a chaffing manner. Then, changing his tone, he said:

"It is not quite so bad as that either. He is the son of Lord St. Paul. He offers you an old and an honorable name, and a distinguished family connection."

"If he were the eldest son and heir of Lord St. Paul, instead of being the penniless younger son, I would not think of him for an instant as a husband," retorted Suzy.

And then, again—but that is of little consequence to you—he is my very good friend."

"I am sorry to hear it," said Suzy to herself.

"He shows me many kind attentions," continued Mr. William, as if he had not heard her. "He invites me to dinner, takes me out boating, introduces me to his friends. I might wait a long time before my Lord Wellrose would do anything of the sort."

"I should hope so," said Susan very gravely. "And there is the whole secret of your advocacy of that man Fitzroy! You, my brother, who should be my protector, are weak enough and false enough to be bribed by a few flattering attentions, into favoring the suit of a ruined spendthrift for the hand of your sister! *You* who ought to be my defender from all such!" she added very bitterly.

Mr. William was touched.

"And I am your defender, Susan! And I will be your defender! It is because Fitzroy loves you, and offers you honorable marriage and a noble connection, that I favor his suit. If he should offer anything else, I should pitch into him and thrash him within an inch of his life, if he were the son of fifty noblemen! But I won't tease you any more about him; indeed I won't. Give us your hand, old girl, and let's say good night, for it's three o'clock in the morning!"

Suzy gave him her hand sulkily enough. She could not quite get over the affront she had received.

"Oh, by the way, I forgot. I say, look here! about that languid swell of a butler of yours, who looks like a gentleman in disguise, and is the perfect fac simile of Lord Wellrose! Who the deuce is he? And where did you pick him up?" inquired Mr. William, detaining the hand of his sister.

"Is it possible you did not recognize him?" inquired Susan.

"Him! Who? No, I didn't. I was so taken up with his likeness to Lord Wellrose, that I never once thought whether I ever had seen him before or not. And now that I *do* think, I am *sure* I never saw him before. Who the deuce is he, then?"

"He is Benjamin Hurst," said Susan gravely.

"Ben—jamin—*Who?*"

"Benjamin Hurst."

"Benjamin Hurst! And who the deuce is *he?* Never heard of him in my life before."

"Oh, William! is it possible that you have utterly for gotten Benny? little Benny who used to be my little playmate in the poor old times, in the poor old house in Junk Lane?" said Susan sadly and reproachfully.

"Whe-ew!" commented Mr. William, in a long, low whistle. "So your new butler is little Benny that was! Well, I should never have thought it! Little Benny that was transported for burglary fourteen years ago, because he wouldn't peach on his pals! Why, when did he get back? Where did you pick him up?"

Susan sat down and told her brother where and when she had again met Benny.

"And I knew him the minute I saw him, William—I did, indeed," she added.

"And you gave him a good situation, and made him your butler."

"And house steward. It was the best I could do for him, William. It was the very best he would let me do for him, I mean."

"Suzy, darling, that was bully! You're a trump!" said Mr. William heartily.

"I'm so glad you think so, Will," said Susan, once more rising to bid her brother good-night.

After she had left the little smokery, Mr. William continued to smoke until he had finished his pipe, and then he too retired to bed.

The next day, about the hour of noon, as Benjamin was sitting over his account-books, in his little basement office, the door was opened, and Mr. William Juniper entered and clapped the young man on the back, exclaiming heartily:

"Hallo, Ben, old chap! Is this you? I shouldn't have known you from the Lord Bishop of London, if my sister hadn't told me who you were. I say old fellow, I'm so glad to see you! Give us your paw!"

"Thank you, Mr. William," said Benjamin, rising and placing his thin hand in that of William Juniper.

"I say, look here you know! Wa'n't you a little game-cock, to set all the big wigs at Old Bailey at naught, and allow them to send you over seas for fourteen years, before you'd peach?"

To this question Benjamin made no reply. He only placed a chair and said:

"Will you sit down, Mr. William?"

"Not this time, old fellow! But I'm coming in here to have a crack with you often, and smoke a pipe in honor of old times. I say, you smoke, you know, don't you?"

"No, sir."

"The deuce, you don't! Then you must learn, you know! Now I'm off I only came in to give you a grip of welcome, and to tell you that if ever you want a friend to call on me. I'm the same old Billy, to you, as I was when we used to fall out and get our hands in each other's hair and roll all the way down from the top to the bottom of the stairs before either of us would give in; and afterwards be better friends than ever."

"Thank you, Mr. William."

"'Bill,' except before folks! Now, then, I *am* off," he said, and he went out.

Days passed, and both Susan and William Juniper treated Benjamin Hurst more like a brother than a servant.

And daily he thanked Heaven for the peace that had descended upon him.

CHAPTER XXV.

THE EARL'S LOVE.

> Oh, a woman's like a dew-drop, she's so purer than the purest!
> And her noble heart's the noblest—yes, and sure her faith's the surest.
> —ROBERT BROWNING.

THE young Earl of Wellrose carried the very spirit of honor into all the transactions of his life, yet was his conduct toward the youthful prima donna very ambiguous.

He loved her; there could be no doubt of that in his own mind, in hers, or even in poor Benny's.

The Earl's devotion to the singer was the talk of all the clubs. Happily it had not yet become the gossip of the boudoirs.

He made her munificent presents of the rarest articles of *vertú*, and which she accepted with a sort of deprecating grace. For, in truth, while she was very unwilling to take such magnificent gifts, she was much too gentle to refuse them, especially when they were chosen with so much good taste and propriety, and offered with such tact and deucacy.

He devoted himself to her in almost every way, but—he never spoke of love or marriage!

And *she* loved him; there was no question of that, either in her mind or in his, or in poor Benny's. She had been drawn to him, first of all by his perfect likeness to the lost friend of her childhood, but now she was bound to him by the goodness of his heart, the brilliancy of his mind, and the charm of his manner.

He was what poor Benny might have been, if Benny had been educated. And now "she loved him with a love that was her doom."

Yes, she loved him and she trusted him; yet she feared with a deadly fear to lose him, because he never spoke to her of love or marriage.

And poor Benny! Benny, waiting behind the chair, at the little suppers where the Earl was a favorite guest, and watching with the most devoted affection over the welfare of Suzy—Benny saw the mutual love between the noble Earl and the beautiful singer; saw the hesitation and indecision in the mind of the man, and the fear and dread in the heart of the girl.

He saw it all, because his vision was enlightened by love, for now he too loved Suzy, and no longer only as a brother loves a sister. He loved her as the Earl of Wellrose loved her, only infinitely more.

As he watched them at these little suppers, and saw, evening after evening, the same little drama performed—the attachment between them; the doubt in the mind of the man, the dread in the heart of the woman—he said to himself that had he, Benny, been an earl or even a prince, and had been so blessed as to win her love, he would never have hesitated an instant to ask her to be his wife. The Earl of Wellrose was a gentleman of stainless honor.

What did he mean?

Benny, with his vision enlightened by pure love, saw clearly enough what the Earl of Wellrose meant.

He was waiting for something: possibly for a favorable opportunity to make to his parents the astounding announcement that he wished to marry an opera singer; perhaps for the rising of parliament; perhaps for the marriage of Lady Hinda Moray; but whatever it might be, he was certainly waiting, and meant to wait.

And meanwhile Suzy, loving him with all the deep passion of her awakened heart, trusting him, yet fearing to lose him, grew sick and pale with "hope deferred."

Her brother William gave her no comfort. He never missed an opportunity of reminding her that it was altogether useless for her to expect a proposal of marriage from such a "heavy swell" as he was—meaning the Earl of Wellrose, of course.

Upon these occasions Suzy would burst into tears, and say, with a little self-deception, or perhaps a little hypocrisy, that "she was sure she did not want anybody to propose marriage to her, because she had no wish to be married at all; that she wished everybody would mind their own business; and for the matter of that, dukes had married actresses before now—witness the Duke of St. Albans."

But Suzy grew pale and thin, though scarcely less lovely; for now there was a tender pensiveness in her face, a touching pathos in her tones, more beautiful and endearing than the most brilliant bloom and gayest spirits.

The many worshippers of her genius said that she was wearing herself out; that she would meet the swan's fate and die in music.

Benjamin's heart ached for her sorrow. Night after night he lay awake in his room, wondering when the Earl of Wellrose would put an end to the suspense that was killing the fair young singer.

At length one evening when, as usual, the Earl supped with the young prima donna, and Benny stood behind her chair, he heard his lordship say, in answer to some remark of hers, that as soon as parliament should rise, he, the Earl, should go off in his yacht for a cruise in the Mediterranean.

Benny could not see her face; but he knew, by the sudden silence that came upon her, how heavily the blow had fallen.

The Earl bade good-night, and went away rather earlier than usual.

Suzy remained seated in her chair in the drawing-room.

Benjamin went down to his little office room, deeply troubled in mind.

He remained sitting over his account-books, but doing nothing, until the clock on his chimney-piece struck two.

Then he started up, and remembered a neglected duty.

It was his custom at twelve o'clock, midnight, to go over

the house to see that all was right, and then with his own hands to secure the fastenings of the doors and windows, and to turn off the gas.

And now he had remained so long in his sad reverie, that he was two hours behind his usual time.

He arose and went quickly, but noiselessly, up the stairs.

He looked to the hall doors and windows, which he found fast.

Then he passed into the drawing-room, where the gas was burning very low.

He was crossing the room toward the front windows, when his eyes fell upon an object that chilled his blood with horror!

For there in the large arm-chair sat the form of Suzy, white, cold and still, and to all appearance stone dead.

He flew to her, frantically caught her in his arms, and wildly called upon her name.

But it was as if he held a corpse. There was no warmth in the limbs, no light in the eyes, no breath between the lips of the senseless body.

He laid her down on the sofa and violently rang the bell.

And then, without waiting for any one to answer it, he ran madly up the stairs, calling aloud for help, until he reached the housekeeper's room door, just as that worthy matron put out her night-capped head in terror, and demanded:

"What on the face of the earth is the matter?"

"Oh, Come! Come quickly, Mrs. Brown! I fear that she is quite dead. It is—it is Suzy. Mademoiselle Arielle, I mean! Oh, come quickly! She is in the drawing-room on the sofa. Dead, or in a deathly swoon!" exclaimed Benjamin in great excitement, as he ran down stairs, followed, as fast as her age would permit, by the housekeeper.

"This is a fainting fit! Bring some brandy!" directed

the housekeeper, as soon as she saw the unconscious form of Suzy.

Benjamin flew to do her bidding, while she laid the girl down flat upon the sofa and began to rub and beat the lifeless hands.

Benjamin came back with the brandy, and was immediately sent for smelling salts, which he also quickly brought.

And while the experienced matron was using every proper means to restore the senseless form to consciousness, she closely questioned the young man.

"How on earth did this happen? And how did you find it out? And how came you to be up so late? And she too? Why, it must be near three o'clock in the morning!"

And all the while she hurried these questions one upon the other without waiting for an answer, she was also diligently rubbing the patient's cold hands, or applying the smelling salts to her nose, or putting the brandy to her motionless lips, but without present good effect.

"Why can't you speak, Mr. Hurst, and tell me all about it?" she impatiently exclaimed.

"I can tell you very little, ma'am," answered Benny, who then stated the case, and asked if Mademoiselle was in any danger.

"Not in the least! Though what on earth could have caused her to faint I have not the slightest idea. Have you?"

Yes, he had; but he did not mean to tell Mrs. Brown. So keeping his eyes fixed upon the face of the fainting girl, he said:

"I think she is coming to herself. Is she not?"

"Yes," said the housekeeper, after a scrutinizing look.

And soon, with a deep, gasping sigh, Suzy recovered her breath, opened her eyes, and looked strangely around.

"There, my dear, you are better now. Take a teaspoonful of brandy," said the housekeeper, putting the full spoon to her lips.

Suzy obediently swallowed the fiery liquid, which half strangled her, and caused her to cough a great deal and to weep a little.

"There, never mind its strength and fire; it will do you good," said the housekeeper, patting her on the back.

"Why did you give me that burning stuff? I think it has taken all the skin off the inside of my throat. And what has been the matter here at all, that you are all standing around me?" half angrily demanded Suzy between her gasps.

"You were found here in a dead swoon by Mr. Hurst, when he came in to turn off the gas. He called me to your assistance, and I came, and I have brought you to yourself. Take another teaspoonful of brandy."

"Thanks, no. I am sorry to have given so much trouble," said Suzy, with a weary sigh. Then turning to her dressing maid, who had just now joined the group, she said, "Jenny Smith, give me your arm to my room. I will go to bed."

"Oh, pray let me assist you! The girl is not strong enough to give you much help," pleaded Benjamin Hurst, coming in her sight from the head of the sofa.

"Oh, are you there, Benny? Thanks very much. Yes, certainly you may help me. Give me your arm," she said, rising from the sofa.

He drew her arm within his own, and supported her with firmness and tenderness as she attempted to leave the room.

"Don't look so distressed, Benny. This is really nothing. I am much better now, and I shall be all right to-morrow," she murmured, with a smile, as she noticed Benjamin's troubled countenance.

He tenderly sustained her drooping form up the stairs, and to the door of her bed-chamber, where he left her in charge of Mrs. Brown and Jenny Smith, who had followed her closely.

Benjamin went up another flight of stairs to his own back room.

But he did not go to bed.

The summer day was now breaking, and Benjamin sat down at the back window that opened above the little shrubbery.

And as he sat and thought over all Suzy's long suspense and distress, caused by the hesitation and indecision of her lover, and her recent despair occasioned by the announcement of his approaching departure on an extensive cruise, Benjamin took a sudden resolution.

If no one else would interfere to save her, *he* would. If no one else would speak to the Earl of Wellrose in her interests, *he* would. If no one else would ask the noble Earl what were his lordship's intention in regard to the beautiful young prima donna, whom he had made the object of his devotion, and whose heart he had won by that devotion, *he* would. For Suzy's sake, *he*, poor Benjamin Hurst, would bring the noble Earl of Wellrose to book.

Even as, in his wretched childhood, he had never hesitated to risk his life or liberty in the service of his old protectress, Ruth Drug, or of his poor, suffering acquaintance, Rosy Flowers, so, in the interests of his childhood's playmate, Suzy Juniper, now the celebrated prima donna, Mademoiselle Arielle, he would not hesitate for one moment to take the distinguished young Earl of Wellrose roundly to task, for his thoughtless conduct in regard to her.

"Thoughtless conduct;" Benjamin never considered it anything worse than that. He never once suspected Lord Wellrose of any premeditated wickedness. He, like Suzy, had the utmost confidence in the young Earl's principles. And, moreover, he had the strongest and the most unaccountable affection for him. His heart warmed toward him. He could believe no evil of him. He felt sure that he might safely go to him and say all that was on his mind to say, without being misinterpreted, or in any manner misjudged.

He strangely felt that he might go to him as man to man —almost as brother to brother—and plead the cause of love and faith. And so he firmly resolved to do, before another day should pass over his head.

So resolving, Benjamin, overcome by fatigue, fell asleep with his head on the window-sill.

The sun, shining brightly and hotly in at the window awoke him.

He collected his faculties, arose and made his simple toilet, and then went below stairs to attend to the duties of his office.

There were none of the female servants stirring yet, so he could not hear how Suzy was this morning.

At eight o'clock Mrs. Brown came down stairs, and, in reply to his anxious question, informed him that "Mademoiselle" was fast asleep.

The hours of the forenoon passed heavily away.

At eleven o'clock Mrs. Brown went softly into Suzy's room, and returned and reported her still sleeping quietly.

"But you had better send a message to Covent Garden Theatre, to say that Mademoiselle Arielle is indisposed, and will not be at the rehearsal this morning. She is due there, you know, at this hour, Mr. Hurst."

"I will take the message myself," said Benjamin.

And having got through his morning duties, he dressed himself in his best clothes and went to Covent Garden theatre, where he delivered his message to the expectant manager.

And then he set out to walk to Cheviot House, Piccadilly to seek an interview with the Earl of Wellrose.

CHAPTER XXVI.

THE BROTHERS FACE TO FACE.

You cannot know the good and tender heart,
Its girl's trust and its woman's constancy;
How pure, yet passionate! how calm, yet kind!
How grave, yet joyous! how reserved, yet free
As light where friends are!—ROBERT BROWNING.

In an elegantly furnished sitting-room, belonging to his own private suite of apartments, the young Earl of Wellrose was seated at a table covered with books, papers and writing materials, when the door opened, and his own valet noiselessly entered and bowed.

"Well, what now, Perkins?" inquired the Earl, with a yawn.

"If you please, my lord, a person brought this and waits an answer," said the valet, presenting the little pearl tray, upon which lay a small, neatly folded note.

The Earl took the note listlessly, opened it, and read:

"Will the Earl of Wellrose kindly permit me to see him alone for a few minutes? I come from No. —, Park Lane.
"BENJAMIN HURST."

"Mademoiselle Arielle's steward," muttered the Earl to himself. "He comes with some message or some letter from her, that he is to deliver to me alone." Then speak-up, he said:

"Certainly, Perkins. Tell the young man to come up."

The valet bowed and withdrew, and after a few moments returned and ushered in the visitor, and again retired.

Benjamin Hurst stood a few feet within the door, and bowed.

"Come here, if you please," said Lord Wellrose, moving his seat a little way from the table.

Benny approached and stood near the Earl.

The brothers, so much alike in person and in disposition so widely apart in social standing, so closely connected by the ties of blood, so utterly unconscious of their relationship, stood face to face, and looked at each other with more of deeply curious interest than either could explain to himself.

"You come from Mademoiselle Arielle, I presume?" said the Earl.

"No, my lord; I come only from her house," replied Benny.

"But you bring some message or letter for me?"

"None, my lord."

"Then, my good fellow, what brings you here at all?" inquired the Earl, in some little surprise.

Benjamin Hurst hesitated. He now felt that it was very difficult to enter upon the delicate subject of his visit. Yet he was firmly resolved to do it. After a short pause, during which the young Earl looked at him with a most embarrassing attention, as if waiting for him to go on, he said:

"My lord, I fear that you will think it very presuming in me to come to you as I come this morning, and speak to you as I must speak—"

Here the Earl of Wellrose lifted his eyebrows questioningly, but said nothing.

"But, my lord, I come here in the interests and for the sake of Suzy—" continued Benny.

"Suzy!" repeated the Earl, more and more surprised and perplexed.

"I beg your pardon, my lord. I should have said Mademoiselle Arielle. But perhaps your lordship may know that this is only her pretty *nomme de theatre;* and that she is of English birth, though of French training," Benjamin explained.

"I have heard so from her own lips," the Earl assented.

"Then, my lord, you may have also heard from her, who

has no secrets from her friends, that long before her French training and her splendid success under her French name, long before all that, even in the days of her childhood, when she lived in her humble English home, and bore her obscure English name, she had a child friend, of her own age, dearer to her than brother or sister; for he loved her beyond everything on earth or in heaven," murmured Benny, his voice nearly breaking down

"Yes, my poor fellow, I have heard all that too; and how she wished and endeavored, in memory of that childhood's friendship, to do a friend's part by you, and place you in some better position than that which you now occupy in her house; but that you would accept of nothing better than it I never heard *why* you would not," said the Earl, with a compassionate look; for his heart was strangely, strongly drawn toward the poor outcast.

"A mixed motive of mingled pride and shame, I believe, my lord. She could not have told you the whole of my miserable past, or you would know that I am not even worthy of the place I now, through her goodness, hold in her house. But I am not here to speak of myself, my lord, but of her. And your kindness to me makes it much easier to do so. I have your lordship's permission, I hope."

"Certainly. Speak on," replied the Earl, as a slight shade of annoyance passed over his face. "Go on with what you have to say, and be sure that no injustice shall misinterpret your words or motives."

"I thank your lordship," said Benjamin, drawing a deep breath.

"And pray sit down, while you speak. You do not seem strong," said the Earl kindly.

Benjamin bowed and availed himself of the offered seat.

"And now?" inquired Lord Wellrose.

"My lord, what I had to say to you is this: that there is a rumor everywhere afloat, to the effect that still another peeress is to be recruited from the ranks of art. And from the bottom of my heart I hope that the rumor may be true, which intimately connects the names of the Earl of Wellrose and Mademoiselle Arielle—and—honorably, I mean of course Again let me repeat that from my heart and soul I hope and trust that the rumor may be correct," said Benjamin solemnly.

Without reply, the Earl arose and walked uneasily up and down the room, opened a window, and then, as if annoyed at having shown even so much disturbance, he returned to the table and resumed his seat, and said quietly:

"Well, my good fellow—for you really are a good fellow—well, what of all this?"

Benjamin Hurst lifted his head and looked at the Earl so gravely, earnestly, solemnly, that his lordship's eyelids lowered beneath the steady blue gaze.

"What can it possibly matter," said Lord Wellrose, forcibly keeping down and controlling the extreme sense of annoyance he experienced—"what can it possibly matter whether rumor, which is so often false, so seldom true, should be false or true in this single instance?"

"Nothing whatever, my lord, to the gossips who circulate the report; but little, also, as regards your lordship's name; and not much even as regards hers; for these are all merely external circumstances. But, my lord, there is more involved in this affair than mere town talk, or even than noble and famous names. There is a whole life's happiness involved in it, Lord Wellrose," said Benjamin, with much emotion.

The Earl was beginning to lose some of his cool self-control. He impatiently tapped his slippered foot with the point of a little cane that he held in his hand, and after a short silence, said suddenly:

"For Heaven's sake, man, go on, and say your worst!"

"My lord, forgive me that I must do so. I would

willingly avoid the duty, were there any one else to do it. I am, also, so conscious of a seeming impertinence in my interference, that I can only trust in your lordship's goodness for a favorable consideration."

Here Benjamin paused for a moment. Lord Wellrose impatiently waved his hand; and Benjamin resumed:

"Lord Wellrose, you have been for the last three months constantly visiting Mademoiselle Arielle, both at the opera and at her house. You have lavished upon her the zealous attentions of a devoted lover. These constant and pointed attentions, together with her most favorable acceptance of them, has occasioned the talk in the clubs, and in all other places where such matters are likely to be discussed. It is confidently asserted that you will marry her. It is of very little consequence to the world at large whether this assertion be true or false. But it is of vital importance to her."

"Of vital importance to *her!*" echoed the Earl, as if speaking to himself.

"Yes, Lord Wellrose. Her father, my lord, is an humble but honorable man. He is in Australia now. Had he been present here in England, he would have politely inquired into your lordship's intentions long before this."

The Earl's face flushed.

"Does any one dare to believe that I could have—" he began, but he could not go on. His color deepened, as Benny answered the half-formed question:

"No, my lord; no one ventures to impute evil to you—that is, evil intention. But what says the poet sage? 'More evil is wrought from want of thought, than ever from want of heart.'"

"Explain yourself."

"I will. It is no disparagement to your honor, my lord, to say that your admiration and affection for Mademoiselle Arielle is patent to all observers. It is no reproach to her delicacy to say that your devotion has won her heart."

Lord Wellrose covered his eyes with his hand. Benjamin continued:

"Your devotion, my lord, has not only won her confidence and affection, but has led her—very naturally and properly—led her to expect no less than the offer of your hand in marriage."

"I have been criminally thoughtless!" sighed the Earl.

Benjamin, perceiving the effect he produced, went on to say:

"From day to day she looks for the offer of your hand—naturally and properly looks for it, as I said before."

"I cannot justify my conduct!" said the Earl.

"And from day to day she wastes and sickens with 'hope deferred!'" continued Benjamin.

"I shall never be able to forgive myself," murmured Lord Wellrose.

"Yes, my lord, you will! for you are a noble man *sans reproche*. You will do all that honor requires of you. And then you will forgive yourself, if indeed you will have anything to forgive!—Oh! my God! I know how presumptive and insolent my words must seem!" exclaimed Benny, in much distress.

But the Earl of Wellrose took his hand:

"Presumptive! insolent!" his lordship said. "No; to me they seem good, true, brave words—words in season, for which I thank you! Leave me now, Benjamin Hurst! I need to be alone, and so, probably, do you. Good-bye. Trust the welfare of your childhood's friend to me," said Lord Wellrose earnestly.

"I do, my lord, I do!" answered Benjamin, as he bowed himself out.

The Earl of Wellrose remained immersed in deep thought.

"I wonder if I am awake," he said to himself. "Or is there another man in Europe from whom I would have taken all that I have taken from this poor, pale boy?"

CHAPTER XXVII

THE OUTCAST'S LOVE.

I give thee prayers, like jewels strung
On golden threads of hope and fear,
And thoughts more tender than e'er hung
In a pure angel's pitying tear.—Anon.

Benjamin Hurst returned home, feeling that his mission had been successful. But you know what he had done. He had sacrificed his own heart for her happiness. He loved her more than the Earl did or could; for he had but her in the whole world to love, while the Earl had many others. But then he was born for sacrifice. And besides, he loved her with a love so pure, so holy, so almost divine, that her happiness was essential to his own peace. To purchase her happiness, he would have been willing to pay the price of his own life or liberty; yes, he would have been willing to be put to death, or to be sent back to the penal colonies for life, if necessary. Already he had made what sacrifice he could—the sacrifice of his own heart; for to promote her marriage with the Earl was no less. And ah! too soon the question was to be put to the test whether he would go further, whether he would lay down his life for his love!

The Earl called at Park Lane that afternoon, and sent up his card to Mademoiselle Arielle.

And she came down to receive him.

They had an interview that lasted more than an hour.

And when it was over, and he had taken leave and gone away, Suzy went singing gayly up to her own room, no sign of the night's illness or the morning's languor in her step or voice. And Benjamin knew by these sure tokens that all was well.

He felt satisfied for her; but for himself, a feeling of desolation swept over his soul, like the cold, dark blast of a sudden wintry storm. And he sighed, and found himself wondering whether his life was to be a long one, and hoping that Heaven might make it short.

At dinner-time he waited as usual behind her chair; and he noticed then that her very countenance seemed transfigured with happiness.

There was no one at the table except herself and her brother, and no one waiting on them but Benjamin. And they always spoke freely before him. So Mr. Bill opened the conversation with his usual theme.

"That heavy swell is agoing to the Mediterranean in his own yacht, is he? And a good riddance too! Only, if he was half the gentleman the Honorable Stuart Fitzroy is, he'd invite *me* to go along with him, seeing as he is so sweet on my sister," he said.

At any other time Suzy would have made a sharp reply, but now was so calmly, serenely happy that she could not find it in her heart to rebuke her offending brother.

"It is not certain that he will go to the Mediterranean, Will.," she said.

"Oh, isn't it? Well, I heard him tell you so last night at supper; that's something. Yes, and I saw that you felt very far down in the mouth at it too! That's more. And this morning you've braced up again. That's most of all. And you tell me that it is not certain his lordship will go to the Mediterranean. And that's everything. Now I want to know what the deuce is up?" demanded Mr. Will.

"One thing that is up is this, that if you cannot behave yourself more like a gentleman, we must part company, Will.," said Suzy firmly.

"Well, if gentlemen allow their pretty sisters to receive the particular attention of noblemen who never speak of marriage, and never intend to do so, then be certain I never can act like a gentleman," retorted Will., who, be it observed, could always do a brother's duty by bullying his sister, but never once by calling her suitor to account, as poor Benny had dared to do.

Suzy was half angry—only half angry—and much too happy to quarrel with Will.

"It is all right, Will.—all quite right! Trust in me, and—trust in him. And now let us speak no more about it for the present," she said pleasantly.

"It may be all right. And it had better be all right, for his sake as well as your own. He'll never do you a wrong, Suzy, if he knows what's good for his health and longevity, I could tell him that. For if he were twenty times an Earl, I wouldn't stand any nonsense from him, where you are concerned!" said Mr. William, nodding his head in a very determined manner.

"My doughty brother, you will not be called upon to show your zeal and courage in my defence. Very soon you shall be convinced that there is no sort of necessity for you to do so, and that all is right. So now let us dismiss the subject," said Suzy, smiling.

"In a moment. Tell me first; is he coming here to-night?"

"The Earl?"

"Yes, the Earl."

"No; he is not coming here to-night. His bill for the Improvement of Prison Discipline for the Reclamation of Criminals will be up before the House of Commons. A great debate is expected upon it, and he must be there, perhaps all night."

"Good. Well now, will you do me a favor, Suzy? I assure you I would not ask it if Lord Wellrose was going to be here this evening," said Will., in an almost pleading voice.

"What is it?" inquired Suzy, always dreading to be asked to do anything by William, whose demands were scarcely ever right or reasonable.

His present demand certainly was not. Perhaps he knew it; for he hesitated and cleared his throat before he said:

"Will you let me bring my particular friend, the Honorable Stuart Fitzroy, here this evening?"

"Will.! you know I do not like that man," said Suzy, deprecatingly.

"Well, upon my sacred word and honor, I think you and I a pretty pair of a sister and brother! You do not like *my* friend, the Honorable Stuart Fitzroy, and I do not like *your* friend, my Lord Wellrose. But this is the difference between us: I let your friend come to supper two or three times a week; while you never let mine at all. Blest if I don't think, under all the circumstances, that I am the better fellow of the two!" grumbled Mr. William with an injured air.

He spoke quite as if Suzy's little palace in Park Lane was his own house instead of hers.

But Suzy only smiled at him.

"I think you might let Stuart Fitzroy come here once in a way. He has never once been invited here since you boxed his ears!" growled Mr. William.

"Oh, Will! I never boxed a man's ears in my life!" said Suzy, deeply shocked.

"Well, you as good as did it; so there. And he's never been invited here since. I say, can't he come this evening?" persisted the brother.

"Well, yes, if you wish him to come very much," assented Suzy, with a sigh.

"I do wish it very much," said Mr. William.

"Then it is settled" said Suzy, as she arose and left the table.

Benjamin heard the whole discussion, never dreaming, poor, fated fellow! how deep a stake he had in the issue.

Suzy went up to her room to prepare to go to the opera. She soon came down cloaked, hooded and vailed, and took her seat in the little brougham which was waiting to receive her.

That night it happened that Benjamin's duties permitted him to indulge himself with an evening at the opera.

When the hour came, he went and took his usual modest seat in the crowded parquette.

The opera for the evening was "La Somnambula," and of course Mademoiselle Arielle took the part of Amina.

The house was, as usual, crowded from parquette to gallery.

Lord Wellrose was not in his usual seat in the front row of orchestra stalls. Benjamin, who noticed his absence, knew the reason of it. He had heard Suzy say that Lord Wellrose must be in his seat in the House of Commons that evening, because his lordship's Bill for the Improvement of Prison Discipline for the Reclamation of Criminals was to be up that night, and it behooved his lordship, of all other members, to be present there.

But his stall at the opera was filled — most uncannily filled, Benjamin thought, for the Honorable Stuart Fitzroy occupied it. And by his side sat Mr. William Juniper.

The curtain rose on the village festival in honor of the betrothal of the heroine to the hero of the play. But though the music and singing were excellent, no one paid much attention to them until the entrance of Mademoiselle Arielle as Amina.

She was received with the usual outburst of most enthusiastic applause.

And she smiled and courtesied, and courtesied and smiled until the storm subsided, and then she began to sing.

And never, said her worshippers, had her beauty been so divine, or her voice so enrapturing.

They thought she slurred the pathetic songs in the second act. But in the last scene of the third act, the scene of the reconciliation with her lover, her song burst forth with such a gush of irrepressible rapture, that all the critics then and there declared that there was not, never had been, and never would be such another celestial songstress on earth.

The curtain fell amid an earthquake of enthusiasm

And Mademoiselle Arielle left the theatre weary, but very happy.

Benjamin went out with the crowd.

Near the stage door he saw Mademoiselle's little brougham waiting.

And he saw her come out, leaning on the arm of her brother, and closely followed by the Honorable Stuart Fitzroy.

Mr. William handed her into the carriage, and then pausing with his foot on the step, inquired:

"Can you give myself and Mr. Fitzroy a seat as far as Park Lane, Suzy?"

She looked extremely annoyed, hesitated, and then answered:

"No, Will, I really cannot. You must indeed excuse me."

"Oh, very well. You have accommodated the Earl of Wellrose before now, and even your own house steward, with a seat in your carriage," he growled.

"Will," she whispered in a very low tone, "if you are not ashamed of yourself, *I* am ashamed enough for both of us. Bring your friend to supper in a hansom, if you must bring him at all. And now be so good as to shut the door, and order the coachman to drive home."

Mr. William sulkily obeyed. And the little brougham rolled off at a rapid rate.

"And she did not even pick up my bouquet from the stage, though it contained a ruby ring a royal princess might have envied," grumbled the Honorable Stuart Eitzroy in a very injured tone.

"Perhaps she didn't know it was yours," suggested Mr. William.

"Oh yes, she did, for I didn't throw it until I had caught her eye. Then I threw it, and she saw me throw it, and she knew it was mine, and that was the very reason why she didn't pick it up! I don't know what *you* call that sort of conduct, but *I* call it exceedingly ill-bred," growled the Honorable Stuart Fitzroy.

"Oh, come now! none of that, you know, about my sister! She's *not* ill-bred; but she's capricious! I fancy all girls are so at times, even Royal Princesses. And a man of the world like yourself should make allowances for the weakness of the sex."

"I say it is not very encouraging," said the Honorable Stuart Fitzroy, with a very injured look.

"Not encouraging, when she invites you to supper? Bosh! Come, here's a hansom, with a fairish sort of horse. Let's take it and go on," replied Mr. William, as he signalled the cabman to draw up on the sidewalk.

They entered the cab and ordered the cabman to take them to Park Lane.

Benjamin Hurst hailed a passing omnibus, got upon the top, and started in the same direction.

He was the last to reach the house, for the omnibus set him down at a corner some streets off from the aristocratic neighborhood of Park Lane.

But he was still in good time to attend to his evening duties.

He went to the Rose Parlor, where the elegant little supper was laid, and where the light was subdued by roseate shades and the air filled with fragrance from the Rose Garden beyond.

He saw that all was perfect there.

He heard the voices of the Honorable Stuart and Mr. William, as they entered the adjoining drawing-room.

And soon after he heard the melodious tones of Suzy, as she came in and welcomed them.

The supper hour was eleven. As soon as the clock struck, Benjamin drew the rose damask satin curtains that divided the Rose Parlor from the drawing-room, and said with his usual formula :

" Mademoiselle is served."

Suzy arose and took the offered arm of Mr. Stuart Fitzroy, and led the way to the table, followed by Mr. William conducting Mrs. Brown.

The four sat down, and the feast began.

Benjamin stood behind Suzy's chair, and as usual waited on her alone—filling her glass, passing her plate, watching and anticipating her wants.

The two young footmen, Smith and Jones, attended to the other members of the supper party.

And the wine was passed, and the Honorable Stuart and Mr. William became very merry.

Before they had been an hour at the table, Benjamin knew, to his disgust, what he had strongly suspected even at the theatre—namely, that both these young men were inebriated, and growing more so every five minutes.

Suzy was slow to perceive this. But Mrs. Brown observed it, and tried to catch Suzy's eye, that she might telegraph her to rise and leave the " gentlemen " at the table. But as is usual in such a case, she found it impossible to attract the attention of her subject, though she drew upon herself that of the Honorable Stuart, who, after watching her for a few minutes, probably divining her intention, turned to Mr. William and inquired, in an audible whisper :

" What the deuce is the matter with the old girl ? "

" I'm sure I don't know, unless she's had more champagne than is good for her," replied Mr. William, with a low laugh.

" My love, I think we had better retire," said Mrs Brown, speaking plainly at last, as she calmly arose from her seat.

"I say, she thinks we're at dinner, and she's going to leave us over our wine! hiccupped the Honorable Stuart.

"Don't go, Suzy," said Mr. William, seeing that his sister was preparing to follow her companion.

"Excuse me, for I must leave the table," replied Suzy with gentle dignity, as she moved away.

"Oh, by——, this will not do at all! Our guardian angel must not be permitted to take flight in this way!" said Mr. Stuart Fitzroy, rising and following her.

"Return to your seat, sir, if you have any grace at all!" Suzy haughtily commanded, averting her head.

"So I will return, my dear; but you must return with me," he stuttered, taking her hand and attempting to draw her back.

She snatched her hand from him with a flash of scorn and anger.

"Sit down, Suzy, and don't be a fool!" Mr. William advised.

She turned a look of sorrow and reproach upon her brother, and moved toward the door.

Then the Honorable Stuart caught her around the waist, and laughing in a foolish, coaxing manner, attempted to take her back to the table.

Her brother also laughed.

Benjamin Hurst started forward, his usually gentle blue eyes blazing with wrath. But even before he could come to her rescue, Suzy had thrown her rude assailant off, and gained the door, where, standing for an instant, she said, with dignity:

"Benjamin Hurst, I charge *you* to see that gentleman out of the house, and attend him to his home. He is clearly not in a condition to take care of himself, any more than to be responsible for his ill-breeding."

And so saying, she passed out of sight.

"There! now you *have* done it! You see, you went too far! You were rude, you know," stuttered Mr. William.

"Rude! Really! Indeed! I should have been considered rude to a *lady!* I suppose; but is a gentleman expected to stand on ceremony with *such as she?*" inquired the Honorable Stuart, with a scornful laugh, for he was both very drunk and very angry.

"I say, look here, you know! What the deuce do you mean by that?" hiccupped Mr. William, as he poured out and turned off another bumper of champagne.

"Come, sir!" said Benjamin Hurst, firmly. "Mademoiselle desired that I should see you safe out of this house, and into your own. I am ready to attend you."

"So am I ready!" laughed the inebriate defiantly.

"But hold on! I say, look here, you know!" repeated Mr. William, in half-muddled dignity. "What do you mean, you know?"

"I mean to go home, that's what I mean. Here, you fellow! show me to the door," answered Mr. Stuart Fitzroy, with a reckless air.

Benjamin handed him his hat and gloves, and then took his arm to assist his rather uncertain steps.

Jones held open the room door, while Smith went before and opened the street door.

Benjamin Hurst took his charge out upon the sidewalk and began to lead him along, with the intention of hailing the first empty cab that passed.

The fresh air seemed to help the inebriated man, who walked somewhat more steadily.

Meanwhile, Mr. William sat over the wine at the deserted supper-table, pouring out and drinking champagne as freely as a thirsty man would drink water. And he brooded over the contemptuous words that Fitzroy had used in reference to his sister.

"What devil did he mean by—by '*such's she?*'" he inquired of himself. Then he drank more wine, and muttered:

"Meant something 'fensive, know he did. What dev'l was't?" And he drank still more wine, and grumbled:

"Ought to called—called 'm to 'count for 's words, 'bout my sister." And again he drank yet more wine, and then he staggered to his feet, muttering:

"Do it yet. Do it, sure. Call 'm to 'count for 's 'sulting words, 'bout my sister!"

And so, crazed with drink, he left the house and went in the direction taken by Benjamin Hurst and his charge.

The fresh air helped *him* also, and partly sobered him, so that he was able to walk steadily and quickly, and to overtake speedily the man he was pursuing.

"I say, look here, you know! Hold on! I want to speak to *you!*" he said, laying his hand on the shoulder of Fitzroy.

"Well, fellow! well, what do you want of me?" grandly inquired this last inebriate.

"Want t' know what dev'l you meant by the words y' used in reference t' my sister?"

"Meant what I said—that a gentleman needn't stand on ceremony with such as she," doggedly replied Fitzroy.

"Look here! I say, you know! What dev'l d' you mean by such 's she?" persisted William, following him up.

"I mean she's only a very common person! Now don't bore *me* about your worthless sister!" said Fitzroy scornfully.

"You false-tongued, base hound!" exclaimed William in a fury. "You lie like—"

The words had scarcely left his lips when Fitzroy wheeled around and struck him full upon the mouth, crying:

"Take that, you dog, for daring to insult a gentleman!"

The sting of that blow drove the already infuriated young man to perfect frenzy. He drew back for an instant and threw himself with all his force upon his assailant, seizing him by the throat and hurling him with violence to the ground.

Fitzroy fell heavily, struck the back of his head against the sharp corner of a curb-stone, quivered for a few seconds, and then lay perfectly still.

And all this happened with the rapidity of lightning, so that Benjamin Hurst could not, if he would, have interfered to prevent the catastrophe.

"Come! I say! get up and have it out like a man!" said Mr. William half fearfully, half recklessly.

Benjamin Hurst stooped down and passed his hand under the back of the man's head to raise it from the curb-stone, but quickly withdrew his hand and gazed upon his fingers in consternation and sickening horror.

"Come! up with you, if you've as much heart as a hare. and have it out with me here and now!" repeated Mr. William, bending over the fallen man, and speaking half in dread and half in defiance.

"Mr. William—O my Lord!—he will never get up any more," said Benjamin, in awe.

"Never get— What the devil do you mean?" inquired the young man, almost sobered.

"He is dead, sir," solemnly answered Benny.

"DEAD!" wildly exclaimed William Juniper, his face blanching, his chin falling, and his eyes starting with horror.

"Quite dead!" answered Benjamin, with a shudder. "The back of his head is crushed upon the sharp corner of the curb-stone. Oh, see!" he added, exhibiting his hand stained and smeared with blood and brains.

"Oh, my Lord! my Lord! Am I a murderer? Have I lived to commit a murder, and to perish on the scaffold?" cried William Juniper, wildly wringing his hands and gazing in horror and terror upon the dead man.

"And it will ruin Suzy! and break my poor mother's heart! And I never meant to kill him. Oh, my Lord! my Lord! what shall I do? what shall I do?" he cried, tearing his hair

These frantic, despairing words brought Benjamin to his senses.

With him, to think quickly and act promptly, on an emergency, was quite natural.

"Mr. William," he said, speaking fast, "you intend going to Paris on your sister's business to-morrow, do you not?"

"I did. But where shall I be to-morrow? In Newgate probably!" cried the young man, tearing a handful of hair from his head.

"No; go now! hurry! fly! You have just time to catch the mail train that leaves for Dover at 2:30, to meet the early steamer. Fly, Mr. William, for Suzy's sake! You have money with you?"

"Yes— No, not a shilling!" answered the wretched young man, shaking.

"Take my pocket-book, then! Yes; there, take it! This is no time for hesitation or scruples. That's right. Now fly! I hear footsteps coming around the corner," breathlessly spoke Benjamin, as he forced his porte-monnaie into the hands of the half-frenzied homicide, and hurried him away.

He watched him cross the street, and turn down another leading in the direction of the Dover railway station.

Then Benjamin turned to meet his fate.

CHAPTER XXVIII

THE OUTCAST'S LAST OFFERING.

As earth pours freely to the sea
  Her thousand streams of wealth untold,
So flows my silent love to thee,
  Glad that its very sands are gold.—Anon.

He thought, with pity and horror, of the murdered man; he thought, with pity and terror, of Suzy's brother; with the deepest sorrow and anxiety, of Suzy herself; but he never once thought of the awful peril in which he placed his own life and liberty.

He turned to face the approaching footsteps.

Two policemen came around the corner and up to the fatal spot.

"Now then, what have *you* been up to?" demanded the first one, stopping short, speaking to Benjamin, but looking down upon the fallen man.

Benny instantly took a firm resolution—to give no information that might criminate Suzy's brother.

"What's all this, White? A man dead drunk?" demanded the second officer, coming nearer, and turning the bull's eye of his lantern full upon the face of the murdered man.

"He was certainly drunk when he fell," replied Benjamin truly, but incautiously.

"Fell?" echoed the first man, whom his companion had addressed by the name of White—"Fell, do you say?" And he took the lantern from his comrade, and stooped and examined the body. "This man never fell of himself. Here are marks of violence on his face and throat. He has been knocked down and probably robbed, and seriously injured. Hold the lantern a moment, Sefton."

The second officer took the offered light and held it, while the first one knelt down to raise the head of the corpse but he quickly withdrew his hand, gazed at it in curiosity, and uttered an exclamation of consternation and horror.

"Heaven and earth, here's been a murder! Secure that man!"

In an instant Sefton seized Benny, while White sprung his alarm rattle.

"You need not take so much trouble. I will go with you quietly, for I have nothing to fear. I did not kill the man," said Benny.

"Then of course you'll be all right, you know. But we must take you all the same; for by your own admission you saw him fall, for you know you told us he was drunk when he fell. Now you see he didn't fall. The marks on his face and throat prove that he was knocked down, either by you, or by some one in your presence. So you must go along with us, whether to be considered as a witness or a principal the magistrate will decide," said Sefton, keeping a firm hold of Benny's arm.

With a deep sigh, as though yielding to the inexorable fate that pursued him, and *had* pursued him through all his life, Benny dropped his head upon his breast and was silent.

Meanwhile the alarm rattle was going at a startling rate; so that even at that most lonely hour of the morning in the streets, two o'clock after midnight, a small crowd began to collect, with excited faces and eager inquiries:

"Hallo?"

"What's up?"

"What's the row?"

"Is it a robbery?"

"Is it a murder?"

"Who is killed?"

"Who did it?"

"How did it happen?"

These and a score of other questions were all asked in a breath by the curious crowd.

Policeman White told all he knew of the circumstances as briefly as possible, and they listened as well as they could in the tumult.

"It is the body of a gentleman," said one.

"Will we take it to the St. James?" inquired another

"No," said Policeman White. "We will leave it just here as it lies, until we take this suspected person to the station-house, and then we'll report the case to our Sergeant and take his orders about where it is to be carried."

And then he beckoned two of his companions of the force, and ordered them to guard the body, while he and his comrade Sefton should take the prisoner to the station and report the murder.

And then Benjamin Hurst was marched off between two policemen to the station-house in Little Vine street, where, in a close, ill-favored office, a sleepy Sergeant sat at a desk, with three or four sleepy attendants around him.

"What is it, White?" inquired the Sergeant.

"If you please, sir, a gentleman, name and person still unknown to us, found murdered out here in Piccadilly," answered the policemen.

"A murder, do you say?" inquired the Sergeant, waking up, while all his satellites, startled by the dreadful word, roused themselves and gathered around to hear the particulars.

"Yes, sir, a murder! A gentleman, name and person as yet unknown to us, found murdered out here on the pavement in Piccadilly," repeated the officer.

"Who is this young man that you have here in custody?" inquired the Sergeant, looking with curious interest at the fair, refined face of the prisoner.

"If you please, sir, one who was found under very suspicious circumstances near the dead body, without being able to give any satisfactory account of his being there," answered the officer.

"Bring him forward, and state the whole case," said the Sergeant.

The policemen led Benny up to the desk, and while the Sergeant settled himself to listen attentively, related all the circumstances of his discovery of the dead body on the sidewalk in Piccadilly.

"What is your name, young man?" inquired the Sergeant of Benny, when the officer had finished his story.

"Benjamin Hurst, sir," replied the young prisoner.

"Now I warn you that you need not say a word to criminate yourself; but if you can say anything, and prove anything to clear yourself from suspicion, you had better do so at once."

"I thank you, sir," said Benny, with a slight bend of the head.

"Can you, then, tell us anything about this murder?"

"No, sir, I can tell you nothing about it except this—that I certainly did not kill the unfortunate man," said Benny earnestly.

The sergeant of police listened to him, looked at him and believed him, but had to do his stern duty nevertheless.

"If you can prove that now?" he began.

"I cannot prove it, sir," answered Benny resignedly, as he recognized in all its horror the full import of the awful sacrifice he was about to make to save the life of Suzy's brother, and the peace of Suzy's mind.

"Can you not explain your presence on the premises at the time of the murder?"

"No, sir, I cannot."

"At least you can tell whether you were acquainted with the deceased."

Benny reflected for a moment as to whether it might be safe to answer this simple question; and then still feeling doubtful on the subject, he answered civilly:

"If you please, sir, I prefer not to answer any more questions."

"You may be right. You are at least very discreet. Yet I am sorry for you, for we shall be obliged to lock you up. Officer, remove the prisoner," said the Sergeant.

Policeman White took possession of Benny to lead him away, while Policeman Sefton, coming forward and touching his hat, inquired:

"If you please, sir, what is to be done with the body of the murdered man for the present? There's the St. James near at hand, and quite convenient, and there's—"

"Have the body brought here for the present. The Inspector will be here soon. And the coroner must be notified immediately," said the sergeant.

And Policeman Sefton went out to obey these orders, while Policeman White conducted Benny to a lock-up room occupied by five or six other prisoners, and secured him there for the night.

CHAPTER XXIX.

LOVE'S MARTYRDOM.

Some die, that some may live;
Life—all they have to give.
Some weep, that some may smile;
  Some lose, that some may gain;
And count it good the while,
  And welcome all the pain.

Some freeze, that some may glow;
  Some starve, that some may feed;
Some plant, that some may mow;
  And each shall get his meed;
For those are Christ's, we know,
  And these the world's indeed.—E. D. E. N.

VERY early in the morning, Benjamin Hurst was brought from the station house to the police court for examination.

As his case was the most important one, it was the first one taken up by the sitting magistrate.

The room was filled with the usual ill-looking and ill-favored crowd that flock to such places, like crows to a battle-field.

Besides these, there were nearer to the magistrate's bench a few police officers, with their prisoners, and a few newspaper reporters, with their note-books.

"He looks more like a missionary than a murderer," said one of these gentlemen to another, as they gazed at the young prisoner in his suit of clerical black cloth, and with his golden-haired head and fair, delicate face of almost girlish beauty.

"Yes, decidedly more like a missionary than a murderer," emphatically repeated the first speaker, making a note of his own words, which that afternoon duly appeared in the papers.

"There's nothing in a prisoner's looks. Witness Palmer, who looked more like a philanthropist than a poisoner, didn't he?" inquired the second speaker.

The first one apparently considered the question unanswerable, since he never answered it.

"He looks astonishingly like the Earl of Wellrose; only not in such high health as his lordship—thinner and paler," said one.

"Yes; like his lordship might look after a spell of sickness," said another.

And then everybody became still, because the examination was about to commence.

Each of the two policemen who had discovered the murdered man and arrested the supposed murderer, in turn gave in his report, and their reports corresponded accurately.

"What have you to say to this charge?" inquired the magistrate, sternly regarding the prisoner.

"Nothing, your Worship, except that I did not kill the man," respectfully replied Benny.

"You were with him when he was killed; you saw him fall; you admitted as much to the policeman here."

"I said that he was drunk when he fell," Benny amended.

"Then you saw him fall, of course; and it appears from the marks of violence upon his face and throat, testified to by both these officers, that he fell, not because he was drunk, but because he was murderously assaulted. Now, since you saw him fall, and he fell by assault, you yourself must have made the assault or seen it made. Now then, if you yourself made the assault, you are not expected to criminate yourself here by any admission of the fact. If, on the other hand, you did not make it, but saw it made, you are strongly advised to tell all you know about it, and thus save yourself."

"I did not assault the man, your Worship. That is all I have to say," replied Benny.

"Then I shall have to remand you to prison to await the issue of the Coroner's inquest," said the magistrate.

And Benjamin Hurst was led away.

He passed in charge of two policemen, pressing their way through the densest crowd that had ever filled that room, and out into Little Vine street, now thronged with a vast multitude of people gathered together and attracted to the spot by the astounding report of the murder of the Honorable Stuart Fitzroy, by Benjamin Hurst, steward in the service of Mademoiselle Arielle.

These assailed the prisoner with such hoots and jeers that he was glad to reach the privacy of his prison cell.

Meanwhile the body of the murdered man had been conveyed to a room in the station house, where the Coroner's inquest was to be held upon it at eleven o'clock that morning.

And meanwhile Suzy Juniper, or Mademoiselle Arielle, over-fatigued by her professional and social duties of the evening previous, slept long and sweetly, in blissful unconsciousness that her brother William was a homicide and a fugitive from justice, and her friend Benny a prisoner charged with murder.

The news of the tragedy had not even reached the little palace in Park Lane as yet. It was not in any of the morning papers, for they had all gone to press some hours before it happened.

Suzy slept on very sweetly until eleven o'clock, and would have slept longer still, had she not been aroused by a knock at her chamber door.

"Who is that?" she cried, startled and bewildered.

"It is I, Miss," answered the low voice of her housekeeper.

"Mrs. Brown! Why, what's the matter? Come in!" cried Suzy, frightened, she scarcely knew why, unless it was at the unprecedented circumstance of being suddenly waked up out of her refreshing morning nap.

The housekeeper entered with a face as pale as death.

"I should not have disturbed you, Miss, knowing how needful your morning rest is, if it had not been for— Oh Lord! how shall I tell you!" exclaimed the matron, clasping her hands.

"In the name of Heaven, what do you mean?" cried Suzy, jumping out of bed in great alarm.

"Now please don't be frightened, Miss! I don't know as anything's the matter! I don't indeed! Please don't be frightened!"

"You're frightened yourself — unless you're crazy! What is wanted, then?" demanded Suzy, changing the form of her question, as she hastily drew on a dressing-gown.

"Why, miss, there's a person down stairs, a man in black, who came and asked to see you on most important business. And when I told him it was a rule without an exception that you were never to be disturbed until you rang your bell, and that you hadn't rung it yet, he replied that there must be an exception in this case, for that he *must* see you immediately on a matter of life and death which could not possibly wait."

"Is that all? Bosh! It is probably some poor actor

who wants an engagement, and considers it a matter of life or death whether he gets it or not, as it may indeed be a matter of feeding or starving," added Suzy, with a sigh.

"I hope it's no worse, miss."

"I will see the poor man. Tell him so, and send Jenny Smith here to help me to dress," said Suzy.

Mrs. Brown went down and sent the dressing-maid to her mistress.

Jenny was as pale and scared as her predecessor had been.

"Have you seen this morning visitor, child?" inquired Suzy.

"Yes, miss," answered the maid, in a trembling voice.

"Now what is there in the poor man to frighten you all so, I should like to know?"

"He beant a poor man, miss. And he do look so solemn and act so masterful, let alone refusing to go away and insisting on seeing you immediate, and sitting himself down in the hall as if the house belonged to him, and not to mention his having of two other men outside awaiting for him."

"Two other men outside waiting for him, Jenny! He may be a hall thief!"

"So we thought, miss; and so my brother Joe is staying there watching of him."

"Why didn't you call Mr. William?"

"If you please, Mr. William haven't been seen about the house this morning, and when Joe went to his room, he found it hadn't been slept in at all."

"Why, that is very strange! Will. *never* stays out all night! But— Oh, to be sure, he was to start for Paris this morning, and probably decided to take an earlier train than he had first intended. He has gone to Paris. But why didn't you call Mr. Hurst to see this importunate person? Mr. Hurst was the proper one to see him, after all."

"Oh, miss," said the little maid, beginning to weep,

"Mr. Hurst haven't been seen this morning neither, nor likewise his bed not slept in last night."

"Good Heaven!" exclaimed Suzy, turning pale, and now fully understanding the fright of the housekeeper.

"And so, miss, what with Mr. William being missing, and Mr. Hurst being missing, and this solemn man in black coming and taking possession of the house and ordering of us about, and insisting on seeing of you immediate, whether or no, me and Mrs. Brown do be so knocked over as we don't know whether we stand on our head or our heels."

"Something *has* happened," exclaimed Suzy with sudden energy, as she sprang to her feet and hurriedly completed her toilet.

"Come with me, Jenny Smith. I can't face that man alone, whoever he is," she said, as she left the room, followed by her maid.

In the passage outside she met Mrs. Brown.

"Why did you not tell me that Mr. William and Benjamin Hurst were missing?" demanded Suzy.

"Oh, miss, I did not like to overwhelm you with all the bad news at once!" said the housekeeper.

"Lead the way to my brother's smoking-room, Jenny. I will receive the man there. I cannot bear the idea of having him into one of my own rooms, whoever he is," said Suzy.

And the little maid ran down the steps before her mistress and opened the door of a smoking-room on the first floor.

"Now, Jenny, tell Smith to show the man in here, and do you come too," said Suzy, throwing herself into one of her brother's arm-chairs.

Jenny ran off on her errand, and in about two minutes returned, soon followed by a footman, who opened the door and announced:

"Mr. Ketchum."

Suzy looked up, and saw before her a stout, elderly, gray-haired man of grave appearance, dressed in black.

"You wished to see me on important business, I hear?" inquired Suzy.

"Yes, Miss."

"Will you be so good as to sit down and state your business?"

"Yes, Miss," answered Mr. Ketchum, taking another arm-chair, and taking his time about it.

"Will you state your business?" repeated Suzy.

"It is a very painful one, Miss. Pardon me if I hesitated to mention it to a young lady. You've heard of the murder last night, or early this morning in Piccadilly?"

"MURDER! No! Heaven! Who's murdered?" cried Suzy, growing pale to her lips, and on the very verge of fainting.

"Don't be frightened, Miss. It's no one akin to you, as I'm happy to say. It is the Honorable Mr. Stuart Fitzroy, son of my Lord St. Paul, who is, unhappily, now travelling on the Continent."

"But, Heaven of Heavens, when was it done? How did it happen?" cried Suzy, clasping her hands in an agony of dread, as she remembered the offensive conduct of the deceased on the preceding evening.

"The gentleman was murdered in Piccadilly, about two hours after midnight this morning."

"And is—is—the murderer known or suspected?" gasped Suzy.

"I beg you will not distress yourself, Miss, particularly as it is very desirable that you should be perfectly cool in giving your evidence before the Coroner's jury."

"Coroner's jury!" echoed Suzy faintly, and with white lips.

"Of course, Miss. I am here with a subpœna to take you as a witness to the inquest."

"I—I know nothing about it! Great Heavens! I know nothing about it!" faintly cried Suzy, shaking as with an ague fit.

The Inspector went coolly to a little open cabinet of liquors that stood on a stand in a corner of Mr. William's room, and he filled a small glass and brought it to her, saying:

"Drink this, Miss, and try to brace up a little. I know it is horrible hearing for a young lady, but you, personally, have no cause for distress."

Suzy took the glass and drank the cordial, for she did not want to faint, and was really on the verge of doing so.

"Tell me now, I implore you. Why am I summoned to give evidence in what I know nothing of? Who is the— Is any one suspected of the murder?" she inquired, somewhat restored by the cordial, and also somewhat encouraged by the Inspector's words.

"There was a young man taken on the spot, under the most suspicious circumstances."

"Who—who—who was—?" faltered Suzy, still scarcely able to breathe, much less to speak, and barely able to keep from fainting.

"The young man who is charged with the murder, Miss, has been in your service for several months, and up to this time when he is in jail. His name is—"

"Benjamin Hurst!" exclaimed Suzy, covering her face with her hands and groaning in anguish. "Oh, Benny! Benny! It was my fault again—mine! Oh, Benny! my Benny! I was born to be your evil genius! But he *never*, *never* did it, sir! He *never* did it! I would stake my life, my soul, upon his innocence!" she cried, weeping vehemently.

"He'll have a fair trial, Miss, and if innocent will be found according. But with respects, I think you are deceived in that young man. May be you don't know—

Ah! to be sure you don't, or you would never have taken him into your service. But we have been looking up his record, Miss, and have found out that he is a returned convict. Bless you, Miss, he was one of the worst characters about London from his babyhood. Lord love you, Miss, why, he stole as soon as he could creep; lied as soon as he could talk; became snakesman to a gang of desperate burglars when he was but ten years old, and ended years ago by admitting a burglar into his master's house, who robbed the house and nearly murdered a visitor who was staying there. For which he was lagged for fourteen years. He had just served his time out and returned, when you took him into your service. How he ever got into a respectable house, is a wonder to all. It must have been by a forged recommendation, or a false character, as it is called, Miss?" said the Inspector interrogatively.

Suzy did not answer him; she could not, she was sobbing so convulsively.

"Don't take it so hard, Miss; although of course I know it *is* hard to discover that you have been harboring in your house a returned convict, who might at any time have robbed the premises and murdered the inmates."

Suzy, who had been trying to speak for some time now burst forth with the energy lent by rage.

"Hold your slandering tongue!" she fiercely exclaimed, forgetting the decorum of the palace, and falling back upon the manners of Junk Lane.

"Every word you speak against Benny is a lie, and worse than a lie—cruel injustice!"

"Really, really, Miss," began the astounded Inspector, "this is very extraordinary language—actionable, in fact."

"I don't care if it is; it is true, every word of it. I know all about Benjamin Hurst. I know him better than anybody in the whole world knows him. And I have known him from the time when we were babies in rags together.

And I know that he was unjustly convicted fourteen years ago, and I am sure that he is unjustly accused now. 'Stole as soon as he could creep,' did he? 'Lied as soon as he could speak,' you say? If he did, he was *taught* to do both. Some very young children do both without being taught. It comes natural to them. They require to be taught *not* to steal, and *not* to lie. And who ever said to that poor, gentle child, 'Benny, it is a sin to lie; it is a sin to steal?' No one ever did. Oh, you law officers, with the law-makers at your backs, you are a precious set of impostors, you are!—fools or knaves, I don't know which. For, look you, what fools you are not to use the 'ounce of prevention,' which is so much better than the 'pound of cure;' not to teach the child to be honest and truthful, to save the trouble and expense of trying and convicting and punishing the young criminal! not to build many cheap little infant schools, to save the enormous cost of keeping up your fortress-like prisons, and all the paraphernalia of criminal law! And what knaves, to punish such neglected and ignorant outcasts of society, when you should all—law officers, law makers, judges, juries, Lords and Commons—scourge your own backs till you faint, for your sins against the poor children, who are so completely in your power to make them good or bad!"

"Really, really, really, Miss," began the Inspector, perceiving that Suzy had stopped from mere want of breath to go on—"really this is very intemperate language."

"Call this a Christian and civilized nation, indeed." continued Suzy, recovering her breath, and taking not the slightest notice of the Inspector's interruption. "Call this a Christian and civilized country, where Benny *was*, and thousands upon thousands of innocent children like him *are*, left to bear cold and hunger and nakedness and disease in dens of guilt and misery, where they are taught 'oaths for prayers' and 'sins for duty?'"

"Miss, I beg your pardon," said the Inspector, rising

hastily, "but *I* have a duty to perform here, which I shall set about immediately. I hope I shall meet no opposition in the discharge of my office."

"It is a grim joke," continued Suzy, referring to the boasted civilization and Christianity of the age. Then turning to the Inspector, she answered him: "Certainly you will receive no opposition in the discharge of your duty. If I cannot set the law right, I will not break its conditions. My brother is, unluckily, in Paris, on my business; but my servants will render you every assistance," said Suzy, reaching her hand to the bell-pull.

"Stay, Miss, one moment. We have ascertained, from a respectable cabman who voluntarily came forward to give the information, that he, the said cabman, drove your brother and the deceased from Covent Garden Theatre to this house, between the hours of ten and eleven, last night, and was dismissed at the door, where he left them. It appears that that unfortunate deceased spent the remainder of the evening here, and was on his way home when the fatal assault was made upon him. He was next found dead in Piccadilly, with this Benjamin Hurst standing over him."

Suzy sickened at the words, as she reflected that she herself had sent the unfortunate young man to attend Mr Stuart Fitzroy to his home.

"Therefore, you see, miss, I shall have to summon all the servants in the house as witnesses, to testify as to what occurred here last evening. I shall also have to examine the room and effects of this man Hurst, and I have brought with me a search-warrant for the purpose."

"Very well; you must do your duty, I suppose,' she said, in a dying voice, as she stretched out her hand and pulled the bell-rope.

Smith answered the summons.

"Tell Jones to order my brougham immediately. I am going out. And do you return here and show this person to Mr. Hurst's room," said Suzy

Then, with a slight bow to the detective, she beckoned Jenny Smith to attend her, and left the room to prepare for her painful attendance at the coroner's inquest.

"For goodness' sake, miss, take a cup of coffee before you go out! Remember that you have had no breakfast," said Jenny Smith, anxiously.

"Breakfast! I never thought of it. Well, bring me a cup of strong coffee. Perhaps I had better take it before I go," sighed Suzy.

"And something with it, miss?"

"No; I could not swallow a morsel. It would choke me," said Suzy, bursting into tears.

Jenny Smith left the room, and speedily returned with a cup of strong and fragrant Mocha, which her mistress drank with feverish eagerness.

"You must come with me, Jenny. I cannot go to that horrid place without a woman's attendance. And I would rather have you, Jenny, than Mrs. Brown. Go, and get ready as quickly as you can," said Suzy, as she put down her empty cup and drew on her gloves.

The girl, eager to go to a scene of such intense interest and excitement as a coroner's inquest on the body of a murdered man, and that man Mr. Stuart Fitzroy, went out quickly, and soon returned dressed, to attend her mistress.

The young lady and her maid went down stairs to Mr. William's room, to await the return of the Inspector.

He came at length.

"Well, have you found anything in Benjamin Hurst's possession likely to criminate him?" sarcastically inquired Suzy, with a curl of her lip.

"Not much. I have found a richly embroidered infant's sack and a little sock or shoe, neither of which would seem to be the rightful property of this young man. Therefore I have taken possession of them for the present, as they may lead to something," said the Inspector, producing the articles and exhibiting them to Suzy.

She took them, and looked at them in surprise and curiosity. She too saw the crest of the Barons of Seton-Linlithgow embroidered among the eglantine leaves, and she suddenly recollected the conversation she had held with Benny, when he had inquired of her whether there were any family connection between the Cheviots and the Seton-Linlithgows. And she thought, with a strange thrill of emotion, about the wonderful likeness existing between the Earl of Wellrose and the poor outcast, Benjamin Hurst; and of the agitation betrayed by the Duchess of Cheviot years ago, when, with her son the Earl, she had stood by the bed of the poor unknown outcast in the children's ward of the Middlesex Hospital; and now of these relics found in Benjamin's possession! What on earth did it all mean? Was possibly this poor outcast the unacknowledged brother of the Earl? Oh, no, no, no, that could never be! The high, pure, noble nature of both the Duke and Duchess of Cheviot forbade the injurious thought. What did it all mean then? she asked herself, as she gazed upon the relics.

She was roused from her reverie by the voice of the Inspector.

"We must be going, miss, if you please. The inquest is already in session."

Suzy started, and handed back the little sack and shoe to the officer, murmuring:

"Yes, they may indeed lead to something."

She then turned and told Jenny Smith to see if the brougham was at the door.

It was reported to be waiting.

"Your housekeeper will have to accompany you, miss. She is also summoned as a witness. I took the liberty of telling her to get ready as quickly as she could. And here she comes," said the Inspector, as Mrs. Brown, bonneted and shawled, and very much frightened, entered the room.

"Smith and Jones, who have been subpoenaed to attend

the inquest, will follow in charge of one of my men. And now, if you please, miss," said the Inspector, as he politely escorted Suzy and her attendants to the door, and placed them in the carriage.

He then mounted to a seat on the box, and directed the coachman to drive to the police station house, Little Vine street, Piccadilly.

CHAPTER XXX.

WHAT THE SACRIFICE COST.

It is my life at thy feet I throw.—BROWNING.

As the carriage turned from Piccadilly into Little Vine street, the crowd was so thick that the coachman could scarcely drive through without running over some one.

The news of the murder had not yet had time to get into the afternoon papers, but it had spread far and wide, so that half the West End seemed to be crowding into Piccadilly toward Little Vine street.

As the carriage drew up before the police station house, the crowd so blockaded the sidewalk that the police officers were obliged to open the way before the witnesses could alight and enter.

The Inspector got off the box and opened the door for them, and when Suzy and her companions, both closely vailed, alighted, he gravely escorted them into the station house, and to the room where the coroner's inquest was being held.

It was held with closed doors, guarded by policemen, so that the room when they entered it was not at all crowded.

Here at last was breathing space. But, ah! what a scene!

In the middle of the room stood a long table, and upon it lay the body of the murdered man, covered with a black pall. At the head of this ghastly table sat the coroner, a grave, gray-haired man of some sixty years. At the foot sat the assistant coroner, and on each side of the table sat six jurymen.

At a smaller table or stand near the coroner's right hand, sat a clerk with writing materials before him.

At other stands or tables here and there, sat other officers engaged in the inquest, and also the reporters of the press.

Along the walls, on benches, sat the witnesses summoned on the investigation, and also a few privileged spectators.

It appeared that many witnesses had already been examined: to wit, the policemen who had discovered the body of the murdered man, and the surgeons who had performed the autopsy.

And now Benjamin Hurst had been brought from his prison cell, and was up for examination.

Suzy seemed to see him, and only him, as the Inspector gravely conducted her and her attendants to seats among the witnesses.

Benny was standing before the coroner, undergoing a severe cross-examination.

He was deadly pale, without a vestige of color in his fair, pure face; but he was perfectly firm and steadfast—as one who had made up his mind to a complete sacrifice of himself, and felt all the horror of its conditions.

The coroner having told him that he was already proved to have been with the dead man at the time of his death, demanded that he should inform the jury how that death came about.

All listened for his reply, but none so intently as Suzy. She clasped her hands together, and gazed at him with an intensity of interest that seemed to cause him to turn and meet her eyes. And then for the first time he was aware of her presence in the room.

He met that intense gaze, and utterly misunderstood its meaning. She was only silently beseeching him to be cautious how he answered, and to say nothing to criminate himself. But he thought that she was imploring him to screen her brother, and his resolution was strengthened to do so, even at the sacrifice of his own life.

He answered the coroner as he had answered others, truly.

"The man fell while he was drunk, and striking his head upon the corner of the curb-stone, killed himself."

"He fell because, as has been proved by the post-mortem examination, he was knocked down with great violence. You must have done it, or seen who did it. If you did it, you are not expected to criminate yourself here, by confessing; if, however, you did not do it, but saw who did, you may clear yourself from suspicion by denouncing the murderer."

"I did not do it. I have no more to say," answered Benny.

"You deny having committed this murder. Can you also deny having seen it committed?"

Benny was perfectly silent.

The question was repeated.

"I have said that I have nothing more to tell your Worship, and I *have* nothing more," he repeated.

"You have said enough. Stand aside," ordered the coroner.

The officer who had Benny in charge withdrew him.

Suzy was next called and sworn, and examined as to the hour that the deceased had left her house on the preceding evening; the state that he was in; and whether he left alone or in company, and if so, with whom.

Now if Suzy had not been on her guard, she must have told much that would have gone far to convict Benny. For she might have told how, before leaving the supper-room that night, she had ordered Benny to attend Mr. Stuart Fitzroy to his home.

But she was on her guard, for Benny's sake, and so she baffled investigation by confining herself to answering in the fewest possible words the questions that were put to her.

"The deceased supped with you last night?"

"Yes."

"What occurred at the supper?"

"He got drunk."

"Then he was—drunk when he left the house?"

"I suppose so."

"At what hour did he leave?"

"I don't know."

"You don't know?"

"No."

"How is that? He was your own guest."

"When I saw his condition I left the supper-room. I never saw him in life again."

"A moment, Miss," said the coroner, as poor, inexperienced Suzy made as if she would have sat down. "We have not quite done with you yet. Do you know of any cause of quarrel or enmity between the deceased gentleman and your butler, Benjamin Hurst?"

"Of none whatever. They had not even a speaking acquaintance, so far as I know. It is not likely. Benjamin Hurst is a pure, truthful and honest man; and the deceased is, or was—what his reputation represents him," said Suzy, departing from her rule of short answers, just so soon as she got a chance to defend Benny.

"You may sit down, Miss," said the coroner.

And so Suzy withdrew, and was succeeded by her house keeper, Mrs. Brown, who was the next witness.

Being put upon her oath and questioned to that effect, she said that her name was Martha Brown, and that she now lived at No. —, Park Lane, as housekeeper and companion to Miss Juniper, who was professionally known as Mademoiselle Arielle.

"You are something of a chaperone or duenna also to the last witness, are you not?"

"Yes, sir; if your worship thinks fit to call me so."

"You are, then, usually present at her little suppers?"

"Yes, sir."

"You were present last night, when Mr. Stuart Fitzroy supped with her?"

"Yes, sir."

"Who else was present?"

"Mr. William Juniper and the servants; no others."

"What occurred?"

"Mr. Stuart Fitzroy drank much more wine than was good for him, and behaved in such an ungentlemanly manner that Miss Juniper and myself left the table, and also the room."

"And then?"

"I do not know what happened after we left."

"You may sit down."

Mrs. Brown retired and Suzy breathed freely. She had been intensely anxious lest it should come out in Mrs. Brown's examination that she, Suzy, had sent Benny home with Mr. Fitzroy.

But her relief was not long. Her heart seemed to stand still again when the name of Joseph Smith was called, and her first footman took the stand.

This witness, being sworn and questioned, said that his name was Joseph Smith and that he lived at No. —, Park Lane, as footman in the service of Miss Juniper. He corroborated every part of the testimony given by the two last witnesses as to the little supper party, the wine drinking, and the intoxication and ungentlemanly deportment of Mr. Fitzroy.

Then the coroner inquired:

"What was the nature of this ungentlemanly deportment of which you speak?"

"Profane language at the table, sir. And when Miss Juniper and Mrs. Brown, in consequence, got up to leave the room, he seized Miss Juniper around the waist, and tried to force her back against her will."

"Did her brother resent this rudeness to his sister?" inquired a juryman, who had been very attentively listening to the testimony.

"No sir; he laughed, and sided with Mr. Fitzroy; and told his sister not to be a fool."

"What! How was that?" inquired the same juryman in some surprise.

"Well, you see, sir, Mr. William wouldn't have behaved so, if he too hadn't been some'at the worse for the wine he'd drank."

"Ah! so *he* was drunk also?"

"Well, sir, since you put it so, and I am on my oath, I must say he *was*."

"And so this man was allowed to insult his hostess with impunity?"

"I beg your pardon, sir?" said the witness interrogatively, and not understanding.

"Did no one interfere to save the young lady from insult?" inquired the juryman, changing the style of his question.

"Well, sir, no one but Mr. Hurst. He did. As soon as he saw Mr. Fitzroy seize her around the waist, he sprang forward and made as if he would have knocked him down. But before he got round the table, Miss Juniper had got free, and she ordered him—"

"Ordered whom?" inquired the Coroner.

"She ordered Mr. Hurst to get Mr. Fitzroy's hat and put it on his head, and take him home, as he was no more capable of taking care of himself than he was of behaving decent, she said."

"Ah! and what happened next?"

"Miss Juniper and Mrs. Brown left the room. And Mr. Hurst started out with Mr. Fitzroy, to take him home."

"You know that for a fact?"

"Yes, sir; I let them out."

"And how did Mr. William Juniper then conduct himself?"

"We left him smoking and drinking, sir. And saw no more of him. But I knew that he was going to Paris by an early train this morning, and I heard he had gone."

"Do you *know* that he went?"

"Not of my own knowledge, sir; but I know he made arrangements to go yesterday. And the general impression about the house is that he went."

Joseph Smith was permitted to withdraw. And Aaron Jones was called to the stand, who corroborated every word of the last witness' testimony.

It was done! All that Suzy dreaded had happened. Benjamin Hurst was all but proved to have murdered Stuart Fitzroy.

Pale as marble and as firm, Benny said to himself:

"Her brother is saved, and I—I can die for her peace."

Suzy burst into a storm of sobs and tears, and had to be led from the room.

But she refused to go home; and still attended by Mrs. Brown and Jenny Smith, she sat in her carriage outside to await the news of the verdict.

That Benny never committed that murder, and that he was shielding the real criminal, she felt sure. But who was that criminal for whom he was sacrificing his life? A horrible suspicion whispered that it was no other than her own brother.

She sat and wept, refusing to be comforted, until a great commotion in the crowd outside the police station house advised her that the verdict of the coroner's inquest had been rendered.

It was soon proclaimed from one to another throughout the crowded streets. It was to the effect that the deceased had met his death at the hands of Benjamin Hurst.

The uproar of the streets at the announcement of this verdict was perfectly terrific.

Mrs. Brown was frightened, and she implored Suzy to order the coachman to drive home.

But Suzy, through her storm of sobs and tears, declared that she would wait to see the poor boy brought out on his way to Newgate, so that she might speak to him, and assure him of her love and trust and entire sympathy.

But ah! she waited in vain. She could not see or speak to him, for presently one of her footmen came to the carriage door, and touching his hat, said:

"There he goes, Miss!"

"Who? Where?" inquired Suzy, looking around and seeing no one that she knew.

"The prisoner, Mr. Hurst, Miss, locked up in that ugly vehicle as looks like a tall hearse, and called the Black Maria. He's committed to Newgate jail to wait his trial for wilful murder. Shall I tell the coachman to drive home, Miss?"

"Yes," said Mrs. Brown, taking upon herself to answer, for Suzy had fallen back in her seat, totally overcome by distress.

She was taken home and laid upon her bed.

And that night the manager of the Covent Garden theatre had to come before the curtain and make the best apology he could for the non-appearance of Mademoiselle Arielle.

And, in a word, she never appeared upon that stage again.

CHAPTER XXXI.

THE LOST STAR.

Like the lost Pleiad, seen no more below.—BYRON.

Could'st thou be shaken from thy radiant place,
Even as a dew-drop from the myrtle spray,
Swept by the wind away?—HEMANS.

"MADEMOISELLE ARIELLE" was never seen on the stage again.

The shock of Stuart Fitzroy's tragic death, and Benjamin Hurst's committal on the charge of murder, utterly prostrated her nervous system.

She held herself and her beautiful art in a great degree accountable for the calamities that had occurred.

If she had never been an opera singer, she reasoned Stuart Fitzroy would never have seen and admired her, and sought her acquaintance, and been her guest, and left her house in the charge of Benjamin Hurst, who then would never have been committed for his murder.

As these thoughts pierced her heart like sword blades, suddenly the theatre, with all its allurements became utterly hateful to her. And she longed to leave her brilliant public career, and to find peace in the privacy of domestic life, if only Benny were free—ah, if only Benny were free and out of all danger!

For whom was Benny offering up his life now? she asked herself, as she lay prostrate on her bed.

She feared it was for her brother.

And yet that could scarcely be, she thought; for she remembered that when she had seen her brother and Stuart Fitzroy together, scarcely an hour before the death of the latter, they had been good friends, and also that the evidence before the coroner's jury had proved that Stuart Fitzroy had left the house in the charge of Benjamin Hurst and that they had *left her brother alone at the table over his wine.*

Therefore she concluded that it could not be her brother for whom Benny was sacrificing himself.

For whom, then?

She could not even conjecture.

She longed to go to the prison to see him, and to gain his confidence, so that she might save him, or persuade him to save himself; but ah! the shocks of the preceding day, and the anguish of the night, had left her on this second morning so utterly prostrated that she could scarcely stand.

She had, indeed, arisen from her bed, and attempted to dress herself; but in the process she had so nearly fainted as to be compelled to lie down and rest on the sofa of her boudoir.

It was while she was thus reposing that the manager of the Covent Garden Theatre called in person to inquire about her health, and the probability of her being at rehearsal that morning, or at the opera that evening.

She sent word that he might come up and see her.

He was therefore soon ushered in by the footman, Smith

He entered bowing, and took the seat near her sofa, to which she invited him.

"You see my condition, Mr. ——. It is all over with me. I think I shall never sing in opera again," said Suzy, holding out her hand to him.

"I am extremely grieved to find you ill; but for Heaven's sake don't say that, Mademoiselle! Your engagement with us incomplete, too! You would ruin me!" exclaimed the manager, in consternation.

"I am sorry for you, but I cannot help it; for *I* am worse than 'ruined,' and those I love best in the world are worse than 'ruined,' in your sense of the word. I will pay the forfeit; stand a suit for damages; do anything, suffer anything, in short, rather than go upon the boards again! I have left the stage! I have left it forever!"

"But for the love of Heaven, Mademoiselle, in common honor! in common honesty! consider—"

"I cannot consider! I am too wretched! Look at me! Do you think it possible that even with the aid of drugs I could be got into condition to appear at the opera to-night? No! nor to-morrow night, nor next night. 'In common honesty' I sent for you to tell you this. If it does not satisfy you, I will send for a physician, who will give a certificate to the facts. My engagement with you will terminate next week. That will be before I shall be able to appear, I know. And after that I will never make another with any theatrical manager."

She spoke in a faint and tremulous voice.

"But, my dear young lady, think!"

"I cannot think! I am too wretched! I have been frank with you, and now please to leave me! Do not think me unkind, but please to go," she said, growing fainter and paler.

"The shock you have sustained has certainly unhinged your mind, as well as your nerves."

"Yes, it has. Now go. I recommend you to telegraph to Geneva for Madame S., who is taking her holiday on Lake Geneva. She will come to you in an emergency, no doubt. Now, good-morning," faltered Suzy, kindly and politely dismissing her visitor.

There was no help for it. The manager had to take himself and his disappointment home. There was no doubt that the young prima donna was too much prostrated to appear upon the stage for some days yet. And the only hope he had in her was, that after a little time, she might be able to rally sufficiently to complete her engagement.

"Well," he said to himself, as he left the house, "her excessive grief proves one thing very clearly—that this handsome scamp who was murdered was her favored lover after all, instead of the infatuated Earl of Wellrose, whom everybody thought to be the man. And now to follow her advice and telegraph for Madame S. And, meanwhile, little Fée must take her part, and do the best she can with it."

The manager had scarcely driven away from the house, before the carriage of the Earl of Wellrose drew up before the door.

He too, with all London, had of course heard of the horrible murder of Mr. Stuart Fitzroy, in Piccadilly, as that unfortunate gentleman was returning from a little supper with Mademoiselle Arielle in Park Lane, and of the consequent illness, and absence from her part, of the young prima donna.

And now he came to make anxious inquiries about her health.

He sent up his card and compliments and inquiries.

And he soon received for answer the message that Mademoiselle begged that his lordship would come up and see her.

This was a pleasure he had not expected, and he followed the footman with alacrity.

He found Suzy still reclining on the sofa, very pale, faint and tremulous.

She greeted him with gentle courtesy, and begged that he would sit down near her.

"But I am very much grieved to find you in so much sorrow," said his lordship tenderly.

"It is for Benjamin Hurst! You know he was committed to Newgate on the charge of the murder. And oh Lord Wellrose, he never did it! Benny never, never did it!" she said, bursting into tears, and sobbing hysterically.

"I do not believe that he did; and so take this comfort to your heart, my best beloved—that, being guiltless, he will surely be acquitted," he said, gently taking her hand.

"'Being guiltless, he will surely be acquitted!' Oh, my lord! my lord! does that always follow? A guiltless child, he was sent to the Penal Colonies for fourteen years! A guiltless man, he is now committed to Newgate upon the charge of murder. And he may be convicted, and then—Oh! I cannot bear it! I cannot bear it! Oh, Benny! Benny if they put you to death, I shall die! I shall die! I never could outlive the dark and dreadful day!" she moaned, sobbing, as if her heart would burst.

"My best beloved," said the young Earl gently, and all the more calmly because she was so much excited—"my own dearest Susan, you must not despair because a Coroner's Jury has brought in a verdict against him. It was really upon very insufficient evidence. And coroners, moreover, are mostly Dogberrys. A judge is another sort of man—a man of superior learning and wisdom, who holds his high office in virtue of these qualities. Benjamin will have a fair trial. And as the evidence is really quite insufficient to convict him, he will be acquitted; and after his acquittal, my dearest Suzy, it shall be my very first care to advance him in life."

"Oh, thanks! thanks! thanks! Oh! you give me hope! You think there's good ground for hope? You really do?" eagerly exclaimed Suzy.

"I *know* there is ground for hope, and none for fear. Benjamin's imprisonment and impending trial are misfortunes that we cannot prevent; but they will be the extent of his troubles, and we can mitigate them. I will see to engaging the best counsel for him. It shall be my first business to do so to-day."

"Oh, I thank you so much! And you will go to see him in his cell to-day, and speak some kind words to him?—poor, friendless boy!"

"Indeed I will! And let me tell you, Susan, that there is something in the poor young man that interests me strangely."

"Oh, Lord Wellrose—forgive me for daring to hint it,

but—" Susan hesitated, and her pale face flushed for an instant.

"But what, my dearest? Speak freely," said the young Earl, gently.

"Oh, Lord Wellrose, there may be some deep reason in nature that you know not of, for this strange interest you feel in Benjamin Hurst," she said, and then again paused.

"Truly there are hidden things in nature, dearest Suzy," he said soothingly, though he did not see the drift of her words.

"And that may give you the *right* to help Benny," she continued, and once more paused in embarrassment.

"I have the right to help him, and all who need my help, dearest Suzan. But there is something you have to say to me, and find difficulty in saying. Now, surely you may speak freely to me, my own," he said gently, pressing her hand, that he still held.

"Oh, Lord Wellrose," murmured Susan, in a very low tone, and blushing deeply, "I hope you will forgive me for venturing to make such an assertion; but I must not hesitate to say anything that may serve to deepen your interest in poor Benny. Lord Wellrose, poor Benjamin Hurst, humble as he is, *may be your own poor kinsman.*"

"Impossible!" broke impulsively from the lips of the astonished young man. Then, in a quieter tone he asked: "What makes you think so, dearest?"

"Oh, in the first place, the strong likeness! If you were dressed alike, strangers might take you for twins," said Susan.

The young Earl smiled slightly, as he said:

The likeness is undeniable. But do you not know that such likenesses have been found to exist even between persons of different nationalities?"

"Yes, my lord; but I fancy that in every such case there must have been some blood relationshship, however distant, or even unknown. But the likeness between you, my lord, and my poor friend Benny, is not the only reason I have for believing that he may be your lordship's poor kinsman."

"Then what more, dearest?"

"Lord Wellrose, Benjamin was not the child of the woman whose name he bears, and who brought him up as her own. He was a deserted child, of unknown parentage. All that is known of him is this: that he was born in or near Seton Castle, the seat of your grandfather, the late Baron Linlithgow; and the only relics of his childhood that he possesses, are two little articles, a sack and a sock, both of which are embroidered with the Eglantine, which your lordship knows to be the symbol of the Seton-Linlithgows, just as the Rose was the symbol of the Sinclairs of Roslyn."

"Yes," said the Earl, with a smile, "and many of the daughters of Seton-Linlithgow were named after their flower, as many of the ladies of Roslyn were named after their rose. But go on, my dearest Susan."

"Nor was there so much in all this, had not the crest of the Barons of Seton-Linlithgow been embroidered among the leaves of their symbolic flower, the Eglantine. That fact *alone* would have been worthless. Any lady of the house of Seton-Linlithgow might have given the cast-off garments of her infant to any servant or peasant woman needing clothing for her child; but taken in connection with the strong likeness between your lordship and the ossessor of these relics, I think they mean much. What do *you* think, Lord Wellrose?" inquired Suzy, looking ntently into the face of the Earl.

The son of Eglantine Seton, Baroness Linlithgow, Duchess of Cheviot, mused for a few moments. A vision passed before him of some young scapegrace of his grandfather's having some love affair with some servant in the family peasant girl on the estate, and of Benny's being the consequence of their folly; and of some nurse or housekeeper at the Castle giving the left-off infant dresses to clothe the destitute child. But all was very vague. So he inquired:

"Do you *know* what you have stated to be facts, my dear Susan? And have you seen these relics, as you call them?"

"Let me be accurate," said Suzy. "I know the likeness to be a fact; and so do you. I have seen the relics; and so may you. All the other facts I have from hearsay; but I believe them, and I believe they may be proved."

"Well, my dearest, whether this young man may have any claim upon me from kinship or from mere humanity, he has certainly a claim stronger than either of these: it is that you, my beloved, are interested in his fate. When I leave you, Susan, I shall go as soon as possible to Mr. Percy Melliss, the most eminent lawyer for criminal cases in the world perhaps, and I shall retain him, and any other lawyer or half dozen lawyers that he may recommend to assist him."

"Oh, I *do* thank you so much! And, Lord Wellrose, my purse, my whole fortune is freely at Benny's service, to secure the best counsel for him—yes, if it should take all I possess in the world! Oh, angels in Heaven, bear me witness how freely I would give all I possess in the world to have Benny once more out of prison, and free from the horrible danger!" she exclaimed, with a shudder, bursting again into hysterical sobs and tears.

"Take comfort, dearest one," said the young Earl, with much emotion. "As to the finding and retaining of the best counsel to be had, that shall be my care and my cost, my duty and my pleasure."

"No, no," said Suzy eagerly, through her tears. "You may *perhaps* have the right to help Benny, and I am glad to know that you will do it; but I have *certainly* the right to help him, and I mean to do it; not only because he was a loved and trusted member of my household—though that circumstance, considered in itself, is much—but more because he has always seemed to me like one of my own brothers, only dearer, far dearer than any brother I have, because he was just of my own age, and in our infancy shared my cradle and my food and play like my twin-brother. My lord, help him all you can, but let me bear the cost, for the precious old love's sake. You do not misunderstand me, I hope; do you, Lord Wellrose?" inquired Suzy, in an anxious tone.

"Misunderstand you, true heart, pure spirit? No, indeed. I understand you and confide in you, and love you perfectly. And I go from you now straight to the cell of the imprisoned boy, that I may comfort him for your sake," said the Earl, as he raised and pressed her hand to his lips.

"God bless you for these good words. Give my love to Benny. Tell him that I know he is innocent; and that I will come to see him just so soon as I can stand on my feet."

"I will tell him," said the Earl.

And then he took leave of his love, and left the house.

As he entered his brougham he gave his orders to the coachman in accordance with his resolutions.

And as the carriage bowled along in the right direction, Lord Wellrose fell into a deep reverie on the subject of Benjamin Hurst's possible relationship with his own family, the circumstances of his birth and his deserted condition; of his likeness to himself, Lord Wellrose; of his possession of the relics, and of Suzy's words.

CHAPTER XXXII.

FETTERED LOVE.

I tell you, he walked up and down
That prison crowned with love's best crown,
And feasted with love's perfect feast,
To feel he killed, for her, at least,
Body and mind, and peace and fame,
Alike youth's end and manhood's aim.—BROWNING.

FROM Park Lane, Lord Wellrose went straight to Lincoln Inn Fields, and sought out the chambers of Mr. Percy Melliss, the great criminal lawyer.

So great was now the fame of this learned lawyer and eloquent advocate, that he might have been a Queen's Counsel if he had but chosen to abandon the cause of the poor and needy—the men and women, aye, and little children, "more sinned against than sinning"—the cause of humanity, the cause of Christ, the cause of God.

So when he might have risen to be Queen's Counsel, Queen's Advocate, Solicitor-General, Attorney-General, or even, in time, Lord Chancellor, he chose to remain only the great criminal lawyer, with the questionable reputation and all but reproach that attaches to the name.

Their deep mutual interest in the "cause" had so frequently brought Lord Wellrose and himself into company, that a very warm friendship had grown up between the gifted advocate and the young Earl.

When Lord Wellrose had been preparing his famous "Bill for the Reclamation of Criminals, and the Reform of Prison Discipline," he took frequent occasion to consult Mr. Percy Melliss, who gave him valuable aid in his humane enterprise.

And so their friendship had matured.

And now the young Earl sought the great criminal lawyer in behalf of Benjamin Hurst, a prisoner in Newgate, charged with the murder of the Honorable Stuart Fitzroy son of the Viscount St. Paul.

Arrived at the house, he sent up his card, on which he had written in pencil, under his name, "*life and death.*"

He was at once admitted, and after going up two flights of stairs and passing through two or three rooms, each occupied by two or three clerks, he was shown into a back chamber, where the great advocate sat writing at a table, covered with papers.

Mr. Melliss immediately arose to receive Lord Wellrose.

"Busy?" inquired the Earl, with a smile.

"Always," responded the lawyer, setting a chair for his visitor.

"Nevertheless, you see, I interrupt you," said the Earl, apologetically, as he took the offered seat.

"Your lordship is most heartily welcome," answered the advocate, as he reseated himself at the table, and, turning his face toward his visitor, assumed an attentive expression.

"You have heard all about this murder in Piccadilly, of course? The papers are full of it, and it is the talk of all London."

"The murder of Stuart Fitzroy. Yes, certainly. Who has not?"

"No one, probably. But I come to you this morning in behalf of the young man who is charged with the murder, and whom I believe from my soul to be as guiltless of that crime as you or myself," said the young Earl, earnestly.

"There is, at least, no good evidence against him. But, for the murder of Lord St. Paul's son, I suppose the coroner and his jury thought they must commit somebody, right or wrong, and so they committed this poor young man. Do you know anything of him?" inquired Mr. Melliss.

"Know him?" echoed Lord Wellrose, with some emotion. "Yes, I know him well, and feel the deepest compassion for his misfortunes. I come this morning to ask you to undertake his defence. Can you do it? Are you too busy?"

"I am busy. I am always busy, very busy. And yet I have always time to do everything that I ought to do. I ought to defend this young man, and I will certainly find time to do it."

"Spoken like yourself, good friend! Thanks," said the Earl, as he opened his pocket-book and took from it a Bank of England note for a hundred pounds, which he quietly laid upon the lawyer's table as a retaining fee. Then he arose to depart.

"I will get through a little pressing business this fore-noon, and early this afternoon I will see my new client," said the lawyer, rising to attend his distinguished visitor to the door.

The Earl of Wellrose went next to Newgate.

He was well acquainted with the Reverend Mr. Ross, the Chaplain of the prison, who was also the Duchess of Cheviot's almoner to the poor and friendless prisoners.

His lordship asked for the chaplain, and was shown to his reverence's room.

Mr. Ross was not the same chaplain who had been in office there when Benny, the child, had been incarcerated for burglary, and consequently he knew nothing whatever of the history of the new prisoner, Benjamin Hurst.

But when the Earl of Wellrose entered the chaplain's room, the latter thought his lordship had only come upon some benevolent errand to him as the Duchess of Cheviot's almoner.

The chaplain was quite an old man, with a tall, spare form, clad in a thread-bare suit of black, a fine bald head, adorned with a few thin locks of silver hair, and a pale, thin face, with a holy calm upon it, full of the love of God and man.

He arose to meet the young Earl, and offered him his hand and begged him to sit down, and inquired after the good Duchess, his mother.

Lord Wellrose thanked him, and sat down and replied satisfactorily to his questions, and then opened the subject of his visit by asking the chaplain if he had yet seen the new prisoner, Benjamin Hurst.

"Who is charged with the murder of young Stuart Fitzroy? No, I have not yet seen him. I was indeed about to visit his cell when your lordship's name was announced. Alas!" sighed the aged minister, using a very old-fashioned interjection—"Alas! I have heard this is also another case of neglected childhood growing up to depraved youth and criminal manhood! The papers state that this wretched young man has been a thief and an outcast, and the companion of burglars and cut-throats, from his infancy up. It is said that he has but recently returned from a fourteen years' transportation for burglary. And that he obtained the situation of butler at the house where he was engaged, only by a false character and forged recommendation. All this will tell very much against him in the coming trial. But I must visit him and save him, if through the Lord's help, I may. Our Divine Master 'came not to call the righteous, but sinners to repentance,'" said the chaplain reverently, bowing his head.

The young Earl looked gravely at the speaker for a moment, and then said:

"'WHO *hath sinned, this man or his parents, that he is born blind?*' Even if all the crimes falsely imputed to Benjamin Hurst were committed by him, still let us ask, '*Who* hath sinned, this man, or his parents,' or you or I, and all society, 'that he is born blind'—morally and spiritually blind; and that he has grown up blind—morally and spiritually blind?"

The chaplain reverently bowed his head and answered:

"I know that we all have sinned."

"Yes," said the young Earl. "We have all sinned in this respect, more than in all others."

"Each one of us, the very poorest of us, might save at least *one* little destitute, neglected child from remaining the companion of thieves and outcasts, and from growing up to become a thief or a murderer," added the chaplain.

And there was silence between the two for a while, and then the young Earl said:

"All that the gossipping daily papers have falsely said of Benjamin Hurst might well have been true; and yet still it might have been truly said of him, that he was 'more sinned against than sinning.'"

"Yes, yes; that is what your gracious mother, the Duchess, often says of the worst criminals confined in this prison."

"And she is nearly right. But in this case of Benjamin Hurst, she is entirely right. He is indeed, Heaven knows, more, *much* more, *very* much more, 'sinned against than sinning.' In his ignorant infancy he became the charge of thieves and outcasts; he was taught evil for good, sin for duty. He learned the lessons and performed the tasks for love of those around him. He became, for their sakes, because he knew no better, a beggar, a liar and a thief, just as another more fortunate child, from the same motives of conscience and affection, might have become a philanthropist, an advocate of truth and a benefactor of his kind. One whom I love and trust, and who has known Benjamin Hurst from his babyhood and hers, has told me so much of his sweetness of temper, goodness of heart, gentleness of manners and docility of disposition, that I can see perfectly well how easy it was for the thieves and outcasts who were his only protectors, and who had won his childish heart, to turn all his inherent good qualities to evil uses. But these evil uses were habits, that were no more a part of the boy's nature than were his poor little ragged jacket and trowsers a part of himself. And he was one who only needed to be shown the Right to see its beauty, to love it and prefer it to the Wrong; just as he would have preferred clean and whole clothes to ragged and filthy ones. And almost the first glimpse he had of the Right was caught within these prison walls, from your venerable predecessor, the then chaplain. I have heard how eagerly and gratefully he learned the good lessons taught him here. And I have seen for myself how he has profited by them. I have only recently known Benjamin Hurst well, but all I have seen of him has shown me a young man true, pure, brave, just and singularly refined in person, in manner and in spirit; a young man rare in any rank of life, and wonderfully rare in his."

"Your lordship is very earnest in your advocacy of this young prisoner. I trust your lordship may be right," said the chaplain.

"When you see and talk with Benjamin Hurst you will know that I am right. I think you said that you were about to visit him in his cell. If so, I should be obliged if you will take me with you. I wish to see him privately, or at least with no other witness than yourself. Can you gratify me?" inquired the young Earl.

"Certainly, my lord, with pleasure," answered the chaplain. And he touched the bell.

An officer of the prison answered the summons.

The chaplain whispered a few words to him. He went out, and after some moments a turnkey entered and respectfully intimated that he was "at the service of his reverence."

Mr. Ross arose and invited Lord Wellrose to accompany him.

The turnkey led the way, and the Earl and the chaplain followed through many passages, and up and down many flights of stairs, until they came to a row of cells, at one of which the man stopped and suddenly thrust in a key, opened the door, and admitted the visitors.

The poor young prisoner, when suddenly exposed to view,

was found sitting on the side of his rude bunk, engaged in reading a small volume.

On seeing his visitors, he quickly turned down the leaf of the volume he was reading, laid the book aside, and arose to greet that one visitor whom he recognized, with the heartfelt acknowledgment:

"I knew your lordship would come to see me in my trouble! I thank your lordship very much."

"My poor fellow, I am very sorry to see you here," said the Earl, taking his hand and pressing it, and still continuing to hold it, while he added, "This gentleman who accompanies me is the Reverend Mr. Ross, the prison chaplain, and he wishes to be your friend." Then turning to Mr. Ross, he said, "Reverend sir, this is Benjamin Hurst, who, though a prisoner here, charged with a crime I feel sure that he did not and could not commit, possesses my entire confidence and esteem."

"Oh, thanks, thanks for these good and gracious words!" said the young prisoner earnestly.

"I hope and trust in the Lord, that I may be able to serve you, my young friend," said the chaplain, kindly shaking hands with the prisoner.

There were few accommodations for visitors in these rude prison cells. Therefore the three sat down on the side of the bunk, that did the double duty of bed by night and bench by day.

"What have you been reading?" inquired the chaplain, taking up the little book that Benny had laid aside. "Ah, I see!" he said, as he opened it.

The book was the New Testament, and the leaf was folded down at the twenty-sixth chapter of St. Matthew's Gospel, describing the Saviour's agony in the garden of Gethsemane.

"Why did you select this particular part of the Scripture to read this morning?" inquired the chaplain.

Benny looked down at his own fettered limbs, and around upon the heavy stone-walls and strong iron gratings of his prison cell, and then raised his mournful blue eyes to the face of the chaplain. And the good man was answered.

"I see," he said with a sigh, as he laid down the book and arose and stood with his back to the grated door, facing the two young men, the unconscious brothers, who were still seated side by side on the edge of the bunk. And as he looked at them his aged face grew deep in interest.

How much alike these young men, though severed so far in rank and position; only that one was so pale, thin and wasted, and the other was in such ruddy health, that the one seemed but the faded-out image of the other!

"They are enough alike to be the children of the same parents," thought the minister. "And yet what a contrast!" And at the thought the good man sighed.

The young Earl with almost womanly tenderness, held the white transparent hand of his unknown brother and wondered at the more than sympathy, at the warmth of affection, he felt for the poor, patient young prisoner.

And as for Benny, a strange feeling of protection and peace came over his spirit.

"It grieves me very much to see you here, Hurst, even for a few days. But it can only be for a few days, my friend, for the Sessions are near at hand, when you will be tried and most certainly acquitted. I hope you know this?"

"I know that I am not guilty, my lord; but whether the jury will believe so, I do not know. But it seems to me that I am fated. It does not matter though," answered Benny sadly.

"Are you a Christian, Benjamin?"

"Yes, my lord, however unworthy to bear that name."

"Then you must not be a fatalist. You will be acquitted, Benjamin. But I wish you to be more than acquitted. I wish you to be vindicated. I wish your character to come pure from this ordeal as fine gold from the fiery furnace For this reason I have to-day retained for your defence, the most learned lawyer and eloquent advocate in the country. I mean Mr. Percy Melliss, of whom, no doubt, you have heard."

"Oh, yes," said Benny, immediately recollecting the name of the young lawyer who, years before, had so successfully defended his, Benny's, foster-mother—"Oh, yes, my lord, I have heard of Mr. Melliss. But, oh, how shall I ever be able to thank you enough for all your goodness and kindness to me?" inquired Benny, raising his sad eyes gratefully to the eyes of the Earl.

"My poor boy, by letting me serve you as much as I wish to do," said the Earl, caressing the thin, pale, fettered hand that he held between his own. "I like you, Benjamin. I wish to see you prosperous and happy. And when you shall be acquitted and vindicated, you must let me do a great deal for you, indeed. You must take a great deal from me. We can, any of us, take anything from one who loves us, can we not, Benjamin?"

The poor young man, overcome by this gentleness of sympathy, dropped his face upon his fettered hands, burst into tears and sobbed. After a little while he composed himself, and said:

"Forgive this weakness, my lord. I have not been used to such kindness, except from one."

"There, there; it is perfectly natural. You are not physically strong, and you have been severely tried. Now let us look beyond this dark present to the fair future, not so far off. When you are fully acquitted and vindicated, both by the court and the press, we must see to giving you a fresh start in life. You are not fit for service, Benjamin. You must not go into it again. You must select some profession that will be more to your taste. You are quite young enough to study law or medicine; or, if you prefer it, as all England is arming now for the Crimean war, you might enter the army. It would give me the greatest happiness to purchase a commission for you in some good regiment, or to enter you at some law school, or medical college."

"Too much! too much, my lord! You—you—" Benny began, but his voice was choked with emotion.

"Ah, Hurst, if you would but keep in mind that we are the sons of one Father, you would not then think or feel that I, the fortunate brother, could do too much for you, the unhappy one," said Lord Wellrose.

He spoke, of course, of the universal human brotherhood, yet Benny's pale face flushed at the words.

"Benny," said the Earl suddenly, yet with great gentleness, "do you remember the time when we first met?"

"In London, my lord?" inquired Benjamin.

"No, in Brighton."

A smile lighted up the wan features of the young man as he answered:

"Oh, yes, my lord. I remember well the little gentleman who emptied his own pockets and levied contributions from the purses of his little sisters, to buy shoes and stockings for the barefooted boy they met on the Esplanade. I remember well, my lord. I remember, also, how, a few days later, the little angels, as they seemed to me then, had me brought off the dark, snowy sidewalk into their bright, warm parlor, and gave me a piece of their Twelfth-day cake. I remember all the incidents of that evening. Such bright spots in my dark life were too few to be forgotten. I remember, my lord. And the first time I saw you in London, I recognized you at once. But it was not for me to speak."

"I very soon recognized you also, Hurst. And now remember, my boy, that this friendship of ours began in our boyhood. And trust me as an old friend," said the young

Earl, with a smile. And then he gave place to the almost forgotten chaplain, who came and sat down by the young prisoner and talked with him for a few moments, and then proposed prayer, in which Lord Wellrose joined them.

When they arose from their knees, the young Earl, looking around upon the bare, comfortless cell, said:

"I see, Benjamin, that you require a good many articles here to make you decently comfortable. I will call on the Governor and obtain leave to fit up this place for you. I will also send you some books to while away the tedious hours. Mr. Melliss, your counsel, will call this afternoon. I hope you will confide entirely in him. And another faithful young friend of yours will come to see you to-morrow. She bade me tell you so, with her love."

"Ah! my lord, how is she? I have been wishing to ask you all this time, but could not bear to breathe her name in a place like this. How is she?" earnestly inquired Benny.

"She is suffering from the shock she has received, of course. But she hopes to be well enough to come to see you to-morrow."

"Does she think me guilty of this murder?" inquired Benny, with quivering lips.

"No. She would stake her life upon your innocence. She will tell you so when she sees you to-morrow. Keep up your spirits, Benjamin," said the Earl, in the cheerful, encouraging tone which he had maintained during the whole interview.

"Oh, I thank Heaven that she, at least, does not think me guilty!" said the young man, earnestly.

"Very few people can believe you to be so, Benjamin," observed the Earl.

"Does she suspect who did the deed?" inquired the young prisoner hesitating, anxiously.

"No; but she suspects that you know who did it, and will not tell even to clear yourself. She suspects that you as shielding the real murderer, even at the risk of your own life," said the young Earl, gazing wistfully into the face of the prisoner, who started, turned white as death, and met the Earl's gaze with a look so conscious, that in an instant as by a flash of revelation, Lord Wellrose knew whom it was that Benjamin Hurst was shielding—Suzy's brother, who had fled, and left Benjamin Hurst to suffer for him—possibly even to die for him!

The conviction was so sudden and overwhelming that the young Earl felt himself obliged to sit down again to recover from the shock.

And at the same moment the door was opened by the guard, and Mr. Percy Melliss entered.

CHAPTER XXXIII.

COUNSEL AND CLIENT.

Stone walls do not a prison make,
Nor iron bars a cage,
For spirits pure and calm do take
These for a hermitage.—SIR WALTER RALEIGH.

THE Earl of Wellrose aroused himself from his preoccupation, and presented the counsel to his client.

And then, having promised to visit the prisoner again on the ensuing morning, he bade good day to both, and, attended by the chaplain, left the cell.

He took leave of the reverend gentleman at the gate, entered his carriage and directed his coachman to drive home. When he arrived at Cheviot House, he shut himself in his own apartments, and gave his mind to painful reflections.

He felt convinced that Benjamin Hurst was shielding the real murderer with his life · and that that murderer was William Juniper!

And yet, when he came to review the evidence given

before the Coroner's jury, he could find nothing whatever to connect young Juniper with the crime, while there was very much to criminate young Hurst.

When Suzy had been affronted by Mr. Stuart Fitzroy, it was not William Juniper, but Benjamin Hurst, who became fired with just anger.

When Stuart Fitzroy left the house, in a state of intoxication that rendered him incapable of taking care of himself, it was not William Juniper, but Benjamin Hurst who attended him.

And finally, when the body of the murdered man was discovered within three minutes after the fatal deed, it was not William Juniper, but Benjamin Hurst that was found standing over the corpse!

And yet in the very face of these facts the Earl of Wellrose felt convinced, not only of Benjamin Hurst's innocence but also of William Juniper's guilt.

Under these circumstances how should he proceed?

Should he denounce Suzy's brother to the proper authorities, and thus become the fatal agent in bringing him to trial, and perhaps to condemnation and death?

It was a horrible thought!

But even if he could bring himself to accuse William Juniper of the murder of Stuart Fitzroy, what evidence had he to put forward in support of his accusation?

None whatever, except his own firm moral conviction. And moral conviction however firm, is not legal evidence.

But yet, believing and feeling as he did, should he leave poor Benjamin Hurst to suffer for William Juniper, the innocent for the guilty?

His painful reverie was interrupted by the dressing bell, and by the entrance of his valet.

He dressed and went down to the drawing-room, where he found his mother and sisters, the still beautiful Duchess and her fair daughters.

They were discussing some matter of very distressing interest, for even their fair, calm faces bore signs of much disturbance.

"How very shocking!" murmured the Duchess with pale cheeks.

Lord Wellrose thought his mother was referring to the recent murder in Piccadilly, and as she had not addressed herself to him, he did not feel called upon to make any comment. The next words undeceived him.

"How many did you say were injured, mamma?" inquired Lady Hester.

"There were thirteen unfortunates killed outright, my love, and thirty-nine dangerously wounded," answered the Duchess.

"Why, what has happened?" inquired Lord Wellrose, aroused from his abstraction.

"Oh, a shocking accident, my dear, on the Paris and Marseilles Railroad!—A collision between the express and a freight train, in which a number of lives have been lost or endangered," answered the Duchess with a shudder.

"Shocking, indeed! Why, I had not heard of it!" said the Earl.

"The news came by telegraph to the evening papers. There are but few particulars given. But I suppose we shall see all about it in to-morrow morning's papers," replied the Duchess.

And at that moment the sliding doors were run back, and the groom of the chambers appeared, and said:

"Her Grace is served."

"My father does not dine at home to-day?" inquired the Earl, as he gave his mother his arm, to lead her in to dinner.

"No, he is at Windsor. There is a cabinet council," answered the Duchess, and the subject was dropped

The next morning the young Earl called by appointment

at Park Lane, to escort Suzy on her distressing visit to poor Benjamin Hurst.

On reaching the house, he was shown at once into the Rose Parlor where he found Suzy with her bonnet on, waiting for him. The poor girl had changed, even within the last twenty-four hours. She was fearfully pale and wasted though her manner was more composed than it had been on the preceding day.

"Oh, Lord Wellrose, you did not quiet me with false hopes yesterday, did you? You would not have given me false hopes even for that purpose, would you?" she inquired, in a beseeching voice.

"Indeed I would not, my dearest one!" he answered earnestly.

"And Benny is really in no imminent danger?"

"Indeed, no. He is nearly sure to be acquitted."

"Nearly sure!" sighed Suzy. "Oh, Lord Wellrose, how awful to think that there should be the remotest chance of his conviction!" she cried, wringing her hands.

"Believe me, I do not think that there is. The evidence is not sufficient to convict him; and besides, we have retained Mr. Percy Melliss, the greatest criminal lawyer in Europe, for his defence."

"Oh, a hundred thousand thanks for all your goodness—" began Suzy, but the Earl gently stopped her by inquiring if they should set out for their visit then.

She readily assented, and he led her to the carriage that stood waiting at the door.

"And oh, Lord Wellrose, I wished to speak to you about another matter. You must know that my brother left me four days ago to proceed to Paris on my affairs."

"I understood so; yes," replied the Earl, wondering.

"He was to see the manager of the Theatre Français by appointment, and make arrangements for my engagement there."

"Yes," said the Earl, seeing that Suzy paused.

"Well, he should have been there the evening of the same day upon which he left here."

"Certainly."

"And now, the queerest part of the business is, that he did not get there at all!"

"No!" exclaimed the Earl, all the more interested because of the suspicion that had entered his mind, connecting Suzy's missing brother with the murder of Stuart Fitzroy.

"No, indeed. And while I have been waiting here, expecting every hour either to see or to hear from my brother, this morning comes a telegram from the manager of the Theatre Français, inquiring what has delayed my agent, that he does not come to treat with him according to agreement. Now, what do you think of that, Lord Wellrose?"

"He may have been taken sick on the road," suggested his lordship, doubtfully.

"So he may; but then he would have written, or he would have got some one else to write," said Suzy. "And oh, Lord Wellrose, there has been a most awful railway accident in France!" she added, growing paler.

"I know it, my love; a very horrible catastrophe indeed, profoundly to be deplored. But it does not concern your brother in the least."

"Ah, I don't know. He may have been one of the victims."

"But, my dearest, your brother was travelling, if I understand you, from Dover to Paris. And this accident happened between Paris and Marseilles."

"Yes, I know; I thought of that, but still—" She paused and sighed.

"Still?" echoed the Earl, with an inquiring smile.

"Still I fear—I know not what, or why. Perhaps I am a woman naturally born to fears,' as poor Constance says

And where there is doubt or danger, I fear the worst rationally or irrationally."

As she spoke, the carriage drew up before the gloomy walls of Newgate.

Upon the Earl's application, they were at once admitted within the building, and conducted first to the chaplain's room.

The venerable man received the young Earl with grave respect. And when the latter presented Suzy, he shook her hands with much kindness of manner.

At the Earl's request, he willingly consented to accompany them to the cell of the prisoner Hurst.

He rang for the proper officer to attend the party, and they immediately went thither.

They found the young prisoner in consultation with his counsel, who had arrived about an hour before.

"We interrupt you," said the chaplain, who preceded the party into the cell.

"Not at all. I was just leaving," replied Mr. Percy Melliss, gathering up his papers to go.

He shook hands with his client, bade him keep up his spirits, and then came out of the cell and bowed to the Earl and the lady, and hurried away.

"That is Percy Melliss, the great criminal advocate. I should have presented him to you, had he not hurried away so fast," said the Earl, as they, in their turn, entered the cell.

The care of the Earl had already improved its appearance.

The stone floor was covered with a thick carpet, two comfortable chairs and a small stand covered with books stood against the wall, and clean bedding and white draperies covered the bunk.

"I owe you many thanks, Lord Wellrose, for the many comforts you have so kindly sent me. The upholsterer was here as soon as the doors were opened this morning, to fit up my cell. I thank your lordship very much indeed!" said Benjamin, earnestly, as he arose to welcome the Earl.

"There, there! I have done nothing worth mentioning, my good fellow. But here is a friend come to see you," said the Earl, as he handed Suzy into the cell.

"Oh, my dear Benny!" exclaimed Suzy, in a low voice, as she held out both hands to the young prisoner and burst into tears.

"Don't cry. Indeed it is not so very bitter to be here, when friends are so kind," said Benny, earnestly.

"Ah! poor brother! You have had so little kindness and sympathy in your life, that you reconcile yourself even to a prison when it brings friends around you," wept Suzy.

"And who would not? 'Love is the greatest good in the world.' And I did not know that any loved me, until I got into this trouble," said the young man, smiling.

"Oh, Benny!" sighed Suzy. Then changing her tone as she sat down beside him, she said, "Benny, you are doing now exactly what you did fifteen years ago. You are innocently suffering for the guilt of another. You are shielding with your own person the real criminal! Oh, Benny! if not for your own sake, for *my* sake, clear yourself by giving him up to justice. Yes, even if he were my own brother, I should still implore you not to sacrifice yourself for him, but to clear your own innocent name and fame by giving him up to justice," said Suzy, utterly unsuspicious that it *was* her own brother, for whom the poor young man was offering himself up.

"Dear Suzy," said the prisoner, "If you really care for me, speak no more of this. I cannot stir from the ground I have taken."

"Then you admit that you are *shielding* some one?" inquired the weeping girl.

"No, I do not admit anything of the sort," said Benny

gently. "But listen, Suzy. I am in no sort of danger of conviction. My counsel assures me that the prosecution has no case to go upon at all—that I shall be certainly acquitted by the jury."

"Oh, Benny, yes! but will you be acquitted by public opinion? Will not suspicion cling to you for the rest of your life? Will not you still suffer and continue to suffer for the guilt of another?"

"Suzy, even if your theory were correct, which I do not admit, still, would it not be better that I should suffer some suspicions than that another, more unfortunate than guilty, should suffer the extreme penalty of the law; and all connected with him should be plunged in unmerited shame and sorrow?"

"No," answered Suzy, with sudden energy. "'Let justice be done, though the Heavens fall.' A guilty man had better die for his crime than an innocent one suffer the slightest unjust suspicion through him! What do you think, Lord Wellrose?" she inquired, turning to the Earl, confident also of his answer.

"I agree with you perfectly; a falsely accused man should clear himself at whatever cost to the real criminal," answered the Earl.

"But if the falsely accused man should be quite alone in the world, while the guilty man should have father and mother, brothers and sisters, who would be brought to shame and sorrow by his exposure and punishment, then would not the falsely accused be justified at least in keeping silence?" earnestly inquired Benny.

"By no means," emphatically answered the Earl.

As he spoke the door was opened, a visitor was announced, and a lady dressed with Quakerly simplicity, in a gray gown, shawl and bonnet, entered the cell.

She bowed to the lady and gentleman present, without recognizing either, and then advanced to speak to the young prisoner.

"Benjamin Hurst! how little you are changed except in growth! Benjamin, I should be so glad to meet you again, if it were anywhere else than here," she said, taking his hand and pressing it affectionately.

But the young prisoner gazed on her in dumb amazement.

"Why, Benny, you don't seem to know me at all! And I should have known *you* anywhere! Look at me, my boy Don't you recognize me now?"

"Miss Rachel Wood!" exclaimed Benny, in joyful surprise, starting up as if he would have embraced her, then recollecting himself, blushing and sinking back on his seat, but adding, in a more subdued manner: "Oh, I am so rejoiced to see you! It was so good of you to come! And, Miss Rachel, I want to tell you at once, I did not commit the murder for which I am to be tried."

"I did not believe you did, Benny! But I am glad to hear you say so, for all that," said Rachel, warmly.

"Ah, but he knows who did! And he is suffering innocently for the guilty, just as he did when he was a poor friendless child!" said Suzy, suddenly breaking into the conversation.

The quiet, Quakerly looking woman turned with surprise to gaze upon the elegantly dressed young lady who had spoken to her.

"You do not recognize me, Miss Rachel. There is some one else besides Benny, it seems, who has a short memory for faces. I am Suzy, and I am very glad to see you again," said the young lady, offering her hand.

"Suzy Juniper!" echoed Rachel Wood in surprise, as she took the delicately gloved little hand and held it while she gazed in the lovely face of the young girl.

"Yes, Suzy Juniper! And now do you recognize me?" inquired Suzy, smiling.

"Now I do. But I should scarcely have done so, if you

had not told me your name. You are more changed than Benjamin Hurst is," said the quiet, Quakerly woman, gazing on the lovely young creature before her.

"Externally I am. But not at heart, for I am *so* glad to see you, Miss Rachel! It is like old times. Are you not a little glad to see me, too?" inquired Suzy, in a plaintive voice.

"Indeed I am, my dear, and greatly surprised," said Rachel Wood, taking the kiss that Suzy offered in the overflowing love of her faithful young heart.

"And the Earl of Wellrose? Surely, Miss Rachel, you know Lord Wellrose? He is one of the visitors of the Duchess' school, where you are the matron," said Suzy.

And the Earl, at the mention of his own name, arose and bowed, and resumed his seat.

"I have the honor of some slight acquaintance with his lordship,' said Rachel, returning the bow, "but the gentlemen visitors of the school have more to do with the teacher's department than with the matron's."

"Rachel!" broke in Suzy, once more, "I began by telling you that Benjamin Hurst is doing now in his manhood precisely what he did fifteen years ago, in his friendless childhood! He is shielding the guilty at the risk of his own life! Oh, Rachel, please unite with us in trying to persuade him to clear himself from the false imputation of this crime."

"Miss Rachel, I implore you, do not attempt to do so. Do not distress yourself or me by urging a course that I cannot pursue," entreated the young man.

"We must trust in Providence to the clearing up of this mystery. It is evident that Mr. Hurst will not clear himself at the expense of another, even when that other is the guilty party. Let us not pursue the discussion," said Lord Wellrose.

Benjamin Hurst thanked his lordship with a grateful look.

And soon after this the visitors departed, after having promised to return the next day.

Suzy went home and telegraphed, and then wrote to the manager of the Theatre Français, to say that her brother and accredited agent, Mr. William Juniper had left London for Paris on the third of the current month, to treat with him concerning an engagement for herself and troupe at the theatre; that she had been daily and hourly expecting to see him, or to hear from him on the subject of his mission; but up to the date of her letter, she had neither seen nor heard from him; that she was suffering great anxiety on her brother's account; and she besought the manager to have inquiries set on foot in Paris, as she feared that her brother had met with foul play.

The manager wrote back by return mail to say that he had notified the Parisian police as to the disappearance of the missing young gentleman, and that he would write again to inform Mademoiselle, as soon as anything should be ascertained on the subject.

But day after day passed and no news of William Juniper came from the other side of the Channel, and Suzy's anxiety daily increased.

The term of her engagement at the Covent Garden theatre expired, and she positively declined all overtures toward a reëngagement there, or a new engagement anywhere else.

The newspapers reported that Mademoiselle Arielle had abruptly left the stage, and left it for ever; that she was suffering from a slight indisposition, and had retired only for a short season; that she had entirely lost her voice, and would never sing a note again; that she was about to start on a professional tour through the United States of America; that she was going to be married to a German grand duke; that she was going into a French convent to take the vail; that she had gone to the Insane Asylum.

Every rumor was inconsistent with every other.

And every new report contradicted the last preceding one.

Meanwhile Suzy lingered in London, living in strict retirement at her little palace in Park Lane, seeing no company but the Earl of Wellrose, and going nowhere but to Newgate, to visit the poor prisoner there.

Benny bore his confinement with his usual patience and fortitude, and waited for the opening of the Sessions at the Old Bailey.

A fortnight had passed in this way, when one morning an event occurred that changed the whole aspect of affairs so far as the young prisoner at Newgate was concerned.

It was the day before the opening of the Sessions.

CHAPTER XXXIV.

STARTLING NEWS.

Ring out the old! Ring in the new!—TENNYSON.

THE Earl of Wellrose was sitting with Benny in his cell, and speaking words of comfort and encouragement, to prepare him to meet his arraignment with cheerfulness and strength, when the door was suddenly thrown open, and Percy Melliss, accompanied by the governor of the jail, and the high sheriff of the county, entered the cell. The faces of all three bore signs of unusual disturbance, though it seemed to be of a pleasant nature.

Lord Wellrose and Benjamin Hurst looked at them and at each other, expecting—they knew not what.

The three new-comers bowed to the Earl and then Mr. Percy Melliss turned to Benny, and said, with some excitement:

"Mr. Hurst, you can bear trouble with great fortitude Can you bear happiness as well?"

Benny looked at his questioner with surprise, and then, as a gleam of his old humor twinkled in his eyes, he answered:

"I don't know. The experiment has never been tried upon me."

"I think you can bear it, however," said the lawyer, with a smile. "Now listen, Mr. Hurst. And Lord Wellrose, you too will be astonished! I am glad, however, that Miss Suzy is not here to-day. If she had been, our communication must have been deferred until her departure.

"It seems to me that you are taking unusual pains to prepare us for something," said Lord Wellrose, with a smile not devoid of curiosity.

"Yes, I am preparing you for something. Benjamin Hurst!" he said, turning to the prisoner, "we bring an order for your immediate discharge. You are entirely cleared from all imputation of guilt. You are a free man from this hour."

"Thank God!" exclaimed the astonished and delighted prisoner, even without knowing or suspecting the cause of his deliverance. "Oh, thank God!"

And he burst into tears of joy and gratitude.

"Mr. Hurst, I am delighted," added Percy Melliss, warmly grasping and shaking the hand of the young man.

"I congratulate you with all my heart though I do not, in the least, understand the turn affairs have taken. God bless you, Benjamin Hurst," said Lord Wellrose, earnestly shaking his hand.

"Thanks, thanks," said Benny, half choked with emotion.

The Governor of the gaol then begged permission to read the order for the prisoner's discharge, and he read it.

"But how came all this about?" inquired the Earl.

"Let us get out of this place first, and then I will tell you. It is a strange story, not without its sorrow for some concerned, though in fact my pleasure at the vindication of my client here made me forget that. Come! I have a four-wheeled cab at the door. Come, Mr. Hurst. My Lord will you accompany us?

"Certainly," said Lord Wellrose, rising.

Benny was already standing with his hat in his hand.

They left the dark and gloomy prison and went out into the street, where the afternoon sun was shining brightly.

"We will drive to the Morley House and take a private parlor for an hour or two, if your lordship pleases?" said Mr. Melliss.

"Certainly," said the Earl.

And they all entered a cab that was waiting before the door, and Mr. Melliss gave the order to drive to the Morley House.

When they arrived there, Mr. Melliss, who acted for the little party, got out and engaged a private parlor, to which he ordered refreshments to be brought, and in which the three soon found themselves comfortably seated around a table, with a bottle of light wine and a plate of biscuits before them.

Here Mr. Percy Melliss told his strange story. It was in brief this:

That among the victims of the fatal accident on the Paris and Marseilles Railroad, was William Juniper, who, though not instantly killed, was fatally injured.

He had been dragged from beneath the ruins of a railway carriage, and conveyed, in an insensible condition, to the nearest house, where, for several days, he lingered in a state of coma.

Just before his death, as often happens in such cases, he came to his senses, and to the full consciousness of his condition.

His first act was then to ask for the attendance of a clergyman and a magistrate.

And in answer to his call, the venerable cure of the parish and a notary from the village came to his bedside.

To them he made a full confession of the unintentional murder that he had committed, and that had driven him from his native country.

This confession was taken down from his lips in writing, and duly sworn to, signed, witnessed, sealed and dispatched to the proper authorities in London.

It had arrived on that day. And the order for the release of Benjamin Hurst had been immediately sent to the sheriff and the governor of Newgate.

These two officers, glad to be the emissaries of deliverance to the prisoner, were on their way to his cell, for the purpose of discharging him, when they were joined by Mr. Percy Melliss, who, ignorant of what had happened, had come for a last consultation with his client before the trial.

The sheriff told him of the pleasing nature of their errand, and he was of course sincerely delighted with the turn affairs had taken.

So Mr. Percy Melliss had scarcely heard the good news two minutes before he communicated it to his client.

"But, oh Heaven! this news that has saved me, what will it do for *her*, the dead man's sister?" sighed Benny.

"She is just and right-minded. And although there will be the natural grief for the lost brother, yet she will suffer less than she would have done, had you remained under the heavy imputation of blood-guiltiness. She will know, besides, that there has been no murder in the case, since there was no intention to kill. In due time she will take comfort," said Mr. Percy Melliss.

"Ah, she will be awfully shocked by the news. Who will venture to break it to her?" murmured the young man sorrowfully.

"That will I," answered the Earl of Wellrose gravely, as he arose from the table.

"Ah, my lord, it will be a most painful task!" said Benny.

"I know it," murmured the Earl. And then, after a pause, he said: "Mr. Hurst, will you do me a favor?"

"Assuredly, my lord."

"Will you then, follow my advice to you—which is, to take a room here for the present, and wait till I can have an opportunity of consulting with you about your future career?"

"I will, Lord Wellrose, with thanks," replied Benjamin, who, from some occult reason, arising out of their unconscious blood relationship, or from some hidden sympathy or pure love and trust, or from all these causes combined, never felt the slightest sense of humiliation in receiving favors from his unknown brother.

"Quite right. Good-day, then. I will see you to-morrow morning. Good-day, Mr. Melliss," said the Earl. And bowing to both his late companions, he left the room.

Outside he took a hansom and drove to Park Lane to break the news of her brother's death to Suzy.

He sent in his card, and in a few moments was invited into the drawing-room, where he was received by Mrs. Brown.

The housekeeper's face wore the traces of recent tears, and her manner was very grave as she greeted Lord Wellrose, and said:

"I hope your lordship will excuse Miss Juniper this morning. She has just heard of the shocking death of her brother, and—"

"She has heard it then! From whom? Who has incautiously shocked her with the news?" exclaimed the Earl.

"No one did, sir. She received a letter this morning from the French priest who attended her brother on his death-bed. He died a Christian, I am happy to say, sir. Poor young man! His head was a little turned with the company he kept, but his heart was not bad," said the housekeeper, willing to say all the good she could of the poor boy cut off in the flower of his wild youth.

"No," said the Earl. And then, "How is Miss Juniper this morning?"

"Sir, she has been in hysterics ever since she got the news until about fifteen minutes ago, when we gave her an opiate, which composed her. She is now sleeping quietly."

"Keep her so," said the Earl, as he arose to go. "And please to tell her when she awakes that I have been here, and will call at this hour to-morrow, when I hope she will be able to receive me."

And he bowed and left the house.

The next morning, when he called at Park Lane, Suzy received him in her Rose Parlor. And though she was deadly pale, she was perfectly calm and collected, and she met him with quiet courtesy.

In reply to his expressions of sympathy and condolence, and to his implied rather than expressed questions as to herself, she answered that she should leave that day for France to be present at her brother's funeral; that soon afterward she should sail for Australia, to make a visit of duty to her parents.

"They must inevitably hear of their bereavement, you know, Lord Wellrose. And it is better that they should have the comfort of a visit from me at the same time," said Suzy.

"You are quite right, dearest," said the Earl kindly.

He staid a long time with her that morning, and with a promise to meet her at the railway station, and escort her to Dover to see her on board the Calais boat, he left her.

From Park Lane he went immediately to Trafalgar Square, and called at the Morley House to see Benny.

The young man received his visitor in his small bed room on the third floor—the only apartment that his limited means could command.

"Now, my dear fellow, I have come on business. I wish to settle with you to-day about your future career. You are quite young enough to strike out into a new path. Now what path would you like to take—the church, the law medicine, the army, or the navy? Take time to think, before deciding," said the Earl kindly.

"If I might choose—" began Benny. And then he blushed like a girl, and paused.

"Choose! It is what I desire you to do. What would you like?"

"All young England is arming for the Crimean war. I should like to enter the army."

Ah, poor boy! He had never known his father, yet he had inherited his father's martial passion. William Douglas had also wanted "to enter the army."

Lord Wellrose reflected for a few moments, during which Benny misinterpreted his silence, and hastened to say:

"Ah, forgive me, my lord! I spoke impulsively and without discretion. I know now how improper my wish is, since I have not the physical powers of endurance that would fit me to be a common soldier in war time, nor yet the education that would prepare me for the duties of an officer. You are right, my lord."

"You mistake me, my dear Hurst. I have been turning over in my mind the best and quietest way of meeting your views. And I have found it now. I have a young friend—Ensign Charley Blount, of the —— Regiment of foot. His regiment is ordered to the Crimea, and he does not want to go there. He wishes to sell out and stay at home. Good! His commission shall be purchased for you. You shall enter the army and go to the war, Mr. Hurst; and although you enter it only as an Ensign, which is the lowest grade of commissioned officer, yet I feel persuaded that you will rise."

CHAPTER XXXV.

BENJAMIN'S NEW NAME.

> Howe'er it be, it seems to me,
> 'Tis only noble to be good.
> Kind hearts are more than coronets,
> And simple faith than Norman blood.—TENNYSON.

AND since "'tis only noble to be good," the young Earl of Wellrose was noble, in the best and highest sense of the word, for he was good—and not only good, but wise and brave.

So thought poor Benjamin Hurst, as he gazed upon his unknown brother and generous benefactor, with a heart too full of gratitude for words.

"This is the third day of this month. The regiment is expected to sail on the first of the next month. You will have four weeks for preparation; ample time; and if I can give you any assistance in any shape, I am very heartily at your service," said Lord Wellrose cordially.

"My lord," faltered Benny, in a voice choked with emotion, and with eyes full of tears, "I cannot express the thanks that fill my heart to breaking. Oh, my good lord, I am not worthy of your goodness, and if you knew all my past life, you would not think me fit to fill the honorable position your generosity would obtain for me! I do wish t enter the army, but I am only fit to be a common soldie and scarcely fit for that; for what honest soldier would con sort, if he knew it, with a returned convict? Not one Ah, no! ah, no! my woeful past can never be blotted out said Benny, burying his face in his hands and groaning deeply.

The young Earl laid his hand affectionately on the outcast's shoulder and said:

"Your past life of bitter wrong and unmerited shame can

and shall be blotted out. You are but a youth still. You shall begin life anew from this day. You are true, honest, courageous and very intelligent. You have educated yourself under difficulties that might well have discouraged the firmest heart. In the midst of undeserved degradation you have prepared yourself for an honorable career, and you shall have it," said the Earl, with much emotion.

"Oh, my lord, my lord, you overwhelm me with your goodness! But still I must tell you, that you do not know all of my past life. If you did you would never think me a fit—" Benny's voice broke down.

"My boy, I *do* know all your past life, and I pronounce you blameless in it all; and I have nothing but sympathy and compassion, and finally forgetfulness, to bestow upon it," said the Earl kindly.

"Oh, Lord Wellrose, there is something behind that you do not know, and that you must be told before you get this Ensign's commission for me, and throw me into the company of gentlemen," said Benny.

"Well, well, my dear boy, if there be any circumstance connected with your past life with which you think I am not acquainted, and which you wish to tell me, speak now understanding, however, that it will make no difference in my views and purposes toward you."

"Ah, Lord Wellrose, you think you know the worst, but you do not. You know, indeed, that I was brought up among thieves and beggars, and taught to do their deeds."

"You were not to be blamed, but very much to be pitied for that misfortune."

"You know that I was tried for burglary and convicted, and sent to the penal colonies, where I passed fourteen years in the company of felons."

"I know that you were most cruelly and unjustly convicted, and that you passed your time there blamelessly, doing your appointed work, and using every opportunity for self-improvement, and that you educated yourself in the face of the most appalling obstacles. Yes, I know all that. What more am I to be told as 'the worst?'"

"My lord, you know that I was the companion of thieves, that I was a convict; but you do not know, that before all that I was—" Benny's voice broke down, so that he could scarcely go on. "I was—the child of sin and shame, nameless and abandoned from my birth."

The Earl took the outcast's hand, and held it affectionately while he gravely replied:

"I know the whole story, as far as any one knows it—as far even as you know it yourself. The sin and the shame were not yours—*not yours*," he repeated.

"No, not mine," sighed Benny, "but yet the penalty and the punishment must fall on me; for I put it to you, Lord Wellrose—I put it to you, in common honor, whether you can properly purchase a commission for me that will put me in the company of gentlemen—whether these gentlemen, if they knew my antecedents, would not demand my expulsion from among them?"

"My dear Benjamin, if they should know your antecedents without knowing your true character—if they should know your penal sufferings without knowing your perfect guilelessness—no doubt their judgment would be harsh and their actions severe. But since they cannot know the whole, they shall not know a part. Half truth is always so deceptive! They shall know nothing of your past, Benjamin. It is, in fact, none of their business."

"Oh, Lord Wellrose, my very name—my name, which has figured so much in the police reports connected with this murder—my name would betray me!" said Benny despondently.

"I have been thinking of that, and have been providing for it," said the Earl.

Benjamin looked up inquiringly.

"The name you bear, that of Benjamin Hurst, is not your own."

"No," said the poor outcast sadly, "I have not even a legal right to the name I bear, since I am not the son of Magdalene Hurst; nor have I even a Christian right to it, since I have never been baptized."

"Then give it up. Cast it off with the slough of your past life. Begin your new life with a new name—a name that I will give you, if you will accept it at my hands—a right noble old name too, my family name—Seton Douglas! And Heaven knows that you may have a natural, if not a legal right to it, for though my dear father is a sort of saint, yet I have heard that there have been some wild men in our family. What do you say to the name, Benjamin?"

Benny had turned pale as death. In his secret soul he had lately believed that he was a disowned or unknown relative of that family, and he had longed with a hopeless unuttered longing, to bear that very name.

"Oh, Lord Wellrose, nothing on earth that you could bestow on me would make me so happy and so grateful as the possession of that name. I will never do anything to dishonor it!" he said.

"I am very sure that you will not. So, as you have never been baptized, we will go to church some day and have you baptized and registered as Benjamin Seton Douglas. And when your commission shall be purchased, as it shall be in a day or two, you will enter her Majesty's service as Ensign Seton Douglas. And now I must leave you for the present. God bless you!" said the Earl, rising to go.

"One moment, my lord. I distrust myself sadly. Have I education enough to do the duties of an ensign? I know nothing whatever of military tactics," said Benny, modestly.

"You have education enough. You do not require to know much of military tactics to be an ensign. And even if you did, the drill sergeant of your company would soon instruct you. But the duty of an ensign is very simple—just to bear the colors of his company. Besides—bless us! —do you suppose that half the young gentlemen who receive commissions in the army have graduated at military academies? By no means. Not a tenth part of them. They have to go into camp or garrison and be drilled by a sergeant. And some of them are too lazy, stupid and careless to learn. You are neither, I am sure, so take heart of grace," said the Earl, smiling happily as he left the room, leaving Benny also happier than he had ever been in his life.

Lord Wellrose, since he had seen so much of Benjamin, and noticed the extraordinary likeness the poor outcast bore to himself, the Earl, and heard so much of his early history, became gradually convinced of some unknown or unacknowledged relationship existing between them.

"I feel sure that the poor boy is our cousin in some degree—perhaps in a very near degree. He may be our first cousin. At all events, since he has been so cruelly abandoned and bitterly wronged, I will do what I can to repair his injuries and atone for the sins of his parents," he thought, as he entered his cab and gave the order:

"To Cheviot House."

He thought of speaking to his mother of Benjamin's sad story. Ah! if he only had done so! But the subject was a delicate one for him to broach, and so, upon reflection, he abandoned the idea.

The next morning the Earl of Wellrose set about the business that was so dear to his heart. His name, influence and wealth so soon effected his object, that in two days more he had the happiness of placing in his *protegé's* hand the document that commissioned him as Ensign Benjamin Seton Douglas, in her Majesty's —— regiment of Foot. He received his commission on the sixth of the month, with orders to join his Regiment on the twenty-first.

The same day Benjamin called by appointment on Suzy. This was the first occasion upon which he had seen her since her brother's death and death-bed confession, and his own consequent release from prison.

Suzy received him in a plainly furnished little sitting-room. She had never occupied the gay and beautiful Rose Parlor since the death of her brother. She was dressed in deep mourning, and it may have been that the intense blackness of her dress made her face appear even paler than it was, for it seemed marble white now.

She advanced to meet her visitor very kindly, saying softly.

"Oh, Benny, I am so rejoiced that you are free, and fully vindicated! Oh, my dear boy, when I think of the sacrifice you were about to make for me—more than the sacrifice of your life—when I think of how you meant to die with a load of unmerited ignominy on your memory for my sake, to save my brother's life and my name from reproach, O Benny, I think that I and all my fame and all my fortune, if I could give all to you, would be too little to repay you! But you are vindicated and released. Oh, I rejoice, and thank God that you are, my brother! my dearest brother!" she said, taking both his hands and pressing them to her heart.

"Dear Suzy, it is very sweet to hear you say this—very sweet and comforting. But, little sister, I cannot fully rejoice in my freedom, since it has come at such a cost to you," said the young man, with emotion, as he took the seat she offered him.

"Don't, Benny, don't say that. *It is best as it is.* Since my poor misguided brother had the misfortune to do that fatal deed that made him a fugitive from justice, and left you to suffer unjustly in his place, it is best—oh, so much best—as it is! Think, Benny, deep as my sorrow is for the sudden loss of my poor brother, how much deeper it must have been had you suffered death in his stead, for his deed! Think what my anguish and despair must have been, to have discovered that when it was too late! Benny, the knowledge would have sent me to my grave, or to a lunatic asylum. It is best as it is. This I can bear. I have the comfort of knowing, through his death-bed confession, that he did not intentionally commit murder. The man Fitzroy richly deserved to be knocked down by the brother of the woman whom he had insulted and traduced. But his death was as much an accident as if he had fallen down. My brother was guiltless of intentional homicide; and you are vindicated and released. It is best as it is. And now let us talk of something else—of your new name and your commission. Ensign Douglas, I congratulate you!" she said, with a smile, as she offered him her hand.

He took the little hand and pressed it to his lips.

"Oh, my dear Benny, I am so glad, for your sake!" she continued, now speaking earnestly. "I honor the Earl of Wellrose even much more than I ever did before, for his appreciation of and kindness to you. You are going out as an Ensign; come back as a General, Benny! And then who knows but it may be, 'Rise up, Sir Benjamin Douglas!' Stranger things have happened," she said, with a smile.

Benny laughed.

"All cannot rise like you, dear Suzy. I shall do my best; but I never expect to rise higher than a lieutenancy, at the very most," he said.

"Where is your regiment stationed, Benny?" she asked.

"At Southampton."

"And when do you join it?"

"On the 20th of this month."

"Just two weeks from to-day," said Suzy, after some little calculation.

"Yes."

"And when does the regiment sail for the Crimea?"

"On or about the first of next month, Suzy."

"Let me see: an ensign is the color-bearer of his company, is he not?" she inquired, with some interest.

"Yes, in a company of Foot; but in a company of Horse, the color-bearer is called a cornet," explained the young man.

"I wish you had been commissioned as a cornet in a company of horse, then. I like Horse better than Foot," said Suzy.

"So do I; but 'beggars must not—' You know the proverb, Suzy."

"Oh, yes; and you are very fortunate—very, very fortunate! And the Earl is very kind. Commissions are not always to be got, even by those who are able to buy them—and a *choice* of commissions hardly ever. Well, so you are the color-bearer of your company! Then I shall do myself the honor of presenting your company with as handsome a pair of colors as can possibly be manufactured. And, mind you, be sure to plant them on the towers of St. Petersburg, if there be any towers there—I know nothing about them myself."

"I will do it, if I die for it!" said Benny, rashly, never stopping to consider that the allies might never be permitted to reach St. Petersburg, or that, if they did, *his* regiment might not be with them, or if it should be, *he* might not be living; he never thought, in a word, of the thousand accidents that might prevent him from keeping his rash vow—a thousand chances to one against his ever doing so.

"All right! I knew you would, Benny," she said, as if it were a feat already accomplished.

"Now, dear sister of my heart, tell me of your own plans and purposes. Lord Wellrose told me that you intended to go out to Australia. Do you still really mean to take that long voyage?"

"Yes, Benny. I have never been there, you know. And I have not seen my parents since they went there, four years ago. It seems a long time. I must go now to see my father and mother, and try to comfort them for the loss of my brother. They are growing old now, Benny," she added sadly.

"Yes," answered the young man, "but they are growing old in much peace and comfort, secured to them by their dutiful daughter. And they have the happiness of seeing all their children healthy and prosperous."

"Yes, except one," sighed Suzy.

"How long shall you be absent, Suzy?" inquired the young man.

"Many months—perhaps a year or more, Benny," she said, growing very serious. "Benny, my brother, my brother, who would have died for my sake, Benny, I will tell you a secret. I am going out to Australia, it is true, to see and to comfort my aged father and mother. But, Benny, I shall stay out there to give the Earl of Wellrose time to forget me. This is my secret."

Benjamin looked at her in unbounded astonishment.

"Yes," she said, smiling sadly. "I know what you are thinking of, my brother. You are thinking how, a little while ago, I was nearly breaking my heart about the Earl of Wellrose. Very true, Benny; but that was because, while I loved and honored him so much, and while he visited me every day, I had no assurance from him that he loved or respected me, or had any good intentions toward me. Your timely interference, delicately conducted as such a thing possibly could be, brought matters to a crisis. The Earl came and told me that he loved me, and that he wished to make me his wife just so soon as he could obtain his father's and his mother's consent. That it would take time and reason to gain this. But that, after waiting a reasonable time for their consent, if they should still withhold it, he should fee. not only free to marry me without their consent, but also bound in honor, as well as drawn by love, to do so."

"He is a pure and noble soul!" said Benny, with enthusiasm, though not without a natural pang at seeing how utterly Suzy was lost to *his* hopes forever.

"Yes," said the young girl warmly. "He is indeed a pure and noble soul. His words made me very happy, so happy that I forgot myself, so happy that I allowed him to place a betrothal ring on my finger and to bind himself to me for ever. He had selected it that morning, and brought it to put upon my finger as the pledge of his faith, so that I might never doubt him, again. See, here is the ring. I could show you the motto on it only I do not wish to draw it from my finger. The motto is—*In truth*," she said, holding out her hand and exhibiting a pure solitaire diamond of priceless value, plainly set in a heavy gold circle.

"I have noticed it before, though I did not know it was the Earl's gift. It is a gem of the purest water, I should judge. And I notice that you have not lately worn any other ring."

"Never! For love of this ring, I have discarded all others from my hand, even the rich ruby ring that I liked so much because it was the gift of the Empress of Russia, and she is such a lovely lady. I sang before Her Majesty three times in the Opera-house of St. Petersburg. I shall never sing on any stage again," said Suzy, with a sigh.

"No, certainly—if you marry the Earl," said Benny.

"I shall never marry the Earl," said the young girl very gravely. "And that brings me back to what I was about to say of my motives. For a little time I was very happy in the Earl's love—forgetting that I was unfit to be his wife."

"Unfit to be his wife, Suzy!" echoed the young man, who, in his own blind and passionate love, believed her fit to be a king's wife

"Yes," she said calmly, "for he is the Earl of Wellrose, and he will be the Duke of Cheviot. And I am the daughter of a poor stage carpenter, and only by accident elevated to be a popular opera singer. I do not blame his family for objecting to me; for though, in my silly vanity, I once boasted that actresses and opera singers had *often* been raised by marriage to the peerage, yet I know now that this has been but seldom so, and that these cases were very exceptional ones, by no means to be taken as precedents or examples, I know that I, the poor stage carpenter's daughter, developed into an opera singer, am not fit to be a countess now and a duchess hereafter. The very idea terrifies me."

"But I thought you were happy and contented in the Earl's love," said Benny, simply.

"And so I was—very happy and confident in the Earl's love; deliriously happy and confident. But the awful events of the last few weeks have sobered me down, and brought me to my senses, Benny—have made me remember that it is not fit I should marry the Earl and bring discord into his family. Oh, yes, I honor the Earl as much as ever—as much as ever! Ah, Heaven truly knows I honor him more than ever! And my soul is satisfied with the knowledge of his esteem for me. And it is this satisfaction which gives me strength to make a sacrifice for his sake—to renounce him for his own good. I will not shock or wound him by giving him up suddenly. But I will go out to Australia, as in duty bound, to visit and console my poor old father and mother. And I will stay out there until absence shall have broken the force of habit, and the Earl of Wellrose shall have forgotten his indiscreet love for the lowly-born opera singer."

"I do not think that he will ever forget that," said Benny, judging the young Earl's heart by his own.

"Ah, yes; I am not so vain as to believe otherwise," sighed Suzy.

"But tell me; does Lord Wellrose know or suspect this design of deserting him?" gravely inquired the young man.

"Why, no; assuredly not! If I were to let him even suspect it, that would defeat my whole purpose. No, I will do nothing suddenly; but I will go away and stay away until his heart has cooled toward me, and then, when time has prepared him for the change, I myself will propose the annulment of our betrothal," said the young girl.

"Suzy," said Benny very gravely, "you mean well, but you do ill. You are betrothed to the Earl of Wellrose, and bound to him by every tie of honor. And in common loyalty to him, you should not take this important step without his knowledge and consent. If you really intend to try the effect of absence on his love and constancy, with the view of finally freeing him from what you deem a rash and indiscreet engagement, you should tell him so. He would probably reply to you, that his love and faith would stand the test. But in any case you should tell him."

"Do you really think so, Benny?" inquired the young girl, with a startled look.

"Assuredly I do. It is his right to be told."

"Then I will think of it, Benny," she said very thoughtfully.

And the young man, who had made quite a long call, arose and took leave of his friend, with a promise to come again. Suzy kept her word with Benny, but that was all. As she had promised to think about his advice, she thought about it; but the more she thought about it, the more disinclined she felt to follow it.

"No," she said to herself, "no; if I am to do Lord Wellrose any good by absenting myself from him, I must be silent as to my motives. If I were to tell him that I go for the purpose of giving him an opportunity of forgetting me, that would only strengthen his resolution to remember e No; I will go, and I will be silent as to my last move in going. *I* will do right; I know that. And if, at ie end of two years' separation, he is not cured of his inscreet love — if then again he claim my hand, he shall ave it, certainly."

So saying, Suzy ordered her brougham, and went to Oxrd street, to the establishment of a celebrated manufacurer of regalia, to order the magnificent pair of colors that ie designed to present to Benjamin's company, for Benjain's sake.

She told the proprietor the purpose of her visit, and ientioned the company of the regiment she wished to onor. And he showed her a book of appropriate designs, nd she chose the most elegant one she saw, and ordered a air of colors to be made from it.

The proprietor promised to have them put in hand immeiately, and sent home within the week.

CHAPTER XXXVI.

TO THE WAR!

> Sound, sound the clarion! fill the fife!
> To all the sensual world proclaim:
> One crowded hour of glorious life
> Is worth an age without a name.—SIR WALTER SCOTT.

MEANWHILE the month slipped swiftly away, and the lay approached when Ensign Douglas must leave London o join his regiment at Southampton.

Benjamin went to take leave of Suzy the day before he vas to start.

"Our parting is not to be here, my dear, you know. I hall go down to Southampton by the same train with yourself, in order to present the colors to your company.

And I shall remain at Southampton until your regiment sails," said the young girl, as she kindly took the young soldier's hand.

Benjamin's face lighted up with pleasure.

"Then I shall see you occasionally, for the next ten days?" he said gayly.

"You shall see me *daily*, for the next ten days, dear Benny," she answered affectionately.

"But the Earl?" suggested Benjamin, as a doubt crossed his mind as to whether Lord Wellrose would approve of the journey of his betrothed.

"Oh, the Earl!" said Suzy, smiling. "You are very much devoted to his lordship's interests."

"There is only one person in the world whom I love more than I do the Earl; and there is no one on earth whom I honor so much. Yes, Suzy, I am devoted to his lordship's interests; they are dearer to me than my own life, than my own happiness. He treats me as a brother. He gave me his name. What more could he do for me than that?" answered Benny, very seriously.

"He *loves* you as a brother, Benny. I know that I never saw anything like it in my life. You are going to take leave of him to-day, I suppose?"

"Yes, dear."

"Then he will tell you more about my journey. And you must meet me at the railway station to-morrow" said Suzy, as Benny arose to go.

From Park Lane, Benjamin went to Cheviot House, to bid good-bye to Lord Wellrose. He sent up his card

ENSIGN DOUGLAS.

And he was almost immediately admitted, and shown to the private apartments of the Earl, and announced as:

"Ensign Douglas."

As he entered the room, his heart suddenly seemed to stand still in his bosom; his breath was suspended; for the

Duchess of Cheviot, "the beautiful Duchess"—still beautiful with her family grown up around her—was passing out. She bowed slightly and smiled on her son's visitor, and so disappeared.

Benjamin caught his breath, and recovered himself as the young Earl arose and came forward to greet him.

"You leave London to-morrow, Benjamin, I believe?" he inquired.

"Yes, my lord, I do. And I have come to-day to take leave of your lordship, and to thank you again, and to say that I shall never cease to thank you for all your kindness—much more than kindness to me," said the young man, with much emotion.

"Say no more about it, Benjamin. It is enough that it makes me very happy to be of service to you. But we do not part to-day. I go down to Southampton with you," said the young Earl pleasantly.

"My lord! you!" exclaimed Benny, pleasure beaming in his eyes.

"Yes. My little queen in Park Lane goes down to present the colors to your company, and has accepted my escort for herself and her companion, Mrs. Brown. So we will make up a party and take a compartment together. What do you say?"

"I am delighted, my lord."

"I have another motive in going down with you. I wish to introduce you to some of the officers of your regiment, especially to the Senior Surgeon, Doctor Christopher Kinlock. He is a very good man indeed. And he has a sort of claim upon us. He comes from Scotland, from my mother's neighborhood, from her estate indeed, being a native of the village of Seton. He was the adopted son and the heir of old Doctor Seton, a distant kinsman or clansman of the Seton-Lnlithgows, and so, as I said, has a sort of claim on us. My father procured him a commission as surgeon in the same regiment you are about to join, and he goes ou with it, of course. I think that in him you will find a val uable friend," added the young Earl, very far from dream ing of the important discoveries that would result from th meeting of Ensign Douglas and Doctor Kinlock.

Benny, after again trying to express his sense of obliga tion to the Earl, took leave and departed.

Early the next morning the travelling party of four namely, Lord Wellrose, Benny, Suzy and Mrs. Brown, witl his lordship's valet and the young lady's maid, met at th railway station and secured a compartment to themselves ir a first class carriage.

The train was the express, and soon steamed down to th seaport upon which the eyes of the world were now fixed for there were gathered the vast British army about to se sail for the East.

In due time the train reached Southampton.

Lord Wellrose and his party went to a hotel, where they took a handsome suit of apartments, and established the two ladies comfortably.

It was yet early in the afternoon; so after a refreshing toilet and lunch, Lord Wellrose proposed to take Ensign Douglas to the quarters of his regiment, to report for duty.

They sat out and in due time reached the quarters of the colonel commanding, where Ensign Douglas was introduced, and where he formally reported.

This ceremony being over, Lord Wellrose took his protegé to the quarters of the senior surgeon and introduced him to Doctor Kinlock.

The Scotch surgeon was a man of about forty-five years of age, prematurely bald and grey, but with an erect form, clear eyes and a resolute countenance.

He received Lord Wellrose with much deference, and welcomed the young Ensign with kindness.

"Ensign—Douglas, my lord, did you say? Oh, aye, a

kinsman of the family, I presume?" said the Surgeon looking from one to the other of his two visitors, and then answering his own question by adding, "Oh, aye, certainly. The likeness shows that, my lord. I never saw twin brothers so much alike in person as your lordship and this young gentleman.

Lord Wellrose did not contradict Doctor Kinlock. He felt that he could not. And then and there the surgeon received an impression that he afterwards transferred to all the officers of his regiment—namely, that the new ensign was a near kinsman of the Earl of Wellrose.

His lordship commended his young "kinsman" to the good offices of the surgeon and then took leave.

And soon after a messenger from the quartermaster came after Ensign Douglas and took him to his tent.

The next day the Earl of Wellrose called again on the Colonel of the regiment, and obtained leave for Miss Juniper to present a pair of colors to Company ——.

It was arranged that the colors should be presented at parade the next morning.

When this matter was settled, Lord Wellrose sought out Benjamin, told him the arrangement that had been made for the presentation and reception of the colors, and laughingly added that he, Ensign Douglas, who was destined to bear them on to victory, must be prepared with a little speech for the occasion.

Then he returned to the hotel and told the news to Suzy, who received it half in delight and half in terror.

And he, seeing her comic dismay, thought to tease her a little by telling her that *she* must be prepared with an appropriate speech to deliver when presenting the colors.

But Suzy, who saw his drift, and meant to defeat it, reminded him, that in her professional capacity, she had been as much accustomed to public speaking as to public singing, and should not in the least mind addressing the gallant "Greys."

The Earl bowed in deference to this self-assertion.

Suzy had told a vain story, however, for early the next da she came to the Earl of Wellrose and implored his lordshi to save her from the most trying part of the exhibition, b presenting the colors and making the speech in her name.

"For after all, you know," she said, "that it is a very dif ferent thing from playing a part. It is much easier for m to sing or speak as Amina or Norma, in the presence of mixed audience, than it would be for me to speak directl in my own person to a company of soldiers; and I can't d it, Lord Wellrose," she added.

"I will relieve you of that duty, my dearest. But you— the donator of the colors—will stand by my side at the cere mony, I hope?"

"Oh, yes; certainly I will do that," said the young gir smiling.

It was the hour of the grand parade when the colors wer finally presented.

Lord Wellrose, who presented them "in the name of th fair donor," made a short speech, full of patriotism.

Ensign Douglas, who received them on behalf of his com pany, also made, in reply, a short speech, eloquent with dee emotion, in which he said, in effect, that he was prepared t die in defence of these colors if necessary; that they shoul never be taken by the enemy except from his dead hand finally, the highest ambition of his life was this—that fat would permit him to plant these colors on the walls of th imperial palace of St. Petersburg!

It was an absurd burst of youthful enthusiasm an extravagance, and yet it was highly applauded.

And so the ceremony of the presentation of the colo ended.

A few days after this, the army, consisting in all of thirt thousand men, embarked and set sail for the East.

Lord Wellrose and Suzy, after having taken the mo

affectionate leave of Benjamin, and given and received promises touching a frequent correspondence, returned to London.

Suzy's next business was to give up her little palace in Park Lane, and take lodgings, while waiting for the sailing of the ship that was to carry her to the antipodes.

It was just three weeks after the sailing of the English forces fr the East, that Suzy took leave of Lord Wellrose and all her London friends, and accompanied by her companion, Mrs. Brown, and her maid Jenny Smith, embarked on board the East Indiaman *Wendover*, bound for Sydney.

Lord Wellrose felt her loss severely, but he was not the sort of man to yield to despondency. He devoted himself to the interests of his great bill for the "Reform of Prison Discipline and the Reclamation of Criminals," and in good works soon recovered his good spirits.

CHAPTER XXXVII.

LOVE'S MISTAKES.

Let them stand
In thy thoughts, untouched by blame.
Could they help it, if her hand
He had claimed with hasty claim?
That was wrong, perhaps; but then
Such things be, and will again.—E. B. BROWNING.

THE Earl of Wellrose occupied himself with the humane cause to which he had consecrated his life. And he found in his work an antidote to that depression of spirits consequent upon his separation from his betrothed, and from his *protegé* whom he had grown to love with more than the love of a brother.

But busily engaged as he was with public affairs, he still found time to go into society more frequently than he had done when "Mademoiselle Arielle" was at Covent Garden theatre and at Park Lane, and all his leisure time given to her.

Yet with all his public and private engagements, he felt the time long while waiting to hear from his betrothed.

He knew that unless the *Wendover* should chance to "speak" some homeward-bound ship, many weary months must elapse before he could hope for a letter from her.

Meanwhile he wrote by every Australian mail, that his letters might reach her soon after her arrival at Sydney.

At length Parliament was prorogued, and the London season closed.

The Earl of Wellrose, released from official duties, would have gone on a yachting excursion to the Mediterranean, but his mother, the Duchess of Cheviot, made it a point that he should join her autumn party at Seton Court, in Scotland.

The family had not been there for so many years, she said, that it was now quite time they should visit the estate and look into the condition of their tenantry. And besides, she urged, there was no better place for game of all sorts, from blackcock to red deer, than Seton Court and Chase; and furthermore, if Wellrose wished to invite any number of his young friends to meet him there, they should be made very welcome.

His married sisters with their husbands and children, were all to join the party. The Earl and Countess of Ornoch and Lady Hinda Moray were also coming. And the venerable General and Mrs. Chimboza were expected. But the gathering would not be complete, or at all satisfactory, if her son Wellrose was absent from it.

Now Lord Wellrose cared very little for blackcock shooting or red deer stalking; but being social and affectionate, like all his brave and tender race, he cared a great deal for the dear friends and relatives who would be gathered at Seton Court, and he cared a great deal more for his mother's wishes; so he promptly gave up his expedition to the Mediterranean, and placed his yacht, the *Arielle*, at the disposal of the Duchess and her friends, if her grace should please to go to Scotland by sea. He also proposed to keep the *Arielle* at anchor at the little port of Killford during the autumn, in the event that the Duchess and her visitors should please to diversify their inland amusements by a sea voyage up the wild and picturesque west coast of Scotland.

The Duchess was delighted with the plan, and thanked her thoughtful and affectionate son, and accepted the offer of his yacht.

And when Lord Wellrose saw the real pleasure he had given his mother, he felt that in resigning his expedition to the Mediterranean for her sake, he had made no sacrifice at all.

The yacht was then at Portsmouth, quite ready for sea.

An agreeable family party was immediately made up for the voyage. It consisted of the Duke and Duchess of Cheviot, their son the Earl of Wellrose, and their sons-in-law and married daughters, as follows: the Viscount and Viscountess Moray, Mr. Albert and Lady Clemence Elphinstone; and their young unmarried daughters, the Ladies Hester and Eva Douglas; and lastly their cousins, the Earl and Countess of Ornoch, and Lady Hinda Moray.

There were no others.

"I prefer that for the voyage this should be exclusively a family party. Our visitors will join us at the appropriate time at Seton Court," said the Duchess, who ordered all the arrangements.

It was agreed that the whole family party should meet at Cheviot House on the evening of a certain day, and that they should take a special train for Portsmouth the next morning.

Consequently on the evening of the twentieth of August a pleasant circle was assembled in the drawing-room of

Cheviot House. This circle included all the individuals named for the yachting party; among them, of course, the lovely Lady Hinda Moray—the most beautiful girl in Europe, as all the clubs declared. She was, perhaps, the most beautiful *brunette* in the world; with a perfect form and perfect features; with a stately little head adorned with a profusion of bright, soft, purple black ringlets; with large, brilliant, tender, purple black eyes, arched with slender black eyebrows, and fringed with long black eyelashes, and with a rich complexion deepening into vivid crimson upon the delicate oval cheeks and plump, ripe lips.

All the men in London were in love with her, except the Earl of Wellrose. He had not even seen her for some months.

But now, as he looked upon her this last evening, seated in the drawing-room of Cheviot House, and with her beauty enhanced by a toilet that was perfectly tasteful and becoming, he thought that she was the most beautiful creature he had ever seen in his life, and he wondered why he had never thought so before.

Then he repented, and hoped that he had not, in thinking this, committed treason against his betrothed.

Yet withal he was glad that this sweet girl was going with the family party to Scotland.

"She is my cousin, and I have always liked her, and always shall, though I never noticed what a perfect beauty she really is, until to-night," he said to himself as he furtively gazed at her.

That night, after he had retired to his own apartments, he found upon his dressing-table a letter from Suzy, the first he had received from her since her departure. He seized it with eager joy. It bore two postmarks—"CORVETTE REVENON," and "HAVRE."

It had been brought them by a French ship homeward bound, that had been spoken by the *Wendover*, and it had come by the way of Havre.

So much he saw by the envelope.

This was not only the first letter he had received from his betrothed since her departure, but the first he had received from her at any time.

As they had never been separated since their first acquaintance, there had never been any necessity, nor even any opportunity for a letter correspondence between them.

Now, after their first parting, to get her first letter was an event of great importance and interest to him.

How would she write to him, he asked himself as he eagerly opened the envelope and unfolded the letter.

The letter disappointed and depressed him by what he considered its coldness and formality.

Suzy had indeed written to her lover in a very matter-of-fact, though friendly sort of way. She dated her letter "On board the ship *Wendover*, Atlantic Ocean." And she commenced it with, "Dear Lord Wellrose." She told him all the incidents of her voyage; what sort of a man the captain was; who her fellow-passengers were; what kind of weather they had had; what ships they had spoken; what fish and water-fowl they had seen; who were seasick, and who were sea-worthy. But not one word about her own feelings. She ended her letter by a paragraph written some days later than the first date, in which she told him that they had just spoken the French ship *Revenon*, homeward bound, and that they would send a boat out to her to take out letters, and bring hers. And she signed herself "Yours affectionately, Susan Juniper."

"She might as well have sent me a leaf from the ship's log-book," said the lover impatiently, as he refolded the formal little letter, and thought how earnest, fervent, ardent, his letters to her had been.

It was true he remembered that she had not received them yet, and could not receive them until her arrival at Sydney

And then he went to bed, and fell to dreaming of the

brilliant, tender, flashing, melting eyes of the Lady Hinda Moray.

Very early in the morning, the yachting party assembled in the breakfast-room, already dressed in their travelling suits.

They were all very merry over the prospect of their sea voyage, and of the fine weather which every sign in the heavens seemed to promise them.

After dispatching a good breakfast, they entered the carriages that were in waiting to take them to the railway station.

Lord Wellrose found himself in the same carriage with the Duke and Duchess of Cheviot. There was a fourth seat vacant.

"Where is Hinda?" inquired the young Earl, glancing at the vacant seat.

"She is in the coach with Albert and Jessie," answered the Duchess, referring to her son-in-law and daughter, the Viscount and Viscountess Moray.

"I thought she was to have come with us," said the Earl, in a tone of disappointment.

"She was to have done so, but allowed herself to be carried off at the last moment by Jessie. However, we shall all be together on the train, as we have engaged a double compartment for ourselves," said the Duchess, with a smile.

In due time they reached the railway station, where, in a few moments, they found themselves comfortably seated in the capacious double compartment that had been secured for the party.

Lord Wellrose, to his complete satisfaction, found himself seated by his beautiful cousin, the Lady Hinda Moray.

And they were all scarcely settled in their places before the train began to move out of the station, and in a few moments, with accelerating speed, to steam swiftly toward Portsmouth.

Lord Wellrose talked with his cousin of the past season in London, with all its trials, triumphs and defeats, artistic, social and political. And he found Lady Hinda as brilliant, witty and attractive in conversation as she was in person.

He afterward remembered that railway ride to Portsmouth as one of the shortest and pleasantest he had ever enjoyed.

It was but a little past noon when they reached the seaport.

They did not go to a hotel, but took carriages from the station directly to the water side, where the beautiful yacht was waiting to receive them.

It was fitted up with every comfort, convenience and luxury that wealth, taste and skill could command.

A sumptuous repast was awaiting them in the elegant saloon.

And the travellers partook of it with an appetite sharpened by their long morning's ride.

As soon as the tide served the yacht sailed.

The voyagers were blessed with beautiful weather, with long, clear, mild days, and with soft, mild, moonlight nights.

All day long it was delightful to sit on deck, breathing the pure air and looking out upon the blue sky, the calm sea, and the wildly beautiful distant coast. And even late at night it required some resolution to leave the moonlit scene, the starry heavens, the silvery ocean, the shadowy shore, to take needful rest.

So they sailed down the south coast, doubled Land's End, and up the wild western shore.

The weather was almost too fine for a quick passage, for though the wind was fair, there was but little of it.

It was the evening of the fourth day of the voyage that the yacht ran into the little harbor of Killford and dropped anchor.

There they found the little steamer *Sprite* waiting to take them through the Straits that connected the harbor of Killford with the Loch.

"We e'en expectit your Grace yestreen; aye, and the day before. We hae been doon here ilka day sin' Sunday," complained old Saundy Gaunt, a gray-haired retainer of the family, as he stood, bonnet in hand, to welcome the Duchess, as the steamer ran alongside of the yacht.

The Duchess smiled as she gave him her hand, and answered:

"But you see we are here at last, Saundy. 'All good things come to us, if we wait long enough for them,' it is said."

"Aye? Do they so? I did na ken. I hae been waiting all my life lang for gude luck, and it has na coom yet," grumbled the old man.

"And what sort of good luck have you been waiting for, Saundy?" laughingly inquired the Duchess, as she took her seat on the deck of the steamer, surrounded by the party.

"Just a wee sheiling c' my ain, wi' a bit ait field attached," promptly answered the old man.

"Why, I thought you had that, Saundy?"

"Na; only a cutty stool beside Duncan Gray's peat fire."

"Then you shall certainly have a cottage and garden of your own, Saundy. And I will direct the new bailiff, Mr. McDonald, to see to it at once. There now, I told you that everything good comes to us, if we wait long enough for it," smiled the Duchess.

"Aye, sure, when ladies like your Grace hae the power and the will to send them," replied the old man, as he deeply bowed his thanks.

Meanwhile the little steamer turned about and headed up the Straits, that were anything but straight, tacking frequently from right to left, and from left again to right, to round the points of the high rocks reaching from each side to the middle of the channel, and almost interlocking each other.

So, at length, they passed through the Straits, and entered the loch.

There a scene of beauty and grandeur unsurpassed and indescribable broke upon their view: the broad loch, entirely surrounded by fir-crowned hills, and at its upper end the white turrets of Seton Court, the whole bathed in moonlight.

They steamed up this beautiful loch, and landed at the stairs leading up into Seton Chase.

At the head of the stairs, carriages were waiting, that took them all up to the house, where the housekeeper, Mrs. Bruce, had all things in readiness for the reception of the family.

The Duke and Duchess, with all their party, passed through a double line of servants drawn up in the hall to welcome them home.

Then the guests were shown to their apartments.

CHAPTER XXXVIII.

BENNY'S RISE.

The death-shot hissing from afar—
The shock—the shout—the groan of war;
Though few the numbers, theirs the strife
That neither spares nor speaks of life.—BYRON.

THE Earl of Wellrose knew where to find his own.

And there, on his table, he found letters awaiting him.

The mail had travelled much faster than the yacht had sailed, and these letters had been forwarded every day from London, and had been accumulating for the last four days.

Lord Wellrose carelessly looked them over until he came to two, lying side by side—one from Suzy, and the other from Benny.

He eagerly snatched up Suzy's letter and hastily opened it.

It was very short and disappointing. She commenced as before, with:

"Dear Lord Wellrose—"

Then she told him that she had *nothing* to tell him. She reminded him that in her first letter she had described the ship, officers, crew and passengers, and that she had nothing left to write about. Since they had spoken the French Corvette *Revenon*, they had not seen a single sail, no, nor a shark, nor a whale, nor an iceberg, nor anything. The voyage was insupportably dull and tedious, and she would be glad of anything for a change, even a tempest or a pirate!

Then there was a short concluding paragraph, dated a few days later, and announcing the approach of a homeward-bound ship, made out to be the *Lord Stanley*, from Sydney to Southampton, and which would take letters home to England.

"I am sorry now that I grumbled," she wrote in conclusion, "for we have been very fortunate in this—that in the last six weeks we have spoken two homeward-bound ships, and have been able to send letters. And I am informed that it often happens that an outward-bound ship does not meet a homeward-bound one in the whole voyage, which must be very dreary.

She signed herself his "affectionate friend, Suzy."

The lover sighed as he laid this letter down, and wondered why she wrote in such a coolly kind and matter-of-fact manner, and whether she loved him still, and whether indeed she had ever loved him at all.

And then a vision of Lady Hinda's melting dark eyes passed before him. But with a self-condemning shudder he turned from them and took up Benny's letter.

Ah! here was no lack of warmth indeed! Gratitude, affection and enthusiasm filled its pages.

It was dated at Gallipoli, a little town on a peninsula to the west of the Dardanelles, where some divisions of the allied armies were still encamped. It told him of the quaint little town, of the strange race that inhabited the place, of the condition of the French and English camps, and of a rumor in camp that they were soon to move higher up the country.

There was a letter also from the surgeon, Dr. Christopher Kinlock, in which he spoke very highly of Ensign Douglas, and of the esteem in which he was held by the whole regiment.

Lord Wellrose laid his letters aside, and made a hasty toilet to join his party at their late dinner.

There had been a little womanly diplomacy in the plan of the Duchess when she made up her party for the Highlands. She wished to bring her son, Lord Wellrose, and his beautiful cousin, Lady Hinda Moray, together under the same roof, where, meeting every day for many weeks, she hoped they might form that mutual attachment for which both their families wished.

And very soon the Duchess saw, with almost equal pain and pleasure, that the dark-eyed Anglo-Indian, Hinda, had given her ardent young heart to the noble and handsome young Earl.

With "equal pain and pleasure," because only half her wish was accomplished in that Hinda loved Wellrose; but she doubted and feared that the other half would never be fulfilled—that Wellrose would never love Hinda. And if not—ah! what life-long sorrow for that lovely girl!

The autumn weeks went swiftly by. The company assembled at Seton Court amused themselves with excursions to celebrated localities in the neighborhood rich in historic interest, and in voyages to the coast isles, rides to the mountain fastnesses, or, nearer home, in archery meetings on the lawn, or billiards in the house.

Not until October did the pleasant circle break up.

And then the Duke and Duchess of Cheviot, with their own immediate family circle, and with the Earl and Countess of Ornoch and the Lady Hinda Moray, left Seton Court for their marine residence at Brunswick Terrace, Brighton.

It was here that bad news reached them from the East.

The allied forces at Varna had been attacked by Asiatic cholera, which was making fearful ravages among them.

"Hitherto," wrote Surgeon Kinlock to Lord Wellrose, "Ensign Douglas has escaped the plague; but he devotes himself with unflagging zeal to the suffering soldiers. It is next to impossible but that he must fall a victim to his own labors."

On reading this, the Earl of Wellrose was filled with the most painful anxiety on Benny's account.

He wrote to Benny, imploring him to take care of himself, and not to throw his life away.

He wrote also to Doctor Kinlock, urging him to use every means in his power to prevent the young ensign from sacrificing himself.

And he wrote to the Colonel of the regiment, much to the same effect, adding with emphasis:

"He is my kinsman and adopted brother. If he were my *own* brother, he could not seem nearer or dearer to me; I could not feel a warmer and deeper interest in his life and well-being."

These letters, and especially the one addressed to the Colonel, probably saved the life of the devoted young officer, for shortly after their receipt at Varna, Ensign Douglas was detailed on duty that took him far from the possibility of sacrificing his life for the cholera patients.

There came no more letters from Suzy. Since the letter brought by the ship *Lord Stanley*, the lover had heard nothing of his beloved. And whatever cause he may have had to doubt her love, he certainly never doubted her friendship or her punctuality. He justly concluded that if no more letters arrived from her, it was because the *Wendover*, in which she went out, had spoken no other homeward-bound ships since the *Revenon* and the *Lord Stanley*. She would write to him, he thought, as soon as she should reach port, and in due time he should receive her letter.

And meanwhile his beautiful dark-eyed cousin, the Lady Hinda was so charming!

More news came from the Orient—very important news now. The allied forces had invaded the Crimea, had been met by the Russians on the the banks of the Alma, and the great battle had been fought and won, and the allies were in full march for Sebastopol.

A private letter from Surgeon Kinlock to his patron the Earl of Wellrose conveyed the additional information that Ensign Douglas had greatly distinguished himself on the field; that he had not only preserved his own colors, but—wounded and bleeding as he was—he had rescued the regimental colors and borne them into the English lines, where he fell, fainting from loss of blood.

He had been very severely wounded, but was now doing well, and in a very fair way of recovery. He had also been recommended for promotion.

How the affectionate and generous heart of the young Earl filled and glowed with pride and pleasure, at reading of the gallant conduct of the brave young "kinsman!"

"I *knew* he would do honor to the name I gave him," he said to himself.

And then he inclosed the surgeon's letter in a letter of his own to Suzy, in Australia, bidding her read the inclosed and see what Benny had already done with his colors, and predicting that he would yet plant them, if not on the walls of St. Petersburg, certainly on those of Sebastopol.

Just as he was about to send these letters off to Suzy, he received one from her, dated on the day of her arrival at Sydney, where her father met her.

The letter was written in a very friendly style, and was filled with descriptions of the town, the country and the people, as far as Suzy had had the opportunity of observing them.

But there was not one word of love from beginning to end, except perhaps in the rather formal greeting of "Dear Lord Wellrose," and the formal ending "Affectionately yours."

And Lord Wellrose would have grieved very much over this "cool friendliness" in his betrothed, if it had not been for his lovely cousin Hinda, who comforted him.

After this, the news from the Crimea came thick and fast.

Balaclava had been taken, and the cry of the allies was still, "On to Sebastopol!"

Another private letter from Surgeon Kinlock to Lord Wellrose informed his lordship that Ensign Douglas had been promoted to a lieutenancy, and placed upon the staff of his Colonel, with whom he was now a deserving favorite.

The next mails from the East brought proud news. The great battle of Inkerman had been fought, and a glorious victory won. And the allied armies had made a splendid march to Sebastopol, and were now before the walls of the city.

Another letter from Dr. Kinlock to Lord Wellrose informed his lordship that Lieutenant Douglas had signally distinguished himself at Inkerman, and had again been recommended for promotion.

And again the generous soul of the young Earl rejoiced in the well-doing of his *protegé*. And this letter also was sent off to Suzy in Australia.

In due time—a long time—her answer came back to him. Among other things, she wrote .

"You have plucked 'a brand from the burning,' which I trust, will light all your onward life with joy."

After this there came a lull in the war-storm. The allied armies were before Sebastopol. And the siege threatened to be a long one.

Meanwhile, in February, Parliament met.

The Duke and Duchess of Cheviot, with all the rest of the great world, came up to London for the season.

Lord Wellrose resumed the labors of humanity to which he had devoted his time and talents.

Lady Hinda Moray was again the belle of Belgravia, and generally pronounced more beautiful than ever.

And this was certainly true. She was more beautiful than ever, because she was happier than ever. The light of a pure and peaceful love beamed in her face; for she loved the noble young Earl of Wellrose, and she knew that he loved her in return.

He had never told her so, but all his self-control had failed to conceal the blissful truth from her eyes.

How he struggled with his passion! How he told himself, day and night, that he should be false to every principle of honor and manhood, should he suffer his affections to stray from his betrothed.

He avoided Hinda as much as possible; though, as she was his mother's guest at Cheviot House that season, common courtesy required him to be frequently in her society.

He would have left London to escape temptation, had not his parliamentary duties kept him in town.

He wrote to Suzy by every mail, and told her all the news of the day, and sent her papers, magazines, new books and new music.

But his letters were no longer the ardent outpourings of passionate love they had once been. They were as coolly friendly and matter-of-fact as her own had always been.

And meanwhile the months slipped away, and brought

near the time when the allied armies should achieve their great triumph.

CHAPTER XXXIX.

VICTORY AND DEATH.

Come when his task of fame is wrought—
Come with her laurel wreath, blood-bought—
  Come in her crowning hour—and then
Thy sunken eye's unearthly light
To him is welcome as the sight
  Of sky and stars to prisoned men.
Thy grasp is welcome as the hand
Of brother in a foreign land.—HALLECK.

IN September came the most important news. The allied armies had taken Sebastopol, and the Crimean war was virtually at an end.

This news found the Duke and Duchess of Cheviot, with the Earl of Wellrose and the ladies Hester and Eva Douglas, at Cheviot Castle, where they were spending the early autumn.

While they were still discussing the great victory, a private letter arrived from Doctor Kinlock to the Earl of Wellrose.

After describing the taking of the city, he went on to write:

"Your brave kinsman, Lieutenant Douglas, has kept his word. With his own hand he planted his colors on the walls of Sebastopol. But ah! in doing this, in the face of a murderous fire, he has been severely wounded by a bullet through the left lobe of the lungs. He has been recommended for promotion, but, it is doubtful whether he will live to profit by it. Certainly he will not, if he stays here. I have advised him to be sent home with the invalid troops who are to sail for England in a few days."

Lord Wellrose groaned as he laid this letter aside, and half his joy in the great victory was turned into grief.

And even thus, throughout the land, the public rejoicing at the national triumph was tempered by the private mourning of those whose beloved ones had bought the victory with their blood.

In a few days there came another letter from Doctor Kinlock, in which he wrote:

"Young Douglas has received his promotion. He is now a captain, but not yet assigned to any company. I fear he never will be. He is sinking slowly, but surely. All his desire, now that the war may be said to be over, is to get back to England, to press your hand once more and die. If I were not hoping from day to day that his desire may be granted, and that he may be sent home, I should even entreat your lordship to come out here and comfort the dying boy, whose only earthly wish is to see your face."

"I will go," said Lord Wellrose to himself; then, suddenly recollecting all the circumstances, he added: "But I might miss him. Ah! he might be on his way home while I should be on my way out. I must wait for another letter from Kinlock, I suppose. And Douglas is so ill! he may die in the interval."

As these troubled thoughts passed through his mind, he turned over a leaf of his letter and read a paragraph dated a day later, and which was as follows:

* * * "I had written so far when I received a message summoning me to head-quarters. I immediately reported there, and instantly received orders to go to England, by the *Relief*, in charge of a party of invalid troops. Captain Douglas goes with us. I am extremely glad of this, as I shall be able to attend personally on him during the voyage. We sail for Southampton the day after to-morrow.

So you may expect us very soon after the receipt of thi letter, if you do not see us before."

"And so he is coming home, and I shall see him again, poor, brave, gentle boy! I thank the Lord for this. And who shall say that home air and kind friends and good nursing may not save his life and restore his health?" said the Earl to himself, as he folded this letter and laid it aside.

Then he rang for his valet, who immediately appeared.

"Perkins, pack my portmanteau, and order the trap for four o'clock, to take us to the railway station. We leave for London by the 5:45 train," said the Earl, as he passed out of his room to notify his mother of his sudden journey.

He found the Duchess and her daughters in their delightful morning room, with the great bay-windows overhanging the sea.

They were at work on various little fancy articles for a charity fair, to be held in aid of the widows and orphans of the war.

They looked up from their graceful work and welcomed the beloved son and brother with smiles.

And the Duchess drew a chair near to herself, for him to take.

"Thanks, mother, dear: no. I cannot sit. I am leaving for London by the 5:45 train," he said, leaning over the back of the chair.

"This is very sudden, Wellrose," she remarked, raising her brows in surprise.

"Yes; but I go to meet a friend who is returning from the Crimea wounded, perhaps dying."

"Oh, go, then, at once, if you can be of any service to him. It is a holy duty. Who is he?" inquired the Duchess.

"Captain Douglas, of the — Regiment of Foot."

"Douglas? Is he a connection of our family?"

"Most probably; there are so many Douglases—as many Douglases as Campbells, I should think."

"Very true. But your friend—how does he come?"

"He comes in the *Relief*, which sailed from Gallipoli for Southampton, with invalided troops on board in charge of Dr. Kinlock."

"Kinlock is coming home, then?"

"Yes; having charge of these sick and wounded men, as I said. The ship may be expected at Southampton any day now; and I wish to be there to meet my poor friend."

"You are quite right. Go, dear. And remember, that if we can be of any use to your wounded friend, you must call upon us," said the kind-hearted Duchess, as she embraced and dismissed her son to his humane errand.

The "trap" was announced.

And the Earl, attended by his valet, entered it, and was driven rapidly to the rustic station, which he reached just in time to catch the night express to London.

His servant took tickets in a great hurry.

And in a few minutes Lord Wellrose found himself comfortably seated in a first-class carriage, flying southward.

He reached London in the small hours of the morning, and passed from the Great Northern to the South-Western railway train, with which it connected; and so he continued his flight to the sea as if he had been flying for his life.

He reached Southampton in time for an early breakfast.

He took apartments at the "Lord Admiral." And after a refreshing bath and change of dress, and a good breakfast, he set out to walk down to the docks, to inquire for the expected ship.

He was more fortunate than he could have hoped to be. The ship had just arrived, and was at anchor about half a mile from the land.

A steam tender was already leaving the shore to bring her passengers to land.

By presence of mind and promptitude in passing a few shillings to the men who were withdrawing the gang piank, Lord Wellrose succeeded in boarding the "tender" at the last moment, and was soon steaming out toward the *Relief.*

In a few moments the tender was alongside of the ship.

The decks of the *Relief* was crowded with—what ?

Were these men "ghosts" or shadows ?

They might have been Charon's passengers crossing the Styx. So pale, so thin, so ghastly they were !

Living skeletons crowned with death's heads !

Here were the maimed, the halt and the blind ; the sick, the dying and the dead.

Yes, and 'the dead.' Many had died on the passage, and had been buried in the sea. But some had died within a few hours ; so recently, so near home, that their bodies had been saved, to be given to their friends.

Lord Wellrose, from his youth up, had been accustomed to sights of misery, in his frequent personal ministrations to the wretched. But he had never seen anything like this. And he grew sick and dizzy as he gazed.

Soon the bustle of transferring these poor wrecks of manhood from the ship to the tender attracted his attention.

Some managed to crawl without assistance, and then drop down helplessly upon the deck of the tender.

Some crept on, leaning on the arms of comrades.

And some were carried bodily, like dead weights

Lord Wellrose was a stranger to all present. In his breathless anxiety to know the fate of Benny, he would have questioned one or more of the men. But their suffering seemed so great, their self-absorption so complete, that the young Earl restrained himself, forbore to trouble them and endured his suspense as well as he could.

At length the form for which he so eagerly watched, appeared. But, oh ! how changed !

Was this a man in the flesh, or a disembodied spirit, that

approached, leaning on the arm of the middle-aged surgeon, Dr. Kinlock?

Benny was clothed in his old, war-worn, battle-stained uniform, that hung loosely upon his emaciated figure. His face was so thin that it had taken an almost triangular shape from the broad forehead, down the hollow cheeks to the sharp chin. His complexion was so bloodless, that "pale" would not describe it; it was a clear, fair, transparent bluish white. His large blue eyes, sunk in their deep, shadowy hollows, seemed larger, bluer and brighter than before. His golden hair had faded to a silvery fairness. And in a word, if Benny was dying, he was as beautiful in death as is a setting star.

So thought the Earl of Wellrose, as he came gently forward and took the wan hand, and said, with suppressed emotion:

"Oh, my dear Benjamin! I thank God that you have lived to get home. And now we will hope that good air and good nursing will restore your health."

The face of the young soldier grew radiant with joy, as he grasped the hand of the Earl between both his own, exclaiming:

"Yes, thank God! I thank God that I live to see you once more! Now I am willing to die!"

"We will not talk of death. We will not have you die. You have everything to live for now, Benjamin," said the Earl.

But a violent fit of coughing seized the invalid, and he turned and crept away to the side of the ship, and sank down upon a seat to recover himself.

"And now, Dr. Kinlock, welcome home. And much thanks for your devotion to my—cousin, here," said the young Earl, cordially shaking hands with the surgeon, whom, however, in the first moments of meeting Benny, he had forgotten.

"Thanks, my lord. I am very happy myself in the thought that I have brought Captain Douglas safe to England. *And for more reasons than one*," added the surgeon so emphatically, that the young Earl looked inquiringly at him, as though he would have asked:

"What do you mean?"

"He is your cousin, you say, my lord," remarked the surgeon, in answer to the unuttered question.

"*All* the Douglases are cousins, you know," replied the Earl, with a smile.

"Like the Stuarts, and the Campbells, and the other Scottish clans. But is that all, my lord?" inquired the doctor, in a low voice.

"That is all, so far as I know," replied the Earl, in a grave and somewhat surprised and questioning manner.

"Then, my lord," said Dr. Kinlock solemnly, "I have something to tell you that I fear will startle your lordship considerably. But not now; not now! See, my patient is recovering himself. Ah, poor fellow! he is so sensitive! When he gets into those violent fits of coughing, he shrinks from observation like a wounded animal. But here he comes," added the surgeon, as he arose and gave Benny his arm to support him to the side of the ship.

Lord Wellrose also lent his aid, and thus the Earl and the surgeon got the invalid on board the tender, and placed him on some cushions in the stern of the deck.

Benny sank down with a sigh of relief, and wearily closed his eyes and dropped off into the sleep of prostration.

The young Earl, standing over him, gazed mournfully down upon the fair, wan, wasted face, and then raised his eyes inquiringly to the surgeon.

Doctor Kinlock gravely shook his head, and sighed.

And the Earl was answered.

The sick and wounded men were still coming on board.

"Where are all these poor creatures to be taken, doctor?"

inquired the young Earl, regarding the suffering crowd compassionately.

"To the Military Hospitals at Walworth, for the present, where I have orders to deliver them over to the surgeon in charge," replied the surgeon.

"Is Captain Douglas expected to go with them?"

"That will be at his own option. He is on sick leave. He can go to the hospital to be treated, if he please, or he can go anywhere else, if he prefer," replied the surgeon.

"And yourself, doctor?" inquired the young Earl, after a pause.

"Oh, I shall be on leave also. After I have delivered over my charge, I shall be at liberty to go anywhere. I have scarcely thought yet where I shall go. My old home at Seton is standing still; but I am an old bachelor, without any particular attraction there more than elsewhere," said the surgeon with a bitter-sweet smile.

"Then, doctor, I have a proposal to make you, and I shall be very glad if it meet your views. I have nothing in this world to occupy me at present, and I think I cannot employ my leisure better than by devoting it to this brave young man, who has no near relative to look after him. I shall invite him to be my guest, and so I shall take charge of him. And if you can kindly favor us with your company, we shall be very happy to have you. What do you say?" inquired Lord Wellrose.

"Thanks, my lord; but where do you propose to go?" asked the surgeon.

"I must take your advice upon that question. We have all Britain to choose from. And of course, Captain Douglas' health must be our first consideration. What do you counsel?"

The surgeon reflected for a moment, but did not reply. And the Earl continued:

"I am willing and anxious to go anywhere to benefit the

health of Douglas. I wish to save his life, if possible. I would spare neither pains nor cost to do so."

"And — in other respects, is it equally immaterial to your lordship where you go?" inquired Doctor Kinlock.

"Equally, I assure you. I have but one wish in this matter—to save Douglas, if it be possible. Here is the Isle of Wight not far off. What do you say to that?"

"I don't recommend it, my lord."

"The south coast here, then—Brighton, Torquay, Penzance?"

"No, my lord; he has had enough of the sea air."

"Then, my dear Kinlock, suggest something yourself," said the Earl.

"Then, my lord, I should certainly recommend the bracing air of the Highlands."

"The Highlands!" echoed Lord Wellrose in some surprise.

"Yes, my lord, the Highlands—decidedly the Highlands," repeated the surgeon.

"This is certainly the season when many invalids go to the Highlands, but not consumptive invalids. And Captain Douglas I should take to be consumptive."

"He is not so, in the usual acceptation of the word, my lord. He is suffering more from general debility than from any other cause. And by general debility, in his case, I mean a general and profound depression of body, mind and spirit. Look at him now, as he sleeps. He scarcely seems to live or breathe. He lies as one dead."

The young Earl followed the direction of the doctor's glance, and sighed deeply. And then he said:

"He shall go to the Highlands. And I deem myself very fortunate in being able to offer him a home quieter and more comfortable than any hotel or lodging-house to be found in those regions. The family are at Cheviot Castle this season. And thus Seton Court is left in charge of the housekeeper and steward and a few old retainers, who will all be glad to see us. What do you say to the plan, Doctor?"

"It is an excellent one."

"Then, as soon as we get back to my hotel, I will telegraph to the housekeeper to have tne rooms aired and everything ready for us. Of course you will go with us. That is understood, I hope?"

"Yes, my lord, I shall be most happy."

"Right. You will also be near your old village home, which will be an advantage," added the Earl.

And while he spoke, as the last of the sick and wounded had been brought on board, the tender dropped away from the side of the great ship, and steamed toward the shore.

As soon as she touched the pier, the bustle of landing the invalided troops began. Many among them had friends who had come down to meet them. And their meeting added to the confusion.

The noise awoke Benny, who opened his eyes and looked wearily around until his glance met the face of the Earl when he smiled radiantly.

Dr. Kinlock was very much engaged in superintending the landing of the invalids under his charge.

But Lord Wellrose himself went on shore and engaged a carriage, and had it drawn up as near as permissible to the steamer. And then he raised Benny, and supported him tenderly to the carriage. and placed him comfortably in it.

And Lord Wellrose, taking Benny's fair head upon his breast, gave the order to the coachman to drive slowly to the "Lord Admiral."

On reaching that hotel, his lordship's groom and valet were found to be in attendance.

And with their assistance, Captain Douglas was taken up to the rooms that had been engaged for his accommodation, and laid upon a comfortable lounge.

Lord Wellrose ordered a dainty luncheon, such as he hoped might tempt the invalid's delicate appetite. And then he came and sat by Benny's lounge, and took his wasted hand, and said:

"We will soon bring you around, my boy. English air and English fare will soon restore you."

"It is rest and peace—it is meat and drink—only for me to lie here and look at you," said Benny, with a tone and glance of such pure love and perfect content, that reached the young Earl's heart.

"I really do believe you like me, Douglas," said the Earl, with a smile.

"Like you!" echoed Benny, with a look of ineffable affection—"like you! Why, you have changed all my life from darkness to light! You have made life bright to me, and even death easy!"

"But we will not talk of death. We will have nothing to do with death at present, on any terms whatever. You are going home with me to Seton Court, where you and I will live together, *en garcon*, for a few weeks, and where our good, motherly old housekeeper will nurse you back to health. Seton Court is at the foot of the mountain, and at the head of the loch. It is one of the most sublime and beautiful places in the Highlands. Tourists make pilgrimages to it; artists paint it; poets be-rhyme it. I feel sure that you will like it."

"I feel sure that I shall like any place where I may only lie and look at you till I die," said Benny, affectionately.

"Die again! I say we will have no dying. And here comes luncheon, which looks more like living," said the young Earl pleasantly, as the waiter entered to lay the cloth, followed by an assistant with a well-laden tray in his hands.

By the Earl's direction, the waiter drew a table up by the side of the invalid's lounge, laid the cloth and arranged the luncheon upon it. There were fresh oysters, fragrant soup, a roasted pheasant; some light, delicious wine; ripe peaches, apricots and grapes.

And then, because Lord Wellrose with his own hand served the invalid with the most choice of the viands spread before him, Benny tried to eat, and found, to his surprise, that he really could do so, for appetite came with touch and taste and smell.

"And now try a little of this Moselle," said the Earl. And though two waiters were in attendance, with his own hand he filled Benny's glass and passed it to him, knowing that the wine would really do him more good when poured by a loved hand.

For these two unconscious brothers loved each other "with a love passing the love of woman."

After luncheon, Benny fell asleep again, with his hand clasped in the hand of the Earl.

Lord Wellrose did not leave him until night. And then he left him comfortably in bed, with his own valet, Perkins, to sleep in the room.

Lord Wellrose was engaged in looking over the evening paper, when Dr. Kinlock's card was brought to him.

He requested that the doctor should be shown up.

And in a few moments Dr. Kinlock entered the room.

"I've got them all off my hands at length, poor fellows, and heartily glad I am of it," said the surgeon, as, at the Earl's invitation, he dropped into a chair.

The Earl congratulated him. And then he reported Benny's condition, and inquired of the doctor what the chances might be for his restoration to health.

But the doctor was very reserved in giving his opinion. He said that young Douglas must always have been constitutionally very delicate, and that he would seem to have suffered, in his childhood, from much neglect, privation and exposure, that had still further undermined his fragile health.

"I fear it has been so indeed," sighed the Earl.

"You care very much for this young man, my lord," said the surgeon.

"I care so much for him that there is not another man on earth, except my father, that I prefer before him," said the Earl earnestly.

"You have known him long, my lord, I presume."

"I have known him since his childhood, though for many years I lost sight of him."

"And you do not know, I think you once said, exactly in what degree of relationship, if in any, he stands to your lordship?"

"I do not indeed," said the Earl, gazing upon the surgeon in surprise and questioning.

"Then, my lord, I fear I am going to startle your lordship very much. I have not yet let the secret pass my lips even to him. But it is my painful duty to reveal it to your lordship. I wish you could—could spare me by anticipating it. But your lordship has no suspicion of the parentage of this young man?"

"None."

"LORD WELLROSE, HE IS YOUR OWN BROTHER!"

CHAPTER XL.

PROOFS.

Concealment is no more. They speak
All circumstance that may compel
Full credence to the tale they tell.—BYRON.

"GOOD Heaven, man!" exclaimed the Earl, standing up and staring at the surgeon as if he thought him insane.

"Your *own* brother, Earl of Wellrose, the son of your own father and mother," continued the surgeon.

"MAN, you are mad to say it!" exclaimed the Earl.

"Your *elder* brother, my lord; born two years before you saw the light," persisted the surgeon, rising and standing before the Earl.

"You must utterly have lost your reason. Sit down, I beg you, and try to collect your thoughts," said Lord Wellrose, who was himself profoundly agitated, not only by the suddenness, strangeness and importance of this revelation, but by something also in his own mind that assured him of its truth.

"I will sit down, and be very quiet. And do you also follow your own advice and my example," calmly replied the surgeon, as he resumed his seat.

The Earl of Wellrose sank into a chair, saying:

"Now, in the name of Heaven, give me your reasons, if you can possibly have any, for making this most astounding statement."

"My lord, I will. But permit me first to put a question. Does your lordship remember ever to have heard of an elder brother, the son of your parents' early marriage, who was said to have died in his infancy?" gravely inquired Doctor Kinlock.

"Oh, yes; quite often. My dearest mother has frequently spoken with me about that little lost one," said the Earl, thoughtfully.

"Your lordship is then aware of all the circumstances under which that child was born, and was supposed to have died?"

"Yes."

"Will your lordship pardon me for asking you, in the interests of justice, to recount those circumstances?"

"Most certainly. My father and mother, as is now generally known, were first privately married in London. Their first child, my elder brother, was born some ten months afterward at Ornoch Castle, in Scotland. For certain reasons he was taken by Dr. Seton, the attendant physician, to be put out at nurse. But being very fragile, he died the same night, while under the charge of the doctor."

"Those are the circumstances as known to your lordship?"

"Those are the circumstances as known to me."

"Then, Lord Wel'rose, I have this to add: That brother did not die, as was supposed. That brother lives now, in the person of Benjamin Seton Douglas," said the surgeon, gravely.

"After your first startling disclosure, I expected to hear this also. But now tell me what proofs you possess of the truth of this story," said the Earl, with more calmness than could have been expected.

"Certainly, my lord. I should surely never expect you to receive this statement without proof. To begin with, then, I must remind your lordship that at the time of your elder brother's birth, I was the pupil and assistant of Doctor Seton, the medical attendant of your mother."

"I know."

"On that wild March night, when your elder brother was born, I sat up till morning, waiting for the doctor's return. In the gray dawn of the morning he came home, bringing with him the dead body of a newly born male child, which he represented to be the child of a charity patient named Magdalene Hurst. He said that he had brought it to the house for post-mortem examination and then burial. With my assistance he performed the autopsy. And the same day the death was duly registered, and the child was buried."

"And this child was not my elder brother?"

"No. This child was what Doctor Seton represented him to me to be—the child of a charity patient who was too poor to bury him. Your infant brother, very fragile indeed, but still living, lay then upon the bosom of that woman, Magdalene Hurst, who, while in a state of unconsciousness, had been bereaved of her own babe, and had had this one, your infant elder brother, dressed in its clothes and put in its place by her side, and so palmed off upon her as her own. Pardon me, Lord Wellrose, for telling you these truths."

"It is your duty to tell me them, since you believe them. And you say that you have proof."

"I have proof, my lord."

"Go on, then!"

"The child of Magdalene Hurst died, and was buried, as I said. The child of William and Eglantine Douglas, now Duke and Duchess of Cheviot, lay on her bosom in its stead. And yet Magdalene Hurst knew nothing of this fraud that had substituted the living noble for the dead peasant."

"Go on! go on!"

"At length, however, the old nurse, who had been Dr. Seton's only confederate in this '*pious fraud*'—as the old doctor honestly considered it—came upon her death-bed, and being smitten with remorse, summoned Magdalene Hurst to receive her confession. And when Magdalene came, she told the astonished woman of the fraud that had been put upon her. And then, before she could utter another word, she died, leaving the woman in perfect ignorance of the real parentage of her foster-child, or of any clue by which she might discover it."

"The last part of this story I have heard already, from Benjamin; but there was nothing in the part told me to lead me to suspect that Benjamin was more than a distant kinsman of the family. Oh! good Heaven! if your story be true, as you believe it, how much, how dreadfully, how awfully has my brother been wronged!" said the young Earl, earnestly.

The surgeon looked at him in amazement and admiration. Here was no selfish consideration of his own lost rank as eldest son and heir—only the thought how much his brother had been wronged!

"As yet, Lord Wellrose," he said, "I have produced no proof of the truth of what I have advanced. I proceed to do so now. I was, as I said before, and as your lordship knows, a pupil and assistant of Dr. Seton. I was with him in the latter years of his life, and I attended him in his last illness, and on his death-bed. I was with him when he sent in haste for your father and mother, saying that he had a disclosure to make to them. I was with him when they came to his death-bed side. But they came too late—the power of speech had left him. And it was awful to stand there and see his agonizing efforts to make the disclosure he had summoned them to hear. He died and took the secret with him to the grave, as every one supposed."

"My mother always feared it concerned her first-born son," said the Earl.

"Her maternal instincts were true. It did concern him. Dr. Seton died, and was buried; and I, his assistant and heir, Christopher Kinlock, succeeded to his property and to his practice. And years passed on. The doctor's death was a thing of the past. His unrevealed secret was forgotten."

"Not by all! Not by my father and my mother! I think that all their lives they have been troubled, at times, by the recollection of the doctor's death-bed and speculation as to the nature of that disclosure which he tried and failed to make them. But I interrupt you. Pray go on!"

"A long time passed. A generation grew up. This Russian war broke out. I wished for a surgeon's commission in the army, and through the Duke of Cheviot's kindness I obtained it. I had to break up my bachelor's establishment in Seton—the establishment, in fact, I had inherited from my predecessor. Among the furniture that I had determined to dispose of was an old writing desk and bookcase. I had emptied it of all its apparent contents, and then ordered it to be carried away to the auctioneer. But in moving the old mouldering desk it fell to pieces, and revealed a secret drawer filled with papers. I took possession of the papers which at first glance seemed to be only old love-letters and old memoranda of debts—secret debts, I mean. I had no time to look into them then. Your lordship knows how sudden my appointment was, and how quickly I was called upon to report for duty,"

"Yes, of course I know."

"So, having no time to examine these papers, which I did not indeed think of much importance, but which a morbid curiosity incited me to read when I should find time, I bundled them all up and packed them into my trunk to look over at my leisure. I took them with me to the Crimea. I had no idea of their immense value to *one.* I had put them in the bottom of my trunk. And in the terrible scenes that followed I forgot them. Later on, my young friend, Lieutenant Douglas, was dangerously wounded. 'If I die, Dr. Kinlock, take charge of my effects, and send them to Lord Wellrose,' he said, as he lapsed into unconsciousness. I took charge of his boxes, as he had desired. It was in the simple action of giving out his linen that I came now and then across the name of Benjamin Hurst. I took little account of it at the time."

"It was the name he bore once, as I suppose you now know," said the Earl.

"Yes. And when the young man recovered sufficiently to permit of conversation, I called his attention to the fact that this strange name was marked upon some of his clothing. He smiled, but gave me no explanation."

"Poor fellow! He kept silence, in regard for me. *I* had given him his new name."

"Aye, my lord; so I thought. And a mere instinct of justice, if not of brotherly love, must have guided your action. But I did not know it then. In a few days the order came to me to sail for England, in charge of the invalided troops. Among these was Captain Douglas, to whom, for good reasons, I gave particular attention. It was during our voyage home that I had ample leisure to look over that old bundle of yellow, mildewed papers that I had discovered in the secret drawer of my guardian's writing-desk when the old worm-eaten book-case was accidentally broken to pieces, in the attempt to move it. I really felt not the slightest interest in those old papers beyond the languid curiosity of an idle voyager in want of amusement. So I looked but carelessly over the old love-letters of the bachelor doctor's boyhood, and the memoranda of old debts sometime to be paid, and old wrongs to be set right by post obit restitution. At length I opened a paper that took away my eyesight and my breath for a full minute. Aye, my lord, it did. As I gazed upon it, a mist passed before my vision, and I gasped. Here, my lord, is the paper; look at it for yourself," said the surgeon, placing in the Earl's hand a folded paper, yellow with age and speckled with mildew.

The Earl took it with calmness, and opened it with care.

First there dropped from the paper a little fine, white, knitted sock, which his lordship picked up and examined with much interest.

"I have seen the fellow to this," he said, as he scrutinized the wreath of eglantines and the crest of Seton-Linlithgow embroidered in the instep.

"You have seen the fellow to that, my lord?" echoed the surgeon.

"Yes, in the hands of Captain Douglas. It was a relic of his childhood. He showed it to me before he left England for the Crimea. No doubt he has it still in his possession," replied the Earl, as he carefully laid the mute witness aside, and proceeded to the examination of the faded writing on the paper. He read as follows

Seton, March, 18—.

"**Memoranda** of the facts relating to the secret birth and concealment of the first-born son of Eglantine, Baroness of Linlithgow, and William Douglas of Douglas Cheviot, late a lieutenant in her Majesty's —— Regiment of Foot, stationed in Canada. I was called to Ornoch Castle, in this shire, on the night of March —, 18—, to attend the Baroness of Linlithgow in her confinement.

"At twelve, midnight, she gave birth to a male child, and immediately fell into syncope.

"Besides myself, only Lady Shetland and the nurse were present. Circumstances that are known to all the parties interested in this statement—and none others need see it—rendered it expedient, for the sake of the family honor, to conceal the birth of this child, and he was committed to me to be disposed of.

"After I had recovered my patient from her syncope, and got her, under the influence of morphia, into a refreshing sleep, I took the child, and while the mother slept in unconsciousness, I carried him to the little seaport of Killford, and to the house of the woman whom I had already engaged to take charge of a new-born child when it should arrive, without telling her the real parentage of the child.

"This woman, by name Magdalene Hurst, was stewardess of the coasting steamer *Shaft*, but was at this time confined of her first child, a boy.

"On reaching the hut where the woman Magdalene Hurst lodged with an old midwife by the name of Jean Craig, I found that my patient was in a profound sleep, and that her child had died while she slept.

"Immediately occurred to me a means by which I might conceal the existence of Eglantine Seton's child more effectually than by simply putting him out to nurse. I broached my plan to the old woman in attendance, and used such arguments as convinced her of the expediency and propriety of substituting the living infant for the dead one. I clenched my arguments by the gift of a few guineas. And I secured her secrecy by a threat of the consequences to herself, as well as to others, should she betray the trust.

"The clothing of the dead and the living child was then exchanged. The living child was laid at the bosom of the foster-mother, and the dead one was taken to Seton Old Church, and buried.

"Magdalene Hurst was led to believe that the child on her bosom was her own, and Eglantine Seton was told that the child who filled the nameless coffin at Seton Old Church, was *hers*.

"In a few weeks, Magdalene Hurst, stewardess of the *Shaft*, went back to London, taking with her the foster-child whom she believed to be her own, and whom she had named Benjamin, after his supposed father.

"Feeling now the infirmities of old age creeping upon me, and knowing that I may be called suddenly hence, and not wishing to take such a secret away with me to the grave, nor yet deeming it expedient to divulge it at this present time, I make these memoranda, for the information of those whom it may in future concern, and for those only, knowing that they will guard, as I have guarded, the honor of the house of Seton-Linlithgow.

"Signed with my hand, and sealed with my seal. ALEXANDER SETON, of the village of Seton, physician and surgeon."

After reading this strange document to the end, Lord Wellrose folded it carefully and held it in his hand and fell into deep thought.

Dr. Kinlock refrained from breaking in upon his reverie. At length Lord Wellrose inquired:

"Does Captain Douglas know of the existence of this document?"

"No, my lord, he does not," answered the surgeon.

"Have you mentioned, or hinted to him, in any way, the fact of the discovery you have made?"

"No, my lord; no. I deemed it best, for many reasons, not to do so. In the first place he was in a condition of weakness, with tendency to hemorrhage of the lungs, that made absolute quietness vitally necessary. Any excitement must have been very dangerous, and would have been probably fatal to him. In the second place I thought it due to your family to make the communication first to yourself, my lord, or to your father, the Duke of Cheviot. In the third place, we were very near England when I made the discovery; and before I had thought over the subject many days, I found myself in Southampton waters. I hope your lordship thinks that I did well."

"You did well," said the Earl, with much emotion.

"Your lordship thinks the proof of your brother's birth conclusive?"

"Yes, I think it conclusive. With the corroborative testimony we have in our hands, I think it quite indisputable. But, oh, gracious Lord of Heaven, how bitterly has my brother been wronged in all these years!" groaned the Earl, covering his face with his hands.

"Your lordship takes no thought of yourself at all in this matter," said the surgeon in amazement.

"Why should I? No one has injured me. But, Great Heaven! how *he* has been wronged! Doctor, we must save him. The best medical skill in England—in Europe—in the world, must be engaged for his restoration to life and health!"

The surgeon gravely shook his head.

"My lord," he said, "I tell you frankly I have no hopes of saving Captain Douglas' life. He was *born* with a constitution enfeebled by the sufferings of his mother even before his birth; that feeble constitution was further undermined by the privations and exposures of his infancy and childhood; and it has received its death-blow in that awful winter before Sebastopol, and in that last fatal wound received when he planted his colors upon the walls of the citadel."

"I tell you, no! He must and shall be saved! All my fortune shall be devoted to his service. The best medical skill in the world shall be secured for him."

"Ah! my lord, there is a limit to the power of wealth and to the skill of physicians. They cannot raise the dead they cannot restore the dying!"

"Then God can! Prayer shall aid work, and we shall save him yet!" said the young Earl, in holy triumph.

CHAPTER XLI.

AT SETON ON THE LOCH.

Face to face with the true mountains
 Standing silently and still,
Drawing strength from Fancy's dauntings,
 From the air about the hill,
And from Nature's open hauntings,
 And most debonaire good will.—E. B. BROWNING.

WHEN the surgeon had left the room, the Earl of Wellrose went to his newly discovered brother's chamber. He found the invalid sleeping calmly. He stood by the bed and gazed compassionately upon the fair, wan, unconscious face.

"He must take my titles and estates away from me, and yet Heaven only knows how much I love him! And ah Lord of Heaven! how cruelly and bitterly he has been wronged!" the young Earl murmured as he gazed.

Then with his own hands, and with almost womanly tenderness and care, he drew the coverlet up over the delicate chest, closed the curtains and lowered the gas.

Then he opened the communicating door and passed silently into his own room.

His valet was there ready to attend him.

"I shall not require anything more to-night, Perkins. You can go," said his lordship.

The valet bowed and withdrew.

Lord Wellrose threw himself into an arm-chair beside a table, with his elbow resting upon the top and his head bowed upon his hand. He felt no disposition to retire to rest. His mind was oppressed with thoughts of the startling revelation he had received from the surgeon. He could not for an instant doubt its truth. Beyond all question Benjamin Douglas was his elder brother, the son of his parents by their first rash, childish marriage.

But the heaviest of all was the thought how that elder, even in helpless infancy, had been cast down into the lowest depths of the social hells, while he, the younger, had always lived in the heaven of family love, and moral, religious and intellectual culture, enjoying privileges that should have been the blessings of both.

But now full justice must be done to that deeply injured elder brother, at whatever cost to himself, the younger, or to any one else.

As he could not sleep, he drew his chair closer to the table, drew writing materials toward him and wrote two letters. The first and least important was a short one addressed to Mrs. Bruce, the housekeeper at Seton Court, directing her to have the house opened and aired, and rooms got ready to receive himself and his guests, who expected to reach Seton on the evening of the fourth day from the date of that letter. The second, and most important one, was addressed to his father, the Duke of Cheviot, at Cheviot Castle, earnestly requesting the Duke and Duchess to join their son at Seton House, at the end of a week from date, assigning as a reason for this request, very important business, that would be better discussed at Seton than at Cheviot.

He closed and sealed these letters, and rang for a late waiter, into whose hands he placed them, with the order that they should go by the first mail.

And then, having done all that it was possible to do in the premises that night, he retired to rest.

The next morning, the Earl of Wellrose, Captain Douglas and Doctor Kinlock left Southampton for London by an early train. A double compartment in a first-class carriage had been engaged and fitted up comfortably, with additional cushions and rugs. So the journey was accomplished with more ease to the invalid officer than could have been hoped from his weakened condition.

On reaching London they took rooms at the nearest hotel, the Paddington, where they passed the remainder of the day and the night.

The next morning, with precautions for Captain Douglas' comfort, the party started by the Great North-western train for York, *en route* for Scotland.

They reached that old cathedral town in the afternoon, rested there until the next morning, and then resumed their journey. The afternoon of the third day brought them into Edinburg. And thus, by short and easy stages they in turn reached Glasgow, Stirling, Callender, and finally, on the evening of the fourth day, they reached by coach the little port of Killford, where the steamer *Sprite* was waiting Lord Wellrose's orders to take them up the loch to Seton Castle.

Immediately on leaving the coach the party went on board the steamer.

It was a cold, clear, starlight night, and to Benjamin, who sat on deck, wrapped in his old camp overcoat, the majestic scenery of loch and mountain was but dimly apparent, but the very obscurity of the landscape lent the weird charm of awe to its beauty. They passed the narrow, winding "straits" that connected the sea with the loch, and where the turns were so short that every few minutes it seemed as if the bows of the boat were going straight up to the land. At length a final turn brought them out upon the broad expanse of the loch, encircled by its lofty mountains, row looming dimly through the clear, starlight night.

Benny uttered a low exclamation of delight.

"You should see the loch by daylight, or by moonlight, when indeed it is exceedingly beautiful," said the Earl.

"It is beautiful exceedingly now, under the dim light of the stars," answered Benjamin, in a low, hushed tone.

And then the brothers relapsed into that silence which is more eloquent than words, as they gazed upon the darkly glorious scene.

A few minutes more brought them to the foot of the water-stairs leading from the loch up into the wooded hills of Seton Chase.

Lord Wellrose gave his arm to his brother, and supported him in going up the stairs, at the top of which they found a large and commodious close carriage waiting to take the travellers to the house.

Lord Wellrose, Captain Douglas, and Doctor Kinlock took their seats, and the horses started.

They drove up a winding road through the thick woods, to the top of the hill, where they entered an avenue of oak-trees that presently led them up to the front of the house, where the windows were shining with hospitable lights.

Mrs. Bruce, the aged housekeeper, with the household servants at her back, received the party at the door. She had been the Earl's nurse a quarter of a century back, and this circumstance constituted a bond of strong affection between herself and her foster-child. She had been promoted from the nursery to the head of the house at Seton Court, and was passing her old age in ease and comfort.

She now stood there in the lighted hall, looking trim and neat in her black silk dress and white muslin cap, neckerchief and apron, smiling and courtesying her welcome.

"How do you do, Mrs. Bruce?" said the young Earl, affectionately, shaking her hands and kissing her rough cheeks.

"I'm weel, and blithe to see ye, my bairn—my laird, I mean!" replied the old nurse, suddenly correcting herself.

"Your 'bairn' always, dear nurse! Whatever I may be to others, I am your 'bairn,'" said the young Earl, with his kindly smile. "And now here is my kinsman, Captain Douglas, who has come back from the war wounded and ill, and in need of tender and skillful nursing. You must take as much care of him as you used to take of me when I was ailing," he added.

"Ah! God bless his bonny face! he's unco like the family, and might be your lordship's ain brither, by the looks of him. But eh, sirs! he's unco fair and fragile, to hae been a soldier, noo. Aweel, laddie, the guid mountain air, wi' my ain nursing, will sune bring ye round again," she said, nodding and courtesying to the invalid guest, who smiled and thanked her.

There were spacious, comfortably furnished old-fashioned bed-rooms, lighted with wax candles in tall silver candlesticks, and heated with glowing wood fires in the massive open fire-places, waiting for the travellers. Here they refreshed themselves with a wash, and then went down to the smaller dining-room, where a good supper was ready for them.

Soon after supper they went to bed.

In the morning Benny arose early, and with the assistance of a footman whom Lord Wellrose had appointed to wait on him, he made his toilet, and went to the morning parlor, to which the footman showed the way.

This parlor had a modern French window opening upon a balcony, and overlooking the loch.

As the morning was very fine, Benny ventured to step out upon the balcony, where a magnificent and beautiful scene burst upon his view—the loch with its clear, deep blue waters glittering in the morning sun, and its girdle of lofty mountains, with their base clothed in deep evergreens, and the sharp, bare peaks gleaming in the morning light with all the colors of the rainbow. Benny, always sensitive to beauty, fairly caught his breath as he gazed.

A light hand was laid upon his shoulder.

He turned, and saw the Earl standing by his side.

"What do you think of the view?" inquired his lordship with a smile.

"What do I think?" echoed Benny, in a calm ecstacy. "There is Paradise still on earth. Eden could not have been fairer than this. Only to breathe and see here, seems joy enough. It is a heavenly place to live in—*or to die in*," he added, in a lower tone.

"To live in, yes. But, as I observed once before, we will have no dying. I most decidedly object to that sort of thing, except in centenarians. They have a right to die, if they insist upon doing so. But as for a young man like yourself, he has no right to think of such a proceeding; and therefore—"

As the Earl said these last words he stepped back into the parlor, and presently returned with a tartan shawl, which he carefully placed around his brother's shoulders, saying, with a smile:

"If you do not take better care of yourself, Douglas, I shall have to be your valet. What would Kinlock say if he saw you out here without a wrap?"

"He would say," exclaimed the surgeon, who at that moment joined them, "that standing shivering on a bleak balcony, while gazing at a magnificent scene, is taking the poetry without the comforts of life, the elegancies without the necessaries; or, to bring it right home to your hearts and stomachs, it's like having the dessert without the dinner! There, the tea and muffins are cooling on the break fast table, to say nothing of the haddock and eggs."

Lord Wellrose laughed, and they all went in to breakfast.

And after breakfast Benny was obliged to lie down on the

sofa of his room. Whether it was from the reaction of his excitement on reaching his native shores, or whether it was the fatigue of his long journey, or from the progress of an incurable malady, or from all these causes combined, Bonny was again prostrated with weakness, so he was compelled to keep his sofa.

"How is this, Kinlock? Why does he not get stronger?" inquired the Earl of the surgeon, as soon as they found themselves alone together.

"I told your lordship the truth from the beginning. I never deceived your lordship," said the surgeon, gravely.

"Do you mean to say that he will never be better?"

"He will be better and then worse, as is the way with people suffering as he does; but, my lord, he will never recover," gravely replied the doctor.

"You medical gentlemen *may* sometimes be mistaken, may you not?"

"Certainly."

"Then I will cling to the hope that you are mistaken in this instance," said the Earl, as he arose and went to his brother's apartment.

CHAPTER XLII.

NEWS OF SUZY.

> I loved . . . . Forty thousand "lovers"
> Could not, with all their quantity of love,
> Make up my sum.—SHAKESPEARE.

HE found Benjamin reclining on the sofa.

"How do you feel now?" he inquired, taking a seat by his side.

"Tired—a little tired, but very comfortable and happy," replied Benjamin, holding out his hand to his brother.

"It is but the effect of your long journey," said Lord Wellrose, taking the thin white hand and holding it in his own.

"My lord," began Benny, after a short silence, "ever since I reached home, I have been longing to ask you more particularly about—"

He hesitated in some embarrassment, and his pale face flushed.

"About Suzy?" suggested the Earl.

"Yes, my lord; about Suzy."

"And I, also, have been wishing to speak to you of her; but as you did not mention—"

And here Lord Wellrose paused, in a little less embarrassment than Benny had betrayed.

The fact is, there had been, and still was, a singular reticence in both these brothers on the subject of Suzy. And the reason was obvious: both loved each other with a brotherly love, and both loved, or had loved, Suzy, with a love that was certainly not brotherly.

"You hear from her often?" said Benny, half-questioningly.

"I hear from her, and write to her by every mail. We exchange letters about once a fortnight."

"She is well, I hope?"

"She is well; but our correspondence is by no means what you would suppose it to be."

"Indeed!"

"Indeed no. She writes to me as though I might be her respected pastor instead of her betrothed. You shall see a recent letter she wrote me. It is a sample one. And it will be no breach of confidence, since there is not a word in it that might not be proclaimed from the church-steeple," said the Earl, as he arose and left the room.

He returned in a few moments with Suzy's letter. He put it open into Benny's hand.

And oh, he saw and marked that frail hand tremble as it touched the paper!

Benny began to read the letter—a cool, friendly, formal letter, such as any girl might have written to a male relative, with whom duty compelled her to correspond, but such as certainly no girl ever before wrote to her betrothed lover.

Benny finished reading the letter, raised his eyes to the face of the Earl, and stared with surprise and perplexity.

Lord Wellrose smiled.

"Why, what on earth does she mean? What in the world is the matter?" inquired Benny.

"Nothing is the matter. The child has found out her mistake in having fancied that she ever loved me with a real and lasting love," said the Earl, calmly.

"How long has she written to you in this style?"

"Always — that is, ever since she began to answer my letters at all."

"Then it must have been, and must still be, mere timidity that caused her to write so coldly. Suzy was timid in some respect."

"It was not timidity in this case. I will prove it to you. The letter that you have just read is the last but one I received from her. This one that I am now about to show you is the very last. In it you will see that she deliberately requests me to free her from her engagement to me, assigning as reasons the unsuitableness of the proposed marriage, the opposition of my family, her own personal unfitness for the rank I offered her, and more than all, the change in her own feelings, which has taught her that she never truly loved me as she once thought she did. Moreover, she gives me no chance to refuse her request, for she tells me, in conclusion, that she is coming home to England, and shall be on the seas before another letter from me can reach her."

While the Earl spoke, Benny's memory was busy with the past.

He remembered that just before they parted, Suzy to go to Australia, and himself to go to the Crimea, she had confessed to him a plan she had formed of absenting herself from England until the Earl should be cured of his indiscreet attachment. He remembered that he himself had begged Suzy to impart her plan to her lover, and get his consent that this test should be put to the strength of his love. And she had said that she would think of his advice. He wondered now whether she had told her purpose. And now he asked the question:

"Did your lordship suspect that she would change in this way?"

"Never! It has taken nearly two years for the truth to gradually reach me."

Benjamin looked anxiously at his brother.

How calmly the Earl took his disappointment! But perhaps he was only exercising self-control. Benny ventured another question:

"And you, Lord Wellrose! You! How is it with you? What shall you do?"

"It is well with me, Benjamin. Just so soon as Suzy shall arrive in England, I shall take great pleasure in seeing the child, and freeing her from her foolish engagement."

Benjamin stared at the Earl in speechless astonishment.

"Don't look so shocked, my dear fellow. Our harmless passion was a brief hallucination, and nothing more. I was fascinated and dazzled by the beautiful singer, and she—" the Earl paused.

"Was fascinated and dazzled by the splendid young nobleman, the lion of Parliament, and the idol of society," said Benjamin, finishing the sentence in his own way, with fond enthusiasm.

"There!" said the Earl, patting Benny's hand, and laughing quietly. "How much I wish that all the world had as great faith in me as *you* have. But to come back to Suzy. It is all over between us. I shall always love the child as a dear, good little sister. But for the rest, I only wait to comply with her request, and free her from her engagement, before offering my hand to Lady Hinda Moray; who has long had my heart."

As the Earl ceased speaking he looked at Benjamin, and was startled to see the change that had come over his wan face and wasted form. His face was marble white and half concealed under his trembling hands, and his form was shaking as with a chill.

"Douglas! Douglas!" said the Earl, bending anxiously over him.

"Oh! if I could only live now! Oh! I wish I could live now!" murmured Benny, in a very low tone.

"Live! my dear boy, you must and shall live. You have so much to live for now; so much more than you know. Never give up! Despair kills more than disease does. *Ah, that cruel cough!*" murmured the Earl, suddenly breaking off from his discourse, as a violent paroxysm seized and shook the invalid, as if it would have shaken his fragile frame to dissolution.

"Yes, I have her to live for now," said Benny, as soon as the paroxysm had passed off. "Yes, Lord Wellrose, I will tell you all now. I *loved* her, my lord. Oh, Heaven, how I loved her! With no 'brief passion,' with no transient hallucination; but with a deep, true, vital love, that 'grew with my growth, and strengthened with my strength,' from infancy to childhood, to youth, to manhood; through good and through evil; in presence and in absence; in hope and in despair!"

"Ah! I suspected this!" murmured the Earl, in an almost inaudible voice.

"It is little to say that I would have died for her. Any man might have done that for his beloved. But I would have died an ignominious death on the scaffold and left my poor memory to infamy, only to have saved her brother from a felon's grave, and her fair name from the shadow of reproach. That was how I loved Suzy, Lord Wellrose," said Benny, with an unusual outburst of emotion.

The Earl was deeply moved.

"You loved her so, and yet you would have promoted her marriage with me!" he said.

"Yes, my lord, because I thought she loved you, even as I loved her. And her happiness--yes, and yours too—was dearer to me than my own," said Benny, earnestly.

"But now you know she never loved me so—never really loved me at all. She only fancied so: drawn first to like me by my strong resemblance to you, her life love. The tremendous sacrifice of your life and good name that you were about to make for her sake, naturally awoke her heart to the knowledge of your great love and her own. And she did well and wisely in going away to her parents at the antipodes, and there to wait for time and Providence to set us all right. Be comforted, my dear Douglas, for she returns your love."

As the Earl spoke there was a knock at the door, presently followed by the entrance of a footman, who said respectfully:

"My lord, their Graces, the Duke and Duchess of Cheviot have arrived, and wish to see your lordship."

"So soon! I did not expect them quite yet," said the Earl to himself. "Tell their Graces I will attend them immediately," he added, to the servant, who went away with the message.

"Dear Douglas, you hear that my father and mother have come. I must leave you for a little while, but I will soon return," said the Earl, as he left the room.

"What a comfort it must be to have a father and mother

living," murmured Benny to himself as his brother closed the door.

Then the racking cough seized and tore him with violence.

CHAPTER XLIII.

NEWS FOR THE DUKE AND DUCHESS.

Alas! the mother that him bore
Had not known her son.—SIR WALTER SCOTT.

MEANWHILE Lord Wellrose went down to the drawing room to welcome his parents. But he had to wait a few moments for the Duke and Duchess, who had gone to their dressing-rooms to change their travelling suits.

At length they both entered together. And after an affectionate greeting, they sat down, and the Duchess said:

"Your letter surprised us very much, Wellrose."

"We set off at once, to know what was the matter," added the Duke.

"Heavens, Wellrose! how your face changes! What can have happened?"

"Out with your bad news at once! It will not improve by keeping," said the Duke, uneasily.

"There is no bad news, father, though there is something te tell that will startle you very much."

"Tell it then."

"First let me offer my mother a glass of wine and a biscuit," said the Earl. And he rang and gave the order.

After the refreshments had been brought and tasted, the Duchess said:

"For mercy's sake, my son, do not keep us longer in suspense."

"No, do not," added the Duke.

"Then read this document, my father; and see if you recognize this little relic, my mother," said the Earl, as he drew a small parcel from his bosom, and placed Doctor Seton's confession in the Duke's hand, and the little embroidered sock on the Duchess' lap.

The Duke unfolded the paper, and began to read.

The Duchess picked up the little sock, looked at it, and with a half-suppressed cry, turned her eyes on Wellrose. Her color came and went; she trembled much; she could scarcely articulate the question:

"Where did you find it?"

"Folded in the document that my father is reading," replied the Earl, in a low tone.

She rose pale and trembling, and stood behind the Duke's sofa, and leaned over his shoulder to look at the document. His face was as pale as hers. His eyes seemed starting from their sockets, as they followed the lines of that written confession. But, conscious of his wife's approach, without taking his eyes from the paper, he put out his hand and drew her to a seat at his side, wound his arm protectingly around her, and let her read as he did.

Their faces paled and paled as they read. Sometimes her head dropped upon his shoulder, and a great heaving sob convulsed her bosom. And then his arm closed tighter around her; but his eyes never left following the lines of that paper until he had read it to its close. Then he turned toward his wife, and their eyes met, in grief and horror.

The Duchess found her voice first:

"Oh, my son! my son! my first-born! my best beloved! Oh, my innocent! my helpless! what has become of you? What has been your fate?" she cried, wringing her hands in an anguish too deep for tears.

The Earl of Wellrose, who had been standing pale and silent before them, now dropped on one knee beside her saying:

"Dear mother, be comforted. Your son, my brother, lives."

"Lives!" echoed the parents, in a breath.

"Yes, lives! Be assured of it; for I know it."

"Lives!" said the Duke again. "Aye, but his life may be worse than death."

"Not so," said the Earl hastily. "He has won honor in the service of his country. He was foremost in the glorious charge at Inkermann. His hand placed his regimental colors on the walls of Sebastopol. And though he has returned wounded and ill, he will yet do well."

They listened to him with breathless interest. Suddenly the Duchess caught his arm, strained her eyes into his and murmured hoarsely:

"He is—he is—he is—"

"Yes, dear mother, he is the Captain Douglas, of whom you heard me speak so often, and whom I went to Southampton to meet; though at that time I neither knew nor suspected his near relationship to us."

"Thank Heaven, the boy will do us no discredit," exclaimed the Duke, in happy ignorance of his poor son's miserable childhood and youth.

"Amen! Aye, thank God!" murmured the Duchess Then turning to the Earl, she hastily inquired:

"But where is he? tell me! Let me go to him at once! Ah! I have been away from him long enough—his whole lifetime! Let me see him at once! Sick and wounded, too! Let me go to him at once!"

And the Duchess arose and drew her shawl around her.

"Dear mother, be patient. He is not far off. You shall see him very soon. He is in the neighborhood," said the Earl, diplomatically.

"Why did you not bring him to this house?" inquired the Duchess. But before the Earl could answer the question, the Duke put another one:

"How did you make this discovery, Wellrose?"

The Earl addressing both his parents, related the history of Dr. Christopher Kinlock's accidental discovery of the documents hidden away in the secret drawer of Dr. Seton's secretary.

"So Kinlock knows all about it?" said the Duke.

"Yes; but he is discretion itself," replied Lord Wellrose.

"Does—your brother also know the secret of his birth?"

"No, my father. Dr. Kinlock and myself thought it due to you and my mother, that you should be told of it first. So I wrote, requesting you to meet me here."

"You were right. But I might repeat your mother's question, and inquire why you did not bring your brother here."

"My father, he *is* here. I left his sofa side when I came down here to see you," replied the Earl.

The duchess arose, with a slight cry.

"Take me to him at once," she said.

"Dear mother, be patient for a few moments, for his sake. He knows nothing of this secret yet. And in his weakened condition it will be necessary to break it to him gradually. My father, if you will trust that duty to me, I think I shall perform it more judiciously than another could," said the Earl.

"You counsel wisely, Wellrose. It shall be as you say. But when will you do this?"

"My dear father, when he wakes, refreshed from his noontide nap, he will be in the best condition to bear the excitement of such a revelation."

"And how soon will that be?" inquired the Duchess, anxiously.

"In about two hours, mother, dear," replied the Earl.

Then, after a little while, the question of the confused inheritance naturally arose.

"Heaven knows how glad I am of the restoration of our

eldest son. But without doubt it will complicate the question of property very much," said the Duke, uneasily.

"Oh, do not think of property at such a time," pleaded the Duchess.

"And I am sorry for you, Wellrose. This may deprive you of your heirship," continued the Duke.

"Do not think of me, dear father. My brother must have justice, and he can have it. I see clearly enough how all this may be arranged," said the young Earl, earnestly.

"You were always unselfish, Wellrose. But let us examine this question in a legal point of view for a moment. You may not be so great a loser as at first sight it would appear," said the Duke reflectively.

Eglantine and her son both looked up inquiringly.

"Our first youthful marriage, secretly solemnized in England, and afterward openly acknowledged in Scotland, was certainly legal in the last-mentioned country, though not in the first. The son of that first marriage would certainly be the lawful heir of all his father's and his mother's estates in Scotland."

"Most assuredly," put in Lord Wellrose.

"But not in England," continued the Duke. "And although he is even now Master of Seton, and will be, after his mother, Baron of Linlithgow, he cannot possibly become, after me, the Duke of Cheviot. This title, with all its appendences, in England, will be the inheritance of yourself, Wellrose, as the sole son of the second marriage, which was legal everywhere," said the Duke.

"And yet, father, in strict justice, if not in law, my elder brother should have been heir to all."

"In strict justice, yes," admitted the Duke.

"Then, I repeat, my brother shall have strict justice. It can be managed. A petition to the House of Lords would surely get a decree constituting that first marriage legal in England, as it is in Scotland, and making my elder brother the heir to all your titles and estates in both countries. Such decrees, under such justifiable circumstances, have been granted heretofore, and will be hereafter," urged the Earl.

"I am, of course, aware of that, Wellrose. But you, my son—you who have been brought up to consider yourself the heir?" said the Duke, with tears in his eyes.

"I repeat, that I must not be thought of in this matter. I have held my brother's birthright long enough. I must hold it no longer. Besides, I can make my own place in the world, dear father."

"Heaven bless you, my boy; you have a noble heart," said the Duke.

"Kinlock is here, father. Would you like to see him?"

"Yes, I should. I should like to hear from his own lips further details of this discovery."

"Then I will send him here to talk with you, while I gc up to my brother's room and break this news to him."

And the Earl kissed his mother's hand and left the room.

He found Dr. Kinlock pacing up and down the hall.

"Have you seen my brother lately?" inquired Lord Wellrose.

"I have just left him," answered the doctor.

"He is awake, then?"

"Oh, yes, awake, and much refreshed."

"Then I will go to him. Tho hour for the revelation has come. Go you, dear doctor, to my parents. They are in the blue drawing-room waiting for you," said the Earl, as he bowed and passed up the stairs.

He found Benjamin still reclining on his sofa, but looking brighter and stronger from his sleep.

The Earl sat down beside the invalid, took his hand in his own, and while he held it, said:

"My father and mother are here for a few days. They wish to see you, Benjamin, as soon as you are strong enough to see them."

"It is very kind of their Graces. I thank them very much. I hope they are well?" replied Benny.

"They are very well. They both take a great interest in you, Douglas. They feel sure that you must be a near relative of the family."

Benny lifted his eyes inquiringly to the face of the Earl. He seemed to think that there was something to be told.

"And I, Douglas, have told you often, that I feel convinced you are very nearly related to us."

"Indeed I hope it may be so. I would like to be your cousin, Lord Wellrose."

"You may be even nearer kin to me than that. Very singular, your exact resemblance to myself, and your earliest garments marked with the crest of my mother's family."

"It was," admitted Benny, still looking inquiringly into the face of his brother.

"Would it surprise you much to find out for a certainty that you are very related nearly to us indeed?" inquired the Earl, looking wistfully into the clear eyes that were upturned to his.

Benny's color came and went; he breathed fast, but faltered forth the words:

"No; I do not think it would."

"Then, my dear Douglas, read this paper," said the Earl placing in his hand the written confession of Dr. Seton, and watching him closely.

As Benny read, his wan face paled and flushed alternately. And when he finished, he let the paper slip from his hold, and he lifted his hands and laid them over his face.

"Douglas! Douglas! my brother!" murmured the Earl, anxiously bending over him.

"My brother!" echoed Benny, in a tone of infinite tenderness, as he uncovered his face and took the hand of the Earl, and pressed it to his heart.

"This has startled you very much, Benjamin," said the Earl.

"Yes, yes; and yet it should not have done so. My heart told me the truth long ago, long ago!—that night when, at Brunswick Terrace, in Brighton, I kneeled at her feet to offer her the crown of Christmas roses, and burst into tears, I knew not why; and that day in the Middlesex Hospital, when her tears fell upon my sleeping face, and I tried to wake in vain, my heart told me the truth. But I did not understand its language," said Benny, in strong emotion.

"But now you do. And now you know you have a father, and above all, a mother, and a brother, and many fair sisters. Your mother, *our* mother, longs to see you, Benjamin, just as soon as you are strong enough to receive her."

"Oh! now! now! let me look upon her lovely and gracious face again! It has never left my memory since that bright day at Brunswick Terrace," he said, as again his color came and went in quick successions of flush and pallor.

The Earl pressed the invalid's hand, and arose to leave the room; but, at a strange gurgling sound from the direction of the sofa, he turned.

Then he uttered an exclamation of horror unspeakable.

Benny had fallen back, white as death, and his bosom and pillow were crimsoned with his life blood.

CHAPTER XLIV.

"PASSING THE LOVE OF WOMAN."

"Kind friends may be to thee,
But love like HIS thou'lt see
Never again."

LORD WELLROSE had great presence of mind. He laid the fainting form flat upon the sofa, and then went and rang the bell.

To the footman who answered it, he said:

"Go, and request Dr. Kinlock to come here immediately, and quietly."

The man went away to do his errand, and the surgeon quickly made his appearance.

The Earl pointed in silence to the form lying on the sofa.

"I thought so," said the doctor, going up to his patient and feeling his pulse. "But you need not be alarmed, my lord. This is not much of a hemorrhage. A very little blood makes a great show. And see, it has quite ceased to flow," he added, as he went to the washstand and wetted a towel to wipe the face of his patient.

Then he administered restoratives. And finally, as Benny breathed again, he settled him more comfortably on the sofa, and enjoined the strictest quiet.

He even recommended Lord Wellrose to withdraw from the room and leave him alone to attend to his patient; adding, that if he should need assistance in the duty, he would ring for Mrs. Bruce.

As Lord Wellrose went out, he beckoned Dr. Kinlock to follow him into the hall, and there inquired:

"What shall I say to my mother? She expects to see him this afternoon."

"Tell her Grace that he has had as much excitement as he can bear for one day. He must rest quietly until to-morrow morning, when, if he should be better, it will be safe for her to see him."

Lord Wellrose went below stairs with this intelligence.

He found his mother alone in the drawing-room.

He said nothing of the hemorrhage, but spoke only of the patient's weakness and fatigue, and of the doctor's orders.

"And you told him all?" inquired Eglantine.

"I told him all," replied her son.

"And how did he take it? How did he take it?"

"With very great emotion, and yet with less than I expected. He said that his heart had told him the truth long ago, and he should have known it, had he understood the language of his heart."

"But what, then, did the poor boy mean? His heart had told him the truth? How could his heart tell him anything, since he never saw his mother's face?"

"Dear mother, he has seen you often. You have touched him and spoken to him more than once."

"Heaven of heavens! When and where?" she asked, in profound agitation.

Then Lord Wellrose told much of the story of his hapless brother's life, suppressing only such parts of it as would have overwhelmed his hearer with shame, as well as with pain.

Then the Duchess learned, for the first time, that the pale infant in the beggar's arms, whom she had pitied and succored at the church door, on the morning of her second bridal; the starving street boy, whom her kind-hearted children had called in from the sidewalk on that winter night, at Brunswick Terrace, and had treated with a portion of their Twelfth-day cake; the poor, dying child she had wept over in the Middlesex Hospital; and the fair, refined looking young man she had met in the bookseller's shop in the Strand, were one and the same, and her son!

Oh! how she wept to hear even thus much! How much more bitterly she must have wept, had she heard all!

"And *my* heart also spoke; but, ah! I too misunderstood its language!" she said, weeping vehemently.

At that moment the Duke came in. And she hastily dried her tears, and smiled.

"You have missed hearing our poor boy's story, Willie but I will tell it you to-night."

"Yes, dear, you shall do so. I shall feel deeply interested in hearing it. Take comfort, my dear Eglantine. Surely all is well now. We have two sons instead of one."

"And now, dear Wellrose, tell me how he came by the name of Douglas, since no one could have known his right to bear it until the surgeon's discovery?" she inquired.

"I gave it him," answered the Earl.

"Ah! *you* did not misunderstand the language of *your* heart, when it claimed him as a brother," said Eglantine, with emotion.

"I felt sure, by his close resemblance to the family, connected with other circumstances he communicated to me, that he was our kinsman. How near a kinsman I never guessed. So when he told me the name he bore was not his own, and not a very desirable one either, and that he had no name, and had never even been baptized—well, by a sudden impulse, or inspiration, I offered him mine. I told him how I could make it his own—if not directly by law, yet by Christianity. And so took him to Christ's Church, and got him baptized by the name of Benjamin Seton Douglas. Under that name, I got him his commission as ensign in a regiment of Foot. Under that name, he has distinguished himself in the Crimean war."

"Under that name he may hereafter claim the Barony of Seton-Linlithgow," said the Duchess.

"And the Dukedom of Cheviot, mother," added Lord Wellrose.

The Duchess looked up inquiringly.

"It is his right, dear mother. I have pointed out to my father how this right may be secured to him. And whatever it may cost to you, to me, or to any other, he should have it."

"And you, Wellrose?"

"I! Oh, I shall be the founder of another line of nobles from the ancient house of Douglas," said the Earl, jestingly

"After all I think more of the hour when I shall press the poor boy to my heart, than of anything else. It is hard to have to wait until to-morrow. Ah! I see what you are thinking of, Willie," she said, as she noticed her husband's grave smile. "You are thinking that if I have managed to wait all these years for my first-born, I can wait these few hours. Yes, but I did not know he was on earth all that time; now that I know he is here, in this very house, hours seem ages till I see him."

"'Time and the hour weareth away the weariest day,'" said the Duke, with a kindly smile.

So the day and the night passed, and the morning came.

At eleven o'clock in the forenoon, the autocrat of the sick-room, Doctor Christopher Kinlock, came down stairs and notified to the Duke and Duchess that they had his professional authority for visiting his patient.

The Duke arose and drew the Duchess' arm within his own. Her heart was beating fast; her color went and came; she panted with emotion.

"Come with us, Wellrose," she faltered.

And the young Earl arose to attend them.

He went up stairs before them, and led the way to his brother's room.

He opened the door, and the three entered together.

They found Benny lying on the sofa, propped up with pillows, his fair, wan face turned toward them in eager expectation, his golden hair flowing loose.

"How beautiful he is!" thought the Duchess; and as she met the full gaze of those clear, gentle blue eyes, and caught the smile of the delicate features, she felt as if her heart must break at that moment. A rush of tenderness, pity, love, filled her bosom, and almost overwhelmed her.

She left her husband's arm and tottered toward him, and sank beside his sofa and dropped her head upon his heart sobbing:

"My son, my son! Oh, my poor, poor, wronged boy!"

He would have risen and knelt at her feet, but for his great weakness. But he put his wasted arms around her neck and murmured:

"Mother, mother! sweetest name on earth."

Then both were silent, looking into each other's eyes, for a while, she sobbing at intervals; he with his pale hand caressing her hair.

But soon she remembered that there was another present waiting to welcome their son. And she arose from her posture and said, in a low tone:

"Your father, my dear."

And the Duke came and knelt, and silently embraced his fading boy. For at first he could find no words to speak. Then, after some inarticulate murmurs of affection, he said, with much emotion:

"You know how it was that we lost you so long, my poor boy? You know, I hope, that neither I"—his voice faltered—"nor your dear mother"—he choked—"could have been so heartless, so cruel—" here he broke down altogether.

Benjamin took his hand, and kissed it.

"I know all, dear father," he said. "It was no one's fault; it was my misfortune. It was *kismet.*"

"*Kismet!* Ah, you have been in the East. A Turk is killed in battle. He falls, crying, '*Kismet,*' and dies contentedly," said the Duke, with that strange mingling of irrelevant matter with the most solemn business on hand, that we sometimes meet in the most awful crises in life.

"Yet I am indeed no fatalist, dear mother," said Benny, turning to the Duchess, who seemed longing for a glance or a word from her new found son.

"No; for I am sure you are too good a Christian to be that, my boy?" she said.

"I have heard of your gallant conduct in the Crimea, my son; of your heroism at Balaklava, at Inkermann, at Sebastopol. You did honor to the name you bore there," said the Duke, proudly.

"I did but my duty," murmured Benny.

"And where got you the wound with which you are suffering now, my brave and modest boy? At the taking of Sebastopol, if I have heard aright—in planting the colors of your regiment on the walls, in the face of a murderous fire. Was every man a hero that day also?"

"I do not know," said Benny, smiling; "but I *do* know that I never should have had the chance of doing what I did, if it had not been for—"

He paused and looked all around the room until his eyes lighted on the form of the Earl of Wellrose, standing apart; and then his face grew radiant, and he held out both his hands. For more than princely father or beautiful mother, Benny loved this dear brother.

The Earl came to him, smiling.

"If it had not been for *him*, my father, Heaven knows where *I* should have been now!" said Benny, clasping his brother's hands.

"We know all that he was to you, my boy, even before he suspected you to be his brother. And now that he knows your position, he is ready to unite with us in restoring you to all your rights."

"What rights?" asked Benny simply, looking from one to the other.

For he had not given so much as a thought to the worldly advantages he would gain from the establishment of his birthright. He had thought only of the rich inheritance of love he would receive.

"What rights?" he asked again, seeing that they only looked at him in surprise.

"Your rights as our eldest son and heir—your rights to the inheritance of all my titles and estates," said the Duke of Cheviot gravely and firmly.

Benny turned paler than ever before, and looked from his father's face to his dear brother's.

"Does your Grace wish me to understand then, that I shall displace, disinherit—HIM?"

"Yes, my boy, lawfully, naturally, inevitably. You are the eldest son, and must take the rank that he has so long erroneously held," replied the Duke, as one speaking from authority.

"THEN I'LL DIE FIRST," said the "elder brother."

"BENJAMIN!" exclaimed father, mother and brother, in one breath.

"I will go down to the grave first! I shall die if I do not try *hard* to live; and I will not try to live: I will try to die, rather than displace, disinherit *him*," repeated Benny. And oh! the ineffable tenderness he threw into that little monosyllable "*him*."

They gazed at him in amazement. Such love, such disinterestedness even *they* had never known.

"My dear brother," said the young Earl, "your love your magnanimity touches me deeply. But you may not make this sacrifice; for if you cannot think of yourself, you must think of her—Suzy."

"I love Suzy. I have *proved* how I love her. And I know—I *know* that she also would never wish to dispossess you. Had she been born with a nature so selfish I could never have loved her."

"You hope to marry Suzy some day?" anxiously said the Earl.

"If I live, which is doubtful."

"Then for your posterity you should take your rights."

"Posterity!—shadows! dreams! Leave all that to time and Providence. That does not exist now. But what see visibly before me — what I touch tangibly — is my brother, my dear brother," he said, with infinite tenderness in his tone and look, as he took the hand of the Earl and pressed it to his heart, while he gazed in his face with unutterable love.

And then the cough seized and shook him.

His mother begged him to be calm, and not to excite himself.

But just as soon as he had recovered from the paroxysm, he, still gazing in his loved brother's face, murmured softly

"My brother, my dear, dear brother, you were more than a brother to me in my bitterest need—more than a brother to me when you did not even suspect our brotherhood. I could not even *live*, knowing that I had dispossessed you."

Again the cruel cough seized and shook him, as if it would have shaken him to dissolution.

They implored him not to talk.

The warning came too late. The new excitement had brought on the hemorrhage again. Blood gushed in torrents from his lips, and he fell back in syncope.

CHAPTER XLV.

VICTORY OF LOVE.

Oh, for some heavenly token,
By which I may be sure
The vase shall not be broken—
Dispersed the essence pure!

Then spake the Angel of Mothers
To me, in gentle tone:
Be kind to the children of others,
And thus deserve thine own.—I. W. H.

In a moment all was grief, terror and confusion. The surgeon, the only self-possessed person about the bed, cleared the room of every one except himself and the old nurse, Mrs. Bruce.

"No, your Grace, he is not dead, nor dying; but his life depends upon quiet," he said, in answer to the questions of the agonized mother, as he led her out into the hall.

"Then Heaven bless you for the words," she said.

And he went back to his patient. And she paced up and down the hall, wringing her hands and moaning:

"Oh, my son! my son! Oh, my poor, poor boy! To find you, only to lose you! to see you die! Not to be able to make your future atone for your bitter, bitter past!"

"Dear Eglantine, do not weep so bitterly," pleaded the Duke, coming to her side.

"Ah, if he had had a happy life, I could have better borne to see him die! But he has had such a miserable, most miserable life, and now he must die without even ever enjoying happiness!"

"Dear mother, it is not certain that he will die. He may recover," said the young Earl, coming up to her other side.

"Oh, Wellrose, no one ever lost so much blood and lived. His poor face is white as snow! Oh, my child! my child! Oh, my poor, wronged, dying child!" she moaned, weeping and wringing her hands.

At this moment the surgeon came out of the room, whispered to Lord Wellrose, and immediately returned.

"What did the doctor say? How is my boy?" anxiously inquired the mother.

"He is just the same. And the doctor wishes me to telegraph to Glasgow for Dr. Kerr, who is one of the most eminent surgeons of the day," answered the young Earl.

"Oh, do so at once! Lose not an instant of time," urged the anxious mother.

And the brother hurried away to dispatch a servant with a message to the nearest telegraph station.

Meantime the Duchess continued to pace up and down the hall, occasionally stopping to listen at the door of the sick-room.

The daily routine went on. Luncheon was announced at the usual time. And the family sat down at table; but no one ate.

Early in the afternoon a telegram came from the Glasgow surgeon, in answer to the one that had been sent him. He would come down, he said, by the night train, and be at Seton early the next morning.

This was promising news.

Later in the day the doctor brought a report from the sick-room. "The hemorrhage had entirely ceased, and the patient had recovered from his syncope, but was as weak as he could possibly be to live."

"Is there any hope?" almost breathlessly inquired the Duchess.

"There is *always* hope, your Grace," said the doctor to the mother.

"Do let me see him. I will be very calm. Do let me see him," pleaded the Duchess.

"Not to-day, your Grace. The most absolute quiet is vitally necessary to him," said the doctor resolutely.

The Duke took his arm and walked him off to the oriel window at the end of the hall, and inquired:

"Now how much hope is there really?"

"Not the faintest shadow of a hope, your Grace," answered the doctor.

"Even so I feared. But in this case, why may not his poor mother be permitted to see him?"

"Because, your Grace, although we may not hope to save his life, we must not therefore hasten his death. And any such agitation as a visit from his mother under present circumstances would cause, might be instantly fatal to him. He could not survive another hemorrhage five minutes."

The Duke sighed deeply, and went down stairs to give orders that a boat should be sent down the loch, to Seton, to meet the Glasgow surgeon on his arrival.

And the Duchess returned to her chamber, and passed the night in praying as only a mother can pray for her child.

Early in the morning the Glasgow surgeon arrived.

After a short interview with the Duke and Duchess, he was shown to the chamber of his patient.

After a very careful examination of the case, and a very close consultation with Dr. Kinlock, he entirely coincided with the army surgeon's opinion, and approved his treatment. The patient, he declared, could not possibly be in better hands than in those of the country doctor.

He remained at Seton Court twenty-four hours, and then went back to Glasgow, promising to revisit the patient at the end of the week, or sooner, if called upon.

And the next morning, being the third from the day of the last terrible hemorrhage, the Duchess was permitted to see her son.

She had schooled her soul to calmness; had promised herself and others that she would preserve a perfect composure, and neither do, nor say, nor *look* anything that might disturb the sufferer.

And so she went into his room.

He was propped up in bed, and the light from the bay-window fell full upon him.

She went up to his side. She could control her words and actions, but not her looks; so when her eyes fell upon his colorless and fleshless face, and met the gaze of his hollow eyes, her own face expressed all the deep anguish of her soul.

He held out both his pale hands to her. Evidently he thought that he was dying, and thought that she knew he was dying; for his first words were:

"Sweet mother, it seems very hard for you, very, very hard for you, to lose your poor boy almost as soon as you have found him."

She could scarcely restrain her tears as she pressed his thin hands to her lips and bosom, and then stooped and pressed her lips to his in a passionate kiss.

"But, dear mother, it is so much better for me to die. See how my life would compromise you all, and complicate the question of inheritance, and above all, how it would injure my dear brother," he whispered, speaking faintly and with difficulty, and caressing her hair with his poor hand.

She lost all her self-control, and forgot all her promises She fell sobbing on his neck, exclaiming:

"Oh, my son! my son! Oh, my poor, poor wronged boy! Live! live! live!—oh, try to live, for my miserable sake! Oh, do not die and leave me to a life-long remorse! Oh live! live! that I may make your future life so bright and happy that you may forget your past!"

"Sweet mother!" he murmured, still with his pale hand caressing her beautiful hair—"sweet mother, you have faith, I know. Have then a RADIANT faith. Believe that, in the better world, your poor son's life will be brighter and happier far than even your dear love could ever make it here. Have a glad, RADIANT faith."

"Oh, my child! my child! If you had had a happy life, like all your brothers and sisters, I think I could better bear to let you go!" she sobbed, weeping bitterly. "Oh, oh, if I could—could roll back the years, dear love!—undo your dreadful past, and make that happy, I could—I think I could bear to let you go."

"Dear mother, can any but Heaven do that? Sweet mother, if you sorrow so bitterly over my miserable past, let that sorrow teach you to pity and succor the thousands and thousands of poor, neglected, innocent little ones, *such as I was once*, who every day perish of want, or live—oh mother!—to grow up in ignorance, vice and misery, to fill the prisons or to freight the gallows. Sweet mother! you are very rich and powerful; save the children, for my sake, and I shall not have suffered and died in vain!" he said, and his brow grew radiant as the face of an angel.

The doctor came quietly to lead the lady away. The interview, he whispered, had been too long already.

She stooped and kissed her boy's bright brow again and again, and then she went away.

The doctor came back to the bedside of his patient.

"You must not give way to thoughts of death," he said encouragingly; for, though he had not a hope in the world of saving Benny's life, yet he continued to flatter him with delusions.

"It is better that I should die, doctor. My position is a false one. Legitimate in one country, illegitimate in another, I am in a false position; and my life compromises everybody, complicates everything connected with me, and most of all my beautiful mother and my beloved brother. Don't you see that I must die?" he murmured faintly.

"Not by any means. All these complications can be straightened out by a simple act of the House of Lords, as has been—"

"Let us talk no more about it, dear doctor. Even if I could live, no such thing should be done, with my consent. And if it were done without it, I would never profit by my dear brother's loss. But I shall die. And there an end."

The doctor said no more then.

Later in the day, when the Earl of Wellrose inquired as to his brother's state, Dr. Kinlock answered:

"The worst of it, and what makes the case so utterly hopeless is, that he does not seem to care to live."

"Oh, if Susan were here! Why does not that ship come in?" murmured the Earl to himself.

At that very moment a footman came in, and brought the mail bag from the Seton post-office.

Lord Wellrose emptied it. There were many letters forwarded from London. Among them was one that Lord Wellrose seized first of all. It bore the Southampton postmark. It was from Suzy, and it announced her arrival in England. Mrs. Brown, the curate's widow, was her companion. They were coming up to London, and should take apartments at the Brunswick Hotel, Berners street, where their letters were to be addressed.

Lord Wellrose, neglecting all the other contents of the mail bag, took Suzy's letter, and went to his mother.

He found the Duchess in her boudoir, weeping.

He put Suzy's letter in her hand, and begged her to read it.

She complied as well as her tear-laden eyes would let her. And then she looked up inquiringly at the face of her son.

"It is from the girl he loves, and whom he resigned because he thought I loved her; and in the magnanimity of his soul preferred my happiness to his own."

"Wellrose! what is all this, my dear?"

"Listen, mother dear, and I will explain," said the young man. And he told the story of his acquaintance with Suzy and Benny, leaving out such portions of it only as must have wounded the spirit of the Duchess.

"And now, dear mother, I wish you to invite this young lady to come here. If anything on earth can rouse and save my brother, it will be the presence of his love."

"She is a pure-spirited and noble-hearted girl, from all you have told me, Wellrose. And if she can do my poor boy any good, she shall be most welcome," said the Duchess.

And she immediately sat down and wrote the letter of invitation, that it might be in time for the first mail.

Lord Wellrose also wrote, telling her that Benjamin was ill at Seton Court, explained as much of the circumstances as he deemed prudent to trust in a letter, and implored her to accept his mother's pressing invitation, and come at once to Seton Court to rouse Benjamin.

These letters dispatched, Lord Wellrose went up to cheer his brother with the intelligence.

"I have good news for you, my dear fellow," he said, cheerfully, as he sat down by his brother's bed.

Benny lifted his blue eyes inquiringly.

"Susan has arrived in England. She is in Southampton. Nay, indeed, by this time she must be in London."

"Suzy has come back! Suzy is in London! Oh! I wish I could see her!" said Benny eagerly, brightening up at once.

"You shall see her in a few days. My mother has written and invited her to come here."

"Suzy coming here!" said Benjamin, joyfully.

"Yes, assuredly, as soon as our letters can reach her, and she can make the journey; for she will not neglect so pressing a call, I am sure, nor will she lose an hour on the road."

"Thank Heaven! And oh! I thank *you* too, Wellrose! I owe all the good I have, under Heaven, to you. I thank you, my dear brother."

"Cheer up, now! Take your nourishment. Resolve to live, for Suzy is coming. And our mother will make her welcome."

"Does our mother know?"

"She knows of your mutual love; for I told her this morning. That is the reason why she wrote for Suzy."

"Bless you! Bless her!" said Benny, fervently.

"Now here comes Mrs. Bruce with your broth. I order you to take it all, and then to go to sleep," said the Earl, as he went out.

Oh, magic of love! Elixir of life! From the time that Benny heard that Suzy was coming, and began to lock forward to her arrival, he brightened and mended day by day.

And his mother saw it and rejoiced.

On the third day from the sending of the letters, Suzy, having travelled day and night, arrived at Seton Court.

She was not at all like the brilliant Mademoiselle Arielle

of that dazzling London season that began in triumph and ended in tragedy. She was a "grave fairy," with golden hair, blue eyes and blooming face, habited in a plain methodistical suit of gray serge, that might have became her grandmother.

The Duchess received her with a kiss, called her her dear child, and took her to a pleasant bedroom where she could change her dress, while Lord Wellrose went to prepare Benny to receive her.

In a few minutes more, Suzy, leaning on the Duchess' arm, entered Benny's chamber.

He was lying as usual propped up by pillows, and with the light of the window falling on his fair, wan, spiritual face. He held out his hands to his love. But as soon as she saw what a mere shadow he was, she sank on her knees beside his bed and burst into tears, and sobbed as though her heart would have broken.

Under other circumstances this violent emotion might have hurt the invalid. But he was stronger now. He put his hands around her fair head, and murmured softly:

"Weep no more, dear Suzy. Dear, dearest Suzy, weep no more. You are here now, and all is well."

But she could not stop weeping all at once. Indeed, she wept the more.

"Mother," inquired Benny, softly, "is she to be my wife?"

"Yes, dearest, if she will," as softly answered the Duchess.

"If she will! Why, of course she will. We have been engaged ever since we were seven years old; have we not, love?" he inquired, caressing the fair hair.

"Yes, Benny, only for one short season when I lost my senses. But oh, my dear! when I saw you about to lay down your life for my sake, I knew how you loved me, and discovered how I loved you also," murmured Suzy, in an almost inaudible voice.

"Engaged since we were seven years old, dear mother and that was nearly twenty years ago," said Benny, brightly smiling up into his mother's face.

"And that is quite a long engagement—quite long enough. It should be ended soon now in marriage," answered the Duchess, smiling back.

"Suzy, love, our childish dreams will be realized," murmured Benny, trying to raise her. But he was as yet too feeble; so she got up and sat by his side, holding his hand, and continuing to hold it until the surgeon came with his peremptory orders that all should now leave the room, that his patient might seek repose in sleep.

A little later in the day Suzy was presented to the Duke, who received her courteously, and kissed her cheek.

A little later still, she had a word apart with the Earl of Wellrose.

"I see that you not only forgive me, but thank me, Lord Wellrose, for setting you free," she said pleasantly.

He bowed and smiled.

"I wish you much joy, fair sister," he said.

"Thanks. And you? When am I to congratulate you?" she archly inquired.

"In a few days, I hope."

And then he gave her his arm, to lead her in to dinner.

From that time Suzy was encouraged to spend the greater portion of every day in Benny's room. And his improvement was thenceforth very rapid. The surgeon expressed astonishment at it. The old nurse declared it was a miracle.

Soon Benny was able to leave his bed, and soon after, his chamber. In a fortnight from the day of Susan's arrival, he dined with the family.

Meanwhile the autumn was waning into winter, and the weather in the Highlands becoming very bleak.

One day the Glasgow surgeon arrived on a visit, and he advised that Captain Douglas should spend the winter on the South coast.

Therefore the family all went down to the Duke's marine residence at Brunswick Terrace, Brighton.

Here they were soon joined by the daughters of the Duke and Duchess, and also by the Lady Hinda Moray.

And here Benjamin—O, triumphs of time!—found himself in the same sea-side palace, the beloved son, the centre of a fond domestic circle, where once he had been taken in, a poor street boy. He was recognized as Captain Benjamin Seton Douglas, Master of Seton, and heir of the old Scottish Barony of Linlithgow, in right of his mother by her first marriage; heir also, in certain contingencies, of the ancient Dukedom of Cheviot.

But Benny would in nowise consent that any step should be taken to reinstate him in any position by which the brother he loved more than life should be a loser. Nay, he declared most positively, that if any movement should be made to establish his right to the heirship of the Dukedom of Cheviot, at his brother's expense, he would at once give up parents, country, and home, and take Suzy and go with her to the uttermost parts of the earth.

And they knew that he would keep his word.

And then he stretched forth his hand, and clasped his father's, saying gayly, and yet tenderly:

"I am the son of 'Bonnie Willie Douglas' and his fair bride Eglantine, and not of the most noble the Duke and the Duchess of Cheviot. You never dreamed of inheriting your great-uncle's dukedom when you married my mother, dear father, did you?" he asked, with a smile. "And after all," he continued, "why all this talk about an inheritance so many happy, happy years off yet? Our father is a man in his prime—not over forty-five or six, and may and probably will live a half century longer. Trust in Providence and in the triumphs of time."

* * * * * * *

Time has accomplished its many triumphs, and will also accomplish many more. It is now fifteen years since

Benjamin Seton Douglas, Master of Seton, married his love, Susan, and took up his residence at Seton Court, on the loch; since the Earl of Wellrose married Lady Hinda Moray, and fixed his abode at Wellrose Park, in Sussex.

The Duke and Duchess of Cheviot are now a handsome, healthy, happy couple, really considerably over sixty years of age, but not looking more than forty, and likely to live to complete their century. Both their sons and all their daughters being married, they have even more grandchildren than her gracious Majesty the Queen, which is saying a great deal.

Captain and Mrs. Seton Douglas have five fair daughters, but no son; and as their youngest daughter is eight years old, it is nearly certain that they never will have one.

But the Earl and Countess of Wellrose have both sons and daughters.

And the complicated question of inheritance will clear itself in this way:

The eldest son of the Earl of Wellrose, styled Viscount Douglas, is of course the lineal heir, after his father, of the Dukedom of Cheviot. He is a dark, gipsyish looking youth of fourteen, with much of his mother's warm Hindoo blood in his veins. With the precocity of his part Eastern nature, he has fallen in love with his fair cousin Eglantine, the eldest daughter of Captain Seton Douglas, and she certainly returns his affection; while the parents on both sides, for excellent reasons, favor their attachment. And in the future marriage of these young people the estates of both brothers will be united.

www.ingramcontent.com/pod-product-compliance
Lightning Source LLC
LaVergne TN
LVHW020057110826
845151LV00001B/3
* 9 7 8 1 4 2 5 5 4 5 2 0 8 *